A BOOK OF
SHORT
STORIES
2

PERSPECTIVES IN LITERATURE

A BOOK OF SHORT STORIES 2

THIRD EDITION

Secondary English Editorial Staff
Holt, Rinehart and Winston, Inc.

Holt, Rinehart and Winston, Inc.

Harcourt Brace Jovanovich, Inc.

Austin • Orlando • San Diego • Chicago • Dallas • Toronto

HBJ

Printed in the United States of America
ISBN 0-03-038439-7

    04 05 06 023 15 14 13 12 11

For permission to reprint copyrighted material, grateful acknowledgment is made to the following sources:

Rudolfo A. Anaya: "Salomon's Story" from *The Silence of the Llano: Short Stories* by Rudolfo A. Anaya (Tonatiuh-Quinto Sol International, 1982). Copyright © 1982 by Rudolfo A. Anaya. Originally published in the novel *Tortuga.*

Toby Cole, Agent and the Pirandello Estate: "War" from *The Medals and Other Stories* by Luigi Pirandello. Copyright © 1932, 1967 by E.P. Dutton, NY.

Delacorte Press/Seymour Lawrence, a division of Bantam, Doubleday, Dell Publishing Group, Inc.: "Tom Edison's Shaggy Dog" from *Welcome to the Monkey House* by Kurt Vonnegut, Jr. Copyright © 1953 by Kurt Vonnegut, Jr. Originally published in *Collier's.*

Doubleday, a division of Bantam, Doubleday, Dell Publishing Group, Inc.: "A Visit to Grandmother" from *Dancers on the Shore* by William Melvin Kelley. Copyright © 1962 by Fawcett Publications.

Farrar, Straus and Giroux, Inc.: "The Lottery" from *The Lottery* by Shirley Jackson. Copyright © 1948, 1949 by Shirley Jackson. Copyright renewed © 1976, 1977 by Laurence Hyman, Barry Hyman, Mrs. Sarah Webster and Mrs. Joanne Schnurer.

Harcourt Brace Jovanovich, Inc.: "Everyday Use" from *In Love & Trouble: Stories of Black Women* by Alice Walker. Copyright © 1973 by Alice Walker.

Johnson Publishing Company, Inc. and Eugenia Collier: "Marigolds" by Eugenia Collier from *Negro Digest,* November 1969. Copyright © 1969 by Johnson Publishing Company, Inc.

Alfred A. Knopf, Inc.: "The Toynbee Convector" from *The Toynbee Convector* by Ray Bradbury. Copyright © 1988 by Ray Bradbury. "My Oedipus Complex" from *Collected Stories* by Frank O'Connor. Copyright 1950 by Frank O'Connor. "The Lucid Eye in Silver Town" from *Assorted Prose* by John Updike. Copyright © 1964 by John Updike.

REVIEWERS:

Flora Foss
Formerly Geneva Middle School
Geneva, IL

H. Edward Deluzain
A. Crawford Mosley High School
Panama City, FL

Kay Tanner
West Orange High School
Winter Garden, FL

CONTENTS

Introduction: Elements of the Short Story   I

INTRODUCTION

As a literary form, the modern short story may be considered America's contribution to literature. Ever since people first began gathering around campfires for companionship as well as warmth, there have been stories—fables, myths, legends, tales—but the short story as we know it today really began in the mid–nineteenth century with Edgar Allan Poe.

As a critic of descriptive "sketches" and imaginative "tales" written in his time, Poe stated that a short story should be unified around a single effect, and that every word of the story should contribute to this effect. Poe's ideas influenced European writers before they were accepted in this country. Over the past one hundred years, French, English, Russian, and Italian, as well as American authors have made contributions to the short story.

You can, of course, enjoy a short story for its own sake, but your appreciation of it will be heightened by a knowledge of the form and the techniques used by a writer to achieve the effects he or she wants. There is great variety in short story form today, but most stories contain such elements as conflict, plot, tone, setting, character, and theme. To develop these, the writer may use such devices as foreshadowing, flashbacks, symbols, methods of characterization, and a particular point of view. (Explanations and examples of all these terms are found in the Glossary, beginning on page 281.)

Conflict in a short story is the basic struggle or problem faced by the hero or heroine. The conflict may be that of (1) person against person, (2) one person or several people against nature, (3) a person or group against society, or (4) an internal conflict, a person struggling against his or her own feelings or values, or (5) a combination of two or more of these types.

The *plot* is the sequence of events in a story, the plan of what happens. Because these events happen to people, at specific times and places, every short story has one or more *characters* and a *setting*.

The *tone* of a short story results from the writer's attitude toward the subject and characters he or she has chosen to write about. And the *theme* of a story is the central insight or idea that the author conveys to the reader through the story.

In many short stories, the theme serves as a unifying element, and conflict, plot, setting, and character all relate to the comment about life that the author is trying to convey to the reader. But not all stories have such controlling ideas. Many adventure and detective stories seek merely to entertain the reader with a suspenseful plot. In some twentieth-century stories, plot and theme may be quite unimportant. Instead, a recurring detail or symbol may dominate a work and give it focus.

The majority of short stories offer more than just diversion. The reader who appreciates good literature and the vision of life it offers will never be satisfied with merely a "What happens next?" approach. Nor is such a reader satisfied with an analysis of technique. It is the realization of the total effect of the story—the idea that underlies and unifies all its elements—that gives a reader the greatest satisfaction. An understanding of *form* as well as *content* provides lasting enjoyment.

MAURICE WALSH
(1879–1964)

Ireland and Scotland provide the setting for the short stories and novels of Maurice Walsh. His fiction is characterized by romantic conflicts, heroic characters, picturesque settings, dialect, humor, and, in many instances, first-rate fights.

Mr. Walsh was born in Kerry, Ireland, and attended St. Michael's College in Listowel, Kerry. He said he did not see the "walls of a city" until he was in his twenties, when he went to Dublin to take the examination for the British Civil Service. He became a customs officer and traveled throughout Ireland, Scotland, Wales, and England. After he married a Scottish woman, he lived in Scotland until the 1920s, when Ireland became a self-governing dominion within the British Empire. Returning to Ireland, Mr. Walsh worked for the Irish government until 1934, when he resigned to devote more time to his writing career.

Ireland in the opening days of the fighting between the I.R.A. and the Black and Tans* is the scene of *Green Rushes* (1935), a collection of five short stories, one of which is "The Quiet Man." In 1952, "The Quiet Man" was made into a film, and it still appears often on television.

THE QUIET MAN

Shawn Kelvin, a blithe[1] young lad of twenty, went to the States to seek his fortune. And fifteen years thereafter he returned to his native Kerry, his blitheness sobered and his youth dried to the core, and whether he had made his fortune or whether

Introduction of main character.

Setting.

---

* **I.R.A. ... Black and Tans:** From 1919 to 1921, there were many violent conflicts between the Irish Republican Army and the Black and Tans. The I.R.A. is a nationalist organization originally formed to obtain Irish independence from British rule. The troops recruited by England to put down the rebellion were popularly called the Black and Tans because they wore black and tan uniforms.
1. blithe (blīth): lighthearted.

Mystery about
Shawn
suggested.

Note the
repetition of the
word quiet.

Physical
description.

Partial
exposition of
Shawn's past;
mystery about it
sustained.

Introduction of
another
character.

Hint given of
future conflict.

The word
quietly is
repeated to stress
this
characteristic.

Foreshadowing
of future
complications.

he had not, no one could be knowing for certain. For he was a quiet man, not given to talking about himself and the things he had done. A quiet man, under middle size, with strong shoulders and deep-set blue eyes below brows darker than his dark hair—that was Shawn Kelvin. One shoulder had a trick of hunching slightly higher than the other, and some folks said that came from a habit he had of shielding his eyes in the glare of an open-hearth furnace[2] in a place called Pittsburgh, while others said it used to be a way he had of guarding his chin that time he was a sort of sparring-partner punching bag at a boxing camp.

Shawn Kelvin came home and found that he was the last of the Kelvins, and that the farm of his forefathers had added its few acres to the ranch of Big Liam O'Grady, of Moyvalla. Shawn took no action to recover his land, though O'Grady had got it meanly. He had had enough of fighting, and all he wanted now was peace. He quietly went among the old and kindly friends and quietly looked about him for the place and peace he wanted; and when the time came, quietly produced the money for a neat, handy, small farm on the first warm shoulder of Knockanore Hill below the rolling curves of heather. It was not a big place but it was in good heart, and it got all the sun that was going; and best of all, it suited Shawn to the tiptop notch of contentment, for it held the peace that turned to his quietness, and it commanded the widest view in all Ireland—vale and mountain and the lifting green plain of the Atlantic Sea.

There, in a four-roomed, lime-washed, thatched cottage, Shawn made his life, and though his friends hinted his needs and obligations, no thought came to him of bringing a wife into the place. Yet Fate had the thought and the dream in

---

2. **open-hearth furnace:** a type of furnace used in making steel. Its open construction requires workers to withstand great heat.

her loom for him.[3] One middling imitation of a man he had to do chores for him, an ex-navy pensioner handy enough about the house and byre,[4] but with no relish for the sustained work of the field—and indeed, as long as he kept house and byre shipshape, he found Shawn an easy master.

Shawn himself was no drudge toiler. He knew all about drudgery and the way it wears out a man's soul. He plowed a little and sowed a little, and at the end of the furrow he would lean on the handles of the cultivator, wipe his brow, if it needed wiping, and lose himself for whole minutes in the great green curve of the sea out there beyond the high black portals of Shannon mouth.[5] And sometimes of an evening he would see, under the glory of the sky, the faint smoke smudge of an American liner. Then he would smile to himself—a pitying smile—thinking of the poor devils, with dreams of fortune luring them, going out to sweat in Ironville, or to bootleg bad whisky down the hidden way, or to stand in a bread line. All these things were behind Shawn forever.

Shawn's character revealed through author's direct analysis and description of his surroundings and behavior.

Market days he would go down and across to Listowel town, seven miles, to do his bartering; and in the long evenings, slowly slipping into the endless summer gloaming,[6] his friends used to climb the winding lane to see him. Only the real friends came that long road, and they were welcome—fighting men who had been out in the "Sixteen":[7] Matt Tobin the thresher, the school-

Introduction of other characters.

---

3. Yet Fate ... for him: The personification of Fate at a loom is the author's variation of the Greek myth of the three goddesses of destiny; Clotho, Lachesis, and Atropos. Clotho spun the thread of life, Lachesis decided its length, and Atropos cut it off.
4. byre (bīr): a cow barn.
5. Shannon mouth: where the Shannon River empties into the Atlantic Ocean.
6. gloaming: dusk, twilight.
7. the "Sixteen": a reference to the Easter Rebellion of 1916 in which Irish rebels unsuccessfully attempted to seize Dublin by force and declare Ireland free from English rule.

master, the young curate[8]—men like that. A stone jar of malt whisky would appear on the table, and there would be a haze of smoke and a maze of warm, friendly disagreements.

Second reference to Shawn's need for a wife.

"Shawn, old son," one of them might hint, "aren't you sometimes terrible lonely?"

"Like hell I am!" might retort Shawn derisively. "Why?"

"Nothing but the daylight and the wind and the sun setting with the wrath o' God."

"Just that! Well?"

"But after the stirring times beyond in the States—"

"Ay! Tell me, fine men, have you ever seen a furnace in full blast?"

"A great sight."

Confirmation of Shawn's experience as an ironworker.

"Great surely! But if I could jump you into a steel foundry this minute, you would be sure that God had judged you faithfully into the very hob[9] of hell."

And then they would laugh and have another small one from the stone jar.

And on Sundays Shawn used to go to church, three miles down to the gray chapel above the black cliffs of Doon Bay. There Fate laid her lure for him.

Narrator's comment advances plot and foreshadows complications.

Sitting quietly on his wooden bench or kneeling on the dusty footboard, he would fix his steadfast, deep-set eyes on the vestmented celebrant and say his prayers slowly, or go into that strange trance, beyond dreams and visions, where the soul is almost at one with the unknowable.

But after a time, Shawn's eyes no longer fixed themselves on the celebrant. They went no farther than two seats ahead. A girl sat there, Sunday after Sunday she sat in front of him, and Sunday after Sunday his first casual admiration grew warmer.

---

8. curate (kyŏŏr'ĭt) : a priest who assists the pastor of a parish.

9. hob: in an open fireplace, a hob is a shelf at the back or side on which something is placed to be kept warm.

She had a white nape to her neck and short red hair above it, and Shawn liked the color and wave of that flame. And he liked the set of her shoulders and the way the white neck had of leaning a little forward and she at her prayers—or her dreams. And the service over, Shawn used to stay in his seat so that he might get one quick but sure look at her face as she passed out. And he liked her face, too—the wide-set gray eyes, cheekbones firmly curved, clean-molded lips, austere yet sensitive. And he smiled pityingly at himself that one of her name should make his pulses stir—for she was an O'Grady.

Description of the girl in the story.

Romantic complication linked to conflict; girl identified as an O'Grady.

One person, only, in the crowded chapel noted Shawn's look and the thought behind the look. Not the girl. Her brother, Big Liam O'Grady of Moyvalla, the very man who as good as stole the Kelvin acres. And that man smiled to himself, too—the ugly, contemptuous smile that was his by nature—and, after another habit he had, he tucked away his bit of knowledge in his mind corner against a day when it might come in useful for his own purposes.

Characterization of Liam.

The girl's name was Ellen—Ellen O'Grady. But in truth she was no longer a girl. She was past her first youth into that second one that has no definite ending. She might be thirty—she was no less—but there was not a lad in the countryside would say she was past her prime. The poise of her and the firm set of her bones below clean skin saved her from the fading of mere prettiness. Though she had been sought in marriage more than once, she had accepted no one, or rather, had not been allowed to encourage anyone. Her brother saw to that.

Additional description and background of Ellen.

Big Liam O'Grady was a great raw-boned, sandy-haired man, with the strength of an ox and a heart no bigger than a sour apple. An overbearing man given to berserk rages. Though he was a churchgoer by habit, the true god of that man was Money—red gold, shining silver, dull copper—the

Description of Liam.

Liam's values.

First mention of
Liam's attitude
toward money.

trinity that he worshipped in degree. He and his
sister Ellen lived on the big ranch farm of Moyvalla, and Ellen was his housekeeper and maid of
all work. She was a careful housekeeper, a good
cook, a notable baker, and she demanded no wage.
All that suited Big Liam splendidly, and so she
remained single—a wasted woman.

Big Liam himself was not a marrying man.

First reference to
dowry.

There were not many spinsters with a dowry[10] big
enough to tempt him, and the few there were had
acquired expensive tastes—a convent education, the
deplorable art of hitting jazz out of a piano, the
damnable vice of cigarette smoking, the purse-
emptying craze for motor cars—such things.

But in due time, the dowry and the place—
with a woman tied to them—came under his nose,
and Big Liam was no longer tardy. His neighbor,
James Carey, died in March and left his fine farm
and all on it to his widow, a youngish woman
without children, a woman with a hard name for
saving pennies. Big Liam looked once at Kathy
Carey and looked many times at her broad acres.
Both pleased him. He took the steps required by
tradition. In the very first week of the following
Shrovetide,[11] he sent an accredited emissary to open
formal negotiations, and that emissary came back
within the hour.

"My soul," said he, "but she is the quick one!
I hadn't ten words out of me when she was down
my throat. 'I am in no hurry,' says she, 'to come to
a house with another woman at the fire corner.
When Ellen is in a place of her own, I will listen to
what Liam O'Grady has to say.'"

"She will, I say!" Big Liam stopped him. "She
will so."

---

10. dowry (dour′ē): the money or property a woman brings to her husband at
marriage.
11. Shrovetide (shrōv′tīd′): *shrove* is the past tense of the verb *shrive*, which means
to make or hear confession. Shrovetide was formerly a time particularly set aside for
going to confession just before and during the forty-day Lenten season.

There, now, was the right time to recall Shawn Kelvin and the look in his eyes. Big Liam's mind corner promptly delivered up its memory. He smiled knowingly and contemptuously. Shawn Kelvin daring to cast sheep's eyes at an O'Grady! The undersized chicken heart, who took the loss of the Kelvin acres lying down! The little Yankee runt hidden away on the shelf of Knockanore! But what of it? The required dowry would be conveniently small, and the girl would never go hungry, anyway. There was Big Liam O'Grady, far descended from many chieftains.

Conflict between Shawn and Liam developed.

The very next market day at Listowel he sought out Shawn and placed a huge, sandy-haired hand on the shoulder that hunched to meet it.

"Shawn Kelvin, a word with you! Come and have a drink."

Shawn hesitated. "Very well," he said then. He did not care for O'Grady, but he would hurt no man's feelings.

They went across to Sullivan's bar and had a drink, and Shawn paid for it. And Big Liam came directly to his subject—almost patronizingly, as if he were conferring a favor.

"I want to see Ellen settled in a place of her own," said he.

Shawn's heart lifted into his throat and stayed there. But that steadfast face with the steadfast eyes gave no sign, and moreover, he could not say a word with his heart where it was.

"Your place is small," went on the big man, "but it is handy, and no load of debt on it, as I hear. Not much of a dowry ever came to Knockanore, and not much of a dowry can I be giving with Ellen. Say two hundred pounds [12] at the end of harvest, if prices improve. What do you say, Shawn Kelvin?"

First mention of a dowry for Ellen.

12. **pounds:** the standard monetary unit of the United Kingdom. In American money, a pound is presently worth about $2.00.

Shawn swallowed his heart, and his voice came slow and cool: "What does Ellen say?"

"I haven't asked her," said Big Liam. "But what would she say, blast it?"

"Whatever she says, she will say it herself, not you, Big Liam."

But what could Ellen say? She looked within her own heart and found it empty; she looked at the granite crag[13] of her brother's face and contemplated herself a slowly withering spinster at his fire corner; she looked up at the swell of Knockanore Hill and saw the white cottage among the green small fields below the warm brown of the heather. Oh, but the sun would shine up there in the lengthening spring day and pleasant breezes blow in sultry summer; and finally she looked at Shawn Kelvin, that firmly built, small man with the clean face and the lustrous eyes below steadfast brow. She said a prayer to her God and sank head and shoulders in a resignation more pitiful than tears, more proud than the pride of chieftains. Romance? Welladay!

Shawn was far from satisfied with that resigned acceptance, but then was not the time to press for a warmer one. He knew the brother's wizened[14] soul, guessed at the girl's clean one, and saw that she was doomed beyond hope to a fireside sordidly bought for her. Let it be his own fireside then. There were many worse ones—and God was good.

Ellen O'Grady married Shawn Kelvin. One small statement; and it holds the risk of tragedy, the chance of happiness, the probability of mere endurance—choices wide as the world.

But Big Liam O'Grady, for all his resolute promptness, did not win Kathy Carey to wife. She, foolishly enough, took to husband her own cat-

---

13. crag (krăg): steep cliff or rock; here, a figurative way of describing Liam's hard, unkindly face.
14. wizened (wĭz'ənd): shriveled, dried up.

tleman, a gay night rambler, who gave her the devil's own time and a share of happiness in the bygoing. For the first time, Big Liam discovered how mordant[15] the wit of his neighbors could be, and to contempt for Shawn Kelvin he now added an unreasoning dislike.

Conflict between Shawn and Liam heightened.

Shawn Kelvin had got his precious, red-haired woman under his own roof now. He had no illusions about her feelings for him. On himself, and on himself only, lay the task of molding her into a wife and lover. Darkly, deeply, subtly, away out of sight, with gentleness, with restraint, with a consideration beyond kenning,[16] that molding must be done, and she that was being molded must never know. He hardly knew, himself.

First he turned his attention to material things. He hired a small servant maid to help her with the housework. Then he acquired a rubber-tired tub cart and a half-bred gelding with a reaching knee action. And on market days husband and wife used to bowl down to Listowel, do their selling and their buying, and bowl smoothly home again, their groceries in the well of the cart and a bundle of second-hand American magazines on the seat at Ellen's side. And in the nights, before the year turned, with the wind from the plains of the Atlantic keening[17] above the chimney, they would sit at either side of the flaming peat fire, and he would read aloud strange and almost unbelievable things out of the high-colored magazines. Stories, sometimes, wholly unbelievable.

Ellen would sit and listen and smile, and go on with her knitting or her sewing; and after a time it was sewing she was at mostly—small things. And when the reading was done, they would sit

Characterization of Shawn and Ellen through description of activities.

15. **mordant** (môr′dənt): biting, sarcastic.
16. **beyond kenning**: beyond one's knowledge (ken) or range of sight.
17. **keening** (kēn′ing): wailing; moaning. A *keen* is a lamentation for the dead. It may be a wordless cry or, sometimes, a rhythmic recounting of the life and character of the dead person.

and talk quietly in their own quiet way. For they were both quiet. Woman though she was, she got Shawn to do most of the talking. It could be that she, too, was probing and seeking, unwrapping the man's soul to feel the texture thereof, surveying the marvel of his life as he spread it diffidently[18] before her. He had a patient, slow, vivid way of picturing for her the things he had seen and felt. He made her see the glare of molten metal, lambent yet searing,[19] made her feel the sucking heat, made her hear the clang; she could see the roped square under the dazzle of the hooded arcs with the curling smoke layer above it, understand the explosive restraint of the game, thrill when he showed her how to stiffen wrist for the final devastating right hook. And often enough the stories were humorous, and Ellen would chuckle, or stare, or throw back her red, lovely curls in laughter. It was grand to make her laugh.

Another reference to Shawn's past—and to his experiences in the boxing ring.

Shawn's friends, in some hesitation at first, came in ones and twos up the slope to see them. But Ellen welcomed them with her smile that was shy and at the same time frank, and her table was loaded for them with scones and crumpets[20] and cream cakes and heather honey; and at the right time it was herself that brought forth the decanter of whisky—no longer the half-empty stone jar— and the polished glasses. Shawn was proud as sin of her. She would sit then and listen to their discussions and be forever surprised at the knowledgeable man her husband was—the way he could discuss war and politics and the making of songs, the turn of speech that summed up a man or a situation. And sometimes she would put in a word or two and be listened to, and they would look to see if her smile commended them, and be a little

18. **diffidently** (dĭf'ə·dənt·lē): unassertively, shyly.
19. **lambent** (lăm'bənt) **yet searing:** softly bright and flickering yet burning.
20. **scones and crumpets:** Scones are a type of tea cake, and crumpets are thin flat cakes cooked on a griddle.

chastened by the wisdom of that smile—the age-old smile of the matriarch from whom they were all descended. In no time at all, Matt Tobin the thresher, who used to think, "Poor old Shawn! Lucky she was to get him," would whisper to the schoolmaster: "Herrin's alive! That fellow's luck would astonish nations."

Women, in the outside world, begin by loving their husbands; and then, if Fate is kind, they grow to admire them; and if Fate is not unkind, may descend no lower than liking and enduring. And there is the end of lawful romance. Look now at Ellen O'Grady. She came up to the shelf of Knockanore and in her heart was only a nucleus of fear in a great emptiness, and that nucleus might grow into horror and disgust. But, glory of God, she, for reason piled on reason, presently found herself admiring Shawn Kelvin; and with or without reason, a quiet liking came to her for this quiet man who was so gentle and considerate; and then, one great heart-stirring dark o'night, she found herself fallen head and heels in love with her own husband. There is the sort of love that endures, but the road to it is a mighty chancy one.

A woman, loving her husband, may or may not be proud of him, but she will fight like a tiger if anyone, barring herself, belittles him. And there was one man that belittled Shawn Kelvin. Her brother, Big Liam O'Grady. At fair or market or chapel that dour[21] giant deigned not to hide his contempt and dislike. Ellen knew why. He had lost a wife and farm; he had lost in herself a frugally cheap housekeeper; he had been made the butt of a sly humor; and for these mishaps, in some twisted way, he blamed Shawn. But—and there came in the contempt—the little Yankee runt, who dared say nothing about the lost Kelvin acres, would not now have the gall or guts to demand the dowry that was due. Lucky the hound to steal

Heightening of conflict.

21. **dour** (door, dour): sullen, surly.

an O'Grady to hungry Knockanore! Let him be satisfied with that luck!

One evening before a market day, Ellen spoke to her husband: "Has Big Liam paid you my dowry yet, Shawn?"

Reference to dowry.

"Sure there's no hurry, girl," said Shawn.

"Have you ever asked him?"

"I have not. I am not looking for your dowry, Ellen."

"And Big Liam could never understand that." Her voice firmed. "You will ask him to-morrow."

Ellen's request adds to complication.

"Very well so, *agrah*,"[22] agreed Shawn easily.

And the next day, in that quiet, diffident way of his, he asked Big Liam. But Big Liam was brusque and blunt. He had no loose money and Kelvin would have to wait until he had. "Ask me again, Shawneen,"[23] he finished, his face in a mocking smile, and turning on his heel, he plowed his great shoulders through the crowded market.

His voice had been carelessly loud and people had heard. They laughed and talked amongst themselves. "Begogs! The devil's own boy, Big Liam! What a pup to sell! Stealing the land and keeping a grip on the fortune! Ay, and a dangerous fellow, mind you, the same Big Liam! He would smash little Shawn at the wind of a word. And devil the bit his Yankee sparring tricks would help him!"

A friend of Shawn's, Matt Tobin the thresher, heard that and lifted his voice: "I would like to be there the day Shawn Kelvin loses his temper."

"A bad day for poor Shawn!"

"It might then," said Matt Tobin, "but I would come from the other end of Kerry to see the badness that would be in it for someone."

22. agrah (à·grō'): *Gaelic,* my love.
23. Shawneen: The suffix *-een* when added to nouns means small; when used in addressing an adult, it means that the person is insignificant or unworthy of consideration.

Shawn had moved away with his wife, not heeding or not hearing.

"You see, Ellen?" he said in some discomfort. "The times are hard on ranchers, and we don't need the money, anyway."

"Do you think Big Liam does?" Her voice had a cut in it. "He could buy you and all Knockanore and be only on the fringe of his hoard. You will ask him again."

"But, girl dear, I never wanted a dowry with you."

She liked him to say that, but far better would she like to win for him the respect and admiration that was his due. She must do that now at all costs. Shawn, drawing back now, would be the butt of his fellowmen.

"You foolish lad! Big Liam would never understand your feelings, with money at stake." She smiled and a pang went through Shawn's breast. For the smile was the smile of an O'Grady, and he could not be sure whether the contempt in it was for himself or for her brother.

Shawn asked Big Liam again, unhappy in his asking, but also dimly comprehending his woman's object. And Shawn asked again a third time. The issue was become a famous one now. Men talked about it, and women too. Bets were made on it. At fair or market, if Shawn was seen approaching Big Liam, men edged closer and women edged away. Some day the big fellow would grow tired of being asked, and in one of his terrible rages half kill the little lad as he had half killed other men. A great shame! Here and there, a man advised Shawn to give up asking and put the matter in a lawyer's hands. "I couldn't do that," was Shawn's only answer. Strangely enough, none of these prudent advisers were among Shawn's close friends. His friends frowned and said little, but they were always about, and always among them was Matt Tobin.

The day at last came when Big Liam grew

First reference to conflict between Shawn and Ellen.

tired of being asked. That was the big October cattle fair at Listowel, and he had sold twenty head of fat, polled Angus beeves at a good price. He was a hard dealer and it was late in the day before he settled at his own figure, so that the banks were closed and he was not able to make a lodgment.[24] He had, then, a great roll of bills in an inner vest pocket when he saw Shawn and Ellen coming across to where he was bargaining with Matt Tobin for a week's threshing. Besides, the day being dank, he had had a drink or two more than was good for him and the whisky had loosened his tongue and whatever he had of discretion. By the powers!—it was time and past time to deal once and for all with this little gadfly[25] of a fellow, to show him up before the whole market. He strode to meet Shawn, and people got out of his savage way and edged in behind to lose nothing of this dangerous game.

He caught Shawn by the hunched shoulder—a rending grip—and bent down to grin in his face.

"What is it, little fellow? Don't be ashamed to ask!"

Matt Tobin was probably the only one there to notice the ease with which Shawn wrenched his shoulder free, and Matt Tobin's eyes brightened. But Shawn did nothing further and said no word. His deep-set eyes gazed steadily at the big man.

The big man showed his teeth mockingly. "Go on, you whelp![26] What do you want?"

"You know, O'Grady."

"I do. Listen, Shawneen!" Again he brought his hand clap on the little man's shoulder. "Listen, Shawneen! If I had a dowry to give my sister, 'tis not a little shrimp like you would get her. Go to hell out o' that!"

---

24. lodgment: deposit.
25. gadfly: a fly that bites cattle; by extension, the word means a person who irritates or persistently bothers another.
26. whelp (hwĕlp)**:** cub or puppy; a contemptuous term.

His great hand gripped and he flung Shawn backward as if he were only the image of a man filled with chaff.[27]

Shawn went backward, but he did not fall. He gathered himself like a spring, feet under him, arms half-raised, head forward into hunched shoulder. But as quickly as the spring coiled, as quickly it slackened, and he turned away to his wife. She was there facing him, tense and keen, her face pale and set, and a gleam of the race in her eyes.

Another example of foreshadowing of outcome of conflict.

"Woman, woman!" he said in his deep voice. "Why would you and I shame ourselves like this?"

"Shame!" she cried. "Will you let him shame you now?"

"But your own brother, Ellen—before them all?"

"And he cheating you—"

"Glory of God!" His voice was distressed. "What is his dirty money to me? Are you an O'Grady, after all?"

That stung her and she stung back in one final effort. She placed a hand across her breast and looked *close* into his face. Her voice was low and bitter, and only he heard: "I am an O'Grady. It is a great pity that the father of this my son is a Kelvin and a coward."

The bosses[28] of Shawn Kelvin's cheekbones were like hard marble, but his voice was as soft as a dove's.

"Is that the way of it? Let us be going home then, in the name of God!"

He took her arm, but she shook his hand off; nevertheless, she walked at his side, head up, through the people that made way for them. Her brother mocked them with his great, laughing bellow.

Another reference to Shawn-Ellen conflict.

"That fixes the pair of them!" he cried,

27. **chaff** (chăf): finely cut straw or hay.
28. **bosses:** the raised, prominent parts of the cheekbones.

brushed a man who laughed out of his way, and strode off through the fair.

There was talk then—plenty of it. "Murder, but Shawn had a narrow squeak that time! Did you see the way he flung him? I wager he'll give Big Liam a wide road after this. And he by the way of being a boxer! That's a pound you owe me, Matt Tobin."

"I'll pay it," said Matt Tobin, and that is all he said. He stood wide-legged, looking at the ground, his hand ruefully rubbing the back of his head and dismay and gloom on his face. His friend had failed him in the face of the people.

Shawn and Ellen went home in their tub cart and had not a single word or glance for each other on the road. And all that evening, at table or fireside, a heart-sickening silence held them in its grip. And all that night they lay side by side, still and mute. There was only one subject that possessed them and on that they dared speak no longer. They slept little. Ellen, her heart desolate, lay on her side, staring into the dark, grieving for what she had said and unable to unsay it. Shawn, on his back, contemplated things with a cold clarity. He realized that he was at the fork of life and that a finger pointed unmistakably. He must risk the very shattering of all happiness, he must do a thing so final and decisive that, once done, it could never again be questioned. Before morning, he came to his decision, and it was bitter as gall. He cursed himself. "Oh, you fool! You might have known that you should never have taken an O'Grady without breaking the O'Gradys."

He got up early in the morning at his usual hour and went out as usual to do his morning chores—rebedding and foddering[29] the cattle, rubbing down the half-bred, helping the servant maid with the milk in the creaming pans—and as usual, he came in to his breakfast and ate it unhungrily

29. **foddering** (fŏd′ər·ĭng): feeding with fodder, a food for domestic animals.

and silently, which was not usual. But thereafter he again went out to the stable, harnessed his gelding and hitched him to the tub cart. Then he returned to the kitchen and spoke for the first time.

"Ellen, will you come with me down to see your brother?"

Rising action.

She hesitated, her hands thrown wide in a helpless, hopeless gesture. "Little use you going to see my brother, Shawn. 'Tis I should go and—not come back."

"Don't blame me now or later, Ellen. It has been put on me and the thing I am going to do is the only thing to be done. Will you come?"

"Very well," she said tonelessly. "I will be ready in a minute."

And they went the four miles down into the vale to the big farmhouse of Moyvalla. They drove into the great square of cobbled yard and found it empty.

On one side of the square was the long, low, lime-washed dwelling house; on the other, fifty yards away, the two-storied line of steadings[30] with a wide arch in the middle; and through the arch came the purr and zoom of a threshing machine. Shawn tied the half-bred to the wheel of a farm cart and, with Ellen, approached the house.

A slattern[31] servant girl leaned over the half-door and pointed through the arch. The master was out beyond in the haggard[32]—the rickyard[33]— and would she run across for him?

"Never mind, *achara*,"[34] said Shawn, "I'll get him.... Ellen, will you go in and wait?"

"No," said Ellen, "I'll come with you." She knew her brother.

---

30. steadings: *British dialect,* farm buildings.
31. slattern (slăt′ərn): untidy; slovenly. From the German word *schlottern* meaning to hang loosely, stouch; used as both a noun and an adjective.
32. haggard (hăg′ərd): a yard for stacking hay.
33. rickyard: on a farm stacks of hay, called ricks, are kept in the open air.
34. achara (ă·kăr′ă): *Gaelic,* dear friend.

Description of noise and activities contrasts with Shawn's quiet determination and heightens the tension at a critical moment.

As they went through the arch, the purr and zoom grew louder, and turning the corner, they walked into the midst of activity. A long double row of cone-pointed cornstacks stretched across the yard and, between them, Matt Tobin's portable threshing machine was busy. The smooth-flying, eight-foot driving wheel made a sleepy purr and the black driving belt ran with a sag and heave to the red-painted thresher. Up there on the platform, barearmed men were feeding the flying drum with loosened sheaves, their hands moving in a rhythmic sway. As the toothed drum bit at the corn sheaves, it made an angry snarl that changed and slowed into a satisfied zoom. The wide conveying belt was carrying the golden straw up a steep incline to where other men were building a long rick; still more men were attending to the corn shoots, shoulders bending under the weight of the sacks as they ambled across to the granary. Matt Tobin himself bent at the face of his machine, feeding the firebox with sods of hard black peat. There were not less than two score of men about the place, for, as was the custom, all Big Liam's friends and neighbors were giving him a hand with the threshing—"the day in harvest."

Big Liam came around the flank of the engine and swore. He was in his shirt sleeves, and his great forearms were covered with sandy hair.

"Hell and damnation! Look who's here!"

He was in the worst of tempers this morning. The stale dregs of yesterday's whisky were still with him, and he was in the humor that, as they say, would make a dog bite its father. He took two slow strides and halted, feet apart and head truculently[35] forward.

"What is it this time?" he shouted. That was the un-Irish welcome he gave his sister and her husband.

---

35. truculently (trŭk′yə•lənt•lē): meanly; savagely.

Shawn and Ellen came forward steadily, and as they came, Matt Tobin slowly throttled down his engine. Big Liam heard the change of pitch and looked angrily over his shoulder.

Focus narrows to Shawn and Liam with the silencing of the engine.

"What the hell do you mean, Tobin? Get on with the work!"

"To hell with yourself, Big Liam! This is my engine, and if you don't like it, you can leave it!" And at that he drove the throttle shut and the purr of the flywheel slowly sank.

"We will see in a minute," threatened Big Liam, and turned to the two now near at hand.

"What is it?" he growled.

"A private word with you. I won't keep you long." Shawn was calm and cold.

"You will not—on a busy morning," sneered the big man. "There is no need for private words between me and Shawn Kelvin."

"There is need," urged Shawn. "It will be best for us all if you hear what I have to say in your own house."

"Or here on my own land. Out with it! I don't care who hears!"

Shawn looked around him. Up on the thresher, up on the straw rick, men leaned idle on fork handles and looked down at him; from here and there about the stackyard, men moved in to see, as it might be, what had caused the stoppage, but only really interested in the two brothers-in-law. He was in the midst of Clan O'Grady, for they were mostly O'Grady men—big, strong, blond men, rough, confident, proud of their breed. Matt Tobin was the only man he could call a friend. Many of the others were not unfriendly, but all had contempt in their eyes, or, what was worse, pity. Very well! Since he had to prove himself, it was fitting that he do it here amongst the O'Grady men.

Shawn brought his eyes back to Big Liam—deep, steadfast eyes that did not waver.

*Simple statement
of the main
conflict of the
story.*

"O'Grady," said he—and he no longer hid his contempt—"you set a great store by money."

"No harm in that. You do it yourself, Shawneen."

"Take it so! I will play that game with you, till hell freezes. You would bargain your sister and cheat; I will sell my soul. Listen, you big brute! You owe me two hundred pounds. Will you pay it?" There was an iron quality in his voice that was somehow awesome. The big man, about to start forward overbearingly, restrained himself to a brutal playfulness.

"I will pay it when I'm ready."

"Today."

"No, nor tomorrow."

"Right. If you break your bargain, I break mine."

"What's that?" shouted Big Liam.

"If you keep your two hundred pounds, you keep your sister."

"What is it?" shouted Big Liam again, his voice breaking in astonishment. "What is that you say?"

"You heard me. Here is your sister Ellen! Keep her!"

"Fires o'hell!" He was completely astounded out of his truculence. "You can't do that!"

"It is done," said Shawn.

Ellen O'Grady had been quiet as a statue at Shawn's side, but now, slow like doom, she faced him. She leaned forward and looked into his eyes and saw the pain behind the strength.

"To the mother of your son, Shawn Kelvin?" she whispered that gently to him.

His voice came cold as a stone out of a stone face: "In the face of God. Let him judge me."

"I know—I know!" That was all she said, and walked quietly across to where Matt Tobin stood at the face of his engine.

Matt Tobin placed a hand on her arm. "Give

him time, *acolleen*,"[36] he whispered urgently. "Give him his own time. He's slow but he's deadly as a tiger when he moves."

Big Liam was no fool. He knew exactly how far he could go. There was no use, at this juncture, in crushing the runt under a great fist. There was some force in the little fellow that defied dragooning.[37] Whatever people might think of Kelvin, public opinion would be dead against himself. Worse, his inward vision saw eyes leering in derision, mouths open in laughter. The scandal on his name would not be bounded by the four seas of Erin. He must change his stance while he had time. These thoughts passed through his mind while he thudded the ground three times with iron-shod heel. Now he threw up his head and bellowed his laugh.

Characterization by revealing character's thoughts.

"You fool! I was only making fun of you. What are your dirty few pounds to the likes of me? Stay where you are."

He turned, strode furiously away, and disappeared through the arch.

Shawn Kelvin was left alone in that wide ring of men. The hands had come down off the ricks and thresher to see closer. Now they moved back and aside, looked at one another, lifted eyebrows, looked at Shawn Kelvin, frowned and shook their heads. They knew Big Liam. They knew that, yielding up the money, his savagery would break out into something little short of killing. They waited, most of them, to prevent that savagery going too far.

Shawn Kelvin did not look at anyone. He stood still as a rock, his hands deep in his pockets, one shoulder hunched forward, his eyes on the ground and his face strangely calm. He seemed the least perturbed man there. Matt Tobin held Ellen's

36. acolleen (ä·kōl′lēn): *Gaelic*, dear girl.
37. dragooning (drə·goon′ing): being forced into submission by violence.

arm in a steadying grip and whispered in her ear: "God is good, I tell you."

Big Liam was back in two minutes. He strode straight to Shawn and halted within a pace of him.

"Look, Shawneen!" In his raised hands was a crumpled bundle of greasy bank notes. "Here is your money. Take it, and then see what will happen to you. Take it!" He thrust it into Shawn's hands. "Count it. Make sure you have it all—and then I will kick you out of this haggard—and look"—he thrust forward a hairy fist—"if I ever see your face again, I will drive that through it. Count it, you spawn!"[38]

Climax.

Shawn did not count it. Instead he crumpled it into a ball in his strong fingers. Then he turned on his heel and walked, with surprising slowness, to the face of the engine. He gestured with one hand to Matt Tobin, but it was Ellen, quick as a flash, who obeyed the gesture. Though the hot bar scorched her hand, she jerked open the door of the firebox and the leaping peat flames whispered out at her. And forthwith, Shawn Kelvin, with one easy sweep, threw the crumpled ball of notes into the heart of the flame. The whisper lifted one tone and one scrap of burned paper floated out of the funnel top. That was all the fuss the fire made of its work.

But there was fuss enough outside.

Big Liam O'Grady gave one mighty shout. No, it was more anguished scream than a shout:

"My money! My good money!"

He gave two furious bounds forward, his great arms raised to crush and kill. But his hands never touched the small man.

"You dumb ox!" said Shawn Kelvin between his teeth. That strong, hunched shoulder moved a little, but no one there could follow the terrific

38. **spawn** (spôn): young produced in great quantity; a contemptuous term.

drive of that hooked right arm. The smack of bone on bone was sharp as whip crack, and Big Liam stopped dead, went back on his heel, swayed a moment, and staggered back three paces.

"Now and forever! Man of Kelvins!" roared Matt Tobin.

But Big Liam was a man of iron. That blow should have laid him on his back—blows like it had tied men to the ground for the full count. But Big Liam only shook his head, grunted like a boar, and drove in at the little man. And the little man, instead of circling away, drove in at him, compact of power.

The men of the O'Gradys saw then an exhibition that they had not knowledge enough to appreciate fully. Thousands had paid as much as ten dollars each to see the great Tiger Kelvin in action, his footwork, his timing, his hitting; and never was his action more devastating than now. He was a thunderbolt on two feet and the big man a glutton.

Big Liam never touched Shawn with clenched fist. He did not know how. Shawn, actually forty pounds lighter, drove him by sheer hitting power across the yard.

Men for the first time saw a two-hundred pound man knocked clean off his feet by a body blow. They saw for the first time the deadly restraint and explosion of skill.

Shawn set out to demolish his enemy in the *Turning point.*
briefest space of time, and it took him five minutes to do it. Five, six, eight times he knocked the big man down, and the big man came again, staggering, slavering, raving, vainly trying to rend and smash. But at last he stood swaying and clawing helplessly, and Shawn finished him with his terrible double hit—left below the breastbone and right under the jaw.

Big Liam lifted on his toes and fell flat on his back. He did not even kick as he lay.

Shawn did not waste a glance at the fallen giant. He swung full circle on the O'Grady men and his voice of iron challenged them:

"I am Shawn Kelvin, of Knockanore Hill. Is there an O'Grady amongst you thinks himself a better man? Come then."

His face was deep-carved stone, his great chest lifted, the air whistled through his nostrils; his deep-set flashing eyes dared them.

No man came.

He swung around then and walked straight to his wife. He halted before her.

His face was still of stone, but his voice quivered and had in it all the dramatic force of the Celt:[39]

"Mother of my son, will you come home with me?"

She lifted to the appeal, voice and eye:

"Is it so you ask me, Shawn Kelvin?"

Dénouement. His face of stone quivered at last. "As my wife only—Ellen Kelvin!"

"Very well, heart's treasure." She caught his arm in both of hers. "Let us be going home."

"In the name of God," he finished for her.

And she went with him, proud as the morning, out of that place. But a woman, she would have the last word.

"Mother of God!" she cried. "The trouble I had to make a man of him!"

"God Almighty did that for him before you were born," said Matt Tobin softly.

---

39. Celt (sĕlt, kĕlt): an individual of any of various Celtic-speaking peoples, of whom the ancient Gauls and Britons and the modern Irish, Scots, Welsh, and Bretons are the best known.

Meaning

1. On his return to his native Kerry, how do Shawn Kelvin's actions show the quiet side of his personality? How does the author hint that Kelvin is not as meek as he seems?

2. After several months of marriage, how have Ellen's feelings about her husband changed? How does the change come about?

3. Shawn, Ellen, and Big Liam have different attitudes toward Ellen's unpaid dowry. What is each character's attitude toward this money? Whose attitude do you find most reasonable? Why?

4. *Conflict,* the struggle between opposing forces, may be external or internal. The fist fight that takes place between Shawn and Liam is an example of *external* or *physical conflict.*

    Inner conflict is the struggle within the mind and heart of a character. Identify three of the inner conflicts in the story.

Method

1. *Suspense* or uncertainty about the outcome of the plot is basic to every good story. It is created **a.** when an author withholds information that would satisfy our curiosity about a character and **b.** when we anxiously await the outcome of a conflict, especially if the person in conflict is someone with whom we sympathize or identify. Illustrate each of these methods of creating suspense with an example from the story.

2. The various *methods of characterization* that an author may use to make an invented character appear lifelike include:
    a. describing appearance.
    b. showing the character in action, especially at key moments in the story.
    c. revealing thoughts and feelings.
    d. presenting conversations.
    e. showing the reactions of others to the character's behavior and in some cases giving their remarks about the character.
    f. contrasting attitudes and values with those of another character in the story.

    How does Maurice Walsh use these methods to develop the personality of Shawn Kelvin? Choose two of the methods and illustrate them with an example from the text.

3. The *climax* is the high point of a story, the moment of greatest interest and intensity. It usually occurs near a narrative's major

turning point, the moment when the fortunes of the main character turn from bad to good or from good to bad, and a probable solution to his or her problem is seen.

At the climax of this story, how does Ellen's decision to open the firebox point the way to a happy solution to the conflict that has developed between her and Shawn? What does her action reveal about her attitude toward money?

What do Shawn's actions at the turning point of this story prove to the O'Grady men?

Language: Denotation and Connotation

As Shawn works on his farm on Knockanore Hill, he thinks of his life in America and "of the poor devils, with dreams of fortune luring them, going out to sweat in Ironville, or to bootleg bad whisky down the hidden way, or to stand in a bread line." The *connotation* of a word refers to the associations that a word has in addition to its explicit literal meaning. The connotations or implications of words such as *bootleg* and *bread line* suggest that Shawn was in the United States during the Depression of the 1930s.

The *denotation* of a word is its exact, dictionary meaning. For example, the denotation of the word *bread line* is "a line of persons waiting to be given bread or other food as charity." However, to those familiar with the Depression, which began with the stock market crash in 1929, a bread line *connotes* widespread unemployment, low wages, and bank failures.

The verb *bootleg,* which is derived from the smuggler's habit of hiding a liquor bottle in the top of his boot, means "to make or sell liquor illegally." The term is usually associated with Prohibition, which lasted from 1920 until 1933, when the Eighteenth Amendment, which forbade the sale of liquor, was repealed. *Bootleg* connotes such things as speakeasies, racketeers, and bribery. Sometimes words have pleasant or unpleasant connotations because of personal experience or associations connected with them.

After each of the following words, write one or two adjectives or nouns that tell what the word connotes to you.

1. athlete	**5.** cigarettes	**9.** winter
2. intellectual	**6.** whale	**10.** textbook
3. spinster	**7.** litter	**11.** drugs
4. husband	**8.** spider	**12.** housewife

Discussion and Composition

1. At the end of the story, Ellen states that she has made a man out of her husband, but Matt Tobin says, "God Almighty did that for him before you were born." Discuss what you think Ellen and Matt mean. Do you agree with Ellen or with Matt? Explain what you think it takes "to make a man."

2. Write an essay about an important decision you or someone you know had to make in order to preserve a value or ideal, such as friendship, honor, honesty, or loyalty. Begin by briefly explaining the situation that caused you or your acquaintance to have to make the decision. Tell what value or ideal was involved, and then explain how and why the decision was made. Include a discussion of the results of that choice.

3. In a short paragraph, describe the face of a person you know well. Before you begin, you may want to review the techniques the author uses to describe Ellen's face. You will also find it helpful to make a list of words or phrases you might use to describe your subject's hair, eyes, nose, cheekbones, mouth, and chin.

ARTHUR CONAN DOYLE
(1859–1930)

Sherlock Holmes, one of the most famous characters in fiction, was the creation of Sir Arthur Conan Doyle, a surgeon who began writing to supplement the income from his medical practice. Doyle was born in Edinburgh, Scotland, and attended schools in Scotland and Germany before studying medicine at the University of Edinburgh. He was a ship's surgeon on a voyage to the Arctic and to Africa before he married and practiced medicine in Portsmouth, England.

Doyle decided that he would try to invent a new kind of story that he hoped would capture a mass readership. He modeled the character of Sherlock Holmes on a medical school instructor whose deductive powers had amazed everyone.

The first Sherlock Holmes story, "A Study in Scarlet" (1887), received little attention when it was published after many rejections. About a year later, an American magazine editor called Doyle and asked Doyle to write another Sherlock Holmes story. That story, "The Sign of Four," launched Doyle's career as a master writer of detective stories. The public demanded and received so many stories about Sherlock Holmes that Doyle became bored with the character he had created. In "The Final Problem" (1893), he had Holmes killed by his arch enemy. Public protest was so great that Doyle had to bring Holmes back to life in the next story he wrote.

Doyle wrote fifty-six stories based on the character of Sherlock Holmes. He also wrote historical novels and nonfiction books. He was knighted in 1902 for his history of the South African (Boer) War, and for his work in a field hospital in South Africa.

THE MUSGRAVE RITUAL

An anomaly[1] which often struck me in the character of my friend Sherlock Holmes was that, although in his methods of thought he was the neatest and most methodical of mankind, and although also he affected a certain quiet primness of dress, he was none the less in his personal habits one of the most untidy men that ever drove a fellow-lodger to distraction. Not that I am in the least conventional in that respect myself. The rough-and-tumble work in Afghanistan, coming on the top of natural Bohemianism[2] of disposition, has made me rather more lax than befits a medical man. But with me there is a limit, and when I find a man who keeps his cigars in the coal-scuttle, his tobacco in the toe end of a persian slipper, and his unanswered correspondence transfixed by a jack-knife into the very centre of his wooden mantelpiece, then I begin to give myself virtuous airs. I have always held, too, that pistol practice should be distinctly an open-air pastime; and when Holmes, in one of his queer humours,[3] would sit in an armchair with his hair-trigger[4] and a hundred Boxer cartridges and proceed to adorn the opposite wall with a patriotic V. R.[5] done in bullet-pocks, I felt strongly that neither the atmosphere nor the appearance of our room was improved by it.

Our chambers were always full of chemicals and of criminal relics which had a way of wandering into unlikely positions, and of turning up in the butter-dish or in even less desirable places. But his papers were my great crux.[6] He had a horror of destroying documents, especially those which were connected with his past cases, and yet it was only once in every year or two that he would

---

1. anomaly (a·nōm′ə·lē): irregularity.
2. Bohemianism: unconventionalism. Because gypsies traveled through Bohemia the adjective *Bohemian* came to be associated with those who like the gypsies chose to live outside the usual life style of those around them.
3. humours: British spelling of *humors,* moods. Humors were thought to be body fluids that determine an individual's health and mood. The four humors were black bile (sadness), yellow bile (anger), phlegm (calmness or stolidity), and blood (cheerfulness).
4. hair-trigger: gun with a trigger that operates with very slight pressure.
5. V. R.: Victoria Regina (1819–1901) queen of Britain. *Regina* is Latin for queen.
6. crux (krŭks): cross; here, most difficult habit.

muster energy to docket[7] and arrange them; for, as I have mentioned somewhere in these incoherent memoirs, the outbursts of passionate energy when he performed the remarkable feats with which his name is associated were followed by reactions of lethargy during which he would lie about with his violin and his books, hardly moving save from the sofa to the table. Thus month after month his papers accumulated until every corner of the room was stacked with bundles of manuscript which were on no account to be burned, and which could not be put away save by their owner. One winter's night, as we sat together by the fire, I ventured to suggest to him that, as he had finished pasting extracts into his commonplace[8] book, he might employ the next two hours in making our room a little more habitable. He could not deny the justice of my request, so with a rather rueful face he went off to his bedroom, from which he returned presently pulling a large tin box behind him. This he placed in the middle of the floor, and, squatting down upon a stool in front of it, he threw back the lid. I could see that it was already a third full of bundles of paper tied up with red tape into separate packages.

"There are cases enough here, Watson," said he, looking at me with mischievous eyes. "I think that if you knew all that I had in this box you would ask me to pull some out instead of putting others in."

"These are the records of your early work, then?" I asked. "I have often wished that I had notes of those cases."

"Yes, my boy, these were all done prematurely before my biographer had come to glorify me." He lifted bundle after bundle in a tender caressing sort of way. "They are not all successes, Watson," said he. "But there are some pretty little problems among them. Here's the record of the Tarleton murders, and the case of Vamberry, the wine merchant, and the adventure of the old Russian woman, and the singular affair of the aluminum crutch, as well as a full account of Ricoletti of the club-foot, and his abominable wife. And here—ah, now, this really is something a little *recherché*."[9]

He dived his arm down to the bottom of the chest and

7. **docket:** label.
8. **commonplace:** reference; here, a book used for reference.
9. **recherché** (rə•shār′shā or rə•shār′•shā): French for rare or unusual.

brought up a small wooden box with a sliding lid such as children's toys are kept in. From within he produced a crumpled piece of paper, an old-fashioned brass key, a peg of wood with a ball of string attached to it, and three rusty old discs of metal.

"Well, my boy, what do you make of this lot?" he asked, smiling at my expression.

"It is a curious collection."

"Very curious, and the story that hangs round it will strike you as being more curious still."

"These relics have a history, then?"

"So much so that they *are* history."

"What do you mean by that?"

Sherlock Holmes picked them up one by one and laid them along the edge of the table. Then he reseated himself in his chair and looked them over with a gleam of satisfaction in his eyes.

"These," said he, "are all that I have left to remind me of the adventure of the Musgrave Ritual."

"I had heard him mention the case more than once, though I had never been able to gather the details. "I should be so glad," said I, "if you would give me an account of it."

"And leave the litter as it is?" he cried mischievously. "Your tidiness won't bear much strain, after all, Watson. But I should be glad that you should add this case to your annals, for there are points in it which make it quite unique in the criminal records of this or, I believe, of any other country. A collection of my trifling achievements would certainly be incomplete which contained no account of this very singular business.

"You may remember how the affair of the *Gloria Scott,* and my conversation with the unhappy man whose fate I told you of, first turned my attention in the direction of the profession which has become my life's work. You see me now when my name has become known far and wide, and when I am generally recognized both by the public and by the official force as being a final court of appeal in doubtful cases. Even when you knew me first, at the time of the affair which you have commemorated in 'A Study in Scarlet,' I had already established a considerable, though not a very lucrative, connection. You can hardly realize, then, how difficult I found it at first, and how long I had to wait before I succeeded in making any headway.

"When I first came up to London I had rooms in Montague

Street, just around the corner from the British Museum, and there I waited, filling in my too abundant leisure time by studying all those branches of science which might make me more efficient. Now and again cases came in my way, principally through the introduction of old fellow-students, for during my last years at the university there was a good deal of talk there about myself and my methods. The third of these cases was that of the Musgrave Ritual, and it is to the interest which was aroused by that singular chain of events, and the large issues which proved to be at stake, that I trace my first stride towards the position which I now hold.

"Reginald Musgrave had been in the same college as myself, and I had some slight acquaintance with him. He was not generally popular among the undergraduates, though it always seemed to me that what was set down as pride was really an attempt to cover extreme natural diffidence. In appearance he was a man of an exceedingly aristocratic type, thin, high-nosed, and large-eyed, with languid and yet courtly manners. He was indeed a scion[10] of one of the very oldest families in the kingdom, though his branch was a cadet[11] one which had separated from the northern Musgraves some time in the sixteenth century and had established itself in western Sussex, where the Manor House of Hurlstone is perhaps the oldest inhabited building in the county. Something of his birth-place seemed to cling to the man, and I never looked at his pale, keen face or the poise of his head without associating him with gray archways and mullioned[12] windows and all the venerable wreckage of a feudal keep.[13] Once or twice we drifted into talk, and I can remember that more than once he expressed a keen interest in my methods of observation and inference.

"For four years I had seen nothing of him until one morning he walked into my room in Montague Street. He had changed little, was dressed like a young man of fashion—he was always a bit of a dandy—and preserved the same quiet, suave manner which had formerly distinguished him.

"'How has all gone with you, Musgrave?' I asked after we had cordially shaken hands.

"'You probably heard of my poor father's death,' said he; 'he

10. **scion** (sī'ən): descendant.
11. **cadet** (kə•dĕt'): younger son.
12. **mullioned** (mŭl'yənd): vertically barred panels between panes of glass.
13. **keep:** fortress.

was carried off about two years ago. Since then I have of course had the Hurlstone estate to manage, and as I am member[14] for my district as well, my life has been a busy one. But I understand, Holmes, that you are turning to practical ends those powers with which you used to amaze us?'

" 'Yes,' said I, 'I have taken to living by my wits.'

" 'I am delighted to hear it, for your advice at present would be exceedingly valuable to me. We have had some very strange doings at Hurlstone, and the police have been able to throw no light upon the matter. It is really the most extraordinary and inexplicable business.'

"You can imagine with what eagerness I listened to him, Watson, for the very chance for which I had been panting during all those months of inaction seemed to have come within my reach. In my inmost heart I believed that I could succeed where others failed, and now I had the opportunity to test myself.

" 'Pray let me have the details,' I cried.

"Reginald Musgrave sat down opposite to me and lit the cigarette which I had pushed towards him.

" 'You must know,' said he, 'that though I am a bachelor, I have to keep up a considerable staff of servants at Hurlstone, for it is a rambling old place and takes a good deal of looking after. I preserve,[15] too, and in the pheasant months I usually have a house-party, so that it would not do to be short-handed. Altogether there are eight maids, the cook, the butler, two footmen, and a boy. The garden and the stables of course have a separate staff.

" 'Of these servants the one who had been longest in our service was Brunton, the butler. He was a young schoolmaster out of place when he was first taken up by my father, but he was a man of great energy and character, and he soon became quite invaluable in the household. He was a well-grown, handsome man, with a splendid forehead, and though he has been with us for twenty years he cannot be more than forty now. With his personal advantages and his extraordinary gifts—for he can speak several languages and play nearly every musical instrument—it is wonderful that he should have been satisfied so long in such a position, but I suppose that he was comfortable and lacked energy to make

14. **member:** member of Parliament.
15. **preserve:** to protect and maintain game for shooting.

any change. The butler of Hurlstone is always a thing that is remembered by all who visit us.

"'But this paragon has one fault. He is a bit of a Don Juan,[16] and you can imagine that for a man like him it is not a very difficult part to play in a quiet country district. When he was married it was all right, but since he has been a widower we have had no end of trouble with him. A few months ago we were in hopes that he was about to settle down again, for he became engaged to Rachel Howells, our second housemaid; but he has thrown her over since then and taken up with Janet Tregellis, the daughter of the head game-keeper. Rachel—who is a very good girl, but of an excitable Welsh temperament—had a sharp touch of brain-fever and goes about the house now—or did until yesterday—like a black-eyed shadow of her former self. That was our first drama at Hurlstone; but a second one came to drive it from our minds, and it was prefaced by the disgrace and dismissal of butler Brunton.

"'This was how it came about. I have said that the man was intelligent, and this very intelligence had caused his ruin, for it seems to have led to an insatiable curiosity about things which did not in the least concern him. I had no idea of the lengths to which this would carry him until the merest accident opened my eyes to it.

"'I have said that the house is a rambling one. One day last week—on Thursday night, to be more exact—I found that I could not sleep, having foolishly taken a cup of strong *café noir*[17] after my dinner. After struggling against it until two in the morning, I felt that it was quite hopeless, so I rose and lit the candle with the intention of continuing a novel which I was reading. The book, however, had been left in the billiard-room,[18] so I pulled on my dressing-gown and started off to get it.

"'In order to reach the billiard-room I had to descend a flight of stairs and then to cross the head of a passage which led to the library and the gun-room. You can imagine my surprise when, as I looked down this corridor, I saw a glimmer of light coming from

16. **Don Juan** (dōn′wän′): lover; Don Juan was a legendary Spanish nobleman who was the hero-villain of countless novels, plays, and poems. Mozart's opera *Don Giovanni* (1787) is based on the Don Juan legend.
17. **café noir** (kä fā nwär): French for black coffee (without cream or milk).
18. **billiard** (bĭl′yərd): table game played with balls and a long stick. The game of pool is one kind of billiard game.

the open door of the library. I had myself extinguished the lamp and closed the door before coming to bed. Naturally my first thought was of burglars. The corridors at Hurlstone have their walls largely decorated with trophies of old weapons. From one of these I picked a battle-axe, and then, leaving my candle behind me, I crept on tiptoe down the passage and peeped in at the open door.

"'Brunton, the butler, was in the library. He was sitting, fully dressed, in an easy-chair, with a slip of paper which looked like a map upon his knee, and his forehead sunk forward upon his hand in deep thought. I stood dumb with astonishment, watching him from the darkness. A small taper[19] on the edge of the table shed a feeble light which sufficed to show me that he was fully dressed. Suddenly, as I looked, he rose from his chair, and, walking over to a bureau at the side, he unlocked it and drew out one of the drawers. From this he took a paper, and, returning to his seat, he flattened it out beside the taper on the edge of the table and began to study it with minute attention. My indignation at this calm examination of our family documents overcame me so far that I took a step forward, and Brunton, looking up, saw me standing in the doorway. He sprang to his feet, his face turned livid with fear, and he thrust into his breast the chart-like paper which he had been originally studying.

"'"So!" said I. "This is how you repay the trust which we have reposed in you. You will leave my service to-morrow."

"'He bowed with the look of a man who is utterly crushed and slunk past me without a word. The taper was still on the table, and by its light I glanced to see what the paper was which Brunton had taken from the bureau. To my surprise it was nothing of any importance at all, but simply a copy of the questions and answers in the singular old observance called the Musgrave Ritual. It is a sort of ceremony peculiar to our family, which each Musgrave for centuries past has gone through on his coming of age—a thing of private interest, and perhaps of some little importance to the archaeologist, like our own blazonings, and charges,[20] but of no practical use whatever.'

19. taper: a slender candle.
20. blazonings, and charges: shields and bearings (symbols of the shield); refers to hereditary coats-of-arms used to distinguish families and individuals. In the West, hereditary symbols (called *heraldry*) were first used on armor and on seals.

" 'We had better come back to the paper afterwards,' said I.

" 'If you think it really necessary,' he answered with some hesitation. 'To continue my statement, however: I relocked the bureau, using the key which Brunton had left, and I had turned to go when I was surprised to find that the butler had returned, and was standing before me.

" ' "Mr. Musgrave, sir," he cried in a voice which was hoarse with emotion. "I can't bear disgrace, sir. I've always been proud above my station in life, and disgrace would kill me. My blood will be on your head, sir—it will, indeed—if you drive me to despair. If you cannot keep me after what has passed, then for God's sake let me give you notice and leave in a month, as if on my own free will. I could stand that, Mr. Musgrave, but not to be cast out before all the folk that I know so well."

" ' "You don't deserve much consideration, Brunton," I answered. "Your conduct has been most infamous. However, as you have been a long time in the family, I have no wish to bring public disgrace upon you. A month, however, is too long. Take yourself away in a week, and give what reason you like for going."

" ' "Only a week, sir?" he cried in a despairing voice. "A fortnight[21]—say at least a fortnight!"

" ' "A week," I repeated, "and you may consider yourself to have been very leniently dealt with."

" 'He crept away, his face sunk upon his breast, like a broken man, while I put out the light and returned to my room.

" 'For two days after this Brunton was most assiduous in his attention to his duties. I made no allusion to what had passed and waited with some curiosity to see how he would cover his disgrace. On the third morning, however, he did not appear, as was his custom, after breakfast to receive my instructions for the day. As I left the dining-room I happened to meet Rachel Howells, the maid. I have told you that she had only recently recovered from an illness and was looking so wretchedly pale and wan that I remonstrated with her for being at work.

" ' "You should be in bed," I said. "Come back to your duties when you are stronger."

" 'She looked at me with so strange an expression that I began to suspect that her brain was affected.

21. fortnight: two weeks.

" " "I am strong enough, Mr. Musgrave," said she.

" " "We will see what the doctor says," I answered. "You must stop work now, and when you go downstairs just say that I wish to see Brunton."

" " "The butler is gone," said she.

" " "Gone! Gone where?"

" " "He is gone. No one has seen him. He is not in his room. Oh, yes, he is gone, he is gone!" She fell back against the wall with shriek after shriek of laughter, while I, horrified at this sudden hysterical attack, rushed to the bell to summon help. The girl was taken to her room, still screaming and sobbing, while I made inquiries about Brunton. There was no doubt about it that he had disappeared. His bed had not been slept in, he had been seen by no one since he had retired to his room the night before, and yet it was difficult to see how he could have left the house, as both windows and doors were found to be fastened in the morning. His clothes, his watch, and even his money were in his room, but the black suit which he usually wore was missing. His slippers, too, were gone, but his boots were left behind. Where then could butler Brunton have gone in the night, and what could have become of him now?

" 'Of course we searched the house from cellar to garret,[22] but there was no trace of him. It is, as I have said, a labyrinth[23] of an old house, especially the original wing, which is now practically uninhabited; but we ransacked every room and cellar without discovering the least sign of the missing man. It was incredible to me that he could have gone away leaving all his property behind him, and yet where could he be? I called in the local police, but without success. Rain had fallen on the night before, and we examined the lawn and the paths all round the house, but in vain. Matters were in this state, when a new development quite drew our attention away from the original mystery.

" 'For two days Rachel Howells had been so ill, sometimes delirious, sometimes hysterical, that a nurse had been employed to sit up with her at night. On the third night after Brunton's disap-

___

22. **garret** (găr′ĭt): attic.
23. **labyrinth** (lăb′ə·rĭnth′): a confusing and difficult place to find one's way. In Greek legend, Daedalus built a labyrinth, or maze, for King Minos of Crete. At the center of the maze was the Minotaur, a monster half-bull, half-man.

pearance, the nurse, finding her patient sleeping nicely, had dropped into a nap in the armchair, when she woke in the early morning to find the bed empty, the window open, and no signs of the invalid. I was instantly aroused, and, with the two footmen, started off at once in search of the missing girl. It was not difficult to tell the direction which she had taken, for, starting from under her window, we could follow her footmarks easily across the lawn to the edge of the mere,[24] where they vanished close to the gravel path which leads out of the grounds. The lake there is eight feet deep, and you can imagine our feelings when we saw that the trail of the poor demented girl came to an end at the edge of it.

"'Of course, we had the drags[25] at once and set to work to recover the remains, but no trace of the body could we find. On the other hand, we brought to the surface an object of a most unexpected kind. It was a linen bag which contained within it a mass of old rusted and discoloured metal and several dull-coloured pieces of pebble or glass. This strange find was all that we could get from the mere, and, although we made every possible search and inquiry yesterday, we know nothing of the fate either of Rachel Howells or of Richard Brunton. The county police are at their wit's end, and I have come up to you as a last resource.'

"You can imagine, Watson, with what eagerness I listened to this extraordinary sequence of events, and endeavoured to piece them together, and to devise some common thread upon which they might all hang. The butler was gone. The maid was gone. The maid had loved the butler, but had afterwards had cause to hate him. She was of Welsh blood, fiery and passionate. She had been terribly excited immediately after his disappearance. She had flung into the lake a bag containing some curious contents. These were all factors which had to be taken into consideration, and yet none of them got quite to the heart of the matter. What was the starting-point of this chain of events? There lay the end of this tangled line.

"'I must see that paper, Musgrave,' said I, 'which this butler of yours thought it worth his while to consult, even at the risk of the loss of his place.'

"'It is rather an absurd business, this ritual of ours,' he an-

24. **mere** (mîr): small lake.
25. **drags:** hooks and nets used to search for a drowned person's body.

swered. 'But it has at least the saving grace of antiquity to excuse it. I have a copy of the questions and answers here if you care to run your eye over them.'

"He handed me the very paper which I have here, Watson, and this is the strange catechism[26] to which each Musgrave had to submit when he came to man's estate. I will read you the questions and answers as they stand.

"'Whose was it?'

"'His who is gone.'

"'Who shall have it?'

"'He who will come.'

"'Where was the sun?'

"'Over the oak.'

"'Where was the shadow?'

"'Under the elm.'

"'How was it stepped?'

"'North by ten and by ten, east by five and by five, south by two and by two, west by one and by one, and so under.'

"'What shall we give for it?'

"'All that is ours.'

"'Why should we give it?'

"'For the sake of the trust.'

"'The original has no date, but is in the spelling of the middle of the seventeenth century,' remarked Musgrave. 'I am afraid, however, that it can be of little help to you in solving this mystery.'

"'At least,' said I, 'it gives us another mystery, and one which is even more interesting than the first. It may be that the solution of the one may prove to be the solution of the other. You will excuse me, Musgrave, if I say that your butler appears to me to have been a very clever man, and to have had a clearer insight than ten generations of his masters.'

"'I hardly follow you,' said Musgrave. 'The paper seems to me to be of no practical importance.'

"'But to me it seems immensely practical, and I fancy that Brunton took the same view. He had probably seen it before that night on which you caught him.'

"'It is very possible. We took no pains to hide it.'

26. **catechism** (kăt′ə•kĭz′•əm): series of questions and answers.

"'He simply wished, I should imagine, to refresh his memory upon that last occasion. He had, as I understand, some sort of map or chart which he was comparing with the manuscript, and which he thrust into his pocket when you appeared.'

"'That is true. But what could he have to do with this old family custom of ours, and what does this rigmarole mean?'

"'I don't think that we should have much difficulty in determining that,' said I; 'with your permission we will take the first train down to Sussex and go a little more deeply into the matter upon the spot.'

"The same afternoon saw us both at Hurlstone. Possibly you have seen pictures and read descriptions of the famous old building, so I will confine my account of it to saying that it is built in the shape of an L, the long arm being the more modern portion, and the shorter the ancient nucleus from which the other has developed. Over the low, heavy-lintelled[27] door, in the centre of this old part, is chiselled the date, 1607, but experts are agreed that the beams and stonework are really much older than this. The enormously thick walls and tiny windows of this part had in the last century driven the family into building the new wing, and the old one was used now as a storehouse and a cellar, when it was used at all. A splendid park with fine old timber surrounds the house, and the lake, to which my client had referred, lay close to the avenue, about two hundred yards from the building.

"I was already firmly convinced, Watson, that there were not three separate mysteries here, but one only, and that if I could read the Musgrave Ritual aright I should hold in my hand the clue which would lead me to the truth concerning both the butler Brunton and the maid Howells. To that then I turned all my energies. Why should this servant be so anxious to master this old formula? Evidently because he saw something in it which had escaped all those generations of country squires, and from which he expected some personal advantage. What was it then, and how had it affected his fate?

"It was perfectly obvious to me, on reading the Ritual, that the measurements must refer to some spot to which the rest of the document alluded, and that if we could find that spot we should

---

27. heavy-lintelled: heavy-beamed. A lintel is a stone or wooden beam over a window or door.

be in a fair way towards finding what the secret was which the old Musgraves had thought it necessary to embalm[28] in so curious a fashion. There were two guides given us to start with, an oak and an elm. As to the oak there could be no question at all. Right in front of the house, upon the left-hand side of the drive, there stood a patriarch among oaks, one of the most magnificent trees that I have ever seen.

" 'That was there when your Ritual was drawn up,' said I as we drove past it.

" 'It was there at the Norman Conquest[29] in all probability,' he answered. 'It has a girth of twenty-three feet.'

"Here was one of my fixed points secured.

" 'Have you any old elms?' I asked.

" 'There used to be a very old one over yonder, but it was struck by lightning ten years ago, and we cut down the stump.'

" 'You can see where it used to be?'

" 'Oh, yes.'

" 'There are no other elms?'

" 'No old ones, but plenty of beeches.'

" 'I should like to see where it grew.'

"We had driven up in a dog-cart, and my client led me away at once, without our entering the house, to the scar on the lawn where the elm had stood. It was nearly midway between the oak and the house. My investigation seemed to be progressing.

" 'I suppose it is impossible to find out how high the elm was?' I asked.

" 'I can give you it at once. It was sixty-four feet.'

" 'How do you come to know it?' I asked in surprise.

" 'When my old tutor used to give me an exercise in trigonometry, it always took the shape of measuring heights. When I was a lad I worked out every tree and building in the estate.'

"This was an unexpected piece of luck. My data were coming more quickly than I could have reasonably hoped.

" 'Tell me,' I asked, 'did your butler ever ask you such a question?'

28. **embalm** (ĕm·bäm'): preserve.
29. **Norman Conquest:** Normans, under the leadership of William the Conqueror, conquered England in 1066. Normandy is an area in Northwestern France.

"Reginald Musgrave looked at me in astonishment. 'Now that you call it to my mind,' he answered, 'Brunton *did* ask me about the height of the tree some months ago in connection with some little argument with the groom.'

"This was excellent news, Watson, for it showed me that I was on the right road. I looked up at the sun. It was low in the heavens, and I calculated that in less than an hour it would lie just above the topmost branches of the old oak. One condition mentioned in the Ritual would then be fulfilled. And the shadow of the elm must mean the farther end of the shadow, otherwise the trunk would have been chosen as the guide. I had, then, to find where the far end of the shadow would fall when the sun was just clear of the oak."

"That must have been difficult, Holmes, when the elm was no longer there."

"Well, at least I knew that if Brunton could do it, I could also. Besides, there was no real difficulty. I went with Musgrave to his study and whittled myself this peg, to which I tied this long string with a knot at each yard. Then I took two lengths of a fishing-rod, which came to just six feet, and I went back with my client to where the elm had been. The sun was just grazing the top of the oak. I fastened the rod on end, marked out the direction of the shadow, and measured it. It was nine feet in length.

"Of course the calculation now was a simple one. If a rod of six feet threw a shadow of nine, a tree of sixty-four feet would throw one of ninety-six, and the line of the one would of course be the line of the other. I measured out the distance, which brought me almost to the wall of the house, and I thrust a peg into the spot. You can imagine my exultation, Watson, when within two inches of my peg I saw a conical depression in the ground. I knew that it was the mark made by Brunton in his measurements, and that I was still upon his trail.

"From this starting-point I proceeded to step, having first taken the cardinal[30] points by my pocket-compass. Ten steps with each foot took me along parallel with the wall of the house, and again I marked my spot with a peg. Then I carefully paced off five to the east and two to the south. It brought me to the very threshold of the old door. Two steps to the west meant now that I was to

30. cardinal: main or primary. The cardinal points of the compass are north, south, east, and west.

go two paces down the stone-flagged passage, and this was the place indicated by the Ritual.

"Never have I felt such a cold chill of disappointment, Watson. For a moment it seemed to me that there must be some radical mistake in my calculations. The setting sun shone full upon the passage floor, and I could see that the old, foot-worn gray stones with which it was paved were firmly cemented together, and had certainly not been moved for many a long year. Brunton had not been at work here. I tapped upon the floor, but it sounded the same all over, and there was no sign of any crack or crevice. But, fortunately, Musgrave, who had begun to appreciate the meaning of my proceedings, and who was now as excited as myself, took out his manuscript to check my calculations.

"'And under,' he cried. 'You have omitted the "and under."'

"I had thought that it meant that we were to dig, but now, of course I saw at once that I was wrong. 'There is a cellar under this then?' I cried.

"'Yes, and as old as the house. Down here, through this door.'

"We went down a winding stone stair, and my companion, striking a match, lit a large lantern which stood on a barrel in the corner. In an instant it was obvious that we had at last come upon the true place, and that we had not been the only people to visit the spot recently.

"It had been used for the storage of wood, but the billets,[31] which had evidently been littered over the floor, were now piled at the sides, so as to leave a clear space in the middle. In this space lay a large and heavy flagstone with a rusted iron ring in the centre to which a thick shepherd's-check muffler[32] was attached.

"'By Jove!' cried my client. 'That's Brunton's muffler. I have seen it on him and could swear to it. What has the villain been doing here?'

"At my suggestion a couple of the county police were summoned to be present, and I then endeavoured to raise the stone by pulling on the cravat.[33] I could only move it slightly, and it was with the aid of one of the constables that I succeeded at last in

31. **billets** (bĭl′ĭts): thick wooden sticks.
32. **muffler:** scarf.
33. **cravat** (krə•vat′): scarf.

carrying it to one side. A black hole yawned beneath into which we all peered, while Musgrave, kneeling at the side, pushed down the lantern.

"A small chamber about seven feet deep and four feet square lay open to us. At one side of this was a squat, brass-bound wooden box, the lid of which was hinged upward, with this curious old-fashioned key projecting from the lock. It was furred outside by a thick layer of dust, and damp and worms had eaten through the wood, so that a crop of livid fungi was growing on the inside of it. Several discs of metal, old coins apparently, such as I hold here, were scattered over the bottom of the box, but it contained nothing else.

"At the moment, however, we had no thought for the old chest, for our eyes were riveted upon that which crouched beside it. It was the figure of a man, clad in a suit of black, who squatted down upon his hams with his forehead sunk upon the edge of the box and his two arms thrown out on each side of it. The attitude had drawn all the stagnant blood to the face, and no man could have recognized that distorted liver-coloured countenance; but his height, his dress, and his hair were all sufficient to show my client, when we had drawn the body up, that it was indeed his missing butler. He had been dead some days, but there was no wound or bruise upon his person to show how he had met his dreadful end. When his body had been carried from the cellar we found ourselves still confronted with a problem which was almost as formidable as that with which we had started.

"I confess that so far, Watson, I had been disappointed in my investigation. I had reckoned upon solving the matter when once I had found the place referred to in the Ritual; but now I was there, and was apparently as far as ever from knowing what it was which the family had concealed with such elaborate precautions. It is true that I had thrown a light upon the fate of Brunton, but now I had to ascertain how that fate had come upon him, and what part had been played in the matter by the woman who had disappeared. I sat down upon a keg in the corner and thought the whole matter carefully over.

"You know my methods in such cases, Watson. I put myself in the man's place, and, having first gauged his intelligence, I try to imagine how I should myself have proceeded under the same circumstances. In this case the matter was simplified by Brunton's intelligence being quite first-rate, so that it was unnecessary to make any allowance for the personal equation, as the astronomers have dubbed it. He knew that something valuable was concealed. He had spotted the place. He found that the stone which covered it was just too heavy for a man to move unaided. What would he do next? He could not get help from outside, even if he had someone whom he could trust, without the unbarring of doors and considerable risk of detection. It was better, if he could, to have his helpmate inside the house. But whom could he ask? This girl had been devoted to him. A man always finds it hard to realize that he may have finally lost a woman's love, however badly he may have treated her. He would try by a few attentions to make his peace with the girl Howells, and then would engage her as his accomplice. Together they would come at night to the cellar, and their united force would suffice to raise the stone. So far I could follow their actions as if I had actually seen them.

"But for two of them, and one a woman, it must have been heavy work, the raising of that stone. A burly Sussex policeman and I had found it no light job. What would they do to assist them? Probably what I should have done myself. I rose and examined carefully the different billets of wood which were scattered round the floor. Almost at once I came upon what I expected. One piece, about three feet in length, had a very marked indentation at one end, while several were flattened at the sides as if they had been compressed by some considerable weight. Evidently, as they had dragged the stone up, they had thrust the chunks of wood into the chink until at last when the opening was large enough to crawl through, they would hold it open by a billet placed lengthwise, which might very well become indented at the lower end, since the whole weight of the stone would press it down on to the edge of this other slab. So far I was still on safe ground.

"And now how was I to proceed to reconstruct this midnight drama? Clearly, only one could fit into the hole, and that one was Brunton. The girl must have waited above. Brunton then unlocked the box, handed up the contents presumably—since they were not to be found—and then—and then what happened?

"What smouldering fire of vengeance had suddenly sprung into flame in this passionate Celtic woman's soul when she saw the man who had wronged her—wronged her, perhaps, far more than we suspected—in her power? Was it a chance that the wood had slipped and that the stone had shut Brunton into what had become his sepulchre?[34] Had she only been guilty of silence as to his fate? Or had some sudden blow from her hand dashed the support away and sent the slab crashing down into its place? Be that as it might, I seemed to see that woman's figure still clutching at her treasure trove and flying wildly up the winding stair, with her ears ringing perhaps with the muffled screams from behind her and with the drumming of frenzied hands against the slab of stone which was choking her faithless lover's life out.

"Here was the secret of her blanched face, her shaken nerves, her peals of hysterical laughter on the next morning. But what had been in the box? What had she done with that? Of course, it must have been the old metal and pebbles which my client had dragged from the mere. She had thrown them in there at the first opportunity to remove the last trace of her crime.

"For twenty minutes I had sat motionless, thinking the matter out. Musgrave still stood with a very pale face, swinging his lantern and peering down into the hole.

"'These are coins of Charles the First,'[35] said he, holding out the few which had been in the box; you see we were right in fixing our date for the Ritual.'

"'We may find something else of Charles the First,' I cried, as the probable meaning of the first two questions of the Ritual broke suddenly upon me. 'Let me see the contents of the bag which you fished from the mere.'

"We ascended to his study, and he laid the débris before me. I could understand his regarding it as of small importance when I looked at it, for the metal was almost black and the stones lustreless and dull. I rubbed one of them on my sleeve, however, and it glowed afterwards like a spark in the dark hollow of my hand. The metal work was in the form of a double ring, but it had been bent and twisted out of its original shape.

"'You must bear in mind,' said I, 'that the royal party made head in England even after the death of the king, and that when they at last fled they probably left many of their most precious

34. **sepulchre** (sĕp'əl·kər): burial place.
35. **Charles the First:** Charles Stuart (1609–1649), an authoritarian British king who dissolved Parliament in 1629 and ruled without a legislative body. After eleven years, he was forced to call Parliament again because he needed money for his war against the Scots. After surrendering to the Scots in 1646, he was convicted of treason and beheaded by Parliamentarian forces.

possessions buried behind them, with the intention of returning for them in more peaceful times.'

"'My ancestor, Sir Ralph Musgrave, was a prominent cavalier and the righthand man of Charles the Second[36] in his wanderings,' said my friend.

"'Ah, indeed!' I answered. 'Well now, I think that really should give us the last link that we wanted. I must congratulate you on coming into the possession, though in rather a tragic manner, of a relic which is of great intrinsic value, but of even greater importance as a historical curiosity.'

"'What is it, then?' he gasped in astonishment.

"'It is nothing less than the ancient crown of the kings of England.'

"'The crown!'

"'Precisely. Consider what the Ritual says. How does it run? "Whose was it?" "His who is gone." That was after the execution of Charles. Then, "Who shall have it?" "He who will come." That was Charles the Second, whose advent was already foreseen. There can, I think, be no doubt that this battered and shapeless diadem once encircled the brows of the royal Stuarts.'[37]

"'And how came it in the pond?'

"'Ah, that is a question that will take some time to answer.' And with that I sketched out to him the whole long surmise and of proof which I had constructed. The twilight had closed in and the moon was shining brightly in the sky before my narrative was finished.

"'And how was it then that Charles did not get his crown when he returned?' asked Musgrave, pushing back the relic into its linen bag.

"'Ah, there you lay your finger upon the one point which we shall probably never be able to clear up. It is likely that the Musgrave who held the secret died in the interval, and by some oversight left this guide to his descendant without explaining the meaning of it. From that day to this it has been handed down from father to son, until at last it came within reach of a man who tore its secret out of it and lost his life in the venture.'

36. Charles the Second: British king, son of Charles the First. Charles the Second (1630–1685) was proclaimed king by the Scots and was restored to the throne in 1660.

37. Stuarts: surname of Scottish family that ruled Scotland, England, and Ireland through most of the seventeenth and eighteenth centuries.

"And that's the story of the Musgrave Ritual, Watson. They have the crown down at Hurlstone—though they had some legal bother and a considerable sum to pay before they were allowed to retain it. I am sure that if you mentioned my name they would be happy to show it to you. Of the woman nothing was ever heard, and the probability is that she got away out of England and carried herself and the memory of her crime to some land beyond the seas."

Meaning

1. At what point in Sherlock Holmes' career did the Musgrave Ritual case take place? Why did Holmes consider this case important?
2. Holmes pulled the following "relics" from a wooden box: a crumpled piece of paper, a brass key, a peg of wood with a ball of string attached to it, and three rusty old discs of metal. Where does each of these items fit into the story?
3. Holmes said that his methods were observation and inference. What are some examples of his use of these methods in the story?
4. What had the maid thrown into the lake?

Method

1. Who is the primary narrator of the story? Who tells the story within the story? At what point is there even a third narrator? Is this method of telling the story confusing, or interesting and important to the plot? Why do you think so?
2. Describe the character of Sherlock Holmes. Do you find him a likeable personality? Why or why not?
3. What questions keep the readers in suspense as the case unfolds?
4. Which element do you think is most important in this story: character, plot, theme, setting, or tone?
5. Why might Doyle's style be described as formal? Consider his choice of words and the length of his sentences. Do you believe a formal style is appropriate for this story? Why or why not?

Language: Differences in British and American Words, Spelling, and Pronunciations

British and Americans sometimes use different words to mean the same thing. In this story, Brunton begs to be allowed to stay on as butler for a fortnight. The American equivalent for *fortnight* is two weeks. Rachel Howells' footprints end at the edge of the *mere*—a word that the British use poetically to mean *lake*.

There are also some differences in British and American spellings. Some words that end in *-er* in this country end in *-re* in England. In this story, for example, *center* is spelled *centre; sepulcher* becomes *sepulchre; lusterless* becomes *lustreless*. In America, words that contain *-or* may be spelled *-our* in England. Instead of *discolored*, the British write *discoloured;* instead of *endeavored*, they write *endeavoured;* instead of *humors*, they spell it *humours*.

Sometimes, even when the spelling is the same, the pronunciation is different. For example, the British pronunciation of *tomato* is tə•mä′tō with a broad *a*, and the words *laboratory* and *schedule* are pronounced lə•bŏr′ə•trē and schĕd′yo͞ol.

See if you can find out the American equivalents of the following British expressions:

1. telly	**4.** underground
2. bobby	**5.** lift
3. cinema	**6.** diversion (a road sign)

Discussion and Composition

1. Discuss why you think Sherlock Holmes stories have been so popular with generations of readers. Do you think these stories will continue to be popular in the future? Why or why not?

2. Write another ending to the story explaining what you think happened to Rachel Howells. Use the information about her in "The Musgrave Ritual" as your starting point. Consider the following questions: Where did she go? How did she get there? Did she have any adventures along the way? What was her new life like? Did she ever think about the events at Hurlston?

WILLIAM MELVIN KELLEY
(born 1937)

Born in New York City, William Melvin Kelley chose writing as a career while he was a student at Harvard University. The success of *A Different Drummer,* published when he was twenty-five, proved that he made the right decision. On the dedication page of *Dancers on the Shore* (1964), the short story collection that includes "A Visit to Grandmother," Kelley explains that the person who listened to him and encouraged his ambition to write rather than choosing "a more secure and respectable occupation" was his grandmother, Jessie Garcia, "who was the only family I had."

Kelley has received several literary awards for his novels and short stories, which have been widely praised. His stories and articles appear in popular magazines such as *Esquire, Mademoiselle, The Negro Digest,* and *The Saturday Evening Post.*

A VISIT TO GRANDMOTHER

Chig knew something was wrong the instant his father kissed her. He had always known his father to be the warmest of men, a man so kind that when people ventured timidly into his office, it took only a few words from him to make them relax, and even laugh. Doctor Charles Dunford cared about people.

But when he had bent to kiss the old lady's black face, something new and almost ugly had come into his eyes: fear, uncertainty, sadness, and perhaps even hatred.

Ten days before in New York, Chig's father had decided suddenly he wanted to go to Nashville to attend his college class reunion, twenty years out. Both Chig's brother and sister, Peter and Connie, were packing for camp and besides were too young for such an affair. But Chig was seventeen, had nothing to do that summer, and his father asked if he would like to go along. His father had given him additional reasons: "All my running buddies got their diplomas and were snapped up by them crafty young gals, and had kids within a year—now all those kids, some of them gals, are your age."

The reunion had lasted a week. As they packed for home, his father, in a far too offhand way, had suggested they visit Chig's grandmother. "We this close. We might as well drop in on her and my brothers."

So instead of going north, they had gone farther south, had just entered her house. And Chig had a suspicion now that the reunion had been only an excuse to drive south, that his father had been heading to this house all the time.

His father had never talked much about his family, with the exception of his brother, GL, who seemed part con man, part practical joker, and part Don Juan; he had spoken of GL with the kind of indulgence he would have shown a cute but ill-behaved and potentially dangerous five-year-old.

Chig's father had left home when he was fifteen. When asked why, he would answer: "I wanted to go to school. They didn't have a Negro high school at home, so I went up to Knoxville and lived with a cousin and went to school."

They had been met at the door by Aunt Rose, GL's wife, and ushered into the living room. The old lady had looked up from her seat by the window. Aunt Rose stood between the visitors.

The old lady eyed his father. "Rose, who that? Rose?" She squinted. She looked like a doll made of black straw, the wrinkles in her face running in one direction like the head of a broom. Her hair was white and coarse and grew out straight from her head. Her eyes were brown—the whites, too, seemed light brown—and were hidden behind thick glasses, which remained somehow on a tiny nose. "That Hiram? That was another of his father's brothers. "No, it ain't Hiram; too big for Hiram." She turned then to Chig. "Now that man, he look like Eleanor, Charles's wife, but Charles wouldn't never send my grandson to see me. I never even hear from Charles." She stopped again.

"It Charles, Mama. That who it is." Aunt Rose, between them, led them closer. "It Charles come all the way from New York to see you, and brung little Charles with him."

The old lady stared up at them. "Charles? Rose, that really Charles?" She turned away, and reached for a handkerchief in the pocket of her clean, ironed, flowered housecoat, and wiped her eyes. "God have mercy. Charles." She spread her arms up to him, and he bent down and kissed her cheek. That was when Chig saw his face, grimacing. She hugged him; Chig watched the muscles in her arms as they tightened around his father's neck. She half rose out of her chair. "How are you, son?"

Chig could not hear his father's answer.

She let him go, and fell back into her chair, grabbing the arms. Her hands were as dark as the wood, and seemed to become part of it. "Now, who that standing there? Who that man?"

"That's one of your grandsons, Mama." His father's voice cracked. "Charles Dunford, junior. You saw him once, when he was a baby, in Chicago. He's grown now."

"I can see that, boy!" She looked at Chig squarely. "Come here, son, and kiss me once." He did. "What they call you? Charles too?"

"No, ma'am, they call me Chig."

She smiled. She had all her teeth, but they were too perfect to be her own. "That's good. Can't have two boys answering to Charles in the same house. Won't nobody at all come. So you that little boy. You don't remember me, do you? I used to take you to church in Chicago, and you'd get up and hop in time to the music. You studying to be a preacher?"

"No, ma'am. I don't think so. I might be a lawyer."

"You'll be an honest one, won't you?"

"I'll try."

"Trying ain't enough! You be honest, you hear? Promise me. You be honest like your daddy."

"All right. I promise."

"Good. Rose, where's GL at? Where's that thief? He gone again?"

"I don't know, Mama." Aunt Rose looked embarrassed. "He say he was going by his liquor store. He'll be back."

"Well, then where's Hiram? You call up those boys, and get them over here—now! You got enough to eat? Let me go see." She started to get up. Chig reached out his hand. She shook him off. "What they tell you about me, Chig? They tell you I'm all laid up? Don't believe it. They don't know nothing about old ladies. When I want help, I'll let you know. Only time I'll need help getting any-wheres is when I dies and they lift me into the ground."

She was standing now, her back and shoulders straight. She came only to Chig's chest. She squinted up at him. "You eat much? Your daddy ate like two men."

"Yes, ma'am."

"That's good. That means you ain't nervous. Your mama, she

ain't nervous. I remember that. In Chicago, she'd sit down by a window all afternoon and never say nothing, just knit." She smiled. "Let me see what we got to eat."

"I'll do that, Mama." Aunt Rose spoke softly. "You haven't seen Charles in a long time. You sit and talk."

The old lady squinted at her. "You can do the cooking if you promise it ain't because you think I can't."

Aunt Rose chuckled. "I know you can do it, Mama."

"All right. I'll just sit and talk a spell." She sat again and arranged her skirt around her short legs.

Chig did most of the talking, told all about himself before she asked. His father only spoke when he was spoken to, and then only one word at a time, as if by coming back home he had become a small boy again, sitting in the parlor while his mother spoke with her guests.

When Uncle Hiram and Mae, his wife, came, they sat down to eat. Chig did not have to ask about Uncle GL's absence; Aunt Rose volunteered an explanation: "Can't never tell where the man is at. One Thursday morning he left here and next thing we knew, he was calling from Chicago, saying he went up to see Joe Louis fight. He'll be here though; he ain't as young and footloose as he used to be." Chig's father had mentioned driving down that GL was about five years older than he was, nearly fifty.

Uncle Hiram was somewhat smaller than Chig's father; his short-cropped kinky hair was half gray, half black. One spot, just off his forehead, was totally white. Later, Chig found out it had been that way since he was twenty. Mae (Chig could not bring himself to call her Aunt) was a good deal younger than Hiram, pretty enough so that Chig would have looked at her twice on the street. She was a honey-colored woman, with long eyelashes. She was wearing a white sheath.

At dinner, Chig and his father sat on one side, opposite Uncle Hiram and Mae; his grandmother and Aunt Rose sat at the ends. The food was good; there was a lot and Chig ate a lot. All through the meal, they talked about the family as it had been thirty years before, and particularly about the young GL. Mae and Chig asked questions; the old lady answered; Aunt Rose directed the discussion, steering the old lady onto the best stories; Chig's father laughed from time to time; Uncle Hiram ate.

"Why don't you tell them about the horse, Mama?" Aunt Rose,

over Chig's weak protest, was spooning mashed potatoes onto his plate. "There now, Chig."

"I'm trying to think." The old lady was holding her fork halfway to her mouth, looking at them over her glasses. "Oh, you talking about that crazy horse GL brung home that time."

"That's right, Mama." Aunt Rose nodded and slid another slice of white meat onto Chig's plate.

Mae started to giggle. "Oh, I've heard this. This is funny, Chig."

The old lady put down her fork and began: Well, GL went out of the house one day with an old, no-good chair I wanted him to take over to the church for a bazaar, and he met up with this man who'd just brung in some horses from out West. Now, I reckon you can expect one swindler to be in every town, but you don't rightly think there'll be two, and God forbid they should ever meet—but they did, GL and his chair, this man and his horses. Well, I wish I'd-a been there; there must-a been some mighty high-powered talking going on. That man with his horses, he told GL them horses was half-Arab, half-Indian, and GL told that man the chair was an antique he'd stole from some rich white folks. So they swapped. Well, I was a-looking out the window and seen GL dragging this animal to the house. It looked pretty gentle and its eyes was most closed and its feet was shuffling.

"GL, where'd you get that thing?" I says.

"I swapped him for that old chair, Mama," he says. "And made myself a bargain. This is even better than Papa's horse."

Well, I'm a-looking at this horse and noticing how he be looking more and more wide awake every minute, sort of warming up like a teakettle until, I swears to you, that horse is blowing steam out its nose.

"Come on, Mama," GL says, "come on and I'll take you for a ride." Now George, my husband, God rest his tired soul, he'd brung home this white folks' buggy which had a busted wheel and fixed it and was to take it back that day and GL says: "Come on, Mama, we'll use this fine buggy and take us a ride."

"GL," I says, "no, we ain't. Them white folks'll burn us alive if we use their buggy. You just take that horse right on back." You see, I was sure that boy'd come by that animal ungainly.

"Mama, I can't take him back," GL says.

"Why not?" I says.

"Because I don't rightly know where that man is at," GL says.

"Oh," I says. "Well, then I reckon we stuck with it." And I turned around to go back into the house because it was getting late, near dinner time, and I was cooking for ten.

"Mama," GL says to my back. "Mama, ain't you coming for a ride with me?"

"Go on, boy. You ain't getting me inside kicking range of that animal." I was eying that beast and it was boiling hotter all the time. I reckon maybe that man had drugged it. "That horse is wild, GL," I says.

"No, he ain't. He ain't. That man say he is buggy and saddle broke and as sweet as the inside of a apple."

My oldest girl, Essie, had-a come out on the porch and she says: "Go on, Mama. I'll cook. You ain't been out the house in weeks."

"Sure, come on, Mama," GL says. "There ain't nothing to be fidgety about. This horse is gentle as a rose petal." And just then that animal snorts so hard it sets up a little dust storm around its feet.

"Yes, Mama," Essie says, "you can see he gentle." Well, I looked at Essie and then at that horse because I didn't think we could be looking at the same animal. I should-a figured how Essie's eyes ain't never been so good.

"Come on, Mama," GL says.

"All right," I says. So I stood on the porch and watched GL hitching that horse up to the white folks' buggy. For a while there, the animal was pretty quiet, pawing a little, but not much. And I was feeling a little better about riding with GL behind that crazy-looking horse. I could see how GL was happy I was going with him. He was scurrying around that animal buckling buckles and strapping straps, all the time smiling, and that made me feel good.

Then he was finished, and I must say, that horse looked mighty fine hitched to that buggy and I knew anybody what climbed up there would look pretty good too. GL came around and stood at the bottom of the steps, and took off his hat and bowed and said: "Madam," and reached out his hand to me and I was feeling real elegant like a fine lady. He helped me up to the seat and then got up beside me and we moved out down our alley. And I remember how colored folks come out on their porches and shook their heads, saying: "Lord now, will you look at Eva Dunford, the fine lady! Don't she look good sitting up there!" And I pretended not to hear and sat up straight and proud.

We rode on through the center of town, up Market Street, and all the way out where Hiram is living now, which in them days was all woods, there not being even a farm in sight, and that's when that horse must-a first realized he weren't at all broke or tame, or maybe thought he was back out West again, and started to gallop.

"GL," I says, "now you ain't joking with your mama, is you? Because if you is, I'll strap you purple if I live through this."

Well, GL was pulling on the reins with all his meager strength, and yelling, "Whoa, you. Say now, whoa!" He turned to me just long enough to say, "I ain't fooling with you, Mama. Honest!"

I reckon that animal weren't too satisfied with the road, because it made a sharp right turn just then, down into a gulley, and struck out across a hilly meadow. "Mama," GL yells. "Mama, do something!"

I didn't know what to do but I figured I had to do something, so I stood up, hopped down onto the horse's back and pulled it to a stop. Don't ask me how I did that; I reckon it was that I was a mother and my baby asked me to do something, is all.

"Well, we walked that animal all the way home; sometimes I had to club it over the nose with my fist to make it come, but we made it, GL and me. You remember how tired we was, Charles?"

"I wasn't here at the time." Chig turned to his father and found his face completely blank, without even a trace of a smile or a laugh.

"Well, of course you was, son. That happened in ... in ... it was a hot summer that year and—"

"I left here in June of that year. You wrote me about it."

The old lady stared past Chig at him. They all turned to him; Uncle Hiram looked up from his plate.

"Then you don't remember how we all laughed?"

"No, I don't, Mama. And I probably wouldn't have laughed. I don't think it was funny." They were staring into each other's eyes.

"Why not, Charles?"

"Because in the first place, the horse was gained by fraud. And in the second place, both of you might have been seriously injured or even killed." He broke off their stare and spoke to himself more than to any of them: "And if I'd done it, you would've beaten me good for it."

"Pardon?" The old lady had not heard him; only Chig had heard.

Chig's father sat up straight as if preparing to debate. "I said that if I had done it, if I had done just exactly what GL did, you would have beaten me good for it, Mama." He was looking at her again.

"Why you say that, son?" She was leaning toward him.

"Don't you know? Tell the truth. It can't hurt me now." His voice cracked, but only once. "If GL and I did something wrong, you'd beat me first and then be too damn tired to beat him. At dinner, he'd always get seconds and I wouldn't. You'd do things with him, like ride in that buggy, but if I wanted you to do something with me, you were always too busy." He paused and considered whether to say what he finally did say: "I cried when I left here. Nobody loved me, Mama. I cried all the way up to Knoxville. That was the last time I ever cried in my life."

"Oh, Charles." She started to get up, to come around the table to him.

He stopped her. "It's too late."

"But you don't understand."

"What don't I understand? I understood then; I understand now."

Tears now traveled down the lines in her face, but when she spoke her voice was clear. "I thought you knew. I had ten children. I had to give all of them what they needed most." She nodded. "I paid more mind to GL. I had to. GL could-a ended up swinging if I hadn't. But you was smarter. You was more growed up than GL when you was five and he was ten, and I tried to show you that by letting you do what you wanted to do."

"That's not true, Mama. You know it. GL was light-skinned and had good hair and looked almost white and you loved him for that."

"Charles, no. No, son. I didn't love any one of you more than any other."

"That can't be true." His father was standing now, his fists clenched tight. "Admit it, Mama ... please!" Chig looked at him, shocked; the man was actually crying.

"It may not-a been right what I done, but I ain't no liar." Chig knew she did not really understand what had happened, what he wanted of her. "I'm not lying to you, Charles."

Chig's father had gone pale. He spoke very softly. "You're about thirty years too late, Mama." He bolted from the table. Silverware and dishes rang and jumped. Chig heard him hurrying up to their room.

They sat in silence for awhile and then heard a key in the front door. A man with a new, lacquered straw hat came in. He was wearing brown and white two-tone shoes with very pointed toes and a white summer suit. "Say now! Man! I heard my brother was in town. Where he at? Where that rascal?"

He stood in the doorway, smiling broadly, an engaging, open, friendly smile, the innocent smile of a five-year-old.

Meaning

1. What reason does Chig's father give for having left home when he was fifteen? What was the real reason?
2. What kind of man has Charles Dunford become? How does his personality change when he is with his mother?
3. What reason does Dr. Dunford offer for his mother's treatment of GL? What reason does the mother give?
4. Something that turns out to be the reverse of what is expected is said to be *ironic*. Give three examples of irony in this story.

Method

1. What methods does the author use to arouse suspense in the first two paragraphs of the story?
2. An *anecdote* is a short account of an event or happening. Why does the author include the anecdote about GL and the horse? What function does it serve in the story?
3. How does the author make us aware of GL before he appears at the end of the story?
4. What are the conflicts in this story? Why do you think the author chooses to leave them unresolved?

Language: Nonstandard English and Dialect

Standard English is a general term meaning the type of English which is spoken by most educated people in this country. *Nonstandard English* includes *dialect,* which is the form of a language which is characteristic of a particular place or group of people. It includes differences in word choice, grammar, sentence structure, and pronunciation, especially the distinct intonation given to particular sounds, syllables, and words. The irish dialect in "The Quiet Man" and the black dialect in "A Visit to Grandmother" give each story an authentic quality.

Reread the following sentences from "A Visit to Grandmother." Decide how each sentence would be written in standard

English. Notice how the use of dialect carries out the author's purpose in communicating character and meaning.

1. "...I was sure that boy'd come by that animal ungainly."
2. "I should-a figured how Essie's eyes ain't never been so good.
3. "It may not-a been right what I done, but I ain't no liar."
4. "Well, I'm a-looking at this horse and noticing how he be looking more and more wide awake every minute..."

Discussion and Composition

1. Who has had the most effect on your life so far? Your father, your mother, another relative, a teacher, a coach, a friend? Discuss how one person has affected you in a way that you think may last all of your life.

2. According to one psychological theory, there is a child, more or less hidden, in every adult. What childlike qualities seem good to you and worth keeping as an adult? What childlike qualities might cause pain and embarrassment to you as an adult?

3. Write a character sketch of the grandmother. Was she kind, proud, honest, loving, unfair, resourceful, dense? Refer to specifics in the story to illustrate your characterization. You might begin by listing her three most important character traits. Then, for each of the traits, list at least one way she exhibits this trait in the story. Use this informal outline as a guide to writing your essay.

ERNEST HEMINGWAY
(1899-1961)

One of the most influential writers of the twentieth century was Ernest Hemingway, whose style seems simple, yet is remarkably suited to his characters. His love for adventure and his obsession with death are reflected in his fiction, which often depicts strong people facing ordeals that test their courage.

Hemingway was born in Oak Park, Illinois, the oldest of seven children. His father, a doctor, introduced him to hunting and fishing, which became lifelong interests. Hemingway played football and boxed in high school, where he also began to write stories. Eager to serve in World War I, Hemingway refused to go to college, but his father would not let him enlist. Instead, Hemingway worked as a reporter on the Kansas City *Star.* In 1918, he went to Italy as an ambulance driver for the Red Cross. He was wounded and received a medal for heroism.

After the war, Hemingway worked as a newspaper correspondent in Paris, where the American colony of artists and writers encouraged him to write. His first collection of stories, *In Our Time,* was published in 1925. *The Sun Also Rises* (1926), his first novel, and *A Farewell to Arms* (1929) established him as a success. He won the Pulitzer Prize in 1953, and the Nobel Prize for literature in 1954.

Fascinated by war, big-game hunting, deep-sea fishing, and bullfighting, Hemingway's life and work were filled with adventure. In his early sixties, depressed and ill, Hemingway took his own life or was killed accidentally while cleaning a shotgun.

IN ANOTHER COUNTRY

In the fall the war was always there, but we did not go to it any more. It was cold in the fall in Milan and the dark came very early. Then the electric lights came on, and it was pleasant along the streets looking in the windows. There was much game hanging outside the shops, and the snow powdered in the fur of the foxes and the wind blew their tails. The deer hung stiff and heavy and empty, and small birds blew in the wind and the wind turned their feathers. It was a cold fall and the wind came down from the mountains.

We were all at the hospital every afternoon, and there were different ways of walking across the town through the dusk to the hospital. Two of the ways were alongside canals, but they were long. Always, though, you crossed a bridge across a canal to enter the hospital. There was a choice of three bridges. On one of them a woman sold roasted chestnuts. It was warm, standing in front of her charcoal fire, and the chestnuts were warm afterward in your pocket. The hospital was very old and very beautiful, and you entered through a gate and walked across a courtyard and out a gate on the other side. There were usually funerals starting from the courtyard. Beyond the old hospital were the new brick pavilions, and there we met every afternoon and were all very polite and interested in what was the matter, and sat in the machines that were to make so much difference.

The doctor came up to the machine where I was sitting and said: "What did you like best to do before the war? Did you practice a sport?"

I said: "Yes, football."

"Good," he said. "You will be able to play football again better than ever."

My knee did not bend and the leg dropped straight from the knee to the ankle without a calf, and the machine was to bend the knee and make it move as in riding a tricycle. But it did not bend yet, and instead the machine lurched when it came to the bending part. The doctor said: "That will all pass. You are a fortunate young man. You will play football again like a champion."

In the next machine was a major who had a little hand like a baby's. He winked at me when the doctor examined his hand, which was between two leather straps that bounced up and down and flapped the stiff fingers, and said: "And will I, too, play football, captain-doctor?" He had been a very great fencer, and before the war the greatest fencer in Italy.

The doctor went to his office in a back room and brought a photograph which showed a hand that had been withered almost as small as the major's, before it had taken a machine course, and after was a little larger. The major held the photograph with his good hand and looked at it very carefully. "A wound?" he asked.

"An industrial accident," the doctor said.

"Very interesting, very interesting," the major said, and handed it back to the doctor.

"You have confidence?"

"No," said the major.

There were three boys who came each day who were about the same age I was. They were all three from Milan, and one of them was to be a lawyer, and one was to be a painter, and one had intended to be a soldier, and after we were finished with the machines, sometimes we walked back together to the Café Cova, which was next door to the Scala.[1] We walked the short way through the Communist quarter because we were four together. The people hated us because we were officers, and from a wineshop someone would call out, *"A basso gli ufficiali!"*[2] as we passed. Another boy who walked with us sometimes and made five wore a black silk handkerchief across his face because he had no nose then and his face was to be rebuilt. He had gone out to the front from the military academy and been wounded within an hour after he had gone into the front line for the first time. They rebuilt his face, but he came from a very old family and they could never get the nose exactly right. He went to South America and worked in a bank. But this was a long time ago, and then we did not any of us know how it was going to be afterward. We only knew then that there was always the war, but that we were not going to it any more.

We all had the same medals, except the boy with the black silk bandage across his face, and he had not been at the front long enough to get any medals. The tall boy with a very pale face who was to be a lawyer had been a lieutenant of Arditi and had three medals of the sort we each had only one of. He had lived a very long time with death and was a little detached. We were all a little detached, and there was nothing that held us together except that we met every afternoon at the hospital. Although, as we walked to the Cova through the tough part of town, walking in the dark, with light and singing coming out of wineshops, and sometimes having to walk into the street when the men and women would crowd together on the sidewalk so that we would have had to jostle them to get by, we felt held together by there being something that had happened that they, the people who disliked us, did not understand.

We ourselves all understood the Cova, where it was rich and

---

1. **Scala** (skɔ́'lə): the opera house in Milan.
2. **A basso gli ufficiali!:** Down with officers.

warm and not too brightly lighted, and noisy and smoky at certain hours, and there were always girls at the tables and the illustrated papers on a rack on the wall. The girls at the Cova were very patriotic, and I found that the most patriotic people in Italy were the café girls—and I believe they are still patriotic.

The boys at first were very polite about my medals and asked me what I had done to get them. I showed them the papers, which were written in very beautiful language and full of *fratellanza*[3] and *abnegazione*,[4] but which really said, with the adjectives removed, that I had been given the medals because I was an American. After that their manner changed a little toward me, although I was their friend against outsiders. I was a friend, but I was never really one of them after they had read the citations, because it had been different with them and they had done very different things to get their medals. I had been wounded, it was true; but we all knew that being wounded, after all, was really an accident. I was never ashamed of the ribbons, though, and sometimes, after the cocktail hour, I would imagine myself having done all the things they had done to get their medals; but walking home at night through the empty streets with the cold wind and all the shops closed, trying to keep near the streetlights, I knew that I would never have done such things, and I was very much afraid to die, and often lay in bed at night by myself, afraid to die and wondering how I would be when I went back to the front again.

The three with the medals were like hunting-hawks; and I was not a hawk, although I might seem a hawk to those who had never hunted; they, the three, knew better and so we drifted apart. But I stayed good friends with the boy who had been wounded his first day at the front, because he would never know now how he would have turned out; so he could never be accepted either, and I liked him because I thought perhaps he would not have turned out to be a hawk either.

The major, who had been the great fencer, did not believe in bravery and spent much time while we sat in the machines correcting my grammar. He had complimented me on how I spoke Italian, and we talked together very easily. One day I had said that Italian seemed such an easy language to me that I could not take a great interest in it; everything was so easy to say. "Ah, yes," the major said. "Why, then, do you not take up the use of grammar?" So we took up the use of

3. **fratellanza** (fra·tǝl·lantżǝ): brotherliness, as between allies in combat.
4. **abnegazione** (ab'·nǝ·gat'·zĭ·ō·nä): self-sacrificing.

grammar, and soon Italian was such a difficult language that I was afraid to talk to him until I had the grammar straight in my mind.

The major came very regularly to the hospital. I do not think he ever missed a day, although I am sure he did not believe in the machines. There was a time when none of us believed in the machines, and one day the major said it was all nonsense. The machines were new then and it was we who were to prove them. It was an idiotic idea, he said, "a theory, like another." I had not learned my grammar, and he said I was a stupid impossible disgrace, and he was a fool to have bothered with me. He was a small man and he sat straight up in his chair with his right hand thrust into the machine and looked straight ahead at the wall while the straps thumped up and down with his fingers in them.

"What will you do when the war is over if it is over?" he asked me. "Speak grammatically!"

"I will go to the States."

"Are you married?"

"No, but I hope to be."

"The more of a fool you are," he said. He seemed very angry. "A man must not marry."

"Why, Signor Maggiore?"

"Don't call me 'Signor Maggiore.'"

"Why must not a man marry?"

"He cannot marry. He cannot marry," he said angrily. "If he is to lose everything, he should not place himself in a position to lose that. He should not place himself in a position to lose. He should find things he cannot lose."

He spoke very angrily and bitterly, and looked straight ahead while he talked.

"But why should he necessarily lose it?"

"He'll lose it," the major said. He was looking at the wall. Then he looked down at the machine and jerked his little hand out from between the straps and slapped it hard against his thigh. "He'll lose it," he almost shouted. "Don't argue with me!" Then he called to the attendant who ran the machines. "Come and turn this damned thing off."

He went back into the other room for the light treatment and the massage. Then I heard him ask the doctor if he might use his telephone and he shut the door. When he came back into the room, I was sitting in another machine. He was wearing his cape and had his cap on, and he came directly toward my machine and put his arm on my shoulder.

"I am so sorry," he said, and patted me on the shoulder with his good hand. "I would not be rude. My wife has just died. You must forgive me."

"Oh—" I said, feeling sick for him. "I am so sorry."

He stood there, biting his lower lip. "It is very difficult," he said. "I cannot resign myself."

He looked straight past me and out through the window. Then he began to cry. "I am utterly unable to resign myself," he said and choked. And then crying, his head up looking at nothing, carrying himself straight and soldierly, with tears on both his cheeks and biting his lips, he walked past the machines and out the door.

The doctor told me that the major's wife, who was very young and whom he had not married until he was definitely invalided out of the war, had died of pneumonia. She had been sick only a few days. No one expected her to die. The major did not come to the hospital for three days. Then he came at the usual hour, wearing a black band on the sleeve of his uniform. When he came back, there were large framed photographs around the wall, of all sorts of wounds before and after they had been cured by the machines. In front of the machine the major used were three photographs of hands like his that were completely restored. I do not know where the doctor got them. I always understood we were the first to use the machines. The photographs did not make much difference to the major because he only looked out of the window.

Meaning

1. What do the young soldiers in this story have in common? How are the narrator and the boy with the black silk bandage different from the other young men?
2. What do you think the narrator means when he says that the major "did not believe in bravery"?
3. Why does the major not have much faith in the new machines? How do you think the narrator feels about the machines?

Method

1. The *theme* is the main idea on which a story is based. One clue to the theme of this story is its title. Considering the title and the story itself, what, in your opinion, is the theme of "In Another Country"?
2. "In Another Country" is told by a *first-person narrator,* a character in the story who tells what happens from his point of view, using the pronoun *I*. What are the advantages of using this method? What might be some disadvantages?
3. The narrator points out several times that the major stared at the wall while using the machine. After the doctor puts the photographs on the wall, the major looks out the window. Why does the narrator emphasize this information? Reread the last sentence of the story. Do you think this is an effective ending? Why or why not?

Language: Tone

An author's choice of words and arrangement of sentences can create a *subjective* or an *objective* tone. Writing that clearly and obviously reveals an author's personal beliefs or feelings is called subjective. As you read Maurice Walsh's "A Quiet Man" and William Melvin Kelley's "A Visit to Grandmother," you know how the authors feel about the characters they have created. It is clear, for example, that Walsh does not want his readers to like Liam O'Grady. Every detail that he includes about Liam places the character in an unfavorable light. Kelley's characters are more complicated—that is, some of them have both good qualities, just as people have in real life, but it is clear that Kelley admires Grandmother and sympathizes with Charles Dunford.

Hemingway, on the other hand, is a master of objective writing. His short, simply constructed sentences include physical details, but do not directly reveal his own feelings. Like a good newspaper reporter, he tells what happened, using strong verbs and a minimum of adjectives and adverbs. Although his tone is matter-of-fact, he communicates a strong impression by repeating important details over and over. We are told little or nothing about how Hemingway feels about his characters, but because we see and hear them in action, we know them first-hand, and they seem quite real to us.

Identify the following sentences as either objective or subjective. Make the subjective sentences objective.

1. Our cozy cabin stood at the edge of the beautiful forest.
2. Shane was quiet and strong, a magnificent giant.
3. She weighed 100 pounds and had red hair.
4. The woman at the door was carrying a suitcase.
5. As the brave astronauts landed, the crowd roared their approval.

Discussion and Composition

1. Why do you think the soldiers feel detached from the rest of the world? Are there experiences other than war that might cause people to feel as the soldiers do?

2. Why does the major say a man should not marry? Do you think the major is being realistic or pessimistic? Explain.

3. Write a brief essay explaining why the narrator describes the other soldiers as "hunting-hawks." Your paragraph should explain the characteristics of hawks and show why the soldiers might be like them. You may also want to explain why the narrator does not consider himself a hawk.

ANTON CHEKHOV
(1860–1904)

The short stories and plays of Anton Pavlovich Chekhov portray realistic characters and situations. He once wrote to his brother, "Don't invent sufferings which you have not experienced . . . a lie in a story is a hundred times more boring than in a conversation."

Born in Russia, Chekhov was the grandson of a liberated serf. He worked as a clerk in his father's grocery store and won a scholarship to study medicine at the University of Moscow. To help pay for his studies, he began writing humorous sketches for magazines. Although he earned a medical degree in 1884, he devoted most of his time to writing after his first collection of short stories, *Particolored Stories,* was published when he was twenty-six.

Chekhov wrote more than four hundred short stories and twelve plays about the Russian people and their lives. *The Three Sisters* (1901) and *The Cherry Orchard* (1904), plays that he wrote toward the end of his life, when he was ill with tuberculosis, are considered his masterpieces.

THE BET

It was a dark autumn night. The old banker was walking up and down his study and remembering how, fifteen years before, he had given a party one autumn evening. There had been many clever men there, and there had been interesting conversations. Among other things they had talked of capital punishment. The majority of the guests, among whom were many journalists and intellectual men, disapproved of the death penalty. They considered that form of punishment out of date, immoral, and unsuitable for Christian states. In the opinion of some of them the death penalty ought to be replaced everywhere by imprisonment for life.

"I don't agree with you," said their host the banker. "I have not tried either the death penalty or imprisonment for life, but if one may judge *a priori,* the death penalty is more moral and more humane than imprisonment for life. Capital punishment kills a man at once, but lifelong imprisonment kills him slowly. Which executioner is the more humane, he who kills you in a few minutes or he who drags the life out of you in the course of many years?"

"Both are equally immoral," observed one of the guests, "for they both have the same object—to take away life. The State is not God. It has not the right to take away what it cannot restore when it wants to."

Among the guests was a young lawyer, a young man of five-and-twenty. When he was asked his opinion, he said:

"The death sentence and the life sentence are equally immoral, but if I had to choose between the death penalty and imprisonment for life, I would certainly chose the second. To live anyhow is better than not at all."

A lively discussion arose. The banker, who was younger and more nervous in those days, was suddenly carried away by excitement; he struck the table with his fist and shouted at the young man:

"It's not true! I'll bet you two millions[1] you wouldn't stay in solitary confinement for five years."

"If you mean that in earnest," said the young man, "I'll take the bet, but I would stay not five but fifteen years."

"Fifteen? Done!" cried the banker. "Gentlemen, I stake two millions!"

"Agreed! You stake your millions and I stake my freedom!" said the young man.

And this wild, senseless bet was carried out! The banker, spoiled and frivolous, with millions beyond his reckoning, was delighted at the bet. At supper he made fun of the young man, and said:

"Think better of it, young man, while there is still time. To me two millions are a trifle, but you are losing three or four of the best years of your life. I say three or four, because you won't stay longer. Don't forget either, you unhappy man, that voluntary confinement is a great deal harder to bear than compulsory. The thought that you have the right to step out in liberty at any moment will poison your whole existence in prison. I am sorry for you."

And now the banker, walking to and fro, remembered all this, and asked himself: "What was the object of that bet? What is the good of that man's losing fifteen years of his life and my throwing away two millions? Can it prove that the death penalty is better or worse than imprisonment for life? No, no. It was all nonsensical and

1. **millions:** refers to rubles. A ruble in pre-Revolutionary Russia was worth about fifty cents in American money.

meaningless. On my part it was the caprice of a pampered man, and on his part simple greed for money. . . ."

Then he remembered what followed that evening. It was decided that the young man should spend the years of his captivity under the strictest supervision in one of the lodges in the banker's garden. It was agreed that for fifteen years he should not be free to cross the threshold of the lodge, to see human beings, to hear the human voice, or to receive letters and newspapers. He was allowed to have a musical instrument and books, and was allowed to write letters, to drink wine, and to smoke. By the terms of the agreement, the only relations he could have with the outer world were by a little window made purposely for that object. He might have anything he wanted—books, music, wine, and so on—in any quantity he desired, by writing an order, but could receive them only through the window. The agreement provided for every detail and every trifle that would make his imprisonment strictly solitary, and bound the young man to stay there *exactly* fifteen years, beginning from twelve o'clock of November 14, 1870, and ending at twelve o'clock of November 14, 1885. The slightest attempt on his part to break the conditions, if only two minutes before the end, released the banker from the obligation to pay him two millions.

For the first year of his confinement, as far as one could judge from his brief notes, the prisoner suffered severely from loneliness and depression. The sounds of the piano could be heard continually day and night from his lodge. He refused wine and tobacco. Wine, he wrote, excites the desires, and desires are the worst foes of the prisoner; and besides, nothing could be more dreary than drinking good wine and seeing no one. And tobacco spoiled the air of his room. In the first year the books he sent for were principally of a light character; novels with a complicated love plot, sensational and fantastic stories, and so on.

In the second year the piano was silent in the lodge, and the prisoner asked only for the classics. In the fifth year music was audible again, and the prisoner asked for wine. Those who watched him through the window said that all that year he spent doing nothing but eating and drinking and lying on his bed, frequently yawning and angrily talking to himself. He did not read books. Sometimes at night he would sit down to write; he would spend hours writing, and in the morning tear up all that he had written. More than once he could be heard crying.

In the second half of the sixth year the prisoner began zealously studying languages, philosophy, and history. He threw himself eagerly into these studies—so much so that the banker had enough to do to get him the books he ordered. In the course of four years some six hundred volumes were procured at his request. It was during this period that the banker received the following letter from his prisoner:

"My dear Jailer, I write you these lines in six languages. Show them to people who know the languages. Let them read them. If they find not one mistake, I implore you to fire a shot in the garden. That shot will show me that my efforts have not been thrown away. The geniuses of all ages and of all lands speak different languages, but the same flame burns in them all. Oh, if you only knew what unearthly happiness my soul feels now from being able to understand them!" The prisoner's desire was fulfilled. The banker ordered two shots to be fired in the garden.

Then, after the tenth year, the prisoner sat immovably at the table and read nothing but the Gospel. It seemed strange to the banker that a man who in four years had mastered six hundred learned volumes should waste nearly a year over one thin book easy of comprehension. Theology and histories of religion followed the Gospels.

In the last two years of his confinement the prisoner read an immense quantity of books quite indiscriminately. At one time he was busy with the natural sciences, then he would ask for Byron or Shakespeare. There were notes in which he demanded at the same time books on chemistry, and a manual of medicine, and a novel, and some treatise on philosophy or theology. His reading suggested a man swimming in the sea among the wreckage of his ship, and trying to save his life by greedily clutching first at one spar and then at another.

The old banker remembered all this, and thought:

"Tomorrow at twelve o'clock he will regain his freedom. By our agreement I ought to pay him two millions. If I do pay him, it is all over with me: I shall be utterly ruined."

Fifteen years before, his millions had been beyond his reckoning; now he was afraid to ask himself which were greater, his debts or his assets. Desperate gambling on the Stock Exchange, wild speculation, and the excitability which he could not get over even in advancing years, had by degrees led to the decline of his fortune, and the proud, fearless, self-confident millionaire had become a banker of middling rank, trembling at every rise and fall in his investments. "Cursed bet!" muttered the old man, clutching his head in despair. "Why didn't the man die? He is only forty now. He will take my last penny from me, he will marry, will enjoy life, will gamble on the Exchange; while I shall look at him with envy like a beggar, and hear from him every day the same sentence: 'I am indebted to you for the happiness of my life, let me help you!' No, it is too much! The one means of being saved from bankruptcy and disgrace is the death of that man!"

It struck three o'clock. The banker listened; everyone was asleep in the house, and nothing could be heard outside but the rustling of the chilled trees. Trying to make no noise, he took from a fireproof safe the key of the door which had not been opened for fifteen years, put on his overcoat, and went out of the house.

It was dark and cold in the garden. Rain was falling. A damp, cutting wind was racing about the garden, howling and giving the trees no rest. The banker strained his eyes, but could see neither the earth nor the white statues, nor the lodge, nor the trees. Going to the spot where the lodge stood, he twice called the watchman. No answer followed. Evidently the watchman had sought shelter from the weather, and was now asleep somewhere either in the kitchen or in the greenhouse.

"If I had the pluck to carry out my intention," thought the old man, "suspicion would fall first upon the watchman."

He felt in the darkness for the steps and the door, and went into the entry of the lodge. Then he groped his way into a little passage and lighted a match. There was not a soul there. There was a bedstead with no bedding on it, and in the corner there was a dark cast-iron stove. The seals on the door leading to the prisoner's rooms were intact.

When the match went out the old man, trembling with emotion, peeped through the little window. A candle was burning dimly in the prisoner's room. He was sitting at the table. Nothing could be seen but his back, the hair on his head, and his hands. Open books were lying on the table, on the two easy chairs, and on the carpet near the table.

Five minutes passed and the prisoner did not once stir. Fifteen years' imprisonment had taught him to sit still. The banker tapped at the window with his finger, and the prisoner made no movement whatever in response. Then the banker cautiously broke the seals off the door and put the key in the keyhole. The rusty lock gave a grating sound and the door creaked. The banker expected to hear at once footsteps and a cry of astonishment, but three minutes passed and it was as quiet as ever in the room. He made up his mind to go in.

At the table a man unlike ordinary people was sitting motionless. He was a skeleton with the skin drawn tight over his bones, with long curls like a woman's, and a shaggy beard. His face was yellow with an earthy tint in it, his cheeks were hollow, his back long and narrow, and the hand on which his shaggy head was propped was so thin and delicate that it was dreadful to look at it. His hair was already streaked with silver, and seeing his emaciated,[2] aged-looking face, no one would have believed that he was only forty. He was asleep. . . . In front of his bowed head there lay on the table a sheet of paper on which there was something written in fine handwriting.

"Poor creature!" thought the banker, "he is asleep and most likely dreaming of the millions. And I have only to take this half-dead man, throw him on the bed, stifle him a little with the pillow, and the most conscientious expert would find no sign of a violent death. But let us first read what he has written here. . . ."

The banker took the page from the table and read as follows:

"Tomorrow at twelve o'clock I regain my freedom and the right to associate with other men, but before I leave this room and see the sunshine, I think it necessary to say a few words to you. With a clear conscience I tell you, as before God, who beholds me, that I despise freedom and life and health, and all that in your books is called the good things of the world.

"For fifteen years I have been intently studying earthly life. It is true I have not seen the earth nor men, but in your books I have drunk fragrant wine, I have sung songs, I have hunted stags and wild boars in the forests, have loved women. . . . Beauties as ethereal as clouds, created by the magic of your poets and geniuses, have visited me at night, and have whispered in my ears wonderful tales that have set my brain in a whirl. In your books I have climbed to the peaks of Elburz and Mont Blanc, and from there I have seen the sun rise and have watched it at evening flood the sky, the ocean, and the mountaintops with gold and crimson. I have watched from there the lightning flashing over my head and cleaving[3] the storm clouds. I have seen green forests, fields, rivers, lakes, towns. I have heard the singing of the sirens, and the strains of the shepherds' pipes; I have touched the wings of comely devils who flew down to converse with

2. **emaciated** (ĭ·mā′shē·ā′tĭd): very thin; wasted away.
3. **cleaving** (klēv′ĭng): splitting.

me of God. . . . In your books I have flung myself into the bottomless pit, performed miracles, slain, burned towns, preached new religions, conquered whole kingdoms. . . .

"Your books have given me wisdom. All that the unresting thought of man has created in the ages is compressed into a small compass in my brain. I know that I am wiser than all of you.

"And I despise your books, I despise wisdom and the blessings of this world. It is all worthless, fleeting, illusory, and deceptive, like a mirage. You may be proud, wise, and fine, but death will wipe you off the face of the earth as though you were no more than mice burrowing under the floor, and your posterity, your history, your immortal geniuses will burn or freeze together with the earthly globe.

"You have lost your reason and taken the wrong path. You have taken lies for truth, and hideousness for beauty. You would marvel if, owing to strange events of some sorts, frogs and lizards suddenly grew on apple and orange trees instead of fruit, or if roses began to smell like a sweating horse; so I marvel at you who exchange heaven for earth. I don't want to understand you.

"To prove to you in action how I despise all that you live by, I renounce the two millions of which I once dreamed as of paradise and which now I despise. To deprive myself of the right to the money I shall go out from here five minutes before the time fixed, and so break the compact. . . ."

When the banker had read this he laid the page on the table, kissed the strange man on the head, and went out of the lodge, weeping. At no other time, even when he had lost heavily on the Stock Exchange, had he felt so great a contempt for himself. When he got home he lay on his bed, but his tears and emotion kept him for hours from sleeping.

Next morning the watchmen ran in with pale faces, and told him they had seen the man who lived in the lodge climb out of the window into the garden, go to the gate, and disappear. The banker went at once with the servants to the lodge and made sure of the flight of his prisoner. To avoid arousing unnecessary talk, he took from the table the writing in which the millions were renounced, and when he got home locked it up in the fireproof safe.

Meaning

1. What are the terms of the bet made between the young lawyer and the middle-aged banker?
2. How does the lawyer change during his fifteen years of imprisonment? How does the banker change?
3. What is ironic about the outcome of the bet?
4. Which of the following themes do you consider to be most appropriate for this story? Give reasons for your answer.

   a. Life imprisonment is worse than capital punishment.

   b. The fewer one's material needs and illusions, the greater one's freedom.

   c. One way or another, all human beings discover the vanities of life.

   d. What actually takes place in life often falls far short of our expectations.

   e. Life is a game of chance.

Method

1. This story is told from the third-person omniscient point of view. Explain this method briefly in your own words.
2. The *flashback* is a technique by which an author focuses on, or flashes back to, an episode or incident that took place prior to the opening situation of a story. What is the purpose of the flashback in this story?
3. Dialogue is one means of portraying character. Quote lines from the banker's and lawyer's conversations at the dinner party that reveal their temperaments and attitudes.
4. An author sometimes uses setting and atmosphere to reflect a person's state of mind, as in the following: "It was dark and cold in the garden. Rain was falling. A damp, cutting wind was racing about the garden, howling and giving the trees no rest. The banker strained his eyes, but could see neither the earth nor the white statues, nor the lodge, nor the trees."

   How does this description of the garden reflect the banker's mood as he heads for the lodge where the lawyer is confined?

Language: Words and Phrases from Latin

During the discussion of capital punishment at the dinner party, the banker speaks of reasoning *a priori*. This phrase comes directly from two Latin words: *a* (from) and *prior* (former or first), and literally means "from the preceding." If something is known *a priori,* it is known simply by reasoning from what is self-evident. It does not have to be supported by facts or experience. For example, the banker says, "I have not tried either the death penalty or imprisonment for life, but if one may judge *a priori,* the death penalty is more moral and more humane than imprisonment for life."

Many English words and phrases are derived directly from Latin. Check your dictionary to find the meaning of the Latin word or phrase which is the basis for each of the following:

1. capital
2. *bona fide*
3. executioner
4. conscience
5. *ipso facto*
6. *summa cum laude*
7. voluntary
8. miracle
9. *obiter dictum*
10. *prima facie*

Discussion and Composition

1. If you had to be isolated for three months, what books would you choose to take with you? Give a reason for each choice.

2. Do you agree or disagree with the claim that "to live, regardless of how, is better than not to live at all"? Why? What reasons might others have for disagreeing with you?

3. You have seen how setting can be used to develop and emphasize a tone or mood. Choose a mood, and write a paragraph in which you describe a setting that reflects it. Here are some ideas for moods: happy, sad, bored, angry, impatient, humorous, loving, dream-like, tense, fearful. Your paragraph will be more effective if you use images that appeal to the senses. What colors might reflect the mood you are trying to establish? What smells? What sounds? Can you work the sense of taste into your paragraph? Can the sense of touch be used effectively?

AMY TAN

(born 1952)

As a teenager growing up in a Chinese American family, Amy Tan tried desperately to blend into the American world of "hot dogs and apple pie." She even considered having plastic surgery to make her features look more American. Yet she gradually came to value her cultural heritage, and a trip to China when she was thirty-five helped Tan to rediscover her Chinese roots.

In 1985, Tan—who was working as a freelance business writer—decided to try her hand at writing fiction. In 1985, she submitted a story to a writing workshop. Out of that story, which eventually became "Rules of the Game," she developed her popular and acclaimed first novel, *The Joy Luck Club*. Many of the tales in the novel focus on mother-daughter relationships within Chinese American families. They explore both the joys and difficulties of a dual heritage—particularly the struggles of second-generation Americans who feel torn between two ways of life.

RULES OF THE GAME

My mother imparted her daily truths so she could help my older brothers and me rise above our circumstances.

We lived in San Francisco's Chinatown,[1] on Waverly Place, the street for which I was named. Waverly was my official name for important American documents; my family called me Mei-mei, the "little sister." Like most of the other Chinese children who played in the back alleys of restaurants and curio shops, I didn't think we were poor. Our two-bedroom flat was warm and clean, and I ate three five-course meals every day, beginning with a soup full of mysterious things I didn't want to know the names of.

I was five when my mother taught me the Chinese art of invisible strength. It was a strategy for winning arguments, respect

---

1. **Chinatown:** the 12-block-square Chinese district of San Francisco.

from others, and eventually, though neither of us knew it at the time, chess games.

"Bite back your tongue," hissed my mother when I cried loudly, yanking her hand toward the store that sold bags of salted candy plums. At home she said, "Wise guy, he not go against wind. In Chinese, we say come from south, blow with wind—poom!—north will follow. Strongest wind cannot be see."

The next week I bit back my tongue as we entered the store with the forbidden candies. When my mother finished her shopping, she quietly plucked a small bag of plums from the rack and put it on the counter with the rest of the items.

My oldest brother, Vincent, was the one who actually got the chess set. It was Christmas. The missionary ladies of the First Chinese Baptist Church had put together a Santa bag of gifts donated by members of another church and had organized a party.

One of the Chinese parishioners had donned a Santa Claus costume and a stiff paper beard with cotton balls glued to it. I think the only children who believed he was the real thing were too young to know Santa wasn't Chinese.

When it was my turn, the Santa man asked me how old I was. I thought it was a trick question; I was seven according to the American formula and eight by the Chinese calendar[2]. I said I was born on March 7, 1951. That seemed to satisfy him. He then solemnly asked if I had been a very good little girl this year and did I believe in Jesus Christ and obey my parents. I knew the only answer to that. I nodded back with equal solemnity.

Having watched the other children opening their gifts, I already knew that the big gifts were not necessarily the nicest ones. I peered into the sack and chose a heavy, compact box that was wrapped in shiny silver foil and tied with a red satin ribbon. It was a twelve-pack of Life Savers; I spent the rest of the party arranging the candy tubes in the order of my favorites. My brother Winston chose wisely as well. He got an authentic miniature replica of a World War II submarine.

Vincent's chess set would have been a very decent present to get at a church Christmas party, except that it was obviously used

2. **Chinese calendar:** the Chinese lunar calendar, which differs from the Western (Gregorian) solar calendar.

and, as we discovered later, it was missing a black pawn and a white knight. My mother graciously thanked the unknown benefactress, saying, "Too good. Cost too much." At which point, an old lady with fine, white, wispy hair nodded toward our family and said with a whistling whisper, "Merry, merry Christmas."

When we got home, my mother told Vincent to throw the chess set away. "She not want it. We not want it," she said, tossing her head stiffly to the side with a tight, proud smile. My brothers had deaf ears. They were already lining up the chess pieces and reading the dog-eared instruction book.

"Me next!" I begged between games. Vincent at first refused to let me play, but when I offered my Life Savers as replacements for the buttons that filled in for missing pieces, he relented. He chose the flavors: wild cherry for the black pawn and peppermint for the white knight. The winner could eat both.

As our mother sprinkled flour and rolled out small, doughy circles for the steamed dumplings that would be our dinner that night, Vincent explained the rules, pointing to each chess piece. "You have sixteen pieces, and so do I. The pawns can only move forward one step, except on the first move. Then they can move two. But they can only take other men by moving diagonally."

"Why can't they move more steps?" I asked as I moved my pawn.

"Because they're pawns," he said.

"But why do they go diagonally to take other men? Why aren't there any women and children?"

"Why is the sky blue? Why must you always ask stupid questions?" said Vincent. "This is a game. These are the rules. I didn't make them up. See. Here. In the book." He jabbed a page with a pawn in his hand. "Pawn. P-A-W-N. Read it yourself."

My mother patted the flour off her hands. "Let me see book," she said quietly. She scanned the pages quickly, not reading the foreign English symbols, seeming to deliberately search for nothing in particular.

"This American rules," she concluded at last. "Every time people come out from foreign country, must know rules. You not know, judge say too bad, go back. They not telling you why so you can use their way go forward. They say don't know why, you find out yourself. But they knowing all the time. Better you take it, find out why yourself." She returned the book with a satisfied smile.

I found out about all the whys later. I learned about opening moves and why it's important to control the center early on; the shortest distance between two points is straight down the middle. I learned about the middle game and why tactics between two adversaries are like clashing ideas; the one who plays best has the clearest plans for both attacking and getting out of traps. I learned why it is essential in the endgame[3] to have foresight, a mathematical understanding of all possible moves, and patience; all weaknesses and advantages become evident to a strong adversary and are obscured to a tiring opponent. I discovered that for the whole game one must gather invisible strengths and see the endgame before the game begins.

I also found out why I should never reveal "why" to others. A little knowledge withheld is a great advantage one should store for future use. That is the power of chess. It is a game of secrets in which one must show and never tell.

One cold spring afternoon while walking home from school, I detoured through the playground at the end of our alley and saw two old men playing chess. They were seated across a folding table, surrounded by other old men smoking pipes, eating peanuts, and watching.

I ran home and grabbed Vincent's chess set. I also carefully selected two prized rolls of Life Savers. I came back to the park and approached a man who was observing the game.

"Wanna play?" I asked him. His face widened with surprise, and he grinned as he looked at the box under my arm.

"Little sister, been a long time since I play with dolls," he said, smiling benevolently. I quickly put the box down next to him on the bench and opened it, displaying my retort.

Lau Po, which he allowed me to call him, turned out to be a much better player than my brothers. I lost many games and many Life Savers. But over the weeks, with each diminishing roll of candy, I added new secrets. Lau Po gave me the names: The double attack from the east and west shores. Throwing stones on the drowning man. The sudden meeting of the clan. The surprise from the sleeping guard. The humble servant that kills the king. Sand in the eyes of advancing forces. A double killing without blood.

---

3. **endgame:** the final stages of a game of chess.

There were also the fine points of chess etiquette. Keep captured men in neat rows, as well-tended prisoners. Never announce "check"[4] with vanity, lest someone with an unseen sword slit your throat. Never hurl pieces into the sandbox after you have lost a game, because then you must find them again, by yourself, after apologizing to all around you. By the end of summer, Lau Po had taught me all he knew, and I had become a better chess player.

A small weekend crowd of Chinese people and tourists would gather as I played and defeated my opponents one by one. My mother would join the crowds during these outdoor exhibition games. She sat proudly on the bench, telling my admirers with proper Chinese humility, "Is luck."

A man who watched me in the park suggested that my mother allow me to play in local chess tournaments. My mother smiled graciously, an answer that meant nothing. I wanted to go, but I knew she would not let me play among strangers. So I bit back my tongue. As we walked home, I told her in a small voice that I didn't want to play in the local tournament. They would have American rules, I said, and if I lost, I would bring shame on my family.

"Is shame, you fall down nobody push you," said my mother.

During my first tournament, my mother sat with me in the front row as I waited for my turn. I frequently bounced my legs to unstick them from the cold metal seat of the folding chair. When my name was called, I leapt up. My mother unwrapped something in her lap. It was her chang, a small tablet of red jade that held the sun's fire. "Is luck," she whispered and tucked it into my dress pocket. I turned to my opponent, a fifteen-year-old boy from Oakland. He looked at me, wrinkling his nose.

As I began to play, the boy disappeared, the color ran out of the room, and I only saw my white pieces and his black ones waiting on the other side. A light wind began blowing past my ears. It whispered secrets only I could hear. "Blow from the south," it murmured. "The wind leaves no trail." I saw a clear path, the traps to avoid. The crowd rustled. "Shhh! Shhh!" said the corners of the room. The wind blew stronger. "Throw sand from the east to distract him." The knight came forward ready for the sacrifice. The wind hissed, louder and louder. "Blow, blow, blow.

4. **"check"**: pronounced by a chess player when threatening the opponent's king.

He cannot see. He is blind now. Make him lean away from the wind so he is easier to knock down."

"Check," I said as the wind roared with laughter. The wind died down to little puffs, my own breath.

My mother placed my first trophy next to a new plastic chess set that the neighborhood Tao Society had given me. As she wiped each piece with a soft cloth, she said, "Next time win more, lose less."

"Ma, it's not how many pieces you lose," I said. "Sometimes you need to lose pieces to get ahead."

"Better to lose less, see if you really need."

At the next tournament, I won again, but it was my mother who wore the triumphant grin.

"Lose eight piece this time. Last time was eleven. What I tell you? Better off lose less!" I was annoyed, but I couldn't say anything.

I attended more tournaments, each one farther away from home. I won all the games, in all divisions. The Chinese bakery downstairs from our flat displayed my growing collection of trophies in their window, amid the dust-covered cakes that were never picked up. The day after I won an important regional tournament, the window showcased a fresh sheet cake with whipped-cream frosting and red script saying "Congratulations, Waverly Jong, Chinatown Chess Champion." Soon after that, a flower shop, headstone engraver, and funeral parlor offered to sponsor me in the national tournaments. That's when my mother decided I no longer had to do the dishes. Winston and Vincent had to do my chores.

"Why does she get to play and we do all the work?" complained Vincent.

"Is new American rules," said my mother. "Mei-mei play, squeeze all her brains out for win chess. You play, worth squeeze towel."

By my ninth birthday, I was a national chess champion. I was still some 429 points away from grandmaster[5] status, but I was touted as the Great American Hope, a child prodigy and a girl to boot. They ran a photo of me in Life magazine next to a quote in which Bobby Fischer[6] said, "There will never be a woman grand

---

5. **grandmaster:** a chess player with the highest level of expertise.
6. **Bobby Fischer** (Robert James) (1943–): U.S. chess Champion.

master." "Your move, Bobby," read the caption.

The day they took the magazine picture I wore neatly plaited braids clipped with plastic barrettes trimmed with rhinestones. I was playing in a large high school auditorium that echoed with phlegmy coughs and the squeaky rubber knobs of chair legs sliding across freshly waxed wooden floors. Seated across from me was an American man, about the same age as Lau Po. I remember that his sweaty brows seemed to weep at my every move. He wore a dark, malodorous suit. One of his pockets was stuffed with a great white kerchief on which he wiped his palm before sweeping his hand over the chosen chess piece with a great flourish.

In my crisp pink-and-white dress with scratchy lace at the neck, one of two that my mother had sewn for these special occasions, I would clasp my hands under my chin, the delicate points of my elbows poised lightly on the table in the manner that my mother had shown me for posing for the press. I would swing my patent leather shoes back and forth like an impatient child riding on a school bus. Then I would pause, suck in my lips, twirl my chosen piece in midair as if undecided, and then firmly plant it in its new, threatening place, with a triumphant smile thrown back at my opponent for good measure.

I no longer played in the alley of Waverly Place. I never visited the playground where the pigeons and old men gathered. I went to school and then directly home to learn new chess secrets, cleverly concealed advantages, more escape routes.

But I found it difficult to concentrate at home. My mother had a habit of standing over me while I plotted out my games. I think she thought of herself as my protective ally. Her lips would be sealed tight, and after each move I made, a soft "hmmmph" would escape from her nose.

"Ma, I can't practice when you stand there like that," I said one day. She retreated to the kitchen and made loud noises with the pots and pans. When the crashing stopped, I could see out of the corner of my eye that she was standing in the doorway. "Hmmmph!" Only this one came out of her tight throat.

My family made many concessions to allow me to practice. One time I complained that the bedroom I shared was so noisy that I couldn't think. Thereafter, my brothers slept in a bed in the living room facing the street. I said I couldn't finish my rice; my head didn't work right when my stomach was too full. I left half-finished bowls on the table, and nobody complained. But there was one duty I couldn't avoid. I had to accompany my mother on Saturday market days when I had no tournament to play. My mother would proudly walk with me, visiting many shops, buying very little. "This is my daughter, Wave-ly Jong," she said to whoever looked her way.

One day after we left a shop, I said under my breath, "I wish you wouldn't do that, telling everybody I'm your daughter." My mother stopped walking. Crowds of people with heavy bags pushed past us on the sidewalk, bumping into first one shoulder, then the other.

"Aiii-ya. So shame be with mother?" She grasped my hand even tighter as she looked at me evenly.

I looked down. "It's not that—it's just so obvious. It's just so embarrassing."

"Embarrass you be my daughter?" Her voice was cracking with anger.

"That's not what I meant. That's not what I said."

"What you say?"

I knew it was a mistake to go on, but I heard my voice speaking. "Why do you have to use me to show off? If you want to show off, then why don't you learn to play chess?"

My mother's eyes turned into dangerous black slits. She had no words for me, just sharp silence.

I felt the wind rushing around my hot ears. I jerked my hand out of my mother's tight grasp and spun around, knocking into an old woman. Her bag of groceries spilled to the ground.

"Aii-ya! Stupid girl!" my mother and the woman cried. Oranges and tin cans careened down the sidewalk. As my mother stopped to help the old woman pick up the escaping food, I took off.

I raced down the street, dashing between people, not looking back as my mother screamed shrilly, "Mei-mei! Mei-mei!" I fled down an alley, past dark curtained shops and merchants washing the grime off their windows. I sped into the sunlight, into a large street crowded with tourists examining trinkets and souvenirs. I ducked into another dark alley, down another street, up another alley. I ran hard until it hurt, and I realized I had nowhere to go, that I was not running from anything. The alleys contained no escape routes.

My breath came out hard, like angry smoke. I was cold. I sat down on an upturned plastic pail next to a stack of empty boxes, cupping my chin with my hands, thinking hard. I imagined my mother first walking briskly down one street or another looking for me, then giving up and returning home to await my arrival. After two hours, I stood up on creaking legs and slowly walked home.

The alley was quiet, and I could see yellow lights shining from our flat like two tiger's eyes in the night. I climbed the sixteen steps to the door, stepping quietly on each so as not to make any warning sounds. I turned the knob; the door was locked. I heard a chair moving, quick steps, the locks turning—click! click! click!—and then the door opened.

"About time you got home," hissed Vincent. "Boy, are you in trouble."

He slid back to the dinner table. On the table were the remains of a large fish, its fleshy head still connected to bones swimming upstream in vain escape. Standing there waiting for my punishment, I heard my mother speak in a dry voice.

"We not concerning this girl. This girl not have concerning for us."

Nobody looked at me. Bone chopsticks clinked against the insides of bowls being emptied into hungry mouths.

I walked into my room, closed the door, and lay down on my bed. The room was dark, the ceiling filled with shadows from the dinnertime lights of neighboring flats.

In my head I saw a chessboard with sixty-four black and white squares. Opposite me was my opponent, her eyes two angry black slits. She wore a triumphant smile. "Strongest wind cannot be see," she said.

Her black men advanced across the plane, slowly marching to each successive level as a single unit. My white pieces screamed as they scurried and fell off the board one by one. As her men drew closer to my edge, I felt myself growing light. I rose up into the air and flew out the window. Higher and higher, above the alley, over the tops of tiled roofs, where I was gathered up by the wind and pushed up toward the night sky until everything below me disappeared and I was alone.

I closed my eyes and pondered my next move.

Meaning

1. What is "the Chinese art of invisible strength"? What are some ways in which Waverly uses it?
2. What seems to be the source of the conflict between Waverly and her mother?
3. At the end of the story, who is Waverly's "opponent"? What do you think is the "next move" that Waverly ponders?

Method

1. The title of the story has a literal reference to the rules for playing chess. What other "rules" and what other "game" might the title refer to?
2. How does the mother's way of speaking help to characterize her?
3. In addition to her *external conflicts* with her mother, what *internal conflict* does Waverly experience in the story?
4. What makes the characters of Waverly and her mother particularly vivid? List the techniques the author uses to characterize these two people.

Language: Vivid Verbs

In "Rules of the Game," Amy Tan uses precise, vivid verbs to convey the actions and gestures of her characters. Notice how the verbs in the following passages help to characterize the people performing the actions.

"My mother *imparted* her daily truths. . . ."

"'Bite back your tongue,' *hissed* my mother. . . ."

"He *jabbed* a page with a pawn in his hand."

For each of the following sentences, replace the italicized verb with a stronger, more precise verb. Examine the surrounding words in each sentence to determine exactly what action or gesture the verb should convey.

1. Unable to tempt the baby with the strained carrots, Juan finally *put* a spoonful into the stubborn child's mouth.
2. At the end of the year, Carol *removed* the overflowing stack of papers from her locker.
3. The track star *moved* to the finish line in record time.
4. Whenever a stranger entered the house, the frightened cat *got* onto its owner's head.

Discussion and Composition

1. Waverly's family moved to the United States from China. What are some of the obstacles immigrant families must overcome when settling in a new country? Consider what new things you would have to learn if you moved to China.

2. An ethnic neighborhood is an area populated by people who share the same ancestry, religion, language, and/or culture. How do you think ethnic neighborhoods begin? What keeps them from dissolving?

3. Many of the descriptions in "Rules of the Game" capture the flavor of life in San Francisco's Chinatown. Write a description of an area or place in your life that has a particular flavor or atmosphere. For example, you might describe the main street of your town, the neighborhood in which you live, or the grounds of your school. Include details that will give your reader a vivid picture of the setting and a sense of its atmosphere.

GRAHAM GREENE
(born 1904)

A master of suspense, Graham Greene divides his work into two groups: "entertainments," such as *This Gun for Hire* (1936), which are fast-moving adventure stories, and "serious" novels, such as *The Power and the Glory* (1940), which have themes emphasizing religious and moral issues. He has also written travel books, short stories, and plays.

Born in Hertfordshire, England, Graham Greene was one of six children, and the son of a school headmaster. Bored and unhappy, Greene ran away from home and tried to take his own life when he was a teenager. At twenty-one, while he was a student at Oxford University, he converted to Roman Catholicism, a step that had a profound influence on his life and writing.

After graduation, he worked as an editor for the *London Times* until his first novel, *The Man Within,* was published in 1929. In later years, he has been a film critic, literary editor, and free-lance writer. His travels through Europe, Mexico, Africa, and Southeast Asia have provided background material for much of his writing. Many of his stories have been made into films.

ACROSS THE BRIDGE

"They say he's worth a million," Lucia said. He sat there in the little hot damp Mexican square, a dog at his feet, with an air of immense and forlorn patience. The dog attracted your attention at once, for it was very nearly an English setter, only something had gone wrong with the tail and the feathering. Palms wilted over his head, it was all shade and stuffiness around the bandstand, radios talked loudly in Spanish from the little wooden sheds where they changed your pesos into dollars at a loss. I could tell he didn't understand a word from the way he read his newspaper—as I did myself, picking out the words which were like English ones. "He's been here a month," Lucia said. "They turned him out of Guatemala and Honduras."

You couldn't keep any secrets for five hours in this border town. Lucia had only been twenty-four hours in the place, but she knew all about Mr. Joseph Calloway. The only reason I didn't know about him (and I'd been in the place two weeks) was that I couldn't talk the language any more than Mr. Calloway could. There wasn't another soul in the place who didn't know the story—the whole story of the Halling Investment Trust and the proceedings for extradition.[1] Any man doing dusty business in any of the wooden booths in the town is better fitted by long observation to tell Mr. Calloway's tale than I am, except that I was in—literally—at the finish. They all watched the drama proceed with immense interest, sympathy, and respect. For after all, he had a million.

Every once in a while through the long steamy day a boy came and cleaned Mr. Calloway's shoes: he hadn't the right words to resist them—they pretended not to know his English. He must have had his shoes cleaned the day Lucia and I watched him at least half a dozen times. At midday he took a stroll across the square to the Antonio Bar and had a bottle of beer, the setter sticking to heel as if they were out for a country walk in England (he had, you may remember, one of the biggest estates in Norfolk[2]). After his bottle of beer, he would walk down between the moneychangers' huts to the Rio Grande and look across the bridge into the United States: people came and went constantly in cars. Then back to the square till lunch time. He was staying in the best hotel, but you don't get good hotels in this border town: nobody stays in them more than a night. The good hotels were on the other side of the bridge: you could see their electric signs twenty stories high from the little square at night, like lighthouses marking the United States.

You may ask what I'd been doing in so drab a spot for a fortnight.[3] There was no interest in the place for anyone; it was just damp and dust and poverty, a kind of shabby replica of the town across the river: both had squares in the same spots; both had the same number of cinemas. One was cleaner than the other, that was all, and more expensive, much more expensive. I'd stayed across there a couple of nights waiting for a man a tourist bureau said was driving down from Detroit to Yucatán[4] and would sell a place in his car for

1. **extradition:** the turning over of an accused individual by one state, country, or authority to another.
2. **Norfolk** (nôr′fək): a county in England.
3. **fortnight:** two weeks.
4. **Yucatán** (yōō′kə•tän′): a state in southeastern Mexico.

some fantastically small figure—twenty dollars, I think it was. I don't know if he existed or was invented by the optimistic half-caste in the agency; anyway, he never turned up, and so I waited, not much caring, on the cheap side of the river. It didn't much matter; I was living. One day I meant to give up the man from Detroit and go home or go south, but it was easier not to decide anything in a hurry. Lucia was just waiting for a car going the other way, but she didn't have to wait so long. We waited together and watched Mr. Calloway waiting—for God knows what.

I don't know how to treat this story—it was a tragedy for Mr. Calloway, it was poetic retribution,[5] I suppose, in the eyes of the shareholders he'd ruined with his bogus transactions, and to Lucia and me, at this stage, it was pure comedy—except when he kicked the dog. I'm not a sentimentalist about dogs, I prefer people to be cruel to animals rather than to human beings, but I couldn't help being revolted at the way he'd kick that animal—with a hint of cold-blooded venom, not in anger but as if he were getting even for some trick it had played him a long while ago. That generally happened when he returned from the bridge: it was the only sign of anything resembling emotion he showed. Otherwise he looked a small, set, gentle creature, with silver hair and a silver moustache, and gold-rimmed glasses, and one gold tooth like a flaw in character.

Lucia hadn't been accurate when she said he'd been turned out of Guatemala and Honduras; he'd left voluntarily when the extradition proceedings seemed likely to go through, and moved north. Mexico is still not a very centralized state, and it is possible to get around governors as you can't get around cabinet ministers or judges. And so he waited there on the border for the next move. That earlier part of the story is, I suppose, dramatic, but I didn't watch it and I can't invent what I haven't seen—the long waiting in anterooms, the bribes taken and refused, the growing fear of arrest, and then the flight—in gold-rimmed glasses—covering his tracks as well as he could, but this wasn't finance and he was an amateur at escape. And so he'd washed up here, under my eyes and Lucia's eyes, sitting all day under the bandstand, nothing to read but a Mexican paper, nothing to do but look across the river at the United States, quite unaware, I suppose, that everyone knew everything about him, once a day kicking his dog. Perhaps in its semi-setter way it reminded him too much

---

5. poetic retribution: in plays, short stories, and poems, an outcome in which vice is punished and virtue rewarded in an ideal or appropriate manner.

of the Norfolk estate—though that too, I suppose, was the reason he kept it.

And the next act again was pure comedy. I hesitate to think what this man worth a million was costing his country as they edged him out from this land and that. Perhaps somebody was getting tired of the business, and careless; anyway, they sent across two detectives, with an old photograph. He'd grown his silvery moustache since that had been taken, and he'd aged a lot, and they couldn't catch sight of him. They hadn't been across the bridge two hours when everybody knew that there were two foreign detectives in town looking for Mr. Calloway—everybody knew, that is to say, except Mr. Calloway, who couldn't talk Spanish. There were plenty of people who could have told him in English, but they didn't. It wasn't cruelty, it was a sort of awe and respect: like a bull, he was on show, sitting there mournfully in the plaza with his dog, a magnificent spectacle for which we all had ringside seats.

I ran into one of the policemen in the Bar Antonio. He was disgusted; he had had some idea that when he crossed the bridge life was going to be different, so much more color and sun, and—I suspect—love, and all he found were wide mud streets where the nocturnal rain lay in pools, and mangy dogs, smells and cockroaches in his bedroom, and the nearest to love, the open door of the Academia Comercial, where pretty mestizo⁶ girls sat all the morning learning to typewrite. Tip-tap-tip-tap-tip—perhaps they had a dream, too—jobs on the other side of the bridge, where life was going to be so much more luxurious, refined, and amusing.

We got into conversation; he seemed surprised that I knew who they both were and what they wanted. He said, "We've got information this man Calloway's in town."

"He's knocking around somewhere," I said.

"Could you point him out?"

"Oh, I don't know him by sight," I said.

He drank his beer and thought awhile. "I'll go out and sit in the plaza. He's sure to pass sometime."

I finished my beer and went quickly off and found Lucia. I said, "Hurry, we're going to see an arrest." We didn't care a thing about Mr. Calloway; he was just an elderly man who kicked his dog and

6. **mestizo** (mĕs·tē′zō): of mixed blood; in Mexico and the western United States, of Spanish and Indian ancestry.

swindled the poor, and who deserved anything he got. So we made for the plaza; we knew Calloway would be there, but it had never occurred to either of us that the detectives wouldn't recognize him. There was quite a surge of people around the place; all the fruit sellers and bootblacks in town seemed to have arrived together; we had to force our way through, and there in the little green stuffy center of the place, sitting on adjoining seats, were the two plainclothes men and Mr. Calloway. I've never known the place so silent; everybody was on tiptoe, and the plainclothes men were staring at the crowd, looking for Mr. Calloway, and Mr. Calloway sat on his usual seat staring out over the moneychanging booths at the United States.

"It can't go on. It just can't," Lucia said. But it did. It got more fantastic still. Somebody ought to write a play about it. We sat as close as we dared. We were afraid all the time we were going to laugh. The semi-setter scratched for fleas, and Mr. Calloway watched the U.S.A. The two detectives watched the crowd, and the crowd watched the show with solemn satisfaction. Then one of the detectives got up and went over to Mr. Calloway. That's the end, I thought. But it wasn't, it was the beginning. For some reason they had eliminated him from their list of suspects. I shall never know why.

The man said, "You speak English?"

"I *am* English," Mr. Calloway said.

Even that didn't tear it, and the strangest thing of all was the way Mr. Calloway came alive. I don't think anybody had spoken to him like that for weeks. The Mexicans were too respectful—he was a man with a million—and it had never occurred to Lucia and me to treat him casually like a human being; even in our eyes he had been magnified by the colossal theft and the worldwide pursuit.

He said, "This is rather a dreadful place, don't you think?"

"It is," the policeman said.

"I can't think what brings anybody across the bridge."

"Duty," the policeman said gloomily. "I suppose you are passing through?"

"Yes," Mr. Calloway said.

"I'd have expected over here there'd have been—you know what I mean—life. You read things about Mexico."

"Oh, life," Mr. Calloway said. He spoke firmly and precisely, as if to a committee of shareholders. "That begins on the other side."

"You don't appreciate your own country until you leave it."

"That's very true," Mr. Calloway said. "Very true."

At first it was difficult not to laugh, and then after awhile there didn't seem to be much to laugh at; an old man imagining all the fine things going on beyond the international bridge. I think he thought of the town opposite as a combination of London and Norfolk—theaters and cocktail bars, a little shooting and a walk around the field at evening with the dog—that miserable imitation of a setter—poking the ditches. He'd never been across—he couldn't know that it was just the same thing over again—even the same layout; only the streets were paved and the hotels had ten more stories, and life was more expensive, and everything was a little bit cleaner. There wasn't anything Mr. Calloway would have called living—no galleries, no bookshops, just *Film Fun* and the local paper, and *Click* and *Focus* and the tabloids.

"Well," said Mr. Calloway, "I think I'll take a stroll before lunch. You need an appetite to swallow the food here. I generally go down and look at the bridge about now. Care to come too?"

The detective shook his head. "No," he said, "I'm on duty. I'm looking for a fellow." And that, of course, gave *him* away. As far as Mr. Calloway could understand, there was only one "fellow" in the world anyone was looking for—his brain had eliminated friends who were seeking their friends, husbands who might be waiting for their wives, all objectives of any search but just the one. The power of elimination was what had made him a financier—he could forget the people behind the shares.

That was the last we saw of him for awhile. We didn't see him going into the Botica[7] Paris to get his aspirin, or walking back from the bridge with his dog. He simply disappeared, and when he disappeared people began to talk, and the detectives heard the talk. They looked silly enough, and they got busy after the very man they'd been sitting next to in the garden. Then they too disappeared. They, as well as Mr. Calloway, had gone to the state capital to see the Governor and the Chief of Police, and it must have been an amusing sight there too, as they bumped into Mr. Calloway and sat with him in the waiting rooms. I suspect Mr. Calloway was generally shown in first, for everyone knew he was worth a million. Only in Europe is it possible for a man to be a criminal as well as a rich man.

Anyway, after about a week the whole pack of them returned by the same train. Mr. Calloway traveled Pullman, and the two

7. **Botica** (bō·tē′cä): *Spanish,* drugstore.

policemen traveled in the day coach. It was evident that they hadn't got their extradition order.

Lucia had left by that time. The car came and went across the bridge. I stood in Mexico and watched her get out at the United States Customs. She wasn't anything in particular but she looked beautiful at a distance as she gave me a wave out of the United States and got back into the car. And I suddenly felt sympathy for Mr. Calloway, as if there were something over there which you couldn't find here, and turning around I saw him back on his old beat, with the dog at his heels.

I said "Good afternoon," as if it had been all along our habit to greet each other. He looked tired and ill and dusty, and I felt sorry for him—to think of the kind of victory he'd been winning, with so much expenditure of cash and care—the prize this dirty and dreary town, the booths of the moneychangers, the awful little beauty parlors with their wicker chairs and sofas looking like the reception rooms of brothels, that hot and stuffy garden by the bandstand.

He replied gloomily, "Good morning," and the dog started to sniff at some ordure and he turned and kicked it with fury, with depression, with despair.

And at that moment a taxi with the two policemen in it passed us on its way to the bridge. They must have seen that kick; perhaps they were cleverer than I had given them credit for, perhaps they were just sentimental about animals, and thought they'd do a good deed, and the rest happened by accident. But the fact remains—those two pillars of the law set about the stealing of Mr. Calloway's dog.

He watched them go by. Then he said, "Why don't you go across?"

"It's cheaper here," I said.

"I mean just for an evening. Have a meal at that place we can see at night in the sky. Go to the theater."

"There isn't a chance."

He said angrily, sucking his gold tooth, "Well, anyway, get away from here." He stared down the hill and up the other side. He couldn't see that that street climbing up from the bridge contained only the same moneychangers' booths as this one.

I said, "Why don't *you* go?"

He said evasively, "Oh—business."

I said, "It's only a question of money. You don't *have* to pass by the bridge."

He said with faint interest, "I don't talk Spanish."

"There isn't a soul here," I said, "who doesn't talk English."
He looked at me with surprise. "Is that so?" he said. "Is that so?"

It's as I have said; he'd never tried to talk to anyone, and they respected him too much to talk to him—he was worth a million. I don't know whether I'm glad or sorry that I told him that. If I hadn't, he might be there now, sitting by the bandstand having his shoes cleaned—alive and suffering.

Three days later his dog disappeared. I found him looking for it, calling it softly and shamefacedly among the palms of the garden. He looked embarrassed. He said in a low, angry voice, "I *hate* that dog. The beastly mongrel," and called "Rover, Rover" in a voice which didn't carry five yards. He said, "I bred setters once. I'd have shot a dog like that." It reminded him, I *was* right, of Norfolk, and he lived in the memory, and he hated it for its imperfection. He was a man without a family and without friends, and his only enemy was that dog. You couldn't call the law an enemy; you have to be intimate with an enemy.

Late that afternoon someone told him they'd seen the dog walking across the bridge. It wasn't true, of course, but we didn't know that then—they'd paid a Mexican five pesos to smuggle it across. So all that afternoon and the next Mr. Calloway sat in the garden having his shoes cleaned over and over again, and thinking how a dog could just walk across like that, and a human being, an immortal soul, was bound here in the awful routine of the little walk and the unspeakable meals and the aspirin at the *botica*. That dog was seeing things he couldn't see—that hateful dog. It made him mad—I think literally mad. You must remember the man had been going on for months. He had a million and he was living on two pounds a week, with nothing to spend his money on. He sat there and brooded on the hideous injustice of it. I think he'd have crossed over one day in any case, but the dog was the last straw.

Next day when he wasn't to be seen I guessed he'd gone across, and I went too. The American town is as small as the Mexican. I knew I couldn't miss him if he was there, and I was still curious. A little sorry for him, but not much.

I caught sight of him first in the only drugstore, having a Coca-Cola, and then once outside a cinema, looking at the posters; he had dressed with extreme neatness, as if for a party, but there was no party. On my third time around, I came on the detectives—they were having Coca-Colas in the drugstore, and they must have missed Mr. Calloway by inches. I went in and sat down at the bar.

"Hello," I said, "you still about?" I suddenly felt anxious for Mr. Calloway, I didn't want them to meet.

One of them said, "Where's Calloway?"

"Oh," I said, "he's hanging on."

"But not his dog," he said, and laughed. The other looked a little shocked; he didn't like anyone to *talk* cynically about a dog. Then they got up—they had a car outside.

"Have another?" I said.

"No, thanks. We've got to keep moving."

The man bent close and confided to me, "Calloway's on this side."

"No!" I said.

"And his dog."

"He's looking for it," the other said.

"I'm damned if he is," I said, and again one of them looked a little shocked, as if I'd insulted the dog.

I don't think Mr. Calloway was looking for his dog, but his dog certainly found him. There was a sudden hilarious yapping from the car and out plunged the semi-setter and gamboled[8] furiously down the street. One of the detectives—the sentimental one—was into the car before we got to the door and was off after the dog. Near the bottom of the long road to the bridge was Mr. Calloway—I do believe he'd come down to look at the Mexican side when he found there was nothing but the drugstore and the cinemas and the paper shops on the American. He saw the dog coming and yelled at it to go home—"home, home, home," as if they were in Norfolk. It took no notice at all, pelting toward him. Then he saw the police car coming and ran. After that, everything happened too quickly, but I think the order of events was this—the dog started across the road right in front of the car, and Mr. Calloway yelled, at the dog or the car, I don't know which. Anyway, the detective swerved—he said later, weakly, at the inquiry, that he couldn't run over a dog, and down went Mr. Calloway, in a mess of broken glass and gold rims and silver hair and blood. The dog was on him before any of us could reach him, licking and whimpering and licking. I saw Mr. Calloway put up his hand, and down it went across the dog's neck, and the whimper rose to a stupid bark of triumph, but Mr. Calloway was dead—shock and a weak heart.

"Poor old geezer," the detective said, "I bet he really loved that

8. **gamboled** (găm'bəld): skipped and leaped about.

dog," and it's true that the attitude in which he lay looked more like a caress than a blow. I thought it was meant to be a blow, but the detective may have been right. It all seemed to me a little too touching to be true as the old crook lay there with his arm over the dog's neck, dead with his million between the moneychangers' huts, but it's as well to be humble in the face of human nature. He had come across the river for something, and it may, after all, have been the dog he was looking for. It sat there, baying its stupid and mongrel triumph across his body, like a piece of sentimental statuary. The nearest he could get to the fields, the ditches, the horizon of his home. It was comic and it was pitiable; but it wasn't less comic because the man was dead. Death doesn't change comedy to tragedy, and if that last gesture was one of affection, I suppose it was only one more indication of a human being's capacity for self-deception, our baseless optimism that is so much more appalling than our despair.

Meaning

1. The narrator describes the silver-haired Mr. Calloway as having "one gold tooth like a flaw in his character." What is his fatal flaw? Why is it ironic that he's worth a million?

2. Why does Mr. Calloway want to visit the American town? Why can't he cross the bridge like everyone else?

3. At one point, the narrator says that Mr. Calloway's story was "pure comedy." The classic definition of comedy is that it is a play concerned with humans as social beings rather than as private individuals. In ancient Greece, the writer of comedy wanted to correct the evils of society by making the audience laugh at characters who were immoral or stupid. To what extent does Mr. Calloway's story fit the definition of pure comedy?

4. Explain Mr. Calloway's need to have a setter. What does his mistreatment of the dog reveal about him?

Method

1. The Mexican town is "just damp and dust and poverty." Why are the atmosphere and setting essential to the unfolding of Mr. Calloway's story?

2. What role does the narrator play in the story? What kind of person does he seem to be? Is his attitude toward Mr. Calloway sad and sentimental, amused and sympathetic, or angry and disapproving?

3. A *symbol* is a person, place, event, or object that, besides being itself, also represents or stands for something else. For example, an owl represents wisdom; a sword, power and authority. The reader determines the meaning of each symbol from its context in the story.

In "Across the Bridge," what elements in Mr. Calloway's life do the moneychangers' huts appear to represent? What does the dog symbolize? the bridge?

Language: Abstract and Concrete Terms

Abstract terms are words and phrases that represent ideas, generalities, or characteristics rather than particular objects. They have little or no sense appeal and are difficult to define and analyze. Examples of abstract terms are *patience, optimism,* and *despair.*

Concrete terms stand for objects that can be perceived by the senses or clearly imagined. Examples of concrete terms are *lake, chair,* and *coat.*

Select the abstract terms from among the following words, and define each with a sentence. Modify each concrete term on the list with an adjective so that it will be as specific as possible and appeal to one or more of the senses.

1. affection	**4.** dog	**7.** injustice
2. snow	**5.** triumph	**8.** law
3. death	**6.** bridge	**9.** river

Discussion and Composition

1. Reread the last sentence of the story. Why is Mr. Calloway's story an example of "our baseless optimism"? Do most human beings have a "capacity for self-deception"?

2. If you were suddenly "worth a million"—and the million had been gained honestly—what would you do? Where would you go? How would you change your life?

3. Compare Mr. Calloway's attitude toward animals with that of the narrator and the sentimental detective. With whom do you most agree? Tell why.

4. The reader does not know for sure whether Mr. Calloway is attempting to pet the dog or hit it as he dies. What do you think? Write a paragraph supporting your position. Base your argument on what you know of Mr. Calloway's character. What evidence can you find that he loved the dog? that he hated the dog? Which emotion do you think triumphed? Why?

SHIRLEY JACKSON

(1919-1965)

Many of Shirley Jackson's stories have a haunting, mysterious quality that leave the reader feeling unsettled. The settings and situations of these works are often commonplace, but below the surface lies a powerful undercurrent of meaning. The convincing elements of horror in her stories and novels reflect her extensive study of the supernatural as well as her ability to intertwine reality and fantasy, everydayness and imaginative speculation.

Jackson was born in San Francisco and graduated from Syracuse University. For most of her life she lived in Vermont, where her husband taught at Bennington College. In addition to her works of fiction, she wrote two humorous books about her life as a mother of four lively children: *Life Among the Savages* (1953) and *Raising Demons* (1957). "The Lottery" is the title work of Jackson's first short-story collection and remains one of her most famous works.

THE LOTTERY

The morning of June 27th was clear and sunny, with the fresh warmth of a full-summer day; the flowers were blossoming profusely, and the grass was richly green. The people of the village began to gather in the square, between the post office and the bank, around ten o'clock; in some towns there were so many people that the lottery took two days and had to be started on June 26th, but in this village, where there were only about three hundred people, the whole lottery took only about two hours, so it could begin at ten o'clock in the morning and still be through in time to allow the villagers to get home for noon dinner.

The children assembled first, of course. School was recently over for the summer, and the feeling of liberty sat uneasily on most of them; they tended to gather together quietly for a while before they broke into boisterous play, and their talk was still of the classroom and the teacher, of books and reprimands. Bobby Martin had already stuffed his pockets full of stones, and the other boys soon followed his example, selecting the smoothest and roundest stones; Bobby and Harry Jones and Dickie Delacroix—the villagers pronounced this name "Dellacroy"—eventually made a great pile of stones in one corner of the square and guarded it against the raids of the other boys. The girls stood aside, talking among themselves, looking over their shoulders at the boys, and the very small children rolled in the dust or clung to the hands of their older brothers or sisters.

Soon the men began to gather, surveying their own children, speaking of planting and rain, tractors and taxes. They stood together, away from the pile of stones in the corner, and their jokes were quiet, and they smiled rather than laughed. The women, wearing faded house dresses and sweaters, came shortly after their menfolk. They greeted one another and exchanged bits of gossip as they went to join their husbands. Soon the women, standing by their husbands, began to call to their children, and the children came reluctantly, having to be called four or five times. Bobby Martin ducked under his mother's grasping hand and ran, laughing, back to the pile of stones. His father spoke up sharply, and Bobby came quickly and took his place between his father and his oldest brother.

The lottery was conducted—as were the square dances, the teen-age club, the Halloween program—by Mr. Summers, who had time and energy to devote to civic activities. He was a round-faced, jovial man, and he ran the coal business; and people were sorry for him, because he had no children and his wife was a scold. When he arrived in the square, carrying the black wooden box, there was a murmur of conversation among the villagers, and he waved and called, "Little late today, folks." The postmaster, Mr. Graves, followed him, carrying a three-legged stool; and the stool was put in the center of the square, and Mr. Summers set the black box down on it. The villagers kept their distance, leaving a space between themselves and the stool, and when Mr. Summers said, "Some of you fellows want to give me a hand?" there was a hesitation before two men, Mr. Martin and his oldest son, Baxter, came forward to hold the box steady on the stool while Mr. Summers stirred up the papers inside it.

The original paraphernalia for the lottery had been lost long ago, and the black box now resting on the stool had been put into use even before Old Man Warner, the oldest man in town, was born. Mr. Summers spoke frequently to the villagers about making a new box, but no one liked to upset even as much tradition as was represented by the black box. There was a story that the present box had been made with some pieces of the box that had preceded it, the one that had been constructed when the first people settled down to make a village here. Every year, after the lottery, Mr. Summers began talking again about a new box, but every year the subject was allowed to fade off without anything's being done. The black box grew shabbier each year; by now it was no longer completely black but splintered badly along one side to show the original wood color, and in some places faded or stained.

Mr. Martin and his oldest son, Baxter, held the black box securely on the stool until Mr. Summers had stirred the papers thoroughly with his hand. Because so much of the ritual had been forgotten or discarded, Mr. Summers had been successful in having slips of paper substituted for the chips of wood that had been used for generations. Chips of wood, Mr. Summers had argued, had been all very well when the village was tiny, but now that the population was more than three hundred and likely to keep on growing, it was necessary to use something that would fit more easily into the black box. The night before the lottery, Mr. Summers and Mr. Graves made up the slips of paper and put them into the box, and it was then taken to the safe of Mr. Summers' coal company and locked up until Mr. Summers was ready to take it to the square next morning. The rest of the year, the box was put away, sometimes one place, sometimes another; it had spent one year in Mr. Graves's barn and another year underfoot in the post office, and sometimes it was set on a shelf in the Martin grocery and left there.

There was a great deal of fussing to be done before Mr. Summers declared the lottery open. There were the lists to make up— of heads of families, heads of households in each family, members of each household in each family. There was the proper swearing-in of Mr. Summers by the postmaster, as the official of the lottery; at one time, some people remembered, there had been a recital of some sort, performed by the official of the lottery, a perfunctory, tuneless chant that had been rattled off duly each year; some people believed that the official of the lottery used to stand just so when he said or sang it; others believed that he was supposed to walk among the people; but years and years ago this part of the ritual had been allowed to lapse. There had been, also, a ritual salute, which the official of the lottery had had to use in addressing each person who came up to draw from the box, but this also had changed with time, until now it was felt necessary only for the official to speak to each person approaching. Mr. Summers was very good at all this; in his clean white shirt and blue jeans, with one hand resting carelessly on the black box, he seemed very proper and important as he talked interminably to Mr. Graves and the Martins.

Just as Mr. Summers finally left off talking and turned to the assembled villagers, Mrs. Hutchinson came hurriedly along the path to the square, her sweater thrown over her shoulders, and slid into place in the back of the crowd. "Clean forgot what day it was," she said to Mrs. Delacroix, who stood next to her, and they both laughed softly. "Thought my old man was out back stacking wood," Mrs. Hutchinson went on, "and then I looked out the window and the kids was gone, and then I remembered it was the twenty-seventh and came a-running." She dried her hands on her apron, and Mrs. Delacroix said, "You're in time, though. They're still talking away up there."

Mrs. Hutchinson craned her neck to see through the crowd and found her husband and children standing near the front. She tapped Mrs. Delacroix on the arm as a farewell and began to make her way through the crowd. The people separated good-humoredly to let her through; two or three people said, in voices just loud enough to be heard across the crowd, "Here comes your Mrs., Hutchinson," and "Bill, she made it after all." Mrs. Hutchinson reached her husband, and Mr. Summers, who had been waiting, said cheerfully, "Thought we were going to have to get on without you, Tessie." Mrs. Hutchinson said, grinning, "Wouldn't have me leave m'dishes in the sink, now, would you, Joe?" and soft laughter ran through the crowd as the people stirred back into position after Mrs. Hutchinson's arrival.

"Well, now," Mr. Summers said soberly, "guess we better get started, get this over with, so's we can go back to work. Anybody ain't here?"

"Dunbar," several people said. "Dunbar, Dunbar."

Mr. Summers consulted his list. "Clyde Dunbar," he said. "That's right. He's broke his leg, hasn't he? Who's drawing for him?"

"Me, I guess," a woman said, and Mr. Summers turned to look at her. "Wife draws for her husband," Mr. Summers said. "Don't you have a grown boy to do it for you, Janey?" Although Mr. Summers and everyone else in the village knew the answer perfectly well, it was the business of the official of the lottery to ask such questions formally. Mr. Summers waited with an expression of polite interest while Mrs. Dunbar answered.

"Horace's not but sixteen yet," Mrs. Dunbar said regretfully. "Guess I gotta fill in for the old man this year."

"Right," Mr. Summers said. He made a note on the list he was holding. Then he asked, "Watson boy drawing this year?"

A tall boy in the crowd raised his hand. "Here," he said. "I'm drawing for m'mother and me." He blinked his eyes nervously and ducked his head as several voices in the crowd said things like "Good fellow, Jack," and "Glad to see your mother's got a man to do it."

"Well," Mr. Summers said, "guess that's everyone. Old Man Warner make it?"

"Here," a voice said, and Mr. Summers nodded.

A sudden hush fell on the crowd as Mr. Summers cleared his throat and looked at the list. "All ready?" he called. "Now, I'll read the names—heads of families first—and the men come up and take a paper out of the box. Keep the paper folded in your hand without looking at it until everyone has had a turn. Everything clear?"

The people had done it so many times that they only half listened to the directions; most of them were quiet, wetting their lips, not looking around. Then Mr. Summers raised one hand high and said, "Adams." A man disengaged himself from the crowd and came forward. "Hi, Steve," Mr. Summers said, and Mr. Adams said, "Hi, Joe." They grinned at one another humorlessly and nervously. Then Mr. Adams reached into the black box and took out a folded paper. He held it firmly by one corner as he turned and went hastily back to his place in the crowd, where he stood a little apart from his family, not looking down at his hand.

"Allen," Mr. Summers said. "Anderson. . . . Bentham."

"Seems like there's no time at all between lotteries any more," Mrs. Delacroix said to Mrs. Graves in the back row. "Seems like we got through with the last one only last week."

"Time sure goes fast," Mrs. Graves said.

"Clark. . . . Delacroix."

"There goes my old man," Mrs. Delacroix said. She held her breath while her husband went forward.

"Dunbar," Mr. Summers said, and Mrs. Dunbar went steadily to the box while one of the women said, "Go on, Janey," and another said, "There she goes."

"We're next," Mrs. Graves said. She watched while Mr. Graves came around from the side of the box, greeted Mr. Summers gravely, and selected a slip of paper from the box. By now, all through the crowd there were men holding the small folded papers in their large hands, turning them over and over nervously. Mrs. Dunbar and her two sons stood together, Mrs. Dunbar holding the slip of paper.

"Harburt. . . . Hutchinson."

"Get up there, Bill," Mrs. Hutchinson said, and the people near her laughed.

"Jones."

"They do say," Mr. Adams said to Old Man Warner, who stood next to him, "that over in the north village they're talking of giving up the lottery."

Old Man Warner snorted. "Pack of crazy fools," he said. "Listening to the young folks, nothing's good enough for them. Next thing you know, they'll be wanting to go back to living in caves, nobody work any more, live that way for a while. Used to be a saying about 'Lottery in June, corn be heavy soon.' First thing you know, we'd all be eating stewed chickweed and acorns. There's always been a lottery," he added petulantly. "Bad enough to see young Joe Summers up there joking with everybody."

"Some places have already quit lotteries," Mrs. Adams said.

"Nothing but trouble in that," Old Man Warner said stoutly. "Pack of young fools."

"Martin." And Bobby Martin watched his father go forward. "Overdyke. . . . Percy."

"I wish they'd hurry," Mrs. Dunbar said to her older son. "I wish they'd hurry."

"They're almost through," her son said.

"You get ready to run tell Dad," Mrs. Dunbar said.

Mr. Summers called his own name and then stepped forward precisely and selected a slip from the box. Then he called, "Warner."

"Seventy-seventh year I been in the lottery," Old Man Warner said as he went through the crowd. "Seventy-seventh time."

"Watson." The tall boy came awkwardly through the crowd. Someone said, "Don't be nervous, Jack," and Mr. Summers said, "Take your time, son."

"Zanini."

After that, there was a long pause, a breathless pause, until Mr. Summers, holding his slip of paper in the air, said, "All right, fellows." For a minute, no one moved, and then all the slips of paper were opened. Suddenly, all the women began to speak at once, saying, "Who is it?" "Who's got it?" "Is it the Dunbars?" "Is it the Watsons?" Then the voices began to say, "It's Hutchinson. It's Bill." "Bill Hutchinson's got it."

"Go tell your father," Mrs. Dunbar said to her older son.

People began to look around to see the Hutchinsons. Bill Hutchinson was standing quiet, staring down at the paper in his hand. Suddenly, Tessie Hutchinson shouted to Mr. Summers, "You didn't give him time enough to take any paper he wanted. I saw you. It wasn't fair!"

"Be a good sport, Tessie," Mrs. Delacroix called, and Mrs. Graves said, "All of us took the same chance."

"Shut up, Tessie," Bill Hutchinson said.

"Well, everyone," Mr. Summers said, "that was done pretty fast, and now we've got to be hurrying a little more to get done in time." He consulted his next list. "Bill," he said, "you draw for the Hutchinson family. You got any other households in the Hutchinsons?"

"There's Don and Eva," Mrs. Hutchinson yelled. "Make them take their chance!"

"Daughters draw with their husbands' families, Tessie," Mr. Summers said gently. "You know that as well as anyone else."

"It wasn't fair," Tessie said.

"I guess not, Joe," Bill Hutchinson said regretfully. "My daughter draws with her husband's family, that's only fair. And I've got no other family except the kids."

"Then, as far as drawing for families is concerned, it's you," Mr. Summers said in explanation, "and as far as drawing for households is concerned, that's you, too. Right?"

"Right," Bill Hutchinson said.

"How many kids, Bill?" Mr. Summers asked formally.

"Three," Bill Hutchinson said. "There's Bill, Jr., and Nancy, and little Dave. And Tessie and me."

"All right, then," Mr. Summers said. "Harry, you got their tickets back?"

Mr. Graves nodded and held up the slips of paper. "Put them in the box, then," Mr. Summers directed. "Take Bill's and put it in."

"I think we ought to start over," Mrs. Hutchinson said, as quietly as she could. "I tell you it wasn't fair. You didn't give him time enough to choose. Everybody saw that."

Mr. Graves had selected the five slips and put them in the box, and he dropped all the papers but those onto the ground, where the breeze caught them and lifted them off.

"Listen, everybody," Mrs. Hutchinson was saying to the people around her.

"Ready, Bill?" Mr. Summers asked, and Bill Hutchinson, with one quick glance around at his wife and children, nodded.

"Remember," Mr. Summers said, "take the slips and keep them folded until each person has taken one. Harry, you help little Dave." Mr. Graves took the hand of the little boy, who came willingly with him up to the box. "Take a paper out of the box, Davy," Mr. Summers said. Davy put his hand into the box and laughed. "Take just one paper," Mr. Summers said. "Harry, you hold it for him." Mr. Graves took the child's hand and removed the folded paper from the tight fist and held it while little Dave stood next to him and looked up at him wonderingly.

"Nancy next," Mr. Summers said. Nancy was twelve, and her school friends breathed heavily as she went forward, switching her skirt, and took a slip daintily from the box. "Bill, Jr.," Mr. Summers said, and Billy, his face red and his feet overlarge, nearly knocked the box over as he got a paper out. "Tessie," Mr. Summers said. She hesitated for a minute, looking around defiantly, and then set her lips and went up to the box. She snatched a paper out and held it behind her.

"Bill," Mr. Summers said, and Bill Hutchinson reached into the box and felt around, bringing his hand out at last with the slip of paper in it.

The crowd was quiet. A girl whispered, "I hope it's not Nancy," and the sound of the whisper reached the edges of the crowd.

"It's not the way it used to be," Old Man Warner said clearly. "People ain't the way they used to be."

"All right," Mr. Summers said. "Open the papers. Harry, you open little Dave's."

Mr. Graves opened the slip of paper, and there was a general sigh through the crowd as he held it up and everyone could see that it was blank. Nancy and Bill, Jr., opened theirs at the same time, and both beamed and laughed, turning around to the crowd and holding their slips of paper above their heads.

"Tessie," Mr. Summers said. There was a pause, and then Mr. Summers looked at Bill Hutchinson, and Bill unfolded his paper and showed it. It was blank.

"It's Tessie," Mr. Summers said, and his voice was hushed. "Show us her paper, Bill."

Bill Hutchinson went over to his wife and forced the slip of paper out of her hand. It had a black spot on it, the black spot Mr. Summers had made the night before with the heavy pencil in the coal-company office. Bill Hutchinson held it up, and there was a stir in the crowd.

"All right, folks," Mr. Summers said. "Let's finish quickly."

Although the villagers had forgotten the ritual and lost the original black box, they still remembered to use stones. The pile of stones the boys had made earlier was ready; there were stones on the ground with the blowing scraps of paper that had come out of the box. Mrs. Delacroix selected a stone so large she had to pick it up with both hands and turned to Mrs. Dunbar. "Come on," she said. "Hurry up."

Mrs. Dunbar had small stones in both hands, and she said, gasping for breath, "I can't run at all. You'll have to go ahead and I'll catch up with you."

The children had stones already, and someone gave little Davy Hutchinson a few pebbles.

Tessie Hutchinson was in the center of a cleared space by now, and she held her hands out desperately as the villagers moved in on her. "It isn't fair," she said. A stone hit her on the side of the head.

Old Man Warner was saying, "Come on, come on, everyone." Steve Adams was in the front of the crowd of villagers, with Mrs. Graves beside him.

"It isn't fair, it isn't right," Mrs. Hutchinson screamed, and then they were upon her.

Meaning

1. How do the villagers behave as they gather in the square? What kind of lottery does their manner lead you to expect?
2. Did you begin to suspect before the end of the story that there was something awful about the lottery? If so, what details made you uneasy?
3. What "saying" does Old Man Warner quote about the lottery? What does this saying suggest about the possible origin and purpose of the drawing?
4. Mrs. Hutchinson's last words are: "'It isn't fair, it isn't right.'" Is the lottery conducted in a fair manner? Do you think a thing can be fair without being right? Explain.

Method

1. Many events of the story are commonplace: children play, old friends exchange greetings and remarks, and people look forward to getting home for lunch. How do these details, ordinary in themselves, contribute to the horror of the tale?
2. What is the *climax,* or turning point, of the story?
3. The author points out that Mrs. Delacroix "selected a stone so large she had to pick it up with both hands" and that "someone gave little Davy Hutchinson a few pebbles." Why do these details have such impact? What is the effect of telling them matter-of-factly?
4. *Irony of situation* involves a contrast between what the reader expects will happen and what actually happens. How does this type of irony figure into "The Lottery"? Give examples from the story.

Language: Determining Meaning from Context

As you read "The Lottery," you may have encountered words that were unfamiliar to you. The meaning of a word can often be determined from its *context,* the part of the sentence or paragraph that comes before and after the word.

Use context clues to determine the meanings of the italicized words in the following passages from "The Lottery." Then use a dictionary to check your definitions.

1. "... the flowers were blossoming *profusely,* and the grass was richly green."
2. "[The children] tended to gather quietly for a while before they broke into *boisterous* play...."
3. "A man *disengaged* himself from the crowd and came forward."
4. "... the children came *reluctantly,* having to be called four or five times."
5. "The lottery was conducted—as were the square dances, the teen-age club, the Halloween program—by Mr. Summers, who had time and energy to devote to *civic* activities."

Discussion and Composition

1. Old Man Warner maintains that "'there's always been a lottery.'" What other comments does he offer in support of the lottery? Are his reasons good ones? Have you heard people give similar arguments in defense of long-standing attitudes and customs? Give examples.

2. For some time after she wrote "The Lottery," Shirley Jackson refused to comment on the story. If you had the chance, would you want to hear a writer explain the meaning of a puzzling story, or would you rather draw your own conclusions? Why?

3. When "The Lottery" was first published in the *New Yorker* in 1948, it brought a flood of letters from readers around the globe. Some praised the story; others protested it or expressed perplexity. Write a letter that you might have sent to the editor of the magazine after reading "The Lottery." Give your response to the story, and tell why it affected you the way it did. Offer some comments on particular aspects of the story that impressed, troubled, or confused you.

WILBUR DANIEL STEELE
(1886–1970)

Wilbur Daniel Steele established his reputation as a master craftsman of storytelling during the 1920s. The son of a college professor, Steele studied art for several years after his graduation from the University of Denver in 1907. He chose writing instead of painting as a career in 1912 when the *Atlantic Monthly* accepted his story "A White Horse Winner."

Steele was born in Greensboro, North Carolina. During World War I, he traveled as a naval correspondent to Europe and North Africa. His plays, novels, and short stories often feature the New England coast, where he studied art, and the West, where he lived for several years. *That Girl from Memphis,* set in 1889 in an Arizona mining town, is his best known novel.

FOOTFALLS

This is not an easy story; not a road for tender or for casual feet. Better the meadows. Let me warn you, it is as hard as that old man's soul and as sunless as his eyes. It has its inception in catastrophe, and its end in an act of almost incredible violence; between them it tells barely how one long blind can become also deaf and dumb.

He lived in one of those old Puritan sea towns where the strain has come down austere and moribund,[1] so that his act would not be quite unbelievable. Except that the town is no longer Puritan and Yankee. It has been betrayed; it has become an outpost of the Portuguese islands.

This man, this blind cobbler himself, was a Portuguese from St. Michael, in the western islands,[2] and his name was Boaz Negro.

He was happy. An unquenchable exuberance lived in him. When he arose in the morning he made vast, as it were, uncontrolla-

---

1. **moribund** (môr′ə•bŭnd): approaching extinction; dying.
2. **St. Michael, in the western islands:** the largest island of the Azores, three groups of islands which are part of Portugal, located in the North Atlantic west of Portugal; in Portuguese, São Miguel.

ble, gestures with his stout arms. He came into his shop singing. His voice, strong and deep as the chest from which it emanated, rolled out through the doorway and along the street, and the fishermen, done with their morning work and lounging and smoking along the wharves, said, "Boaz is to work already." Then they came up to sit in the shop.

In that town a cobbler's shop is a club. One sees the interior always dimly thronged. They sit on the benches watching the artisan at his work for hours, and they talk about everything in the world. A cobbler is known by the company he keeps.

Boaz Negro kept young company. He would have nothing to do with the old. On his own head the gray hairs set thickly.

He had a grown son. But the benches in his shop were for the lusty and valiant young, men who could spend the night drinking, and then at three o'clock in the morning turn out in the rain and dark to pull at the weirs,[3] sing songs, buffet one another among the slippery fish in the boat's bottom, and make loud jokes about the fundamental things—love and birth and death. Harkening to their boasts and strong prophecies, his breast heaved and his heart beat faster. He was a large, full-blooded fellow, fashioned for exploits; the flame in his darkness burned higher even to hear of them.

It is scarcely conceivable how Boaz Negro could have come through this much of his life still possessed of that unquenchable and priceless exuberance; how he would sing in the dawn; how, simply listening to the recital of deeds of gale or brawl, he could easily forget himself a blind man, tied to a shop and a last;[4] easily make of himself a lusty young fellow breasting the sunlit and adventurous tide of life.

He had had a wife, whom he had loved. Fate, which had scourged him with the initial scourge of blindness, had seen fit to take his Angelina away. He had had four sons. Three, one after another, had been removed, leaving only Manuel, the youngest. Recovering slowly, with agony, from each of these recurrent blows, his un-quenchable exuberance had lived. And there was another thing quite as extraordinary. He had never done anything but work, and that sort of thing may kill the flame where an abrupt catastrophe fails. Work in the dark. Work, work, work! And accompanied by priva-tion, an almost miserly scale of personal economy. Yes indeed, he had

3. **weirs** (wîrz): nets set in a waterway to catch fish.
4. **last:** a metal or wooden form, shaped like a human foot, over which a shoe is made or repaired.

"skinned his fingers," especially in the earlier years. When it tells most.

How he had worked! Not alone in the daytime, but also sometimes, when orders were heavy, far into the night. It was strange for one passing along that deserted street at midnight to hear issuing from the black shop of Boaz Negro the rhythmical tap-tap-tap of hammer on wooden peg.

Nor was that sound all: no man in town could get far past that shop in his nocturnal wandering unobserved. No more than a dozen footfalls, and from the darkness Boaz's voice rolled forth, fraternal, stentorian:[5] "Good night, Antone!" "Good night to you, Caleb Snow!"

To Boaz Negro it was still broad day.

Now because of this, he was what might be called a substantial man. He owned his place, his shop, opening on the sidewalk, and behind it the dwelling house with trellised galleries upstairs and down.

And there was always something for his son, a "piece for the pocket," a dollar, five, even a ten-dollar bill if he had "got to have it." Manuel was "a good boy." Boaz not only said this, he felt that he was assured of it in his understanding, to the infinite peace of his heart.

It was curious that he should be ignorant only of the one nearest to him. Not because he was physically blind. Be certain he knew more of other men and of other men's sons than they or their neighbors did. More, that is to say, of their hearts, their understandings, their idiosyncrasies,[6] and their ultimate weight in the balance pan of eternity.

His simple explanation of Manuel was that Manuel "wasn't too stout." To others he said this, and to himself. Manuel was not indeed too robust. How should he be vigorous when he never did anything to make him so? He never worked. Why should he work, when existence was provided for, and when there was always that "piece for the pocket"? Even a ten-dollar bill on a Saturday night! No, Manuel "wasn't too stout."

In the shop they let it go at that. The missteps and frailties of everyone else in the world were canvassed there with the most shameless publicity. But Boaz Negro was a blind man, and in a sense their host. Those reckless, strong young fellows respected and loved

5. stentorian (stĕn·tôr′ē·ən): extremely loud.
6. idiosyncrasies (ĭdē·ō·sĭng′krə·sēz): peculiarities.

him. It was allowed to stand at that. Manuel was "a good boy." Which did not prevent them, by the way, from joining later in the general condemnation of that father's laxity—"the ruination of the boy!"

"He should have put him to work, that's what."

"He should have said to Manuel, 'Look here, if you want a dollar, go earn it first.'"

As a matter of fact, only one man ever gave Boaz the advice direct. That was Campbell Wood. And Wood never sat in that shop.

In every small town there is one young man who is spoken of as "rising." As often as not he is not a native, but "from away."

In this town Campbell Wood was that man. He had come from another part of the state to take a place in the bank. He lived in the upper story of Boaz Negro's house, the ground floor now doing for Boaz and the meager remnant of his family. The old woman who came in to tidy up for the cobbler looked after Wood's rooms as well.

Dealing with Wood, one had first of all the sense of his incorruptibility. A little ruthless perhaps, as if one could imagine him, in defense of his integrity, cutting off his friend, cutting off his own hand, cutting off the very stream flowing out from the wellsprings of human kindness. An exaggeration, perhaps.

He was by long odds the most eligible young man in town; good-looking in a spare, ruddy, sandy-haired Scottish fashion; important, incorruptible, "rising." But he took good care of his heart. Precisely that: like a sharp-eyed duenna[7] to his own heart. One felt that here was the man, if ever was the man, who held his destiny in his own hand. Failing, of course, some quite gratuitous[8] and unforeseeable catastrophe.

Not that he was not human, or even incapable of laughter or passion. He was, in a way, immensely accessible. He never clapped one on the shoulder; on the other hand, he never failed to speak. Not even to Boaz.

Returning from the bank in the afternoon, he had always a word for the cobbler. Passing out again to supper at his boarding place, he had another, about the weather, the prospects of rain. And if Boaz were at work in the dark when he returned from an evening at the Board of Trade, there was a "Good night, Mr. Negro!"

7. **duenna** (dōō·ēn′ə): a chaperon; in Spain and Portugal, an elderly woman who serves as a companion and protector to a young girl. Here, it refers to Wood's careful guarding of himself from close relationships.
8. **gratuitous** (grə·tōō′ə·təs): unearned, uncalled for.

On Boaz's part, his attitude toward his lodger was curious and paradoxical. He did not pretend to anything less than reverence for the young man's position; precisely on account of that position he was conscious toward Wood of a vague distrust. This was because he was an uneducated fellow.

To the uneducated, the idea of large finance is as uncomfortable as the idea of law. It must be said for Boaz that, responsive to Wood's unfailing civility, he fought against this sensation of dim and somehow shameful distrust.

Nevertheless, his whole parental soul was in arms that evening when, returning from the bank and finding the shop empty of loungers, Wood paused a moment to propose the bit of advice already referred to.

"Haven't you ever thought of having Manuel learn the trade?"

A suspicion, a kind of premonition, lighted the fires of defense.

"Shoemaking," said Boaz, "is good enough for a blind man."

"Oh, I don't know. At least it's better than doing nothing at all."

Boaz's hammer was still. He sat silent, monumental. Outwardly. For once his unfailing response had failed him, "Manuel ain't too stout, you know." Perhaps it had become suddenly quite inadequate.

He hated Wood; he despised Wood; more than ever before, a hundredfold more, quite abruptly, he distrusted Wood.

How could a man say such things as Wood had said? And where Manuel himself might hear!

Where Manuel *had* heard! Boaz's other emotions—hatred and contempt and distrust—were overshadowed. Sitting in darkness, no sound had come to his ears, no footfall, no infinitesimal creaking of a floor plank. Yet, by some sixth uncanny sense of the blind, he was aware that Manuel was standing in the dusk of the entry joining the shop to the house.

Boaz made a Herculean effort. The voice came out of his throat, harsh, bitter, and loud enough to have carried ten times the distance to his son's ears.

"Manuel is a good boy!"

"Yes—h'm—yes—I suppose so."

Wood shifted his weight. He seemed uncomfortable.

"Well. I'll be running along. I—ugh! Heavens!"

Something was happening. Boaz heard exclamations, breathings, the rustle of sleeve cloth in large, frantic, and futile graspings—all without understanding. Immediately there was an impact on the floor, and with it the unmistakable clink of metal. Boaz even heard that the metal was minted, and that the coins were gold. He understood. A coin sack, gripped not quite carefully enough for a moment under the other's overcoat, had shifted, slipped, escaped and fallen.

And Manuel had heard!

It was a dreadful moment for Boaz, dreadful in its native sense, as full of dread. Why? It was a moment of horrid revelation, ruthless clarification. His son, his link with the departed Angelina, that "good boy"—Manuel, standing in the shadow of the entry, visible alone to the blind, had heard the clink of falling gold, and—*and Boaz wished that he had not!*

There, amazing, disconcerting, destroying, stood the sudden fact.

Sitting as impassive and monumental as ever, his strong, bleached hands at rest on his work, round drops of sweat came out on Boaz's forehead. He scarcely took the sense of what Wood was saying. Only fragments.

"Government money, understand—for the breakwater workings—huge—too many people know here, everywhere—don't trust the safe—tin safe—'Noah's Ark'—give you my word—Heavens, no!"

It boiled down to this—the money, more money than was good for that antiquated "Noah's Ark" at the bank—and whose contemplated sojourn there overnight was public to too many minds—in short, Wood was not only incorruptible, he was canny. To what one of those minds, now, would it occur that he should take away that money bodily, under casual cover of his coat, to his own lodgings behind the cobbler shop of Boaz Negro? For this one, this important night!

He was sorry the coin sack had slipped, because he did not like to have the responsibility of secret sharer cast upon anyone, even upon Boaz, even by accident. On the other hand, how tremendously fortunate that it had been Boaz and not another. So far as that went, Wood had no more anxiety now than before. One incorruptible knows another.

"I'd trust you, Mr. Negro" (that was one of the fragments which came and stuck in the cobbler's brain), "as far as I would myself. As long as it's only you. I'm just going up here and throw it under the bed. Oh, yes, certainly."

Boaz ate no supper. For the first time in his life food was dry in his gullet. Even under those other successive crushing blows of Fate the full and generous habit of his functionings had carried on un-abated; he had always eaten what was set before him. Tonight, over his untouched plate, he watched Manuel with his sightless eyes, keeping track of his every mouthful, word, intonation, breath. What profit he expected to extract from this catlike surveillance it is im-possible to say.

When they arose from the supper table Boaz made another Herculean effort: "Manuel, you're a good boy!"

The formula had a quality of appeal, of despair, and of com-mand.

"Manuel, you should be short of money, maybe. Look, what's this? A tenner? Well, there's a piece for the pocket; go and enjoy yourself."

He would have been frightened had Manuel, upsetting tradi-tion, declined the offering. With the morbid contrariness of human imagination, the boy's avid grasping gave him no comfort.

He went out into the shop, where it was already dark, drew to him his last, his tools, mallets, cutters, pegs, leather. And having prepared to work, he remained idle. He found himself listening.

It has been observed that the large phenomena of sunlight and darkness were nothing to Boaz Negro. A busy night was broad day. Yet there was a difference; he knew it with the blind man's eyes, the ears.

Day was a vast confusion, or rather a wide fabric, of sounds: great and little sounds all woven together—voices, footfalls, wheels, far-off whistles and foghorns, flies buzzing in the sun. Night was another thing. Still, there were voices and footfalls, but rarer, emerg-ing from the large, pure body of silence as definite, surprising, and yet familiar entities.

Tonight there was an easterly wind, coming off the water and carrying the sound of waves. So far as other fugitive sounds were concerned it was the same as silence. The wind made little difference to the ears. It nullified, from one direction at least, the other two visual processes of the blind, the sense of touch and the sense of smell. It blew away from the shop, toward the living house.

As has been said, Boaz found himself listening, scrutinizing with an extraordinary attention this immense background of sound. He heard footfalls. The story of that night was written, for him, in footfalls.

He heard them moving about the house, the lower floor, prowling here, there, halting for long spaces, advancing, retreating softly on the planks. About this aimless, interminable perambulation there was something to twist the nerves, something led and at the same time driven, like a succession of frail and indecisive charges.

Boaz lifted himself from his chair. All his impulses called him to make a stir, join battle, cast in the breach the reinforcement of his presence, authority, good will. He sank back again; his hands fell down. The curious impotence of the spectator held him.

He heard footfalls, too, on the upper floor, a little fainter, borne to the inner rather than the outer ear, along the solid causeway of partitions and floor, the legs of his chair, the bony framework of his body. Very faint indeed. Sinking back easily into the background of the wind. They, too, came and went, this room, that, to the passage, the stairhead, and away. About them, too, there was the same quality of being led and at the same time driven.

Time went by. In his darkness it seemed to Boaz that hours must have passed. He heard voices. Together with the footfalls, that abrupt, brief, and (in view of Wood's position) astounding interchange of sentences made up his history of the night. Wood must have opened the door at the head of the stair; by the sound of his voice he would be standing there, peering below perhaps; perhaps listening.

"What's wrong down there?" he called. "Why don't you go to bed?"

After a moment came Manuel's voice. "Ain't sleepy."

"Neither am I. Look here, do you like to play cards?"

"What kind? Euchre? I like euchre all right. Or pitch."[9]

"Well, what would you say to coming up and having a game of euchre then, Manuel? If you can't sleep?"

"That'd be all right."

The lower footfalls ascended to join the footfalls on the upper floor. There was the sound of a door closing.

Boaz sat still. In the gloom he might have been taken for a piece of furniture, of machinery, an extraordinary lay figure[10] perhaps, for the trying on of the boots he made. He seemed scarcely to breathe, only the sweat starting from his brow giving him an aspect of life.

He ought to have run, and leaped up that inner stair, and pounded with his fists on that door. He seemed unable to move. At

9. **Euchre** (yōō′kər) ... **pitch:** In a game of *euchre*, whoever declares trumps has to make three to five tricks to win a hand; in *pitch*, the first card led or "pitched" by a designated player determines which suit is trump.
10. **lay figure:** a jointed model of the human body used by artists.

rare intervals feet passed on the sidewalk outside, just at his elbow, so to say, and yet somehow, tonight, immeasurably far away. Beyond the orbit of the moon. He heard Rugg, the policeman, noting the silence of the shop, muttering, "Boaz is to bed tonight," as he passed.

The wind increased. It poured against the shop with its deep, continuous sound of a river. Submerged in its body, Boaz caught the note of the town bell striking midnight.

Once more, after a long time, he heard footfalls. He heard them coming around the corner of the shop from the house, footfalls half swallowed by the wind, passing discreetly, without haste, retreating, merging step by step with the huge, incessant background of the wind.

Boaz's muscles tightened all over him. He had the impulse to start up, to fling open the door, shout into the night, "What are you doing? Stop there! Say! What are you doing and where are you going?"

And as before, the curious impotence of the spectator held him motionless. He had not stirred in his chair. And those footfalls, upon which hinged, as it were, that momentous decade of his life, were gone.

There was nothing to listen for now. Yet he continued to listen. Once or twice, half arousing himself, he drew toward him his unfinished work. And then relapsed into immobility.

As has been said, the wind, making little difference to the ears, made all the difference in the world with the sense of feeling and the sense of smell. From the one important direction of the house. That is how it could come about that Boaz Negro could sit waiting and listening to nothing in the shop and remain ignorant of disaster until the alarm had gone away and come back again, pounding, shouting, clanging.

"*Fire!*" he heard them bawling in the street. "*Fire! Fire!*"

Only slowly did he understand that the fire was in his own house.

There is nothing stiller in the world than the skeleton of a house in the dawn after a fire. It is as if everything living, positive, violent, had been completely drained in the one flaming act of violence, leaving nothing but negation till the end of time. It is worse than a tomb. A monstrous stillness! Even the footfalls of the searchers cannot disturb it, for they are separate and superficial. In its presence they are almost frivolous.

Half an hour after dawn the searchers found the body, if what was left from that consuming ordeal might be called a body. The discovery came as a shock. It seemed incredible that the occupant of that house, no cripple or invalid but an able man in the prime of youth, should not have awakened and made good his escape. It was the upper floor which had caught; the stairs had stood to the last. It was beyond calculation. Even if he had been asleep!

And he had not been asleep. This second and infinitely more appalling discovery began to be known. Slowly. By a hint, a breath of rumor here, there an allusion, half taken back. The man whose incinerated body still lay curled in its bed of cinders had been dressed at the moment of disaster, even to the watch, the cuff buttons, the studs, the very scarf pin. Fully clothed to the last detail, precisely as those who had dealings at the bank might have seen Campbell Wood any weekday morning for the past eight months. A man does not sleep with his clothes on. The skull of the man had been broken, as if with a blunt instrument of iron. On the charred lacework of the floor lay the leg of an old andiron[11] with which Boaz Negro and his Angelina had set up housekeeping in that new house.

It needed only Mr. Asa Whitelaw, coming up the street from that gaping "Noah's Ark" at the bank, to round out the scandalous circle of circumstance.

"Where is Manuel?"

Boaz Negro still sat in his shop, impassive, monumental, his thick, hairy arms resting on the arms of his chair. The tools and materials of his work remained scattered about him, as his irresolute gathering of the night before had left them. Into his eyes no change could come. He had lost his house, the visible monument of all those years of "skinning his fingers." It would seem that he had lost his son. And he had lost something incalculably precious—that hitherto unquenchable exuberance of the man.

"Where is Manuel?"

When he spoke his voice was unaccented and stale, like the voice of a man already dead.

"Yes, where is Manuel?"

He had answered them with their own question.

"When did you last see him?"

Neither he nor they seemed to take note of that profound irony.

"At supper."

---

11. andiron (and'ī̇ə′rn): one of a pair of metal supports used to hold wood in an open fireplace.

"Tell us, Boaz; you knew about this money?"

The cobbler nodded his head.

"And did Manuel?"

He might have taken sanctuary in a legal doubt. How did he know what Manuel knew? Precisely! As before, he nodded his head.

"After supper, Boaz, you were in the shop? But you heard something?"

He went on to tell them what he had heard: the footfalls, below and above, the extraordinary conversation which had broken for a moment the silence of the inner hall. The account was bare, the phrases monosyllabic. He reported only what had been registered on the sensitive tympanums[12] of his ears, to the last whisper of footfalls stealing past the dark wall of the shop. Of all the formless tangle of thoughts, suspicions, interpretations, and the special and personal knowledge given to the blind which moved in his brain, he said nothing.

He shut his lips there. He felt himself on the defensive. Just as he distrusted the higher ramifications of finance (his house had gone down uninsured), so before the rites and processes of that inscrutable creature, the Law, he felt himself menaced by the invisible and the unknown, helpless, oppressed; in an abject sense, skeptical.

"Keep clear of the Law!" they had told him in his youth. The monster his imagination had summoned up then still stood beside him in his age.

Having exhausted his monosyllabic and superficial evidence, they could move him no further. He became deaf and dumb. He sat before them, an image cast in some immensely heavy stuff, inanimate. His lack of visible emotion impressed them. Remembering his exuberance, it was only the stranger to see him unmoving and unmoved. Only once did they catch sight of something beyond. As they were preparing to leave he opened his mouth. What he said was like a swan song[13] to the years of his exuberant happiness. Even now there was no color of expression in his words, which sounded mechanical.

"Now I have lost everything. My house. My last son. Even my honor. You would not think I would like to live. But I go to live. I go to work. That *cachorra*, one day he shall come back again, in the dark night, to have a look. I shall go to show you all. That *cachorra!*"

12. **tympanums** (tĭm′pǝ•nǝms): eardrums; a tympanum is the thin membrane, shaped like the head of a drum, that separates the middle ear from the external ear.
13. **swan song:** a farewell. An allusion to the fable that a swan sings a final song before dying.

(And from that time on, it was noted, he never referred to the fugitive by any other name than *cachorra,* which is a kind of dog. "That *cachorra!*" As if he had forfeited the relationship not only of the family, but of the very genus, the very race! "That *cachorra!*")

He pronounced this resolution without passion. When they assured him that the culprit would come back again indeed, much sooner than he expected, "with a rope around his neck," he shook his head slowly.

"No, you shall not catch that *cachorra* now. But one day—"

There was something about its very colorlessness which made it sound oracular. It was at least prophetic. They searched, laid their traps, proceeded with all their placards, descriptions, rewards, clues, trails. But on Manuel Negro they never laid their hands.

Months passed and became years. Boaz Negro did not rebuild his house. He might have done so, out of his earnings, for upon himself he spent scarcely anything, reverting to his old habit of an almost miserly economy. Yet perhaps it would have been harder after all. For his earnings were less and less. In that town a cobbler who sits in any empty shop is apt to want for trade. Folks take their boots to mend where they take their bodies to rest and their minds to be edified.[14]

No longer did the walls of Boaz's shop resound to the boastful recollections of young men. Boaz had changed. He had become not only different, but opposite. A metaphor will do best. The spirit of Boaz Negro had been meadowed hillside giving upon the open sea, the sun, the warm, wild winds from beyond the blue horizon. And covered with flowers, always hungry and thirsty for the sun and the fabulous wind and bright showers of rain. It had become an entrenched camp, lying silent, sullen, verdureless, under a gray sky. He stood solitary against the world. His approaches were closed. He was blind, and he was also deaf and dumb.

Against that, what can young fellows do who wish for nothing but to rest themselves and talk about their friends and enemies? They had come and they had tried. They had raised their voices even higher than before. Their boasts had grown louder, more presumptuous, more preposterous, until, before the cold separation of that unmoving and as if contemptuous presence in the cobbler's chair, they burst of their own air, like toy balloons. And they went and left Boaz alone.

---

14. edified: instructed and improved, especially in a moral or religious sense.

There was another thing which served, if not to keep them away, at least not to entice them back. That was the aspect of the place. It was not cheerful. It invited no one. In its way that fire-bitten ruin grew to be almost as great a scandal as the act itself had been. It was plainly an eyesore. A valuable property, on the town's main thoroughfare—and an eyesore! The neighboring owners protested.

Their protestations might as well have gone against a stone wall. That man was deaf and dumb. He had become, in a way, a kind of vegetable, for the quality of a vegetable is that, while it is endowed with life, it remains fixed in one spot. For years Boaz was scarcely seen to move foot out of that shop that was left him, a small, square, blistered promontory[15] on the shores of ruin.

He must indeed have carried out some rudimentary sort of domestic program under the debris at the rear (he certainly did not sleep or eat in the shop). One or two lower rooms were left fairly intact. The outward aspect of the place was formless; it grew to be no more than a mound in time; the charred timbers, one or two still standing, lean and naked against the sky, lost their blackness and faded to a silvery gray. It would have seemed strange, had they not grown accustomed to the thought, to imagine that blind man, like a mole, or some slow slug, turning himself mysteriously in the bowels of that gray mound—that time-silvered eyesore.

When they saw him, however, he was in the shop. They opened the door to take in their work (when other cobblers turned them off), and they saw him seated in his chair in the half darkness, his whole person, legs, torso, neck, head, as motionless as the vegetable of which we have spoken—only his hands and his bare arms endowed with visible life. The gloom had bleached the skin to the color of damp ivory, and against the background of his immobility they moved with a certain amazing monstrousness, interminably. No, they were never still. One wondered what they could be at. Surely he could not have had enough work now to keep those insatiable hands so monstrously in motion. Even far into the night. Tap-tap-tap! Blows continuous and powerful. On what? On nothing? On the bare iron last? And for what purpose? To what conceivable end?

Well, one could imagine those arms, growing paler, also grow-

15. **promontory** (prŏm′ən•tôr′ē): a high point of land projecting into a body of water; here, used figuratively, it means that the shop, being the only piece of Boaz's property left standing, is distinct and noticeable.

ing thicker and more formidable with that unceasing labor; the muscles feeding themselves omnivorously[16] on their own waste, the cords toughening, the bone tissues revitalizing themselves without end. One could imagine the whole aspiration of that mute and motionless man pouring itself out into those pallid arms, and the arms taking it up with a kind of blind greed. Storing it up. Against a day!

"That *cachorra!* One day—"

What were the thoughts of this man? What moved within that motionless cranium covered with long hair? Who can say? Behind everything, of course, stood that bitterness against the world—the blind world—blinder than he would ever be. And against "that *cachorra.*" But this was no longer a thought: it was the man.

Just as all muscular aspiration flowed into his arms, so all the energies of his senses turned to his ears. The man had become, you might say, two arms and two ears. Can you imagine a man listening, intently, through the waking hours of nine years?

Listening to footfalls. Marking with a special emphasis of concentration the beginning, rise, full passage, falling away, and dying of all the footfalls. By day, by night, winter and summer and winter again. Unraveling the skein[17] of footfalls passing up and down the street!

For three years he wondered when they would come. For the next three years he wondered if they would ever come. It was during the last three that a doubt began to trouble him. It gnawed at his huge moral strength. Like a hidden seepage of water, it undermined (in anticipation) his terrible resolution. It was a sign, perhaps, of age, a slipping away of the reckless infallibility of youth.

Supposing, after all, that his ears should fail him. Supposing they were capable of being tricked, without his being able to know it. Supposing that the *cachorra* should come and go, and he, Boaz, living in some vast delusion, some unrealized distortion of memory, should let him pass unknown. Supposing precisely this thing had already happened!

Or the other way around. What if he should hear the footfalls coming, even into the very shop itself? What if he should be as sure of

16. **omnivorously** (ŏm•nĭv′ər•əs•lē): greedily and indiscriminately.
17. **skein** (skān): a quantity of yarn or thread wound in a loose coil; here, it refers to the confused, complicated, and tangled mass of footfalls.

them as of his own soul? What, then, if he should strike? And what then if it were not that *cachorra* after all? How many tens and hundreds of millions of people were there in the world? Was it possible for them all to have footfalls distinct and different?

Then they would take him and hang him. And that *cachorra* might then come and go at his own will, undisturbed.

As he sat there, sometimes the sweat rolled down his nose, cold as rain.

Supposing!

Sometimes, quite suddenly, in broad day, in the booming silence of the night, he would start. Not outwardly. But beneath the pale integument[18] of his skin all his muscles tightened and his nerves sang. His breathing stopped. It seemed almost as if his heart stopped.

Was that it? Were those the feet, there, emerging faintly from the distance? Yes, there was something about them. Yes! Memory was in travail.[19] Yes, yes, yes! No! How could he be sure? Ice ran down into his empty eyes. The footfalls were already passing. They were gone, swallowed up already by time and space. Had that been that *cachorra*?

Nothing in his life had been so hard to meet as this insidious[20] drain of distrust in his own powers, this sense of a traitor within the walls. His iron-gray hair turned white. It was always this now, from the beginning of the day to the end of the night: how was he to know? How was he to be inevitably, unshakably, sure?

Curiously, after all this purgatory of doubts, he did know them. For a moment at least, when he had heard them, he was unshakably sure. It was on an evening of the winter holidays, the Portuguese festival of *Menin'*[21] *Jesus*. Christ was born again in a hundred mangers on a hundred tiny altars; there were cake and wine; songs went shouting by to the accompaniment of mandolins and tramping feet. The wind blew cold under a clear sky. In all the houses there were lights; even in Boaz Negro's shop a lamp was lit just now, for a man had been in for a pair of boots which Boaz had patched. The man had gone out again. Boaz was thinking of blowing out the light. It meant nothing to him.

He leaned forward, judging the position of the lamp-chimney

18. **integument** (ĭn·tĕg′yə·mənt): covering.
19. **travail** (trăv′āl): strenuous physical or mental labor, especially that involving pain or suffering.
20. **insidious** (ĭn·sĭd′ē·əs): progressing gradually, but harmfully; treacherous.
21. ***Menin'*:** a shortened form of the word *menino,* meaning "child or baby."

by the heat on his face, and puffed out his cheeks to blow. Then his cheeks collapsed suddenly, and he sat back again.

It was not odd that he had failed to hear the footfalls until they were actually within the door. A crowd of merrymakers was passing just then. Their songs and tramping almost shook the shop.

Boaz sat back. Beneath his passive exterior his nerves thrummed; his muscles had grown as hard as wood. Yes! Yes! But no. He had heard nothing; no more than a single step, a single foot-pressure on the planks within the door. Dear God! He could not tell!

Going through the pain of an enormous effort, he opened his lips.

"What can I do for you?"

"Well, I—I don't know. To tell the truth—"

The voice was unfamiliar, but it might be assumed. Boaz held himself. His face remained blank, interrogating, slightly helpless.

"I am a little deaf," he said. "Come nearer."

The footfalls came halfway across the intervening floor, and there appeared to hesitate. The voice, too, had a note of uncertainty.

"I was just looking around. I have a pair of—well, you mend shoes?"

Boaz nodded his head. It was not in response to the words, for they meant nothing. What he had heard was the footfalls on the floor.

Now he was sure. As has been said, for a moment at least after he had heard them he was unshakably sure. The congestion of his muscles had passed. He was at peace.

The voice became audible once more. Before the massive preoccupation of the blind man it became still less certain of itself.

"Well, I haven't got the shoes with me. I was—just looking around."

It was amazing to Boaz, this miraculous sensation of peace.

"Wait!" Then, bending his head as if listening to the winter wind: "It's cold tonight. You've left the door open. But wait!" Leaning down, his hand fell on a rope's end hanging by the chair. The gesture was one continuous, undeviating movement of the hand. No hesitation. No groping. How many hundreds, how many thousands of times, had his hand schooled itself in that gesture!

A single strong pull. With a little *bang* the front door had swung to and latched itself. Not only the front door. The other door, leading to the rear, had closed too, and latched itself with a little *bang*. And leaning forward from his chair, Boaz blew out the light.

There was not a sound in the shop. Outside, feet continued to go by, ringing on the frozen road; voices were lifted; the wind hustled about the corners of the wooden shell with a continuous, shrill note of whistling. All of this outside, as on another planet. Within the blackness of the shop the complete silence persisted.

Boaz listened. Sitting on the edge of his chair, half-crouching, his head, with its long, unkempt, white hair, bent slightly to one side, he concentrated upon this chambered silence the full powers of his senses. He hardly breathed. The other person in that room could not be breathing at all, it seemed.

No, there was not a breath, not the stirring of a sole on wood, not the infinitesimal rustle of any fabric. It was as if in this utter stoppage of sound, even the blood had ceased to flow in the veins and arteries of that man, who was like a rat caught in a trap.

It was appalling even to Boaz; even to the cat. Listening became more than a labor. He began to have to fight against a growing impulse to shout out loud, to leap, sprawl forward without aim in that unstirred darkness—do something. Sweat rolled down from behind his ears, into his shirt collar. He gripped the chair arms. To keep quiet he sank his teeth into his lower lip. He would not! He would not!

And of a sudden he heard before him, in the center of the room, an outburst of breath, an outrush from lungs in the extremity of pain, thick, laborious, fearful. A coughing up of dammed air.

Pushing himself from the arms of the chair, Boaz leaped.

His fingers, passing swiftly through the air, closed on something. It was a sheaf of hair, bristly and thick. It was a man's beard.

On the road outside, up and down the street for a hundred yards, merrymaking people turned to look at one another. With an abrupt cessation of laughter, of speech. Inquiringly. Even with an unconscious dilation of the pupils of their eyes.

"What was that?"

There had been a scream. There could be no doubt of that. A single, long-drawn note. Immensely high-pitched. Not as if it were human.

"God's sake! What was that? Where'd it come from?"

Those nearest said it came from the cobbler shop of Boaz Negro.

They went and tried the door. It was closed, even locked, as if for the night. There was no light behind the window shade. But Boaz would not have a light. They beat on the door. No answer.

But from where, then, had that prolonged, as if animal, note come?

They ran about, penetrating into the side lanes, interrogating, prying. Coming back at last, inevitably, to the neighborhood of Boaz Negro's shop.

The body lay on the floor at Boaz's feet, where it had tumbled down slowly after a moment from the spasmodic embrace of his arms—those ivory-colored arms which had beaten so long upon the bare iron surface of a last. Blows continuous and powerful. It seemed incredible. They were so weak now. They could not have lifted the hammer now.

But that beard! That bristly, thick, square beard of a stranger!

His hands remembered it. Standing with his shoulders fallen forward and his weak arms hanging down, Boaz began to shiver. The whole thing was incredible. What was on the floor there, upheld in the vast gulf of darkness, he could not see. Neither could he hear it, smell it. Nor (if he did not move his foot) could he feel it. What he did not hear, smell, or touch did not exist. It was not there.

But that beard! All the accumulated doubtings of those years fell down upon him. After all, the thing he had been so fearful of in his weak imaginings had happened. He had killed a stranger. He, Boaz Negro, had murdered an innocent man!

And all on account of that beard. His deep panic made him lightheaded. He began to confuse cause and effect. If it were not for that beard, it would have been that *cachorra*.

On this basis he began to reason with crazy directness. And to act. He went and pried open the door into the entry. From the shelf he took down his razor. A big heavy-heeled strop.[22] His hands began to hurry. And the mug, half full of soap. And water. It would have to be cold water. But after all, he thought (lightheadedly), at this time of night—

Outside, they were at the shop again. The crowd's habit is to forget a thing quickly, once it is out of sight and hearing. But there had been something about that solitary cry which continued to bother them, even in memory. Where had it been? Where had it come from? And those who had stood nearest the cobbler shop were heard again. They were certain now, dead certain. They could swear!

In the end they broke down the door.

22. **strop:** a strip of leather used for sharpening a razor.

If Boaz heard them he gave no sign. An absorption as complete as it was monstrous wrapped him. Kneeling in the glare of the lantern they had brought, as impervious[23] as his own shadow sprawling behind him, he continued to shave the dead man on the floor.

No one touched him. Their minds and imaginations were arrested by the gigantic proportions of the act. The unfathomable presumption of the act. As if throwing murder in their faces to the tune of a jig in a barbershop. It is a fact that none of them so much as thought of touching him. No less than all of them, together with all other men, shorn of their imaginations—that is to say, the expressionless and imperturbable creature of the Law—would be sufficient to touch that ghastly man.

On the other hand, they could not leave him alone. They could not go away. They watched. They saw the damp, lather-soaked beard of that victimized stranger falling away, stroke by stroke of the flashing, heavy razor. The dead denuded by the blind!

It was seen that Boaz was about to speak. It was something important he was about to utter; something, one would say, fatal. The words would not come all at once. They swelled his cheeks out. His razor was arrested. Lifting his face, he encircled the watchers with a gaze at once of imploration and of command. As if he could see them. As if he could read his answer in the expressions of their faces.

"Tell me one thing now. Is it that *cachorra?*"

For the first time those men in the room made sounds. They shuffled their feet. It was as if an uncontrollable impulse to ejaculation, laughter, derision, forbidden by the presence of death, had gone down into their boot soles.

"Manuel?" one of them said. "You mean *Manuel?*"

Boaz laid the razor down on the floor beside its work. He got up from his knees slowly, as if his joints hurt. He sat down in his chair, rested his hands on the arms, and once more encircled the company with his sightless gaze.

"Not Manuel. Manuel was a good boy. But tell me now, is it that *cachorra?*"

Here was something out of their calculations; something for them mentally to chew on. Mystification is a good thing sometimes. It gives the brain a fillip,[24] stirs memory, puts the gears of imagination

---

23. impervious (ĭm·pûr′vē·əs): unaffected; impenetrable.
24. fillip: stimulus or incentive. A sharp tap or fillip is made when a finger, pressed down by the thumb, is suddenly released or snapped outward.

in mesh. One man, an old, tobacco-chewing fellow, began to stare harder at the face on the floor. Something moved in his intellect.

"No, but look here now, by God—"

He had even stopped chewing. But he was forestalled by another.

"Say now, if it don't look like that fellow Wood, himself. The bank fellow—that was burned—remember? Himself."

"That *cachorra* was not burned. Not that Wood. You darned fool!"

Boaz spoke from his chair. They hardly knew his voice, emerging from its long silence; it was so didactic and arid.

"That *cachorra* was not burned. It was my boy that was burned. It was that *cachorra* called my boy upstairs. That *cachorra* killed my boy. That *cachorra* put his clothes on my boy, and he set my house on fire. I knew it all the time. Because when I heard those feet come out of my house and go away, I knew they were the feet of that *cachorra* from the bank. I did not know where he was going to. Something said to me—you better ask him where he is going to. But then I said, you are foolish. He had the money from the bank. I did not know. And then my house was on fire. No, it was not my boy that went away; it was that *cachorra* all the time. You darned fools! Did you think I was waiting for my own boy?

"Now I show you all," he said at the end. "And now I can get hanged."

No one ever touched Boaz Negro for that murder. For murder it was in the eye and letter of the Law. The Law in a small town is sometimes a curious creature; it is sometimes blind only in one eye.

Their minds and imaginations in that town were arrested by the romantic proportions of the act. Simply, no one took it up. I believe the man Wood was understood to have died of heart failure.

When they asked Boaz why he had not told what he knew as to the identity of that fugitive in the night, he seemed to find it hard to say exactly. How could a man of no education define for them his own but half-denied misgivings about the Law, his sense of oppression, constraint, and awe, of being on the defensive, even, in an abject way, his skepticism? About his wanting, come what might, to "keep clear of the Law"?

He did say this: "You would have laughed at me."

And this: "If I told folks it was Wood went away, then I say he would not dare come back again."

That was the last. Very shortly he began to refuse to talk about the thing at all. The act was completed. Like the creature of fable,[25] it had consumed itself. Out of that old man's consciousness it had departed. Amazingly. Like a dream dreamed out.

Slowly at first, in a makeshift, piece-at-a-time, poor man's way, Boaz commenced to rebuild his house. That "eyesore" vanished.

And slowly at first, like the miracle of a green shoot pressing out from the dead earth, that priceless and unquenchable exuberance of the man was seen returning. Unquenchable, after all.

---

25. creature of fable: an allusion to the phoenix, a legendary bird of Egyptian mythology. After living for five to six hundred years, the phoenix destroys itself in fire and rises again, renewed and youthful, to live through another long cycle.

Meaning

1. What words and phrases does the narrator use in the first paragraph to describe his story? Do you agree or disagree with his assessment? Explain.
2. How would you describe Boaz Negro's character before the murder? How does he change after the murder? What evidence do you find to indicate that Negro has returned to his old ways?
3. Do you think Negro is justified in taking revenge? Explain.
4. What is the theme of the story?

Method

1. When a writer wants to introduce an important fact in a story, he usually mentions it early and usually quite casually. This is called a *plant*. Where do we first learn that Boaz Negro can recognize people by their footfalls?
2. How does Steele maintain suspense? Why does he have Negro repeatedly use the word *cachorra*?
3. The climax takes place during a Christmas festival. The writer uses this setting to account for the crowds in the street and for their presence in the shop. But he also intends it to be symbolic. How is the season symbolic of the subsequent change in Negro?
4. How are we prepared for the ending? Give some examples of foreshadowing in this story.

Language: Suffixes

"And those footfalls, upon which hinged, as it were, that *momentous* decade in his life, were gone." Anything that is *momentous* is full of importance. The suffix *-ous* means "full of" or "having." The word *moment* by itself may mean a short time or a particular period, such as a moment in history.

A *suffix* comes after the main part of a word and can change its meaning or function. Among the suffixes you should learn to recognize on sight as separate parts of words are *-less*, meaning "without"; *-ity*, meaning "state, condition, or quality of"; and *-ble*, meaning "capable of."

A knowledge of these four suffixes should help you in breaking down each of the following words from "Footfalls" and working out its meaning. Consult your dictionary to see if your analysis of each word is correct.

1. vigorous
2. aimless
3. laxity
4. unquenchable
5. adventurous
6. accessible
7. ruthless
8. infallibility
9. inscrutable

Write a sentence for each of these words.

Discussion and Composition

1. Do you think Negro is correct when he says that Manuel is a good boy? Explain.

2. Is the ending of "Footfalls" a "trick ending"? Why or why not? Write a composition using the following topic sentence and giving reasons to support your point of view: The ending of "Footfalls" is (is not) completely justified by the clues Wilbur Daniel Steele gives in the story. As a prewriting activity, you might make a list of the hints that Steele provides. Examine the list and determine whether these clues could reasonably lead the reader to expect the ending that Steele provides.

EDGAR ALLAN POE
(1809–1849)

Poet, short-story writer, editor, and critic, Edgar Allan Poe was a versatile genius, and the first great writer who grew up in the South. Born in Boston, Poe was the son of traveling actors. When he was two years old, his mother died, and Poe was taken in by a wealthy Virginia family named Allan. In 1826, he entered the University of Virginia, but left a year later when Mr. Allan refused to pay his gambling debts. Poe quarreled constantly with his foster father, who wanted Poe to follow a law career. In 1830, Poe received an appointment to West Point, but he was expelled within a year; Mr. Allan then discontinued his financial support of the young man.

Poe earned a meager living by editing and writing poetry and short stories. In 1835, he became editor of *The Southern Literary Messenger* and in the same year married his young cousin, Virginia Clemm. His wife became seriously ill and died at the age of twenty-four. Two years later, depressed and in debt, Poe died at an age when many writers are just beginning their careers.

"The Cask of Amontillado" (1846) is a horror story intended to produce a single emotional impact on the reader. It adheres to Poe's definition of plot as "that in which no part can be displaced without ruin to the whole."

*THE CASK OF AMONTILLADO**

The thousand injuries of Fortunato I had borne as I best could, but when he ventured upon insult, I vowed revenge. You, who so well know the nature of my soul, will not suppose, however, that I gave utterance to a threat. *At length* I would be avenged; this was a point definitely settled—but the very definitiveness with which it was resolved precluded the idea of risk. I must not only punish, but punish with impunity. A wrong is unredressed when retribution overtakes its

---

* **Amontillado:** sherry wine made near Montilla, a Spanish town.

redresser. It is equally unredressed when the avenger fails to make himself felt as such to him who has done the wrong.

It must be understood that neither by word nor deed had I given Fortunato cause to doubt my good will. I continued, as was my wont,[1] to smile in his face, and he did not perceive that my smile *now* was at the thought of his immolation.[2]

He had a weak point—this Fortunato—although in other regards he was a man to be respected and even feared. He prided himself on his connoisseurship[3] in wine. Few Italians have the true virtuoso spirit. For the most part their enthusiasm is adopted to suit the time and opportunity—to practice imposture upon the British and Austrian *millionaires.* In painting and gemmary[4] Fortunato, like his countrymen, was a quack, but in the matter of old wines he was sincere. In this respect I did not differ from him materially;—I was skillful in the Italian vintages myself and bought largely whenever I could.

It was about dusk, one evening during the supreme madness of the carnival season, that I encountered my friend. He accosted me with excessive warmth, for he had been drinking much. The man wore motley.[5] He had on a tight-fitting parti-striped dress, and his head was surmounted by the conical cap and bells. I was so pleased to see him that I thought I should never have done wringing his hand.

I said to him—"My dear Fortunato, you are luckily met. How remarkably well you are looking today! But I have received a pipe[6] of what passes for Amontillado, and I have my doubts."

"How?" said he, "Amontillado? A pipe? Impossible! And in the middle of the carnival!"

"I have my doubts," I replied; "and I was silly enough to pay the full Amontillado price without consulting you in the matter. You were not to be found, and I was fearful of losing a bargain."

"Amontillado!"

"I have my doubts."

"Amontillado!"

"And I must satisfy them."

1. **wont** (wônt): habit.
2. **immolation** (ĭm′ə•lā′•shən): being killed or sacrificed.
3. **connoisseurship** (kŏn′ə•sûr′ship): the ability to make competent judgments, based on thorough knowledge, in matters of art or taste.
4. **gemmary** (jĕm′•rē): knowledge of gems.
5. **motley** (mŏt′lē): a multicolored garment, especially that of a jester.
6. **pipe**: a large cask.

"Amontillado!"

"As you are engaged, I am on my way to Luchesi. If any one has a critical turn, it is he. He will tell me—"

"Luchesi cannot tell Amontillado from Sherry."

"And yet some fools will have it that his taste is a match for your own."

"Come, let us go."

"Whither?"

"To your vaults."

"My friend, no; I will not impose upon your good nature. I perceive you have an engagement. Luchesi—"

"I have no engagement;—come."

"My friend, no. It is not the engagement, but the severe cold with which I perceive you are afflicted. The vaults are insufferably damp. They are encrusted with niter."[7]

"Let us go, nevertheless. The cold is merely nothing. Amontillado! You have been imposed upon. And as for Luchesi, he cannot distinguish Sherry from Amontillado."

Thus speaking, Fortunato possessed himself of my arm; and putting on a mask of black silk, and drawing a *roquelaure*[8] closely about my person, I suffered him to hurry me to my palazzo.[9]

There were no attendants at home; they had absconded to make merry in honor of the time. I had told them that I should not return until the morning, and had given them explicit orders not to stir from the house. These orders were sufficient, I well knew, to insure their immediate disappearance, one and all, as soon as my back was turned.

I took from their sconces[10] two flambeaux,[11] and giving one to Fortunato, bowed him through several suites of rooms to the archway that led into the vaults. I passed down a long and winding staircase, requesting him to be cautious as he followed. We came at length to the foot of the descent, and stood together on the damp ground of the catacombs of the Montresors.

The gait of my friend was unsteady, and the bells upon his cap jingled as he strode.

---

7. niter (nī′tər): potassium nitrate; a salt deposit which forms on the damp walls of caves.

8. roquelaure (rok′ə•lôr): *French,* a knee-length cloak.

9. palazzo (pä•lot′zō): a palace or elegant town house in Italy.

10. sconces (skŏn′sez): wall brackets for holding candles or other lights.

11. flambeaux (flăm′bōz): burning torches.

"The pipe?" said he.

"It is farther on," said I; "but observe the white web-work which gleams from these cavern walls."

He turned toward me, and looked into my eyes with two filmy orbs that distilled the rheum[12] of intoxication.

"Niter?" he asked, at length.

"Niter," I replied. "How long have you had that cough?"

"Ugh! ugh! ugh!—ugh! ugh! ugh!—ugh! ugh! ugh!—ugh! ugh! ugh!—ugh! ugh! ugh!"

My poor friend found it impossible to reply for many minutes.

"It is nothing," he said at last.

"Come," I said with decision, "we will go back; your health is precious. You are rich, respected, admired, beloved; you are happy, as once I was. You are a man to be missed. For me it is no matter. We will go back; you will be ill, and I cannot be responsible. Besides, there is Luchesi—"

"Enough," he said; "the cough is a mere nothing: it will not kill me. I shall not die of a cough."

"True—true," I replied; "and, indeed, I had no intention of alarming you unnecessarily—but you should use all proper caution. A draft of this Médoc[13] will defend us from the damps."

Here I knocked off the neck of a bottle which I drew from a long row of its fellows that lay upon the mold.

"Drink," I said, presenting him the wine.

He raised it to his lips with a leer. He paused and nodded to me familiarly, while his bells jingled.

"I drink," he said, "to the buried that repose around us."

"And I to your long life."

He again took my arm, and we proceeded.

"These vaults," he said, "are extensive."

"The Montresors," I replied, "were a great and numerous family."

"I forget your arms."[14]

"A huge human foot d'or,[15] in a field azure; the foot crushes a serpent rampant[16] whose fangs are imbedded in the heel."

---

12. rheum (rōōm): a watery discharge from the eyes and nose.

13. Médoc (mā·dôk′): a red wine made in Médoc, France.

14. arms: hereditary insignia of a family.

15. d'or (dôr): *French*, of gold.

16. rampant (răm′pənt): in heraldry, this means rearing up in a threatening manner; the word also means unrestrained, wild, or unchecked.

"And the motto?"

Nemo me impune lacessit."[17]

"Good!" he said.

The wine sparkled in his eyes and the bells jingled. My own fancy grew warm with the Médoc. We had passed through walls of piled bones, with casks and puncheons[18] intermingling, into the inmost recesses of the catacombs. I paused again, and this time I made bold to seize Fortunato by an arm above the elbow.

"The niter!" I said; "see, it increases. It hangs like moss upon the vaults. We are below the river's bed. The drops of moisture trickle among the bones. Come, we will go back before it is too late. Your cough—"

"It is nothing," he said; "let us go on. But first, another draft of Médoc."

I broke and reached him a flagon[19] of De Graves.[20] He emptied it at a breath. His eyes flashed with a fierce light. He laughed and threw the bottle upward with a gesticulation I did not understand.

I looked at him in surprise. He repeated the movement—a grotesque one. "You do not comprehend?" he said.

"Not I," I replied.

"Then you are not of the brotherhood."

"How?"

"You are not of the masons."[21]

"Yes, yes," I said; "yes, yes."

"You? Impossible! A mason?"

"A mason," I replied.

"A sign," he said.

"It is this," I answered, producing a trowel from beneath the folds of my *roquelaure.*

"You jest," he exclaimed, recoiling a few paces. "But let us proceed to the Amontillado."

"Be it so," I said, replacing the tool beneath the cloak and again offering him my arm. He leaned upon it heavily. We continued our

17. **Nemo me impune lacessit** (nĕ′mō mē im•pū′nē la•kes′sit): *Latin,* No one injures me and escapes punishment.
18. **puncheons** (pŭn′chɔnz): large casks for liquor.
19. **flagon** (flăg′ɔn): a large, bulging, short-necked bottle.
20. **De Graves** (gravz; gräv): a white or red wine produced in a district near Bordeaux, France.
21. **masons:** that is, Freemasons, members of a widespread secret fraternal society; the word also means bricklayers.

route in search of the Amontillado. We passed through a range of low arches, descended, passed on, and descending again, arrived at a deep crypt, in which the foulness of the air caused our flambeaux rather to glow than flame.

At the most remote end of the crypt there appeared another, less spacious. Its walls had been lined with human remains, piled to the vault overhead, in the fashion of the great catacombs of Paris. Three sides of this interior crypt were still ornamented in this manner. From the fourth the bones had been thrown down, and lay promiscuously upon the earth, forming at one point a mound of some size. Within the wall thus exposed by the displacing of the bones, we perceived a still interior crypt or recess, in depth about four feet, in width three, in height six, or seven. It seemed to have been constructed for no especial use within itself, but formed merely the interval between two of the colossal supports of the roof of the catacombs, and was backed by one of the circumscribing walls of solid granite.

It was in vain that Fortunato, uplifting his dull torch, endeavored to pry into the depths of the recess. Its termination the feeble light did not enable us to see.

"Proceed," I said; "herein is the Amontillado. As for Luchesi—"

"He is an ignoramus," interrupted my friend, as he stepped unsteadily forward, while I followed immediately at his heels. In an instant he had reached the extremity of the niche, and finding his progress arrested by the rock, stood stupidly bewildered. A moment more and I had fettered[22] him to the granite. In its surface were two iron staples,[23] distant from each other about two feet, horizontally. From one of these depended[24] a short chain, from the other a padlock. Throwing the links about his waist, it was but the work of a few seconds to secure it. He was too much astounded to resist. Withdrawing the key, I stepped back from the recess.

"Pass your hand," I said, "over the wall; you cannot help feeling the niter. Indeed it is *very* damp. Once more let me *implore* you to return. No? Then I must positively leave you. But I must first render you all the little attentions in my power."

"The Amontillado!" ejaculated my friend, not yet recovered from his astonishment.

---

22. fettered (fĕt′ərd): chained.
23. staples: *here*, U-shaped metal loops with pointed ends to be driven into a surface, used to secure a bolt or lock.
24. depended: hung.

"True," I replied: "the Amontillado."

As I said these words I busied myself among the pile of bones of which I have before spoken. Throwing them aside, I soon uncovered a quantity of building-stone and mortar. With these materials and with the aid of my trowel, I began vigorously to wall up the entrance of the niche.

I had scarcely laid the first tier of the masonry when I discovered that the intoxication of Fortunato had in a great measure worn off. The earliest indication I had of this was a low moaning cry from the depth of the recess. It was *not* the cry of a drunken man. There was then a long and obstinate silence. I laid the second tier, and the third, and the fourth; and then I heard the furious vibrations of the chain. The noise lasted for several minutes, during which, that I might hearken to it with the more satisfaction, I ceased my labors and sat down upon the bones. When at last the clanking subsided, I resumed the trowel, and finished without interruption the fifth, the sixth, and the seventh tier. The wall was now nearly upon a level with my breast. I again paused, and holding the flambeaux over the mason-work, threw a few feeble rays upon the figure within.

A succession of loud and shrill screams, bursting suddenly from the throat of the chained form, seemed to thrust me violently back. For a brief moment I hesitated—I trembled. Unsheathing my rapier,[25] I began to grope with it about the recess; but the thought of an instant reassured me. I placed my hand upon the solid fabric of the cata-combs, and felt satisfied. I reapproached the wall. I replied to the yells of him who clamored. I re-echoed—I aided—I surpassed them in volume and in strength. I did this, and the clamorer grew still.

It was now midnight, and my task was drawing to a close. I had completed the eighth, the ninth, and the tenth tier. I had finished a portion of the last and the eleventh; there remained but a single stone to be fitted and plastered in. I struggled with its weight; I placed it partially in its destined position. But now there came from out the niche a low laugh that erected the hairs upon my head. It was succeeded by a sad voice, which I had difficulty in recognizing as that of the noble Fortunato. The voice said—

"Ha! ha! ha!—he! he! he!—a very good joke indeed—an excellent jest. We will have many a rich laugh about it at the palazzo—he! he! he!—over our wine—he! he! he!"

"The Amontillado!" I said.

---

25. rapier (rā'pē·ər): a straight, two-edged sword with a narrow, pointed blade.

"He! he! he!—he! he! he!—yes, the Amontillado. But is it not getting late? Will not they be awaiting us at the palazzo, the Lady Fortunato and the rest? Let us be gone."

"Yes," I said, "let us be gone."

"For the love of God, Montresor!"

"Yes," I said, "for the love of God!"

But to these words I hearkened in vain for a reply. I grew impatient. I called aloud—

"Fortunato!"

No answer. I called again:

"Fortunato!"

No answer still. I thrust a torch through the remaining aperture and let it fall within. There came forth in return only a jingling of the bells. My heart grew sick—on account of the dampness of the catacombs. I hastened to make an end of my labor. I forced the last stone into its position; I plastered it up. Against the new masonry I reerected the old rampart of bones. For the half of a century no mortal has disturbed them. *In pace requiescat!*[26]

---

26. In pace requiescat! (in pə′kə rek′wē•es′kat; in pə′chə rek′wē•es′chat): *Latin,* May he rest in peace.

Meaning

1. Poe quickly reveals Montresor to be a man with extraordinary powers of deception and manipulation. Cite some examples of Montresor's clever use of psychology.
2. Irony pervades "The Cask of Amontillado" and is carefully built into the structure of the story itself—into its setting, dialogue, and choice of characters. The story's setting is an example of *irony of situation* because a carnival is a place for merriment and shouts of laughter, not for intricate plans of murder and cries of terror.

   Montresor hails his friend with the deceptive words, "My dear Fortunato, you are luckily met." This is just one example of Poe's use of *irony of expression,* which means that a character's speech conveys a meaning opposite to what he is thinking. Cite other examples of Montresor's ironic manner of speech.
3. What in the story shows that the murder of Fortunato was premeditated?

4. Consider that Montresor is narrating the story a half-century after he has committed the crime. What has been the effect of the murder on him?

Method

1. When do you first suspect that Montresor is insane? What details cause you to be certain that he will kill Fortunato?
2. How does the setting contribute to the story? Could you change the setting without changing the atmosphere and mood of the story? If so, suggest a different setting.
3. Poe believed that every word in a story should contribute to a single emotional effect. Why do you think he carefully described the luring of Fortunato into a trap and the details of the murder itself, but only casually mentioned the motive for the crime in the first sentence?

Language: Prefixes

A *prefix* placed in front of the root of a word can change its meaning. For example, the word *impunity* is based on the Latin word *poena*, meaning "punishment or pain." The addition of the prefix *im-*, meaning "not," changes the meaning to "not punishable."

When Montresor says, "I must not only punish, but punish *with impunity*," his intent is to punish with safety so that there will be no danger in, or penalty for, his act. In a sense, the perfect crime may be said to be one committed with impunity.

The prefix *im-* can also mean "in, on, or without." Add this prefix to the words *posture* and *pose*. How does it change their meanings? (Both of these words are derived from the Latin verb *ponere*, meaning "to place or put.")

Another common prefix is *re-*, meaning "back or again." Check your dictionary to see how this prefix affects the meaning of the following words taken from the first paragraph of "The Cask of Amontillado": *resolved*, *redresser*, *retribution*, and *revenge*.

Discussion and Composition

1. "The Cask of Amontillado" has fascinated readers for over 150 years. How do you account for this fascination? Do you have a similar response? Explain.

2. Write a paragraph in which you explain how Fortunato's personality and actions contribute to his downfall. Before you begin your first draft, you will find it helpful to answer the following questions: How does Montresor trick Fortunato into coming with him? Why doesn't Fortunato turn back when he begins to feel sick? Why does he allow himself to be fettered?

LESLIE NORRIS

(born 1921)

Leslie Norris's poignant, artfully crafted stories are often set in his native Wales—an environment that, for Norris, included both natural beauty and urban poverty. This contrast is reflected in the themes as well as the settings of his works. His characters often struggle with knowledge of poverty, cruelty, death, and injustice; and yet they also experience beauty, friendship, laughter, and wonder.

Born near an industrial city, Merthyr Tydfil, Norris spent much of his boyhood exploring the surrounding Welsh countryside. His father died while Norris was still a young man, an event that profoundly affected Norris and that has influenced many of his works—particularly the bittersweet story "Shaving," which appears in his second short-story collection.

In 1940, Norris left for England to receive training in the Royal Air Force. He was discharged for a physical disability and returned to Merthyr Tydfil for a few years, but he eventually settled in England. While in England he attended college, worked as a teacher, and married. Norris now lives in Utah and teaches English at Brigham Young University.

Norris's works—particularly his stories—have begun to receive widespread recognition in the United States. Many of the stories that appear in his collections *Sliding* and *The Girl from Cardigan* have been published in magazines such as the *New Yorker* and the *Atlantic,* and they have earned him a devoted readership as well as critical acclaim.

A FLIGHT OF GEESE

My Uncle Wynford wasn't really my uncle; he was my great-uncle, my grandmother's brother. I used to visit him often on my way home from school. He lived in a small house at the edge of the village with his wife and two daughters. He also had two sons, but they lived in London and one of them was a famous footballer[1], an International. A color photograph of him, wearing his International cap and shirt, his arms folded across his chest, stood on the sideboard. My uncle had given up regular work when he was a young man. He had come home unexpectedly early from the engine room at the steelworks and announced his philosophy of leisure. "Anne," he had said to his wife, "I shall not be going to work again. There's too much talk about the dignity of labor. One life is all we have and I'm not spending mine in senseless toil." And he never did.

Not that he was an idle man. His garden was neat and orderly; his workbench, in the shed at the end of the garden, was swept free of dust and shavings; his tools, worn and polished with use, all had their proper place, and were sharp and clean. He could build a freestone wall, clear a chimney, repair plumbing. He was marvellously inventive with metal and stone, those old elements. But most of all he liked to work with wood. His hands held wood intimately, as if he knew all of its lost warmth and offered with his fingers and the flat of his palm a consolation for the tragic falling of trees. He made six crimson soup spoons for my grandmother, carved from the one piece of yew, polished hard and smooth. And he made her a little footstool for her use in chapel on Sundays. Many Sunday evenings I sat on that little stool, my head well below the top of the pew, noiselessly sucking a mint, reading a comic book while interminable sermons thundered above me.

Uncle Wynford made a stool for himself, too—a larger one. His was secular, not intended for Sunday use. It was painted in the most brilliant and glittering colors. The panel of the seat was decorated with an oval centerpiece, a landscape in which a lake of raucous blue lay beneath impossibly dramatic mountains. Water lilies

1. **footballer:** soccer player.

grew close at hand, and birds—swallows, probably—performed their frozen arabesques above the water. Far away the little, leaning sails of yachts and skiffs stood white against the hills. Complex patterns, like those in the *Book of Kells*[2], covered the legs and the undersurface. My uncle normally carried this stool about with him. A short man, he found it useful to stand on in crowds, but mostly he just sat on it whenever he stopped to talk.

For his finest art was conversation. He loved above all else to be among a small circle of old friends, who made together a pattern of articulate life, each in his turn leading the discussion or telling a story, the others an essential, encouraging chorus. At all aspects of this activity my uncle was a master. Nobody could listen more intently to tales told many times before, nobody could time an urgent question more subtly, nobody else could invent such marvellous, rich detail. His voice was like an instrument. He could use it to entice, to chill, to bombard. On early autumn mornings he sat among his friends down at the square, he on his wooden throne, they squatting or sprawled at length on the warm stone.

It was my habit then to go to school very early. I used to run almost all the way, using an exaggerated stride and a very upright stance, arms bent high at the elbow, trying to look like Paavo Nurmi[3] in a photograph I had seen in an old book about the Olympic Games. I was running across the square one morning, driving off the toes just like Nurmi, when my Uncle Wynford called me. "Don't run, boy," he said. "You've no need to run. You have plenty of time."

I tried to tell him that I liked getting to school early, that I liked being alone on the playground when it was silent and empty and the windows of the school were without life, but he just shook his head and held my hand, so that I had to stand by him. I wore a white shirt and gray trousers, and my shadow was very long and thin in the sun.

After a while Mr. Carrington spoke. He was Frankie Carrington's grandfather. He had been a butcher, and kept snuff in a little silver box. He had a walking stick with a handle made of antler and was in every way precise and gentlemanly.

---

2. ***Book of Kells:*** Artfully illustrated eighth-century manuscript found in the monastery in Kells, Ireland.
3. **Paavo Nurmi:** Finnish athlete (1897–1973).

"Going up the street last evening," he said, "I saw Arthur Baker standing at his door with his dog—you know, that blue-roan cocker[4]. It was sitting at Arthur's feet, near the front door. I hadn't seen the dog for some time." Mr. Carrington smiled as he looked back in his mind and saw himself talking to Arthur Baker. "'Well, Arthur,' I said, 'I haven't seen that dog of yours for some time, but there she is, safe and sound.'"

"Quick-tempered fellow," said Ginty Willis. "Arthur Baker has a very quick temper. All the Bakers have. Like living in a box of matches in their house."

"What did he say?" asked my Uncle Wynford. "What did Arthur say to you?"

"That's just it," said Mr. Carrington, leaning forward, widening his eyes, tapping himself on the knee to impress us. "He said nothing at first. He rushed down the path, and then, I swear, he almost shouted at me."

"Angry, was he?" said Ginty Willis. "Oh, a terrible quick temper."

"Not so much angry as puzzled," Mr. Carrington said. "And, yes, a bit frightened."

"Frightened?" my uncle said. "Why should he have been frightened?"

"Because the dog wasn't there!" Mr. Carrington said. "What do you think of that? Not there! 'What are you saying?' Arthur Baker shouted. 'My dog was killed a fortnight ago. Run over by a truck. What do you mean there she is, safe and sound?' And boys, when I looked again, there was no dog anywhere. Gave me quite a turn." Mr. Carrington pursed his lips and took out his snuffbox.

"Was it dark?" said Selby Davis belligerently. He wasn't really bullying; sometimes he stammered, so he pushed his word out quickly and roughly before he tripped over them.

Mr. Carrington considered. "Not dark," he said, "but certainly more than dusk. The house—the Bakers' house—was in deep shadow."

"Could have been a shadow you saw," said Selby Davis.

"It could have been," agreed Mr. Carrington, "but it looked very much like Arthur Baker's dog."

---

4. **blue-roan cocker:** an English cocker spaniel.

"Arthur was very fond of that dog," said my uncle, "and the dog adored him. There was a great bond between them. It could have been some form of manifestation you saw, Jimmy." I hadn't known Mr. Carrington's name was Jimmy, so I looked at him carefully, to see if it suited him.

Eddie D'Arcy progressed across the square, more a parade than a walk. His dark suit was superbly cut, his white shirt was dazzling, his silk tie was rich and sombre, his expensive black shoes utterly without flaw or spot. Despite the perfection of the morning, he carried an umbrella, rolled tight as a sword.

"Good morning, gentlemen," said Eddie, his vowels without fault, his dignity unassailable.

"Good morning, Eddie," the men said, smiling and nodding.

Eddie moved, full-sailed, out of sight, toward the office where he worked as a lawyer.

"Clever chap, Eddie," said my uncle. He turned to Mr. Carrington. "Jimmy," he said, "I'm prepared to believe that what you saw up at the Bakers was a manifestation. Stands to reason that an animal's identity is bound up with its sense of place, and, in the case of a domestic animal like a dog, with its owner." He warmed to his topic. "Our lives—the lives of human beings—are astonishingly manipulated by animals. It is useless to ignore the fact that our lives are deeply influenced by those of animals. Take Eddie D'Arcy as an example."

"What about Eddie D'Arcy?" asked Ginty Willis.

"Did I ever tell you about the D'Arcys' goose?" my uncle said.

Nobody answered.

"Old Mrs. D'Arcy bought a gosling to fatten for Christmas," said Uncle Wynford. "Eddie was a little boy then. The bird had the run of the field at the back of the house. It grew and prospered— oh, it grew into a magnificent goose." We could see that my uncle still admired the bird's every feather. "Yes," he said, "it was a splendid bird."

"I've done it myself, often," said Selby Davis, in his angry voice. "I prefer goose to any other bird. Properly cooked, a goose is lovely."

"This was an unusual goose," my uncle said. "Called at the back door every morning for its food, answered to its name. An intelligent creature. Eddie's sisters tied a blue silk ribbon around its neck and made a pet of it. It displayed more personality and understanding than you'd believe possible in a bird. Came Christmas, of course, and they couldn't kill it."

"Couldn't kill it?" Mr. Carrington said, his professional sense outraged. "It's not all that difficult. The best way...."

My uncle stopped him with a wave of his hand, as if conducting music. "They knew how to kill it," he said, "but they were unable to do so. On moral grounds, if you like. They were fond of it. They loved it. The goose lived another twenty years; Eddie grew up with it. They all cried when, at last, it died. Except Eddie, of course."

"Why not Eddie?" someone asked.

"You know how particular Eddie is?" Uncle Wynford said. "Such clothes, such a dandy? How not a mote of dust shall settle on his linen, how his handkerchief must be pressed to a mathematical nicety? Imagine how it must have been for him, living in that house with an elderly, dictatorial goose. You ever tried to house-train a goose, Ginty?"

"I have not," said Ginty. "I imagine it can't be done."

"It can't," said my uncle, laughing.

"Geese are pretty bright," I said. "They're good guards. Some geese saved Rome from the invaders."[5]

"The boy's right," said Mr. Carrington. "Well done, boy. I can see you're going to be a great scholar."

"I had a cousin in Cardiganshire[6] who was an expert with geese," my uncle said after a silence. "Kept all the varieties in his time. People used to come from all over the country to buy breeding stock from him. Oh, what a sight to see his flocks on the moors—great flocks of geese, marching like Prussians[7]! He used to clip their wings at the elbow so they couldn't fly, and then once they were old enough, out they'd go on the open moors, white geese, gray geese. They never strayed. At dusk they'd come highstepping into his yard and the whole mountain would be full of their voices. I often stayed with him when I was young.

---

5. **"Some geese saved Rome from the invaders.":** The Romans raised geese and held some sacred. Sacred geese were kept on the Capitoline Hill of Rome. According to legend, these geese detected invading Gauls and awakened a sleeping garrison, thus preventing a surprise attack.

6. **Cardiganshire:** a county in Western Wales.

7. **marching like Prussians:** a reference to the supposed militarism and expansionism of the Prussian people.

"He sent us a goose every year—two geese: one for Michaelmas and another for Christmas, always trussed and ready for cooking. He used to send them by bus—a bewildering journey, with many changes—but none of them ever failed to reach us. I used to wait here, on the square, for the bus to come in from Brecon toward late afternoon. The conductor would hand me a large hamper with our goose inside, and I'd stagger home with it. We used to cook it on a spit, rotating it in front of a blaze of a fire, a pan beneath to catch the melting fat. We took turns at basting as it spun slowly—first one way, then the other—so that it wouldn't burn. Every Michaelmas[8] and every Christmas for years. What feasts we had then! Nor was that the end of the goose's usefulness. After the cooking we put the solidified goose grease in jars and kept it as a cure for sore throats and chest colds and bronchitis. I can remember my mother rubbing it on my bare chest and throat when I was a small boy. I can remember its gross smell, the thick feel of the grease on my skin. I hated that, although the old people swore by it as a curative.

"And even the bed I slept on owed its comfort to my cousin's geese, for the bed was stuffed with feathers from his birds. My mother made a huge envelope of blue-and-white striped ticking and filled it with goose feathers, making the whole thing plump and soft as a cloud. We all sleep well when we're young, but nobody could have slept softer and deeper than I did in my goose-feather bed."

My uncle held out his hand in front of him. "You see this hand?" he asked. "The hand is a superb instrument. This hand of mine can do all manner of things: it can wield a hammer, pick up a pin, it can point a chisel to the exact splitting place of a stone, it can create, it can destroy. My cousin's hands were to do with geese. He had huge hands. Here, on the inside of his thumb and forefinger, he had long calluses, incredibly hard, from feathering geese. Every week he would kill and pluck some of his birds for the market, and many more near Christmas and other busy times. He had slaughtered thousands over the years. And when he plucked them he did it swiftly, expertly, and the soft flesh would not be bruised or torn when he finished. I've seen him kill and dress hundreds of birds. He was an artist."

8. **Michaelmas:** Festival of St. Michael and All Angels, September 29.

"How old was he, Wynford?" Mr. Carrington asked.

"Not a lot older than I," said my uncle. "Seven or eight years. But that's a lot when you're young. He was already at work on the farm when I was a young boy visiting there."

"What's he doing now?" asked Selby Davis.

"He's dead," my uncle said softly. "Yes, he's dead these many years." He shifted on his painted stool. He was far away, visiting an old sadness. "He's been dead for years," he repeated. "One Christmas he had many geese, and he set to work early, day after day, killing and preparing them. The weather was intolerably cold. The mountains had a fall of snow, two feet deep and deeper in drifts. It never stopped freezing. Night and day not a gust of wind—only the deep stillness of frost. My cousin kept the dead birds in a long barn, where they hung in rows, heads down. The bitter cold worried my cousin. It was bringing in the wild things off the hills, the rats and foxes. He found himself staying more and more near his filling barn.

"One night he awoke from sleep, bright awake at once, certain that something was wrong. It was just after three in the morning. He hurried into his thick clothes and wrapped a blanket over his shoulders. There wasn't a sound in the yard; even the living birds were silent. The brilliant snow threw back every gleam of light, redoubled it, so the night was unnaturally lit. The barn door was locked and safe. Nothing was out of place. He opened the door and went in. The dead geese hung in their rows before him, untouched, pallid. The night was pitilessly still. My cousin moved along the stiff files, alert, waiting for something to happen.

"Then, in the cold barn, as if from high above him, he heard the call of geese, far away, the crying of wild geese out of the empty sky. He could hear them clearly, although he knew they were not there. He did not move. In an instant the barn was full of their loud honking; their flailing wings beat under the sturdy roof. He closed his eyes in terror, he wrapped his arms about his bent head, and through his barn flew the heavy skeins of great, invisible birds. Their crying filled his ears; the still air was buffeted by their plunging flight, on and on, until the last bodiless goose was flown and the long, wild voices were gone. He stood in the cold of his barn and opened his eyes. What he saw was this: he saw the hanging corpses of his own geese, every one swaying, every one swinging gently. And that was the most frightening of all."

My uncle sighed. "Poor old boy," he said. "Poor old lad. After a while they took him to Swansea, to the mental hospital, and he died there."

"How do you know this?" asked Ginty Willis.

"He told me," said Uncle Wynford. "I went down to see him, and he told me. He was a young man, only thirty-two when he died. He had killed thousands of geese, thousands of them."

"What was his name, Uncle?" I asked. I stood in the warm day as cold as if I were in the heart of that long-dead winter and were standing under the roof among the swaying corpses of Christmas geese.

"Good God!" my uncle said. "Are you still here? Get to school, get to school! You'll be late." I turned and ran.

All day my friends were indolent in the heat of the quiet classroom, moving sleepily through their work, but all I could see were the high arrows of the streaming geese, all I could hear was their faint and melancholy crying, and the imagined winter was all about me.

Meaning

1. The narrator says that his uncle's "finest art" is conversation. In what way is conversation an "art" for Uncle Wynford?

2. How do animals figure into the men's anecdotes? How do they affect the lives of the people in the stories?

3. Do you find Uncle Wynford's story about his cousin's geese believable, or do you think he makes it up to entertain his friends? What evidence is there for either case?

4. How does Uncle Wynford's story affect the narrator? What does the narrator's reaction suggest about his uncle's skills as a storyteller?

Method

1. What does the narrator tell the reader directly about Uncle Wynford? What does he reveal about his uncle's character through indirect details?

2. "A Flight of Geese" is a *framework story,* or a story within a story. What is the relationship between the outer story narrated by the nephew and the inner story told by Uncle Wynford? How does the author move from one story to the other?

3. How does the setting of Uncle Wynford's tale help to create its eerie atmosphere? What is ironic about the fact that the events take place during the Christmas season?

4. Compare the "manifestation" of Arthur Baker's dog with the "appearance" of the ghostly geese. How are these events similar? How are they different?

Language: American Equivalents to British Expressions

In "A Flight of Geese," there are several British expressions that are not usually found in American English. For example, Uncle Wynford refers to D'Arcy as a "chap"; he says his cousins' hands "were to do with" geese.

Use a dictionary to find the American counterpart of each of the following British words.

1. batman		**5.** petrol	
2. bonnet		**6.** smashing	
3. gaff		**7.** tommy	
4. lift		**8.** tram	

Discussion and Composition

1. Long after he hears his uncle's tale, the narrator can see, feel, and hear his uncle's descriptions. Has a story or movie ever affected you like this? What aspects of it stayed in your mind, and why?

2. Uncle Wynford maintains that "our lives—the lives of human beings—are astonishingly manipulated by animals." Do you agree? Why or why not? Give examples.

3. Write a character sketch of someone you know who is good at telling stories. Give examples of anecdotes the person has told that show his or her storytelling technique. Include physical details to help your reader picture the person.

RAY BRADBURY
(born 1920)

Ray Bradbury's novels and short stories have earned him tremendous popularity as a writer. Like many writers of fantasy and science fiction, Bradbury offers the reader more than entertainment: he presents critical, thought-provoking views of modern technology and its role in determining the future of our society.

Born in Waukegan, Illinois, Bradbury was educated in Los Angeles. He began writing when he was seven and became a full-time writer at the age of twenty-three. He considers himself a disciple of Edgar Allan Poe, and the influence of Poe's works is evident in his works.

Like Poe's stories, many of Bradbury's tales have a subtly developed atmosphere of horror. "The Toynbee Convector," however, presents an optimistic view of the future and of the power of the human imagination.

THE TOYNBEE CONVECTOR

"Good! Great! Bravo for me!"

Roger Shumway flung himself into the seat, buckled himself in, revved the rotor and drifted his Dragonfly Super-6 helicopter up to blow away on the summer sky, heading south toward La Jolla[1].

"How lucky can you get?"

For he was on his way to an incredible meeting.

The time traveler, after 100 years of silence, had agreed to be interviewed. He was, on this day, 130 years old. And this afternoon, at four o'clock sharp, Pacific time, was the anniversary of his one and only journey in time.

Lord, yes! One hundred years ago, Craig Bennett Stiles had waved, stepped into his *Immense Clock,* as he called it, and vanished from the present. He was and remained the only man in history to

---

1. **La Jolla:** a resort area in San Diego, California.

travel in time. And Shumway was the one and only reporter, after all these years, to be invited in for afternoon tea. And? The possible announcement of a second and final trip through time. The traveler had hinted at such a trip.

"Old man," said Shumway, "Mr. Craig Bennett Stiles—here I come!"

The Dragonfly, obedient to fevers, seized a wind and rode it down the coast.

The old man was there waiting for him on the roof of the Time Lamasery at the rim of the hang glider's cliff in La Jolla. The air swarmed with crimson, blue, and lemon kites from which young men shouted, while young women called to them from the land's edge.

Stiles, for all his 130 years, was not old. His face, blinking up at the helicopter, was the bright face of one of those hang-gliding Apollo[2] fools who veered off as the helicopter sank down.

Shumway hovered his craft for a long moment, savoring the delay.

Below him was a face that had dreamed architectures, known incredible loves, blueprinted mysteries of seconds, hours, days, then dived in to swim upstream through centuries. A sunburst face, celebrating its own birthday.

For on a single night, one hundred years ago, Craig Bennett Stiles, freshly returned from time, had reported by Telstar[3] around the world to billions of viewers and told them their future.

"We made it!" he said. "We did it! The future is ours. We rebuilt the cities, freshened the small towns, cleaned the lakes and rivers, washed the air, saved the dolphins, increased the whales, stopped the wars, tossed solar stations across space to light the world, colonized the moon, moved on to Mars, then Alpha Centauri.[4] We cured cancer and stopped death. We did it—Oh Lord, much thanks—we did it. Oh, future's bright and beauteous spires, arise!"

---

2. **Apollo:** classical god of music, medicine, and prophecy. Usually portrayed as young, handsome, and brave.
3. **Telstar:** U.S. communications satellite launched in 1962.
4. **Alpha Centauri:** star system that is the brightest object in the constellation Centaurus.

He showed them pictures, he brought them samples, he gave them tapes and LP records, films and sound cassettes of his wondrous roundabout flight. The world went mad with joy. It ran to meet and make that future, fling up the cities of promise, save all and share with the beasts of land and sea.

The old man's welcoming shout came up the wind. Shumway shouted back and let the Dragonfly simmer down in its own summer weather.

Craig Bennett Stiles, 130 years old, strode forward briskly and, incredibly, helped the young reporter out of his craft, for Shumway was suddenly stunned and weak at this encounter.

"I can't believe I'm here," said Shumway.

"You are, and none too soon," laughed the time traveler. "Any day now, I may just fall apart and blow away. Lunch is waiting. Hike!"

A parade of one, Stiles marched off under the fluttering rotor shadows that made him seem a flickering newsreel of a future that had somehow passed.

Shumway, like a small dog after a great army, followed.

"What do you want to know?" asked the old man as they crossed the roof, double time.

"First," gasped Shumway, keeping up, "why have you broken silence after a hundred years? Second, why to *me?* Third, what's the big announcement you're going to make this afternoon at four o'clock, the very hour when your younger self is due to arrive from the past—when, for a brief moment, you will appear in two places, the paradox: the person you were, the man you are, fused in one glorious hour for us to celebrate?"

The old man laughed. "How you *do* go on!"

"Sorry." Shumway blushed. "I wrote that last night. Well. Those are the questions."

"You shall have your answers." The old man shook his elbow gently. "All in good—time."

"You must excuse my excitement," said Shumway.

"After all, you *are* a mystery. You were famous, world-acclaimed. You went, saw the future, came back, told us, then went into seclusion. Oh, sure; for a few weeks, you traveled the world in ticker-tape parades, showed yourself on TV, wrote one book, gifted us with one magnificent two-hour television film, then shut yourself away here. Yes, the time machine is on exhibit below, and crowds are allowed in each day at noon to see and touch. But you yourself have refused fame—"

"Not so." The old man led him along the roof. Below in the gardens, other helicopters were arriving now, bringing TV equipment from around the world to photograph the miracle in the sky, that moment when the time machine from the past would appear, shimmer, then wander off to visit other cities before it vanished into the past. "I have been busy, as an architect, helping build that very future I saw when, as a young man, I arrived in our golden tomorrow!"

They stood for a moment watching the preparations below. Vast tables were being set up for food and drink. Dignitaries would be arriving soon from every country of the world to thank—for a final time, perhaps—this fabled, this almost mythic traveler of the years.

"Come along," said the old man. "Would you like to come sit in the time machine? No one else ever has, you know. Would you like to be the first?"

No answer was necessary. The old man could see that the young man's eyes were bright and wet.

"There, there," said the old man. "Oh, dear me; there, there."

A glass elevator sank and took them below and let them out in a pure white basement at the center of which stood—

The incredible device.

"There." Stiles touched a button and the plastic shell that had for one hundred years encased the time machine slid aside. The old man nodded. "Go. Sit."

Shumway moved slowly toward the machine.

Stiles touched another button and the machine lit up like a cavern of spider webs. It breathed in years and whispered forth remembrance. Ghosts were in its crystal veins. A great god spider had woven its tapestries in a single night. It was haunted and it was alive. Unseen tides came and went in its machinery. Suns burned and moons hid their seasons in it. Here, an autumn blew away in tatters; there, winters arrived in snows that drifted in spring blossoms to fall on summer fields.

The young man sat in the center of it all, unable to speak, gripping the armrests of the padded chair.

"Don't be afraid," said the old man gently. "I won't send you on a journey."

"I wouldn't mind," said Shumway.

The old man studied his face. "No, I can see you wouldn't. You look like me one hundred years ago this day. Damn if you aren't my honorary son."

The young man shut his eyes at this, and the lids glistened as the ghosts in the machine sighed all about him and promised him tomorrows.

"Well, what do you think of my *Toynbee Convector*"? said the old man briskly, to break the spell.

He cut the power. The young man opened his eyes.

"The *Toynbee Convector*? What—"

"More mysteries, eh? The great Toynbee,[5] that fine historian who said any group, any race, any world that did not run to seize the future and shape it was doomed to dust away in the grave, in the past."

"Did he say *that?*"

"Or some such. He did. So, what better name for my machine, eh? Toynbee, wherever you are, here's your future-seizing device!"

He grabbed the young man's elbow and steered him out of the machine.

"Enough of that. It's late. Almost time for the great arrival, eh? And the earth-shaking final announcement of that old time traveler Stiles! Jump!"

Back on the roof, they looked down on the gardens, which were now swarming with the famous and the near famous from across the world. The nearby roads were jammed; the skies were full of helicopters and hovering biplanes. The hang gliders had long since given up and now stood along the cliff rim like a mob of bright pterodactyls, wings folded, heads up, staring at the clouds, waiting.

"All this," the old man murmured, "my God, for *me.*"

The young man checked his watch.

"Ten minutes to four and counting. Almost time for the great arrival. Sorry; that's what I called it when I wrote you up a week ago for the *News*. That moment of arrival and departure, in the blink of an eye, when, by stepping across time, you changed the

---

5. **Toynbee:** Arnold Toynbee, English historian (1889–1975).

whole future of the world from night to day, dark to light. I've often wondered—"

"What?"

Shumway studied the sky. "When you went ahead in time, did *no one* see you arrive? Did anyone at *all* happen to look up, do you know, and see your device hover in the middle of the air, here and over Chicago a bit later, and then New York and Paris? *No one?*"

"Well," said the inventor of the *Toynbee Convector*, "I don't suppose anyone was *expecting* me! And if people saw, they surely did not know what in blazes they were looking at. I was careful, anyway, not to linger too long. I needed only time to photograph the rebuilt cities, the clean seas and rivers, the fresh, smog-free air, the unfortified nations, the saved and beloved whales. I moved quickly, photographed swiftly and ran back down the years home. Today, paradoxically, is different. Millions upon millions of mobs of eyes will be looking up with great expectations. They will glance, will they not, from the young fool burning in the sky to the old fool here, still glad for his triumph?"

"They will," said Shumway. "Oh, indeed, they *will!*"

A cork popped. Shumway turned from surveying the crowds on the nearby fields and the crowds of circling objects in the sky to see that Stiles had just opened a bottle of champagne.

"Our own private toast and our own private celebration."

They held their glasses up, waiting for the precise and proper moment to drink.

"Five minutes to four and counting. Why," said the young reporter, "did no one else ever travel in time?"

"I put a stop to it myself," said the old man, leaning over the roof, looking down at the crowds. "I realized how dangerous it was. I was reliable, of course, no danger. But, Lord, think of it—just *anyone* rolling about the bowling-alley time corridors ahead, knocking tenpins headlong, frightening natives, shocking citizens somewhere else, fiddling with Napoleon's life line behind or restoring Hitler's cousins ahead? No, no. And the government, of course, agreed—no, insisted—that we put the *Toynbee Convector* under sealed lock and key. Today, you were the first and the last to fingerprint its machinery. The guard has been heavy and constant, for tens of thousands of days, to prevent the machine's being stolen. What time do you have?"

Shumway glanced at his watch and took in his breath. "One minute and counting down—"

He counted, the old man counted. They raised their champagne glasses.

"Nine, eight, seven—"

The crowds below were immensely silent. The sky whispered with expectation. The TV cameras swung up to scan and search.

"Six, five—"

They clinked their glasses.

"Four, three, two—"

They drank.

"One!"

They drank their champagne with a laugh. They looked to the sky. The golden air above the La Jolla coast line waited. The moment for the great arrival was here.

"Now!" cried the young reporter, like a magician giving orders.

"Now!" said Stiles, gravely quiet.

Nothing.

Five seconds passed.

The sky stood empty.

Ten seconds passed.

The heavens waited.

Twenty seconds passed.

Nothing.

At last, Shumway turned to stare and wonder at the old man by his side.

Stiles looked at him, shrugged and said:

"I lied."

"You what!?" cried Shumway.

The crowds below shifted uneasily.

"I lied," said the old man simply.

"No!"

"Oh, but yes," said the time traveler. "I never went anywhere. I stayed but made it seem I went. There is no time machine—only something that *looks* like one."

"But why?" cried the young man, bewildered, holding to the rail at the edge of the roof. "Why?"

"I see that you have a tape-recording button on your lapel. Turn it on. Yes. There. I want everyone to hear this. Now."

The old man finished his champagne and then said:

"Because I was born and raised in a time, in the sixties, seventies, and eighties, when people had stopped believing in themselves. I saw that disbelief, the reason that no longer gave itself reasons to survive, and was moved, depressed and then angered by it.

"Everywhere, I saw and heard doubt. Everywhere, I learned destruction. Everywhere was professional despair, intellectual ennui, political cynicism. And what wasn't ennui and cynicism was rampant skepticism and incipient nihilism."

The old man stopped, having remembered something. He bent and from under a table brought forth a special bottle of red Burgundy with the label 1984 on it. This, as he talked, he began to open, gently plumbing the ancient cork.

"You name it, we had it. The economy was a snail. The world was a cesspool. Economics remained an insolvable mystery. Melancholy was the attitude. The impossibility of change was the vogue. End of the world was the slogan.

"Nothing was worth doing. Go to bed at night full of bad news at eleven, wake up in the morn to worse news at seven. Trudge through the day underwater. Drown at night in a tide of plagues and pestilence. Ah!"

For the cork had softly popped. The now-harmless 1984 vintage was ready for airing. The time traveler sniffed it and nodded.

"Not only the four horsemen of the Apocalypse[6] rode the horizon to fling themselves on our cities but a fifth horseman, worse than all the rest, rode with them: Despair, wrapped in dark shrouds of defeat, crying only repetitions of past disasters, present failures, future cowardices.

"Bombarded by dark chaff and no bright seed, what sort of harvest was there for man in the latter part of the incredible twentieth century?

"Forgotten was the moon, forgotten the red landscapes of Mars, the great eye of Jupiter, the stunning rings of Saturn. We refused to be comforted. We wept at the grave of our child, and the child was *us.*"

---

6. four horsemen of the Apocalypse: Biblical figures who represent war, pestilence, famine, and death (Revelations 6:2–8).

"Was that how it was," asked Shumway quietly, "one hundred years ago?"

"Yes." The time traveler held up the wine bottle as if it contained proof. He poured some into a glass, eyed it, inhaled, and went on. "You have seen the newsreels and read the books of that time. You know it all.

"Oh, of course, there were a few bright moments. When Salk[7] delivered the world's children to life. Or the night when *Eagle* landed and that one great step for mankind trod the moon. But in the minds and out of the mouths of many, the fifth horseman was darkly cheered on. With high hopes, it sometimes seemed, of his winning. So all would be gloomily satisfied that their predictions of doom were right from day one. So the self-fulfilling prophecies were declared; we dug our graves and prepared to lie down in them."

"And you couldn't allow that?" said the young reporter.

"You know I couldn't."

"And so you built the *Toynbee Convector*—"

"Not all at once. It took years to brood on it."

The old man paused to swirl the dark wine, gaze at it and sip, eyes closed.

"Meanwhile, I drowned, I despaired, wept silently late nights thinking, what can I do to save us from ourselves? How to save my friends, my city, my state, my country, the entire *world* from this obsession with doom? Well, it was in my library late one night that my hand, searching along shelves, touched at last on an old and beloved book by H. G. Wells.[8] His time device called, ghostlike, down the years. I *heard*! I understood. I truly listened. Then I blueprinted. I built. I traveled, or so it *seemed*. The rest, as you know, is history."

The old time traveler drank his wine, opened his eyes.

"Good God," the young reporter whispered, shaking his head. "Oh, dear God. Oh, the wonder, the wonder—"

There was an immense ferment in the lower gardens now and in the fields beyond and on the roads and in the air. Millions were still waiting. Where was the great arrival?

---

7. **Salk:** Jonas Salk (1914–). Physician who developed a vaccine to prevent polio.
8. **beloved book by H.G. Wells:** English author (1866–1946). In Wells's science fiction novel *The Time Machine*, the narrator travels to the future and returns, warning his friends of the disastrous outcomes unless current ways are changed.

"Well, now," said the old man, filling another glass with wine for the young reporter. "Aren't I something? I made the machines, built miniature cities, lakes, ponds, seas. Erected vast architectures against crystal-water skies, talked to dolphins, played with whales, faked tapes, mythologized films. Oh, it took years, years of sweating work and secret preparation before I announced my departure, left and came back with good news!"

They drank the rest of the vintage wine. There was a hum of voices. All of the people below were looking up at the roof.

The time traveler waved at them and turned.

"Quickly, now. It's up to you from here on. You have the tape, my voice on it, just freshly made. Here are three more tapes, with fuller data. Here's a film-cassette history of my whole inspired fraudulence. Here's a final manuscript. Take, take it all, hand it on. I nominate you as son to explain the father. Quickly!"

Hustled into the elevator once more, Shumway felt the world fall away beneath. He didn't know whether to laugh or cry, so gave, at last, a great hoot.

The old man, surprised, hooted with him, as they stepped out below and advanced upon the *Toynbee Convector*.

"You see the point, don't you son? Life has *always* been lying to ourselves! As boys, young men, old men. As girls, maidens, women, to gently lie and prove the lie true. To weave dreams and put brains and ideas and flesh and the truly real beneath the dreams. Everything, finally, is a promise. What seems a lie is a ramshackle need, wishing to be born. Here. Thus and so."

He pressed the button that raised the plastic shield, pressed another that started the time machine humming, then shuffled quickly in to thrust himself into the *Convector*'s seat.

"Throw the final switch, young man!"

"But—"

"You're thinking," here the old man laughed, "if the time machine is a fraud, it won't work, what's the use of throwing a switch, yes? Throw it, anyway. *This* time, it *will* work!"

Shumway turned, found the control switch, grabbed hold, then looked up at Craig Bennett Stiles.

"I don't understand. Where are you *going?*"

"Why, to be one with the ages, of course. To exist now, only in the deep past."

"How can that *be?*"

"Believe me, this time it will happen. Goodbye, dear, fine, nice young man."

"Goodbye."

"Now. Tell me my name."

"What?"

"Speak my name and throw the switch."

"Time traveler?"

"Yes! *Now!*"

The young man yanked the switch. The machine hummed, roared, blazed with power.

"Oh," said the old man, shutting his eyes. His mouth smiled gently. "Yes."

His head fell forward on his chest.

Shumway yelled, banged the switch off and leaped forward to tear at the straps binding the old man in his device.

In the midst of so doing, he stopped, felt the time traveler's wrist, put his fingers under the neck to test the pulse there and groaned. He began to weep.

The old man had, indeed, gone back in time, and its name was death. He was traveling in the past now, forever.

Shumway stepped back and turned the machine on again. If the old man were to travel, let the machine—symbolically, anyway —go with him. It made a pathetic humming. The fire of it, the bright sun fire, burned in all of its spider grids and armatures and lighted the cheeks and the vast brow of the ancient traveler, whose head seemed to nod with the vibrations and whose smile, as he traveled into darkness, was the smile of a child much satisfied.

The reporter stood for a long moment more, wiping his cheeks with the backs of his hands. Then, leaving the machine on, he turned, crossed the room, pressed the button for the glass elevator and, while he was waiting, took the time traveler's tapes and cassettes from his jacket pockets and, one by one, shoved them into the incinerator trash flue set in the wall.

The elevator doors opened, he stepped in, the doors shut. The elevator hummed now, like yet another time device, taking him up into a stunned world, a waiting world, lifting him up into a bright continent, a future land, a wondrous and surviving planet. . . .

That one man with one lie had created.

Meaning

1. Shumway expects Stiles to announce "a second and final trip through time." Does Stiles make such a journey?

2. What compelled Stiles to tell his lie? What were the results of the lie?

3. Stiles refers to Shumway as his "honorary son." What do you think he means?

4. Stiles maintains that "life has *always* been lying to ourselves" and that "what seems like a lie is a ramshackle need, wishing to be born." How do you interpret these statements? How do they explain Stiles's own lie?

Method

1. What is the *climax,* or turning point, of the story? How does the author build up to it?

2. All science fiction contains some fantastical elements. However, the author must make the story plausible enough that the reader is willing to believe the events are possible within the context of the story. This is called the reader's *willing suspension of disbelief.* Were you willing to suspend your disbelief as you read Bradbury's story? Why or why not?

3. What do you think is the *theme,* or underlying message, of "The Toynbee Convector"?

4. *Science fiction* is a type of fantasy that includes imaginative speculation about the impact of science on individuals or society. What aspects of "The Toynbee Convector" make it a science fiction story? Give examples.

Language: Similes and Metaphors

In "The Toynbee Convector," the author creates images in the reader's mind by means of *similes* and *metaphors* —figures of speech that draw comparisons between basically unlike things. Similes use words of comparison such as *like* or *as* to compare two things. For example, Shumway follows Stiles "like a small dog after a great army." Bradbury does not mean to say that Shumway is like a small dog in every way; instead, this comparison gives a picture of Shumway's eager struggle to keep up with the energetic, purposeful Stiles.

Metaphors state comparisons between two things without using words of comparison such as *like* or *as*. For example, Stiles says that "the economy was a snail." This metaphor gives the reader a concrete image of the sluggish economy Stiles is describing.

Find at least two other similes and two other metaphors in "The Toynbee Convector," and describe the image each comparison creates in your mind.

Discussion and Composition

1. Stiles's lie results in a "wondrous and surviving planet." Consider the possibility that his lie, instead of encouraging people to work toward a better future, might have convinced them that the future would work itself out without their efforts. What could have been the results?

2. Create a journal in which you record your imaginary travels in a time machine. Tell why you have decided to travel, what adventures you have in the future or the past, and what effects your travels have on the eras you visit.

3. Write a different ending for "The Toynbee Convector" in which Shumway tells the world the truth about Stiles's journey through time. Describe the reactions of the people, and tell how public knowledge of the hoax affects the future of the planet. You might give your account from the first-person point of view of a witness, or you might use the third-person point of view that Bradbury uses in his story.

ALICE WALKER

(born 1944)

Born to sharecroppers in Georgia, Walker experienced first-hand the hardships endured by black families in the South. After attending Spelman College and Sarah Lawrence College, Walker began voter-registration work in Georgia and later worked in Mississippi with Head Start, a social services program for under-priveleged children.

Alice Walker's commitment to the liberation of black women has deeply influenced her work. Her female characters face the harsh realities of poverty, racism, and sexism; yet their inner strength allows them to emerge triumphant from their struggles.

Like many of Walker's stories, essays, and poems, "Everyday Use" has been widely anthologized. The story takes a more light-hearted tone than many of her other works, such as the Pulitzer Prize-winning novel *The Color Purple,* but it develops some of Walker's central concerns.

EVERYDAY USE

for your grandmama

I will wait for her in the yard that Maggie and I made so clean and wavy yesterday afternoon. A yard like this is more comfortable than most people know. It is not just a yard. It is like an extended living room. When the hard clay is swept clean as a floor and the fine sand around the edges lined with tiny, irregular grooves, any-one can come and sit and look up into the elm tree and wait for the breezes that never come inside the house.

Maggie will be nervous until after her sister goes: she will stand hopelessly in corners, homely and ashamed of the burn scars down her arms and legs, eying her sister with a mixture of envy and awe. She thinks her sister has held life always in the palm of one hand, that "no" is a word the world never learned to say to her.

You've no doubt seen those TV shows where the child who has "made it" is confronted, as a surprise, by her own mother and father, tottering in weakly from backstage. (A pleasant surprise, of course: What would they do if parent and child came on the show only to curse out and insult each other?) On TV mother and child embrace and smile into each other's faces. Sometimes the mother and father weep, the child wraps them in her arms and leans across the table to tell how she would not have made it without their help. I have seen these programs.

Sometimes I dream a dream in which Dee and I are suddenly brought together on a TV program of this sort. Out of a dark and soft-seated limousine I am ushered into a bright room filled with many people. There I meet a smiling, gray, sporty man like Johnny Carson who shakes my hand and tells me what a fine girl I have. Then we are on the stage and Dee is embracing me with tears in her eyes. She pins on my dress a large orchid, even though she has told me once that she thinks orchids are tacky flowers.

In real life I am a large, big-boned woman with rough, man-working hands. In the winter I wear flannel nightgowns to bed and overalls during the day. I can kill and clean a hog as mercilessly as a man. My fat keeps me hot in zero weather. I can work outside all day, breaking ice to get water for washing; I can eat pork liver cooked over the open fire minutes after it comes steaming from the hog. One winter I knocked a bull calf straight in the brain between the eyes with a sledgehammer and had the meat hung up to chill before nightfall. But of course all this does not show on television. I am the way my daughter would want me to be: a hundred pounds lighter, my skin like an uncooked barley pancake. My hair glistens in the hot bright lights. Johnny Carson has much to do to keep up with my quick and witty tongue.

But that is a mistake. I know even before I wake up. Who ever knew a Johnson with a quick tongue? Who can even imagine me looking a strange white man in the eye? It seems to me I have talked to them always with one foot raised in flight, with my head turned in whichever way is farthest from them. Dee, though. She would always look anyone in the eye. Hesitation was no part of her nature.

"How do I look, Mama?" Maggie says, showing just enough of her thin body enveloped in pink skirt and red blouse for me to know she's there, almost hidden by the door.

"Come out into the yard," I say.

Have you ever seen a lame animal, perhaps a dog run over by some careless person rich enough to own a car, sidle up to someone who is ignorant enough to be kind to him? That is the way my Maggie walks. She has been like this, chin on chest, eyes on ground, feet in shuffle, ever since the fire that burned the other house to the ground.

Dee is lighter than Maggie, with nicer hair and a fuller figure. She's a woman now, though sometimes I forget. How long ago was it that the other house burned? Ten, twelve years? Sometimes I can still hear the flames and feel Maggie's arms sticking to me, her hair smoking and her dress falling off her in little black papery flakes. Her eyes seemed stretched open, blazed open by the flames reflected in them. And Dee. I see her standing off under the sweet gum tree she used to dig gum out of; a look of concentration on her face as she watched the last dingy gray board of the house fall in toward the red-hot brick chimney. Why don't you do a dance around the ashes? I'd wanted to ask her. She had hated the house that much.

I used to think she hated Maggie, too. But that was before we raised the money, the church and me, to send her to Augusta to school. She used to read to us without pity; forcing words, lies, other folks' habits, whole lives upon us two, sitting trapped and ignorant underneath her voice. She washed us in a river of make-believe, burned us with a lot of knowledge we didn't necessarily need to know. Pressed us to her with the serious way she read, to shove us away at just the moment, like dimwits, we seemed about to understand.

Dee wanted nice things. A yellow organdy dress to wear to her graduation from high school; black pumps to match a green suit she'd made from an old suit somebody gave me. She was determined to stare down any disaster in her efforts. Her eyelids would not flicker for minutes at a time. Often I fought off the temptation to shake her. At sixteen she had a style of her own: and knew what style was.

I never had an education myself. After second grade the school was closed down. Don't ask me why: in 1927 colored asked fewer questions than they do now. Sometimes Maggie reads to me. She stumbles along good-naturedly but can't see well. She knows she is not bright. Like good looks and money, quickness passed her by. She will marry John Thomas (who has mossy teeth in an earnest face) and then I'll be free to sit here and I guess just sing church songs to myself. Although I never was a good singer. Never could carry a tune. I was always better at a man's job. I used to love to milk till I was hooked in the side in '49. Cows are soothing and slow and don't bother you, unless you try to milk them the wrong way.

I have deliberately turned my back on the house. It is three rooms, just like the one that burned, except the roof is tin; they don't make shingle roofs anymore. There are no real windows, just some holes cut in the sides, like the portholes in a ship, but not round and not square, with rawhide holding the shutters up on the outside. This house is in a pasture, too, like the other one. No doubt when Dee sees it she will want to tear it down. She wrote me once that no matter where we "choose" to live, she will manage to come see us. But she will never bring her friends. Maggie and I thought about this and Maggie asked me, "Mama, when did Dee ever *have* any friends?"

She had a few. Furtive boys in pink shirts hanging about on washday after school. Nervous girls who never laughed. Impressed with her they worshiped the well-turned phrase, the cute shape, the scalding humor that erupted like bubbles in lye. She read to them.

When she was courting Jimmy T she didn't have much time to pay to us, but turned all her faultfinding power on him. He *flew* to marry a cheap city girl from a family of ignorant flashy people. She hardly had time to recompose herself.

When she comes I will meet—but there they are!

Maggie attempts to make a dash for the house, in her shuffling way, but I stay her with my hand. "Come back here," I say. And she stops and tries to dig a well in the sand with her toe.

It is hard to see them clearly through the strong sun. But even the first glimpse of leg out of the car tells me it is Dee. Her feet were always neat-looking, as if God himself had shaped them with a certain style. From the other side of the car comes a short, stocky man. Hair is all over his head a foot long and hanging from his chin like a kinky mule tail. I hear Maggie suck in her breath. "Uhnnnh," is what it sounds like. Like when you see the wriggling end of a snake just in front of your foot on the road. "Uhnnnh."

Dee next. A dress down to the ground, in this hot weather. A dress so loud it hurts my eyes. There are yellows and oranges enough to throw back the light of the sun. I feel my whole face warming from the heat waves it throws out. Earrings gold, too, and hanging down to her shoulders. Bracelets dangling and making noises when she moves her arm up to shake the folds of the dress out of her armpits. The dress is loose and flows, and as she walks closer, I like it. I heart Maggie go "Uhnnnh" again. It is her sister's hair. It stands straight up like the wool on a sheep. It is black as night and around the edges are two long pigtails that rope about like small lizards disappearing behind her ears.

"Wa-su-zo-Tean-o!" she says, coming on in that gliding way the dress makes her move. The short stocky fellow with the hair to his navel is all grinning and he follows up with "Asalamalakim[1], my mother and sister!" He moves to hug Maggie but she falls back, right up against the back of my chair. I feel her trembling there and when I look up I see the perspiration falling off her chin.

"Don't get up," says Dee. Since I am stout it takes something of a push. You can see me trying to move a second or two before I make it. She turns, showing white heels through her sandals, and goes back to the car. Out she peeks next with a Polaroid. She stoops down quickly and lines up picture after picture of me sitting there in front of the house with Maggie cowering behind me. She never takes a shot without making sure the house is included. When a cow comes nibbling around the edge of the yard she snaps it and me and Maggie *and* the house. Then she puts the Polaroid in the back seat of the car, and comes up and kisses me on the forehead.

Meanwhile Asalamalakim is going through motions with Maggie's hand. Maggie's hand is as limp as a fish, and probably as cold, despite the sweat, and she keeps trying to pull it back. It looks like Asalamalakim wants to shake hands but wants to do it fancy. Or maybe he don't know how people shake hands. Anyhow, he soon gives up on Maggie.

"Well," I says. "Dee."

"No, Mama," she says. "Not 'Dee,' Wangero Leewanika Kemanjo!"

---

1. Asalamalakim: *Salaam aleikhim* (sə-läm′ ä-lä-kŏŏm′), an African greeting meaning "Peace be with you."

"What happened to 'Dee'?" I wanted to know.

"She's dead," Wangero said. "I couldn't bear it any longer, being named after the people who oppress me."

"You know as well as me ~~you was named~~ after your aunt Dicie," I said. Dicie is my sister. She named Dee. We called her "Big Dee" after Dee was born.

"But who was *she* named after?" asked Wangero.

"I guess after Grandma Dee," I said.

"And who was she named after?" asked Wangero.

"Her mother," I said, and saw Wangero was getting tired. "That's about as far back as I can trace it," I said. Though, in fact, I probably could have carried it back beyond the Civil War through the branches.

"Well," said Asalamalakim, "there you are."

"Uhnnnh," I heard Maggie say.

"There I was not," I said, "before 'Dicie' cropped up in our family, so why should I try to trace it that far back?"

He just stood there grinning, looking down on me like somebody inspecting a Model A car. Every once in a while he and Wangero sent eye signals over my head.

"How do you pronounce this name?" I asked.

"You don't have to call me by it if you don't want to," said Wangero.

"Why shouldn't I?" I asked. "If that's what you want us to call you, we'll call you."

"I know it might sound awkward at first," said Wangero.

"I'll get used to it," I said. "Ream it out again."

Well, soon we got the name out of the way. Asalamalakim had a name twice as long and three times as hard. After I tripped over it two or three times he told me to just call him Hakim-a-barber. I wanted to ask him was he a barber, but I didn't really think he was, so I didn't ask.

"You must belong to those beef-cattle peoples down the road," I said. They said "Asalamalakim" when they met you, too, but they didn't shake hands. Always too busy: feeding the cattle, fixing the fences, putting up salt-lick shelters, throwing down hay. When the white folks poisoned some of the herd the men stayed up all night with rifles in their hands. I walked a mile and a half just to see the sight.

Hakim-a-barber said, "I accept some of their doctrines, but farming and raising cattle is not my style." (They didn't tell me, and I didn't ask, whether Wangero (Dee) had really gone and married him.)

We sat down to eat and right away he said he didn't eat collards and pork was unclean. Wangero, though, went on through the chitlins and corn bread, the greens and everything else. She talked a blue streak over the sweet potatoes. Everything delighted her. Even the fact that we still used the benches her daddy made for the table when we couldn't afford to buy chairs.

"Oh, Mama!" she cried. Then turned to Hakim-a-barber. "I never knew how lovely these benches are. You can feel the rump prints," she said, running her hands underneath her and along the bench. Then she gave a sigh and her hand closed over Grandma Dee's butter dish. "That's it!" she said. "I knew there was something I wanted to ask you if I could have." She jumped up from the table and went over in the corner where the churn stood, the milk in it clabber[2] by now. She looked at the churn and looked at it.

"This churn top is what I need," she said. "Didn't Uncle Buddy whittle it out of a tree you all used to have?"

"Yes," I said.

"Uh huh," she said happily. "And I want the dasher,[3] too."

"Uncle Buddy whittle that, too?" asked the barber.

Dee (Wangero) looked up at me.

"Aunt Dee's first husband whittled the dash," said Maggie so low you almost couldn't hear her. "His name was Henry, but they called him Stash."

"Maggie's brain is like an elephant's," Wangero said, laughing. "I can use the churn top as a centerpiece for the alcove table," she said, sliding a plate over the churn, "and I'll think of something artistic to do with the dasher."

When she finished wrapping the dasher the handle stuck out. I took it for a moment in my hands. You didn't even have to look close to see where hands pushing the dasher up and down to make butter had left a kind of sink in the wood. In fact, there were a lot of small sinks; you could see where thumbs and fingers had sunk into the wood. It was beautiful light yellow wood, from a tree that grew in the yard where Big Dee and Stash had lived.

---

2. **clabber:** curdled.
3. **dasher:** the plunger of a churn.

After dinner Dee (Wangero) went to the trunk at the foot of my bed and started rifling through it. Maggie hung back in the kitchen over the dishpan. Out came Wangero with two quilts. They had been pieced by Grandma Dee and then Big Dee and me had hung them on the quilt frames on the front porch and quilted them. One was in the Lone Star pattern. The other was Walk Around the Mountain. In both of them were scraps of dresses Grandma Dee had worn fifty and more years ago. Bits and pieces of Grandpa Jarrell's Paisley shirts. And one teeny faded blue piece, about the size of a penny matchbox, that was from Great Grandpa Ezra's uniform that he wore in the Civil War.

"Mama," Wangero said sweet as a bird. "Can I have these old quilts?"

I heard something fall in the kitchen, and a minute later the kitchen door slammed.

"Why don't you take one or two of the others?" I asked. "These old things was just done by me and Big Dee from some tops your grandma pieced before she died."

"No," said Wangero. "I don't want those. They are stitched around the borders by machine."

"That'll make them last better," I said.

"That's not the point," said Wangero. "These are all pieces of dresses Grandma used to wear. She did all this stitching by hand. Imagine!" She held the quilts securely in her arms, stroking them.

"Some of the pieces, like those lavender ones, come from old clothes her mother handed down to her," I said, moving up to touch the quilts. Dee (Wangero) moved back just enough so that I couldn't reach the quilts. They already belonged to her.

"Imagine!" she breathed again, clutching them closely to her bosom.

"The truth is," I said, "I promised to give them quilts to Maggie, for when she marries John Thomas."

She gasped like a bee had stung her.

"Maggie can't appreciate these quilts!" she said. "She'd probably be backward enough to put them to everyday use."

"I reckon she would," I said. "God knows I been saving 'em for long enough with nobody using 'em. I hope she will!" I didn't want to bring up how I had offered Dee (Wangero) a quilt when she went away to college. Then she had told me they were old-fashioned, out of style.

"But they're *priceless!*" she was saying now, furiously; for she has a temper. "Maggie would put them on the bed and in five years they'd be in rags. Less than that!"

"She can always make some more," I said. "Maggie knows how to quilt."

Dee (Wangero) looked at me with hatred. "You just will not understand. The point is these quilts, *these* quilts!"

"Well," I said, stumped. "What would *you* do with them?"

"Hang them," she said. As if that was the only thing you *could* do with quilts.

Maggie by now was standing in the door. I could almost hear the sound her feet made as they scraped over each other.

"She can have them, Mama," she said, like somebody used to never winning anything, or having anything reserved for her. "I can 'member Grandma Dee without the quilts."

I looked at her hard. She had filled her bottom lip with checkerberry snuff and it gave her face a kind of dopey, hangdog look. It was Grandma Dee and Big Dee who taught her how to quilt herself. She stood there with her scarred hands hidden in the folds of her skirt. She looked at her sister with something like fear but she wasn't mad at her. This was Maggie's portion. This was the way she knew God to work.

When I looked at her like that something hit me in the top of my head and ran down to the soles of my feet. Just like when I'm in church and the spirit of God touches me and I get happy and shout. I did something I never had done before: hugged Maggie to me, then dragged her on into the room, snatched the quilts out of Miss Wangero's hands and dumped them into Maggie's lap. Maggie just sat there on my bed with her mouth open.

"Take one or two of the others," I said to Dee.

But she turned without a word and went out to Hakim-a-barber.

"You just don't understand," she said, as Maggie and I came out to the car.

"What don't I understand?" I wanted to know.

"Your heritage," she said. And then she turned to Maggie, kissed her, and said, "You ought to try to make something of yourself, too, Maggie. It's really a new day for us. But from the way you and Mama still live you'd never know it."

She put on some sunglasses that hid everything above the tip of her nose and her chin.

Maggie smiled; maybe at the sunglasses. But a real smile, not scared. After we watched the car dust settle I asked Maggie to bring me a dip of snuff. And then the two of us sat there just enjoying, until it was time to go in the house and go to bed.

Meaning

1. How does the mother describe Maggie at the beginning of the story? What circumstances might explain Maggie's feelings about herself?
2. Give details from the story that show how Dee felt about her home and family while she was growing up.
3. Dee is outraged at the idea that she can not have the old quilts because they will be Maggie's to "put to everyday use" when she marries. What do the quilts represent for Dee? What do they represent for Maggie?
4. What is ironic about Dee's new appreciation for her "heritage"? Are you convinced that her appreciation is genuine? Why or why not?
5. Maggie offers Dee the quilts, but their mother intervenes. Why do you think the mother does this?

Method

1. Which character do you learn the most about in "Everyday Use": the mother, Maggie, or Dee? How does the author develop this character?
2. How does the description of the mother's dream at the beginning of the story prepare you for meeting Dee? How does the dream point up the conflict between the mother and Dee?
3. The mother's descriptions of Dee suggest that Dee is self-centered and shallow. Which of Dee's actions in the story show the kind of behavior that has made her mother think of her this way?
4. How is the story's setting significant?

Language: Imagery

Imagery refers to words and phrases that appeal to the senses and create pictures, or images, in the reader's mind. For example, when the narrator describes Dee's companion's hair as "a foot long and hanging from his chin like a kinky mule tail," she is appealing to the reader's sense of sight and conjuring up a precise visual image for the reader. Find three other examples of imagery in the story that appeal to your sense of sight and create strong images in your mind.

Discussion and Composition

1. Dee and her mother have conflicting views of their heritage, race, and family. In your experience, do conflicts between older and younger generations often involve a clash between values or ways of life? How are such conflicts resolved?

2. Since leaving home, Dee has come to view objects such as the butter churn and quilts in a new way. What experiences do you think she has had in the city that have affected her attitude toward these things? Why do you think her heritage has become important to her?

3. Although the mother in the story does not have much education or worldly experience, she has the wisdom to understand Dee's behavior. In a brief composition, give your personal definition of "wisdom." First think about the following questions: Do you know people who seem especially wise? What do you think is the source of their wisdom? In general, what makes a person wise? As you develop your definition, give specific examples to support your opinions.

JAMES JOYCE
(1882–1941)

The short stories of James Joyce often seem to have little plot. There is almost no dramatic action in "Araby," for instance, which is part of his short story collection, *Dubliners* (1914). One of Joyce's contributions to the development of the short story was his idea that the story should build toward a moment of clear vision, truth, or self-discovery, which he called "epiphany."

One of the most influential and controversial writers of the twentieth century, James Joyce was born in Dublin, Ireland, the oldest son of a large family that sank deep into poverty as he grew up. He attended a Catholic grammar school on scholarship and graduated from University College in Dublin in 1902. Joyce left Dublin soon after his mother died in 1903, and spent the rest of his life in Paris, Zurich, and Trieste, supporting himself by teaching languages and writing.

Joyce's most important books are *A Portrait of the Artist as a Young Man* (1916), *Ulysses* (1922), and *Finnegans Wake* (1939). Almost all of his writing deals with Dublin and contains elements of his own life, which was often wild and sometimes sad. Although he suffered from eye disease and was sometimes blind, he was always committed to excellence and originality in his writing. Several of his works are considered masterpieces because of his sensitive portrayal of human nature and his brilliant use of language with many levels of meaning. He is credited with developing the stream-of-consciousness technique, which takes the reader inside the mind of a character to experience a free flow of ideas and sensations. Joyce pointed out new and exciting directions to writers who have followed him.

ARABY

North Richmond Street, being blind,[1] was a quiet street except at the hour when the Christian Brothers' School set the boys free. An uninhabited house of two storeys stood at the blind end, detached

1. **blind:** dead-end.

from its neighbours in a square ground. The other houses of the street, conscious of decent lives within them, gazed at one another with brown imperturbable faces.

Personification The former tenant of our house, a priest, had died in the back drawing-room. Air, musty from having been long enclosed, hung in all the rooms, and the waste room behind the kitchen was littered with old useless papers. Among these I found a few paper-covered books, the pages of which were curled and damp: *The Abbot*, by Walter Scott, *The Devout Communicant* and *The Memoirs of Vidocq*. I liked the last best because its leaves were yellow. The wild garden behind the house contained a central apple-tree and a few straggling bushes under one of which I found the late tenant's rusty bicycle-pump. He had been a very charitable priest; in his will he had left all his money to institutions and the furniture of his house to his sister.

When the short days of winter came dusk fell before we had well eaten our dinners. When we met in the street the houses had grown sombre. The space of sky above us was the colour of ever-changing violet and towards it the lamps of the street lifted their feeble lanterns. The cold air stung us and we played till our bodies glowed. Our shouts echoed in the silent street. The career of our play brought us through the dark muddy lanes behind the houses where we ran the gantlet of the rough tribes from the cottages, to the back doors of the dark dripping gardens where odours arose from the ashpits, to the dark odorous stables where a coachman smoothed and combed the horse or shook music from the buckled harness. When we returned to the street light from the kitchen windows had filled the areas. If my uncle was seen turning the corner we hid in the shadow until we had seen him safely housed. Or if Mangan's sister came out on the doorstep to call her brother in to his tea we watched her from our shadow peer up and down the street. We waited to see whether she would remain or go in and, if she remained, we left our shadow and walked up to Mangan's steps resignedly. She was waiting for us, her figure defined by the light from the half-opened door. Her brother always teased her before he obeyed and I stood by the railings looking at her. Her dress swung as she moved her body and the soft rope of her hair tossed from side to side.

Every morning I lay on the floor in the front parlour watching her door. The blind was pulled down to within an inch of the sash so that I could not be seen. When she came out on the doorstep my heart leaped. I ran to the hall, seized my books and followed her. I kept her brown figure always in my eye and, when we came near the point at which our ways diverged, I quickened my pace and passed her. This happened morning after morning. I had never spoken to her, except for a few casual words, and yet her name was like a summons to all my foolish blood.

Her image accompanied me even in places the most hostile to romance. On Saturday evenings when my aunt went marketing I had to go to carry some of the parcels. We walked through the flaring streets, jostled by drunken men and bargaining women, amid the curses of labourers, the shrill litanies[2] of shop-boys who stood on guard by the barrels of pigs' cheeks, the nasal chanting of street-singers, who sang a *come-all-you* about O'Donovan Rossa,[3] or a ballad about the troubles in our native land. These noises converged in a single sensation of life for me: I imagined that I bore my chalice safely through a throng of foes. Her name sprang to my lips at moments in strange prayers and praises which I myself did not understand. My eyes were often full of tears (I could not tell why) and at times a flood from my heart seemed to pour itself out into my bosom. I thought little of the future. I did not know whether I would ever speak to her or not or, if I spoke to her, how I could tell her of my confused adoration. But my body was like a harp and her words and gestures were like fingers running upon the wires.

One evening I went into the back drawing-room in which the priest had died. It was a dark rainy evening and there was no sound in the house. Through one of the broken panes I heard the rain impinge upon the earth, the fine incessant needles of water playing in the sodden beds. Some distant lamp or lighted window gleamed below me. I was thankful that I could see so little. All my senses seemed to desire to veil themselves and, feeling that I was about to slip from them, I pressed the palms of my hands together until they trembled, murmuring: *O love! O love!* many times.

At last she spoke to me. When she addressed the first words to me I was so confused that I did not know what to answer. She asked me was I going to *Araby*. I forget whether I answered yes or no. It would be a splendid bazaar, she said; she would love to go.

—And why can't you? I asked.

While she spoke she turned a silver bracelet round and round

2. **litanies** (lĭt′n·ēs): prayers in which a priest and congregation alternate with recitation and response.
3. **come-all-you ... Rossa:** a ballad about an Irish hero.

her wrist. She could not go, she said, because there would be a retreat [4] that week in her convent. Her brother and two other boys were fighting for their caps and I was alone at the railings. She held one of the spikes, bowing her head towards me. The light from the lamp opposite our door caught the white curve of her neck, lit up her hair that rested there and, falling, lit up the hand upon the railing. It fell over one side of her dress and caught the white border of a petticoat, just visible as she stood at ease.

—It's well for you, she said.

—If I go, I said, I will bring you something.

What innumerable follies laid waste my waking and sleeping thoughts after that evening! I wished to annihilate the tedious intervening days. I chafed against the work of school. At night in my bedroom and by day in the classroom her image came between me and the page I strove to read. The syllables of the word *Araby* were called to me through the silence in which my soul luxuriated and cast an Eastern enchantment over me. I asked for leave to go to the bazaar on Saturday night. My aunt was surprised and hoped it was not some Freemason[5] affair. I answered few questions in class. I watched my master's face pass from amiability to sternness; he hoped I was not beginning to idle. I could not call my wandering thoughts together. I had hardly any patience with the serious work of life which, now that it stood between me and my desire, seemed to me child's play, ugly monotonous child's play.

On Saturday morning I reminded my uncle that I wished to go to the bazaar in the evening. He was fussing at the hallstand, looking for the hat-brush, and answered me curtly:

—Yes, boy, I know.

As he was in the hall I could not go into the front parlour and lie at the window. I left the house in bad humour and walked slowly towards the school. The air was pitilessly raw and already my heart misgave me.

When I came home to dinner my uncle had not yet been home. Still it was early. I sat staring at the clock for some time and, when its ticking began to irritate me, I left the room. I mounted the staircase and gained the upper part of the house. The high cold empty gloomy rooms liberated me and I went from room to room singing. From the

---

4. retreat: a period of prayer and contemplation.
5. Freemason: secret society considered anti-Catholic in Ireland.

front window I saw my companions playing below in the street. Their cries reached me weakened and indistinct and, leaning my forehead against the cool glass, I looked over at the dark house where she lived. I may have stood there for an hour, seeing nothing but the brown-clad figure cast by my imagination, touched discreetly by the lamplight at the curved neck, at the hand upon the railings and at the border below the dress.

When I came downstairs again I found Mrs Mercer sitting at the fire. She was an old garrulous woman, a pawnbroker's widow, who collected used stamps for some pious purpose. I had to endure the gossip of the tea-table. The meal was prolonged beyond an hour and still my uncle did not come. Mrs Mercer stood up to go: she was sorry she couldn't wait any longer, but it was after eight o'clock and she did not like to be out late, as the night air was bad for her. When she had gone I began to walk up and down the room, clenching my fists. My aunt said:

—I'm afraid you may put off your bazaar for this night of Our Lord.

At nine o'clock I heard my uncle's latchkey in the halldoor. I heard him talking to himself and heard the hallstand rocking when it had received the weight of his overcoat. I could interpret these signs. When he was midway through his dinner I asked him to give me the money to go to the bazaar. He had forgotten.

—The people are in bed and after their first sleep now, he said.

I did not smile. My aunt said to him energetically:

—Can't you give him the money and let him go? You've kept him late enough as it is.

My uncle said he was very sorry he had forgotten. He said he believed in the old saying: *All work and no play makes Jack a dull boy.* He asked me where I was going and, when I had told him a second time he asked me did I know *The Arab's Farewell to his Steed.* When I left the kitchen he was about to recite the opening lines of the piece to my aunt.

I held a florin[6] tightly in my hand as I strode down Buckingham Street towards the station. The sight of the streets thronged with buyers and glaring with gas recalled to me the purpose of my journey. I took my seat in a third-class carriage of a deserted train. After an intolerable delay the train moved out of the station slowly. It crept

6. florin: a silver coin equal to two shillings, or 1/10 of a pound, about $.20 in U.S. money.

onward among ruinous houses and over the twinkling river. At Westland Row Station a crowd of people pressed to the carriage doors; but the porters moved them back, saying that it was a special train for the bazaar. I remained alone in the bare carriage. In a few minutes the train drew up beside an improvised wooden platform. I passed out on to the road and saw by the lighted dial of a clock that it was ten minutes to ten. In front of me was a large building which displayed the magical name.

I could not find any sixpenny entrance and, fearing that the bazaar would be closed, I passed in quickly through a turnstile, handing a shilling to a weary-looking man. I found myself in a big hall girdled at half its height by a gallery. Nearly all the stalls were closed and the greater part of the hall was in darkness. I recognised a silence like that which pervades a church after a service. I walked into the centre of the bazaar timidly. A few people were gathered about the stalls which were still open. Before a curtain, over which the words *Café Chantant* were written in coloured lamps, two men were counting money on a salver[7]. I listened to the fall of the coins.

Remembering with difficulty why I had come I went over to one of the stalls and examined porcelain vases and flowered tea-sets. At the door of the stall a young lady was talking and laughing with two young gentlemen. I remarked their English accents and listened vaguely to their conversation.

—O, I never said such a thing!

—O, but you did!

—O, but I didn't!

—Didn't she say that?

—Yes. I heard her.

—O, there's a . . . fib!

Observing me the young lady came over and asked me did I wish to buy anything. The tone of her voice was not encouraging; she seemed to have spoken to me out of a sense of duty. I looked humbly at the great jars that stood like eastern guards at either side of the dark entrance to the stall and murmured:

—No, thank you.

The young lady changed the position of one of the vases and went back to the two young men. They began to talk of the same subject. Once or twice the young lady glanced at me over her shoulder.

7. **salver** (săl′vər): tray.

I lingered before her stall, though I knew my stay was useless, to make my interest in her wares seem the more real. Then I turned away slowly and walked down the middle of the bazaar. I allowed the two pennies to fall against the sixpence in my pocket. I heard a voice call from one end of the gallery that the light was out. The upper part of the hall was now completely dark.

Gazing up into the darkness I saw myself as a creature driven and derided by vanity; and my eyes burned with anguish and anger.

Meaning

1. What kind of person is the boy in "Araby"? What evidence can you find that he has a romantic view of life? How can you tell that the narrator is telling a story about his youth?
2. Why is Mangan's sister unable to go to the bazaar? Why does the boy want to go there?
3. There is little dramatic action in "Araby." It is typical of Joyce's stories in which a character arrives at an *epiphany,* a time when the character discovers an important truth that changes his or her view of life. What discovery about himself does the boy make at the bazaar?
4. Describe the boy's uncle. Why do you think the aunt at first seems to disapprove of the bazaar, but later urges her husband to let the boy go?

Method

1. What is the function of the first two paragraphs in the story?
2. What does the bazaar symbolize? What does the old priest symbolize?
3. *Images* are word pictures and impressions that appeal to our senses. Images of darkness and light pervade "Araby" and help to convey mood and atmosphere. Explain the significance of the following images:

   a. "The career of our play brought us through the *dark muddy lanes behind the houses . . .* to the *back doors of the dark dripping gardens . . .* "

   b. "*The light from the lamp* opposite our door *caught the white curve of her neck, lit up her hair that rested there and, falling, lit up the hand* upon the railing."

   c. "I heard a voice call from one end of the gallery that *the light was out.* The upper part of the hall was now *completely dark.*"

Language: Poetic Prose Style

"Araby" contains several elements that are seen more often in poetry than in prose. In addition to similes and metaphors, Joyce uses a figure of speech called *personification,* that is, he gives human or animal characteristics to inanimate objects and ideas. "Towards it the lamps of the street lifted their feeble lanterns." He also uses the poetic techniques of alliteration and assonance. *Alliteration* is the repetition of initial consonants, as, for example, in the following sentence: "Our *s*houts echoed in the *s*ilent *s*treet." *Assonance* is the repetition of internal vowel sounds in words that occur close to one another in a sentence, for example, "Her dress swung as she moved her body and the soft rope of her hair tossed from side to side." Find other examples of personification, alliteration, and assonance in "Araby."

Discussion and Composition

1. Do you think that "Araby" describes a typical adolescent experience? Tell why or why not.

2. Write about an incident that helped you grow up. It could be a time when you lost some illusions, gained new responsibilities, or did something on your own. To organize your essay, first tell what you were like before the incident. Next describe what happened, using specific details. Then tell how you felt after the incident.

RUDOLFO A. ANAYA

(born 1937)

The myths and traditions of Rudolfo Anaya's Mexican American heritage form the basis for many of his works. His novels and stories are often set in the southwestern United States, and he weaves a magical, mysterious quality into these landscapes that complements the mythical themes of his works.

Anaya has lived in New Mexico all of his life. He teaches at the University of New Mexico and gives readings of his works throughout the Southwest. His award-winning novel *Bless Me, Ultima,* which was published in 1972, earned him wide acclaim for its insights into Mexican American culture. Anaya has published two more novels, *Heart of Aztlán* and *Tortuga,* as well as a short-story collection titled *The Silence of the Llano.* In 1980, his home state honored him with the Governor's Award for Achievement in Literature.

SALOMON'S STORY

Before I came here I was a hunter, but that was long ago. Still, it was in the pursuit of the hunt that I came face to face with my destiny. This is my story.

We called ourselves a tribe and we spent our time hunting and fishing along the river. For young boys that was a great adventure. Each morning I stole away from my father's home to meet my fellow hunters by the river. My father was a farmer who planted corn on the hills bordering the river. He was a good man. He kept the ritual of the seasons, marked the path of the sun and the moon across the sky, and he prayed each day that the order of things not be disturbed.

He did his duty and tried to teach me about the rhythm in the weather and the seasons, but a wild urge in my blood drove me from him. I went willingly to join the tribe along the river. The call of the hunt was exciting, and daily the slaughter of the animals with the smell of blood drove us deeper and deeper into the dark river. I became a member of the tribe, and I forgot the fields of my father. We hunted birds with our crude weapons and battered to death stray raccoons and rabbits. Then we skinned the animals and filled the air with the smoke of roasting meat. The tribe was pleased with me and welcomed me as a hunter. They prepared for my initiation.

I, Salomon, tell you this so that you may know the meaning of life and death. How well I know it now, how clear are the events of the day I killed the giant river turtle. Since that day I have been a storyteller, forced by the order of my destiny to reveal my story. I speak to tell you how the killing became a horror.

The silence of the river was heavier than usual that day. The heat stuck to our sweating skin like a sticky syrup and the insects sucked our blood. Our half-naked bodies moved like shadows in the brush. Those ahead and behind me whispered from time to time, complaining that we were lost and suggesting that we turn back. I said nothing, it was the day of my initiation, I could not speak. There had been a fight at camp the night before and the bad feelings still lingered. But we hunted anyway, there was nothing else to do. We were compelled to hunt in the dark shadows of the river. Some days the spirit for the hunt was not good, fellow hunters quarreled over small things, and still we had to start early at daybreak to begin the long day's journey which would not bring us out until sunset.

In the branches above us the bird cries were sharp and frightful. More than once the leader lifted his arm and the line froze, ready for action. The humid air was tense. Somewhere to my left I heard the river murmur as it swept south, and for the first time the dissatisfaction which had been building within me surfaced. I cursed the oppressive darkness and wished I was free of it. I thought of my father walking in the sunlight of his green fields, and I wished I was with him. But it was not so; I owed the tribe my allegiance. Today I would become a full member. I would kill the first animal we encountered.

We moved farther than usual into unknown territory, hacking away at the thick underbrush; behind me I heard murmurs of dissension. Some wanted to turn back, others wanted to rest on the warm sandbars of the river, still others wanted to finish the argument which had started the night before. My father had given me an amulet to wear and he had instructed me on the hunt, and this made the leader jealous. Some argued that I could wear the amulet, while others said no. In the end the jealous leader tore it from my neck and said that I would have to face my initiation alone.

I was thinking about how poorly prepared I was and how my father had tried to help, when the leader raised his arm and sounded the alarm. A friend behind me whispered that if we were in luck there would be a deer drinking at the river. No one had ever killed a deer in the memory of our tribe. We held our breath and waited, then the leader motioned and I moved forward to see. There in the middle of the narrow path lay the biggest tortoise any of us had ever seen. It was a huge monster which had crawled out of the dark river to lay its eggs in the warm sand. I felt a shiver, and when I breathed the taste of copper drained in my mouth and settled in my queasy stomach.

The giant turtle lifted its huge head and looked at us with dull, glintless eyes. The tribe drew back. Only I remained facing the monster from the water. Its slimy head dripped with bright green algae. It hissed a warning. It had come out of the water to lay its eggs, now it had to return to the river. Wet, leathery eggs fresh from the laying clung to its webbed feet, and as it moved forward it crushed them into the sand. Its gray shell was dry, dulled by the sun, encrusted with dead parasites and green growth; it needed the water.

"Kill it!" the leader cried, and at the same time the hunting horn sounded its too-rou which echoed down the valley. Ah, its call was so sad and mournful I can hear it today as I tell my story. . . . Listen, Tortuga, it is now I know that at that time I could have forsaken my initiation and denounced the darkness and insanity that urged us to the never-ending hunt. I had not listened to my father's words. The time was not right.

"The knife," the leader called, and the knife of the tribe was passed forward, then slipped into my hand. The huge turtle lumbered forward. I could not speak. In fear I raised the knife and brought it down with all my might. Oh, I prayed to no gods, but since then how often I have wished that I could undo what I did. One blow severed the giant turtle's head. One clean blow and the head rolled in the sand as the reptilian body reared back, gushing green slime. The tribe cheered and pressed forward. They were as surprised as I was that the kill had been so swift and clean. We had hunted smaller tortoises before and we knew that once they retreated into their shells it took hours to kill them. Then knives and spears had to be poked into the holes and the turtle had to be turned on its back so the tedious task of cutting the softer underside could begin. But now I had beheaded the giant turtle with one blow.

"There will be enough meat for the entire tribe," one of the boys cried. He speared the head and held it aloft for everyone to see. I could only look at the dead turtle that lay quivering on the sand, its death urine and green blood staining the damp earth.

"He has passed his test," the leader shouted, "he did not need the amulet of his father. We will clean the shell and it will be his shield! And he shall now be called the man who slew the turtle!"

The tribe cheered, and for a moment I bathed in my glory. The fear left me, and so did the desire to be with my father on the harsh hills where he cultivated his fields of corn. He had been wrong; I could trust the tribe and its magic. Then someone shouted and we turned to see the turtle struggling toward us. It reared up, exposing the gaping hole where the head had been, then it charged, surprisingly swift for its huge size. Even without its head it crawled toward the river. The tribe fell back in panic.

"Kill it!" the leader shouted, "Kill it before it reaches the water! If it escapes into the water it will grow two heads and return to haunt us!"

I understood what he meant. If the creature reached the safety of the water it would live again, and it would become one more of the ghosts that lurked along our never-ending path. Now there was nothing I could do but stand my ground and finish the killing. I struck at it until the knife broke on its hard shell, and still the turtle rumbled toward the water, pushing me back. Terror and fear made me fall on the sand and grab it with my bare hands. Grunting and gasping for breath I dug my bare feet into the sand. I slipped one hand into the dark, bleeding hole where the head had been and with the other I grabbed its huge feet. I struggled to turn it on its back and rob it of its strength, but I couldn't. Its dark instinct for the water and the pull of death were stronger than my fear and desperation. I grunted and cursed as its claws cut into my arms and legs. The brush shook with our violent thrashing as we rolled down the bank towards the river. Even mortally wounded it was too strong for me. At the edge of the river, it broke free from me and plunged into the water, trailing frothy blood and bile as it disappeared into the gurgling waters.

Covered with turtle's blood, I stood numb and trembling. As I watched it disappear into the dark waters of the river, I knew I had done a wrong. Instead of conquering my fear, I had created another shadow which would return to haunt us. I turned and looked at my companions; they trembled with fright.

"You have failed us," the leader whispered. "You have angered the river gods." He raised his talisman, a stick on which hung chicken feathers, dried juniper berries and the rattler of a snake we had killed in the spring, and he waved it in front of me to ward off the curse. Then they withdrew in silence and vanished into the dark brush, leaving me alone on that stygian bank.

Oh, I wish I could tell you how lonely I felt. I cried for the turtle to return so I could finish the kill, or return its life, but the force of my destiny was already set and that was not to be. I understand that now. That is why I tell you my story. I left the river, free of the tribe, but unclean and smelling of death.

That night the bad dreams came, and then the paralysis. . . .

Meaning

1. How does the author contrast two ways of life in the story? Why do you think Salomon chooses one way and not the other?
2. Storytellers in every culture have attempted to explain "the meaning of life and death" through images and symbols. What images of life and death does Salomon present in his tale? What meaning do you think these images have?
3. What do you think is the *theme,* or underlying message, of "Salomon's Story"?

Method

1. Reread Salomon's descriptions of the turtle. What details suggest that the turtle represents the life force? What details suggest that it also represents death?
2. Writers often hint at, or *foreshadow,* what will come in a story How does the author foreshadow Salomon's fate?
3. What images in the story do you think you will remember the longest? Why are these images particularly powerful?

Language: Adjectives

The adjectives that Rudolfo Anaya uses in "Salomon's Story" contribute to the *atmosphere* or prevailing feeling of the story. Reread Salomon's description of the tribe's hike to the river (pages 188–189), and write down each descriptive adjective that you find in the passage. Then study your list. What do many of the adjectives have in common? What atmosphere do they help to create?

Composition

Write a different version of the story's ending in which Salomon kills the turtle before it reaches the water. Begin after the sentence, "The brush shook with our violent thrashing as we rolled down the bank towards the river," and rework the last few paragraphs of the story to show Salomon's victory instead of his defeat. For example, you might replace the leader's whispered comment, "'You have failed us,'" with a shout of congratulations. In your version, indicate how Salomon feels about killing the turtle, and tell whether he decides to remain with the tribe.

FRANK O'CONNOR
(1903–1966)

The land and the people of Ireland are the subject of Frank O'Connor's fiction. Born Michael O'Donovan in Cork, Ireland, he was able to attend school only through the fourth grade, but he educated himself by reading widely while holding odd jobs to help support his family. His father was a laborer; his mother, a cleaning woman. He began writing short stories while still a child, and adopted the pseudonym Frank O'Connor.

As a youth, O'Connor spent a year in prison for his political support of the Irish Republican Army. He later worked as a professional librarian and directed the famous Abbey Theater in Dublin during the 1930s. Learning Gaelic as a child from his grandmother, he subsequently taught Gaelic and translated Gaelic literature into English. During the last twenty years of his life, O'Connor lived in the United States, where he taught creative writing at Northwestern University and at Harvard.

O'Connor wrote poetry, plays, and scholarly works, but his major contribution was to the short story. Asked what he believed to be the most important element of a story, he replied, "You have to have a theme, a story to tell. . . . A theme is something that is worth something to everybody." O'Connor recalls his childhood and adolescence in his autobiography, *An Only Child* (1961).

MY OEDIPUS COMPLEX

Father was in the army all through the war—the first war, I mean—so, up to the age of five, I never saw much of him, and what I saw did not worry me. Sometimes I woke and there was a big figure in khaki peering down at me in the candlelight. Sometimes in the early morning I heard the slamming of the front door and the clatter of nailed boots down the cobbles of the lane. These were Father's entrances and exits. Like Santa Claus he came and went mysteriously.

In fact, I rather liked his visits, though it was an uncomfortable squeeze between Mother and him when I got into the big bed in the early morning. He smoked, which gave him a pleasant musty smell, and shaved, an operation of astounding interest. Each time he left a trail of souvenirs—model tanks and Gurkha knives with handles made of bullet cases, and German helmets and cap badges and button-sticks, and all sorts of military equipment—carefully stowed away in a long box on the top of the wardrobe, in case they ever came in handy. There was a bit of the magpie about Father; he expected everything to come in handy. When his back was turned, Mother let me get a chair and rummage through his treasures. She didn't seem to think so highly of them as he did.

The war was the most peaceful period of my life. The window of my attic faced southeast. My mother had curtained it, but that had small effect. I always woke with the first light and, with all the responsibilities of the previous day melted, feeling myself rather like the sun, ready to illumine and rejoice. Life never seemed so simple and clear and full of possibilities as then. I put my feet out from under the clothes—I called them Mrs. Left and Mrs. Right—and invented dramatic situations for them in which they discussed the problems of the day. At least Mrs. Right did; she was very demonstrative, but I hadn't the same control of Mrs. Left, so she mostly contented herself with nodding agreement.

They discussed what Mother and I should do during the day, what Santa Claus should give a fellow for Christmas, and what steps should be taken to brighten the home. There was that little matter of the baby, for instance. Mother and I could never agree about that. Ours was the only house in the terrace without a new baby, and Mother said we couldn't afford one till Father came back from the war because they cost seventeen and six. That showed how simple she was. The Geneys up the road had a baby, and everyone knew they couldn't afford seventeen and six. It was probably a cheap baby, and Mother wanted something really good, but I felt she was too exclusive. The Geneys' baby would have done us fine.

Having settled my plans for the day, I got up, put a chair under the attic window, and lifted the frame high enough to stick out my head. The window overlooked the front gardens of the terrace behind ours, and beyond these it looked over a deep valley to the tall, red-brick houses terraced up the opposite hillside, which were all still in shadow, while those at our side of the valley were all lit up, though with long strange shadows that made them seem unfamiliar; rigid and painted.

After that I went into Mother's room and climbed into the big bed. She woke and I began to tell her of my schemes. By this time, though I never seem to have noticed it, I was petrified in my night-shirt, and I thawed as I talked until, the last frost melted, I fell asleep beside her and woke again only when I heard her below in the kitchen, making the breakfast.

After breakfast we went into town; heard Mass at St. Augus-tine's and said a prayer for Father, and did the shopping. If the afternoon was fine we either went for a walk in the country or a visit to Mother's great friend in the convent, Mother St. Dominic. Mother had them all praying for Father, and every night, going to bed, I asked God to send him back safe from the war to us. Little, indeed, did I know what I was praying for!

One morning, I got into the big bed, and there, sure enough, was Father in his usual Santa Claus manner, but later, instead of uniform, he put on his best blue suit, and Mother was as pleased as anything. I saw nothing to be pleased about, because, out of uniform, Father was altogether less interesting, but she only beamed, and explained that our prayers had been answered, and off we went to Mass to thank God for having brought Father safely home.

The irony of it! That very day when he came in to dinner he took off his boots and put on his slippers, donned the dirty old cap he wore about the house to save him from colds, crossed his legs, and began to talk gravely to Mother, who looked anxious. Naturally, I disliked her looking anxious, because it destroyed her good looks, so I interrupted him.

"Just a moment, Larry!" she said gently.

This was only what she said when we had boring visitors, so I attached no importance to it and went on talking.

"Do be quiet, Larry!" she said impatiently. "Don't you hear me talking to Daddy?"

This was the first time I had heard those ominous words, "talking to Daddy," and I couldn't help feeling that if this was how God answered prayers, he couldn't listen to them very attentively.

"Why are you talking to Daddy?" I asked with as great a show of indifference as I could muster.

"Because Daddy and I have business to discuss. Now, don't interrupt again!"

In the afternoon, at Mother's request, Father took me for a walk. This time we went into town instead of out to the country, and I thought at first, in my usual optimistic way, that it might be an improvement. It was nothing of the sort. Father and I had quite different notions of a walk in town. He had no proper interest in trams, ships, and horses, and the only thing that seemed to divert him was talking to fellows as old as himself. When I wanted to stop he simply went on, dragging me behind him by the hand; when he wanted to stop I had no alternative but to do the same. I noticed that it seemed to be a sign that he wanted to stop for a long time whenever he leaned against a wall. The second time I saw him do it I got wild. He seemed to be settling himself forever. I pulled him by the coat and trousers, but, unlike Mother who, if you were too persistent, got into a wax and said: "Larry, if you don't behave yourself, I'll give you a good slap," Father had an extraordinary capacity for amiable inattention. I sized him up and wondered would I cry, but he seemed to be too remote to be annoyed even by that. Really, it was like going for a walk with a mountain! He either ignored the wrenching and pummeling entirely, or else glanced down with a grin of amusement from his peak. I had never met anyone so absorbed in himself as he seemed.

At teatime, "talking to Daddy" began again, complicated this time by the fact that he had an evening paper, and every few minutes he put it down and told Mother something new out of it. I felt this was foul play. Man for man, I was prepared to compete with him any time for Mother's attention, but when he had it all made up for him by other people it left me no chance. Several times I tried to change the subject without success.

"You must be quiet while Daddy is reading, Larry," Mother said impatiently.

It was clear that she either genuinely liked talking to Father better than talking to me, or else that he had some terrible hold on her which made her afraid to admit the truth.

"Mummy," I said that night when she was tucking me up, "do you think if I prayed hard God would send Daddy back to the war?"

She seemed to think about that for a moment.

"No dear," she said with a smile. "I don't think he would."

"Why wouldn't he, Mummy?"

"Because there isn't a war any longer, dear."

"But Mummy, couldn't God make another war, if he liked?"

"He wouldn't like to, dear. It's not God who makes wars, but bad people."

"Oh!" I said.

I was disappointed about that. I began to think that God wasn't quite what he was cracked up to be.

Next morning I woke at my usual hour, feeling like a bottle of champagne. I put out my feet and invented a long conversation in which Mrs. Right talked of the trouble she had with her own father till she put him in the Home. I didn't quite know what the Home was but it sounded the right place for Father. Then I got my chair and stuck my head out of the attic window. Dawn was just breaking, with a guilty air that made me feel I had caught it in the act. My head bursting with stories and schemes, I stumbled in next door, and in the half-darkness scrambled into the big bed. There was no room at Mother's side so I had to get between her and Father. For the time being I had forgotten about him, and for several minutes I sat bolt upright, racking my brains to know what I could do with him. He was taking up more than his fair share of the bed, and I couldn't get comfortable, so I gave him several kicks that made him grunt and stretch. He made room all right, though. Mother waked and felt for me. I settled back comfortably in the warmth of the bed with my thumb in my mouth.

"Mummy!" I hummed, loudly and contentedly.

"Sssh! dear," she whispered. "Don't wake Daddy!"

This was a new development, which threatened to be even more serious than "talking to Daddy." Life without my early-morning conferences was unthinkable.

"Why!" I asked severely.

"Because poor Daddy is tired."

This seemed to me a quite inadequate reason, and I was sickened by the sentimentality of her "poor Daddy." I never liked that sort of gush; it always struck me as insincere.

"Oh!" I said lightly. Then in my most winning tone: "Do you know where I want to go with you today, Mummy?"

"No, dear," she sighed.

"I want to go down the Glen and fish for thornybacks with my new net, and then I want to go out to the Fox and Hounds, and—"

"Don't-wake-Daddy!" she hissed angrily, clapping her hand across my mouth.

But it was too late. He was awake, or nearly so. He grunted and reached for the matches. Then he stared incredulously at his watch.

"Like a cup of tea, dear?" asked Mother in a meek, hushed voice I had never heard her use before. It sounded almost as though she were afraid.

"Tea?" he exclaimed indignantly. "Do you know what the time is?"

"And after that I want to go up the Rathcooney Road," I said loudly, afraid I'd forget something in all those interruptions.

"Go to sleep at once, Larry!" she said sharply.

I began to snivel. I couldn't concentrate, the way that pair went on, and smothering my early-morning schemes was like burying a family from the cradle.

Father said nothing, but lit his pipe and sucked it, looking out into the shadows without minding Mother or me. I knew he was mad. Every time I made a remark Mother hushed me irritably. I was mortified. I felt it wasn't fair; there was even something sinister in it. Every time I had pointed out to her the waste of making two beds when we could both sleep in one, she had told me it was healthier like that, and now here was this man, this stranger, sleeping with her without the least regard for her health!

He got up early and made tea, but though he brought Mother a cup he brought none for me.

"Mummy," I shouted, "I want a cup of tea, too."

"Yes, dear," she said patiently. "You can drink from Mummy's saucer."

That settled it. Either Father or I would have to leave the house. I didn't want to drink from Mother's saucer; I wanted to be treated as an equal in my own home, so, just to spite her, I drank it all and left none for her. She took that quietly, too.

But that night when she was putting me to bed she said gently: "Larry, I want you to promise me something."

"What is it?" I asked.

"Not to come in and disturb poor Daddy in the morning. Promise?"

"Poor Daddy" again! I was becoming suspicious of everything involving that quite impossible man.

"Why?" I asked.

"Because poor Daddy is worried and tired and he doesn't sleep well."

"Why doesn't he, Mummy?"

"Well, you know, don't you, that while he was at the war Mummy got the pennies from the Post Office?"

"From Miss MacCarthy?"

"That's right. But now, you see, Miss MacCarthy hasn't any more pennies, so Daddy must go out and find us some. You know what would happen if he couldn't?"

"No," I said, "tell us."

"Well, I think we might have to go out and beg for them like the poor old woman on Fridays. We wouldn't like that, would we?"

"No," I agreed. "We wouldn't."

"So you'll promise not to come in and wake him?"

"Promise."

Mind you, I meant that. I knew pennies were a serious matter, and I was all against having to go out and beg like the old woman on Fridays. Mother laid out all my toys in a complete ring round the bed so that, whatever way I got out, I was bound to fall over one of them.

When I woke I remembered my promise all right. I got up and sat on the floor and played—for hours, it seemed to me. Then I got my chair and looked out the attic window for more hours. I wished it was time for Father to wake; I wished someone would make me a cup of tea. I didn't feel in the least like the sun; instead, I was bored and so very, very cold! I simply longed for the warmth and depth of the big featherbed.

At last I could stand it no longer. I went into the next room. As there was still no room at Mother's side I climbed over her and she woke with a start.

"Larry," she whispered, gripping my arm very tightly, "what did you promise?"

"But I did, Mummy," I wailed, caught in the very act. "I was quiet for ever so long."

"Oh, dear, and you're perished!" she said sadly, feeling me all over. "Now, if I let you stay will you promise not to talk?"

"But I want to talk, Mummy," I wailed.

"That has nothing to do with it," she said with a firmness that was new to me. "Daddy wants to sleep. Now, do you understand that?"

I understood it only too well. I wanted to talk, he wanted to sleep—whose house was it, anyway?

"Mummy," I said with equal firmness, "I think it would be healthier for Daddy to sleep in his own bed."

That seemed to stagger her, because she said nothing for a while.

"Now, once for all," she went on, "you're to be perfectly quiet or go back to your own bed. Which is it to be?"

The injustice of it got me down. I had convicted her out of her own mouth of inconsistency and unreasonableness, and she hadn't even attempted to reply. Full of spite, I gave Father a kick, which she didn't notice but which made him grunt and open his eyes in alarm.

"What time is it?" he asked in a panic-stricken voice, not looking at Mother but the door, as if he saw someone there.

"It's early yet," she replied soothingly. "It's only the child. Go to sleep again.... Now, Larry," she added, getting out of bed, "you've wakened Daddy and you must go back."

This time, for all her quiet air, I knew she meant it, and knew that my principal rights and privileges were as good as lost unless I asserted them at once. As she lifted me, I gave a screech, enough to wake the dead, not to mind Father. He groaned.

"That damn child! Doesn't he ever sleep?"

"It's only a habit, dear," she said quietly, though I could see she was vexed.

"Well, it's time he got out of it," shouted Father, beginning to heave in the bed. He suddenly gathered all the bedclothes about him, turned to the wall, and then looked back over his shoulder with nothing showing only two small, spiteful, dark eyes. The man looked very wicked.

To open the bedroom door, Mother had to let me down, and I broke free and dashed for the farthest corner, screeching. Father sat bolt upright in bed.

"Shut up, you little puppy!" he said in a choking voice.

I was so astonished that I stopped screeching. Never, never had anyone spoken to me in that tone before. I looked at him incredulously and saw his face convulsed with rage. It was only then that I fully realized how God had codded[1] me, listening to my prayers for the safe return of this monster.

"Shut up, you!" I bawled, beside myself.

"What's that you said?" shouted Father, making a wild leap out of bed.

"Mick, Mick!" cried Mother. "Don't you see the child isn't used to you?"

"I see he's better fed than taught," snarled Father, waving his arms wildly. "He wants his bottom smacked."

All his previous shouting was as nothing to these obscene words referring to my person. They really made my blood boil.

"Smack your own!" I screamed hysterically. "Smack your own! Shut up! Shut up!"

At this he lost his patience and let fly at me. He did it with the

1. **codded:** tricked.

lack of conviction you'd expect of a man under Mother's horrified eyes, and it ended up as a mere tap, but the sheer indignity of being struck at all by a stranger, a total stranger who had cajoled his way back from the war into our big bed as a result of my innocent intercession, made me completely dotty. I shrieked and shrieked, and danced in my bare feet, and Father, looking awkward and hairy in nothing but a short grey army shirt, glared down at me like a mountain out for murder. I think it must have been then that I realized he was jealous too. And there stood Mother in her nightdress, looking as if her heart was broken between us. I hoped she felt as she looked. It seemed to me that she deserved it all.

From that morning out my life was a hell. Father and I were enemies, open and avowed. We conducted a series of skirmishes against one another, he trying to steal my time with Mother and I his. When she was sitting on my bed, telling me a story, he took to looking for some pair of old boots which he alleged he had left behind him at the beginning of the war. While he talked to Mother I played loudly with my toys to show my total lack of concern. He created a terrible scene one evening when he came in from work and found me at his box, playing with his regimental badges, Gurkha knives and button-sticks. Mother got up and took the box from me.

"You mustn't play with Daddy's toys unless he lets you, Larry," she said severely. "Daddy doesn't play with yours."

For some reason Father looked at her as if she had struck him and then turned away with a scowl.

"Those are not toys," he growled, taking down the box again to see had I lifted anything. "Some of those curios are very rare and valuable."

But as time went on I saw more and more how he managed to alienate Mother and me. What made it worse was that I couldn't grasp his method or see what attraction he had for Mother. In every possible way he was less winning than I. He had a common accent and made noises at his tea. I thought for a while that it might be the newspapers she was interested in, so I made up bits of news of my own to read to her. Then I thought it might be the smoking, which I personally thought attractive, and took his pipes and went round the house dribbling into them till he caught me. I even made noises at my tea, but Mother only told me I was disgusting. It all seemed to hinge round that unhealthy habit of sleeping together, so I made a point of dropping into their bedroom and nosing round, talking to myself, so that they wouldn't know I was watching them, but they were never up to anything that I could see. In the end it beat me. It seemed to depend on being grownup and giving people rings, and I realized I'd have to wait.

But at the same time I wanted him to see that I was only waiting, not giving up the fight. One evening when he was being particularly obnoxious, chattering away well above my head, I let him have it.

"Mummy," I said, "do you know what I'm going to do when I grow up?"

"No, dear," she replied. "What?"

"I'm going to marry you," I said quietly.

Father gave a great guffaw out of him, but he didn't take me in. I knew it must only be pretense. And Mother, in spite of everything, was pleased. I felt she was probably relieved to know that one day Father's hold on her would be broken.

"Won't that be nice?" she said with a smile.

"It'll be very nice," I said confidently. "Because we're going to have lots and lots of babies."

"That's right, dear," she said placidly. "I think we'll have one soon, and then you'll have plenty of company."

I was no end pleased about that because it showed that in spite of the way she gave in to Father she still considered my wishes. Besides, it would put the Geneys in their place.

It didn't turn out like that, though. To begin with, she was very preoccupied—I supposed about where she would get the seventeen and six—and though Father took to staying out late in the evenings it did me no particular good. She stopped taking me for walks, became as touchy as blazes, and smacked me for nothing at all. Sometimes I wished I'd never mentioned the confounded baby—I seemed to have a genius for bringing calamity on myself.

And calamity it was! Sonny arrived in the most appalling hullabaloo—even that much he couldn't do without a fuss—and from the first moment I disliked him. He was a difficult child—so far as I was concerned he was always difficult—and demanded far too much attention. Mother was simply silly about him, and couldn't see when he was only showing off. As company he was worse than useless. He slept all day, and I had to go round the house on tiptoe to avoid waking him. It wasn't any longer a question of not waking Father. The slogan now was "Don't-wake-Sonny!" I couldn't understand why the child wouldn't sleep at the proper time, so whenever Mother's back was turned I woke him. Sometimes to keep him awake

I pinched him as well. Mother caught me at it one day and gave me a most unmerciful flaking.

One evening, when Father was coming in from work, I was playing trains in the front garden. I let on not to notice him; instead, I pretended to be talking to myself, and said in a loud voice: "If another bloody baby comes into this house, I'm going out."

Father stopped dead and looked at me over his shoulder.

"What's that you said?" he asked sternly.

"I was only talking to myself," I replied, trying to conceal my panic. "It's private."

He turned and went in without a word. Mind you, I intended it as a solemn warning, but its effect was quite different. Father started being quite nice to me. I could understand that, of course. Mother was quite sickening about Sonny. Even at mealtimes she'd get up and gawk at him in the cradle with an idiotic smile, and tell Father to do the same. He was always polite about it, but he looked so puzzled you could see he didn't know what she was talking about. He complained of the way Sonny cried at night, but she only got cross and said that Sonny never cried except when there was something up with him— which was a flaming lie, because Sonny never had anything up with him, and only cried for attention. It was really painful to see how simple-minded she was. Father wasn't attractive, but he had a fine intelligence. He saw through Sonny, and now he knew that I saw through him as well.

One night I woke with a start. There was someone beside me in the bed. For one wild moment I felt sure it must be Mother, having come to her senses and left Father for good, but then I heard Sonny in convulsions in the next room, and Mother saying: "There! There! There!" and I knew it wasn't she. It was Father. He was lying beside me, wide awake, breathing hard and apparently as mad as hell.

After a while it came to me what he was mad about. It was his turn now. After turning me out of the big bed, he had been turned out himself. Mother had no consideration now for anyone but that poisonous pup, Sonny. I couldn't help feeling sorry for Father. I had been through it all myself, and even at that age I was magnanimous.[2] I began to stroke him down and say: "There! There!" He wasn't exactly responsive.

"Aren't you asleep either?" he snarled.

"Ah, come on and put your arm around us, can't you?" I said,

2. **magnanimous** (măg-năn′ə-məs): generous and forgiving.

and he did, in a sort of way. Gingerly, I suppose, is how you'd describe it. He was very bony but better than nothing.

At Christmas he went out of his way to buy me a really nice model railway.

Meaning

1. Explain the title of the story. What is an "Oedipus Complex"? How does the term express Larry's relationship with his parents?
2. What is the conflict between Larry and his father?
3. How do Larry and his father become allies?

Method

1. How are the relative sizes of father and son used humorously in this story?
2. Why does the author have Larry tell his story some time after the main events have happened? What is the advantage of learning about the boy through is own words and actions?
3. How does this story illustrate Frank O'Connor's idea about the most important element in a story (see biographical introduction)?

Discussion and Composition

1. Frank O'Connor has said that a short story "doesn't deal with problems; it doesn't have any solutions, it just states the human condition." Discuss how this applies to several stories you have read.

2. Larry thought he wanted a new baby in the house. When Sonny arrived, Larry soon regretted ever having asked for a baby. In a humorous composition, tell about a time when something you wished for was granted but turned out to be undesirable. You might use the following thesis statement: Be careful what you wish for because you might get it. Devote the first paragraph of your composition to explaining what you wished for and why. In the next paragraph, explain how your wish was granted. Finally, discuss the results of having gotten what you thought you wanted.

ANNE TYLER
(born 1941)

Anne Tyler's characters often strike a familiar chord in the reader: they are memorable for their ordinariness as well as for their quirks. Tyler credits southern writer Eudora Welty with inspiring her to write about the details of everyday lives; like Welty, she chronicles these ordinary lives with wit and compassion.

Born in Minneapolis, Minnesota, Tyler spent most of her childhood in the South. She graduated from high school at the age of sixteen and entered Duke University in North Carolina, where she studied Russian. She continued her studies with graduate work at Columbia University.

In addition to her many novels, which include the award-winning *Dinner at the Homesick Restaurant* and *The Accidental Tourist,* Tyler has published more than fifty short stories. She currently lives in Baltimore, Maryland, with her family, and she continues to devote much of her time to writing.

TEENAGE WASTELAND

He used to have very blond hair—almost white—cut shorter than other children's so that on his crown a little cowlick always stood up to catch the light. But this was when he was small. As he grew older, his hair grew darker, and he wore it longer—past his collar even. It hung in lank, taffy-colored ropes around his face, which was still an endearing face, fine-featured, the eyes an unusual aqua blue. But his cheeks, of course, were no longer round, and a sharp new Adam's apple jogged in his throat when he talked.

In October, they called from the private school he attended to request a conference with his parents. Daisy went alone; her husband was at work. Clutching her purse, she sat on the principal's couch and learned that Donny was noisy, lazy, and disruptive; always fooling around with his friends, and he wouldn't respond in class.

In the past, before her children were born, Daisy had been a fourth-grade teacher. It shamed her now to sit before this principal as a parent, a delinquent parent, a parent who struck Mr. Lanham, no doubt, as unseeing or uncaring. "It isn't that we're not concerned," she said. "Both of us are. And we've done what we could, whatever we could think of. We don't let him watch TV on school nights. We don't let him talk on the phone till he's finished his homework. But he tells us he doesn't have any homework or he did it all in study hall. How are we to know what to believe?"

From early October through November, at Mr. Lanham's suggestion, Daisy checked Donny's assignments every day. She sat next to him as he worked, trying to be encouraging, sagging inwardly as she saw the poor quality of everything he did—the sloppy mistakes in math, the illogical leaps in his English themes, the history questions left blank if they required any research.

Daisy was often late starting supper, and she couldn't give as much attention to Donny's younger sister. "You'll never guess what happened at..." Amanda would begin, and Daisy would have to tell her, "Not now, honey."

By the time her husband, Matt, came home, she'd be snappish. She would recite the day's hardships—the fuzzy instructions in English, the botched history map, the morass of unsolvable algebra equations. Matt would look surprised and confused, and Daisy would gradually wind down. There was no way, really, to convey how exhausting all this was.

In December, the school called again. This time, they wanted Matt to come as well. She and Matt had to sit on Mr. Lanham's couch like two bad children and listen to the news: Donny had improved only slightly, raising a D in history to a C, and a C in algebra to a B-minus. What was worse, he had developed new problems. He had cut classes on at least three occasions. Smoked in the furnace room. Helped Sonny Barnett break into a freshman's locker. And last week, during athletics, he and three friends had been seen off the school grounds; when they returned, the coach had smelled beer on their breath.

Daisy and Matt sat silent, shocked. Matt rubbed his forehead with his fingertips. Imagine, Daisy thought, how they must look to Mr. Lanham: an overweight housewife in a cotton dress and a too-tall, too-thin insurance agent in a baggy, frayed suit. Failures, both of them—the kind of people who are always hurrying to catch up, missing the point of things that everyone else grasps at once. She wished she'd worn nylons instead of knee socks.

It was arranged that Donny would visit a psychologist for testing. Mr. Lanham knew just the person. He would set this boy straight, he said.

When they stood to leave, Daisy held her stomach in and gave Mr. Lanham a firm, responsible handshake.

Donny said the psychologist was a jackass and the tests were really dumb; but he kept all three of his appointments, and when it was time for the follow-up conference with the psychologist and both parents, Donny combed his hair and seemed unusually sober and subdued. The psychologist said Donny had no serious emotional problems. He was merely going through a difficult period in his life. He required some academic help and a better sense of self-worth. For this reason, he was suggesting a man named Calvin Beadle, a tutor with considerable psychological training.

In the car going home, Donny said he'd be damned if he'd let them drag him to some stupid fairy tutor. His father told him to watch his language in front of his mother.

That night, Daisy lay awake pondering the term "self-worth." She had always been free with her praise. She had always told Donny he had talent, was smart, was good with his hands. She had made a big to-do over every little gift he gave her. In fact, maybe she had gone too far, although, Lord knows, she had meant every word. Was that his trouble?

She remembered when Amanda was born. Donny had acted lost and bewildered. Daisy had been alert to that, of course, but still, a new baby keeps you so busy. Had she really done all she could have? She longed—she ached—for a time machine. Given one more chance, she'd do it perfectly—hug him more, praise him more, or perhaps praise him less. Oh, who can say . . .

The tutor told Donny to call him Cal. All his kids did, he said. Daisy thought for a second that he meant his own children, then realized her mistake. He seemed too young, anyhow, to be a family man. He wore a heavy brown handlebar mustache. His hair was as long and stringy as Donny's, and his jeans as faded. Wire-rimmed spectacles slid down his nose. He lounged in a canvas director's chair with his fingers laced across his chest, and he casually, amiably questioned Donny, who sat upright and glaring in an armchair.

"So they're getting on your back at school," said Cal. "Making a big deal about anything you do wrong."

"Right," said Donny.

"Any idea why that would be?"

"Oh, well, you know, stuff like homework and all," Donny said.

"You don't do your homework?"

"Oh, well, I might do it sometimes but not just exactly like they want it." Donny sat forward and said, "It's like a prison there, you know? You've got to go to every class, you can never step off the school grounds."

Smile

"You cut classes sometimes?"

"Sometimes," Donny said, with a glance at his parents.

Cal didn't seem perturbed. "Well," he said, "I'll tell you what. Let's you and me try working together three nights a week. Think you could handle that? We'll see if we can show that school of yours a thing or two. Give it a month; then if you don't like it, we'll stop. If I don't like it, we'll stop. I mean, sometimes people just don't get along, right? What do you say to that?"

"Okay," Donny said. He seemed pleased.

"Make it seven o'clock till eight, Monday, Wednesday, and Friday," Cal told Matt and Daisy. They nodded. Cal shambled to his feet, gave them a little salute, and showed them to the door.

This was where he lived as well as worked, evidently. The interview had taken place in the dining room, which had been transformed into a kind of office. Passing the living room, Daisy winced at the rock music she had been hearing, without registering it, ever since she had entered the house. She looked in and saw a boy about Donny's age lying on a sofa with a book. Another boy and a girl were playing Ping-Pong in front of the fireplace. "You have several here together?" Daisy asked Cal.

"Oh, sometimes they stay on after their sessions, just to rap. They're a pretty sociable group, all in all. Plenty of goof-offs like young Donny here."

He cuffed Donny's shoulder playfully. Donny flushed and grinned.

Climbing into the car, Daisy asked Donny, "Well? What did you think?"

But Donny had returned to his old evasive self. He jerked his chin toward the garage. "Look," he said. "He's got a basketball net."

Now on Mondays, Wednesdays, and Fridays, they had supper early—the instant Matt came home. Sometimes, they had to leave before they were really finished. Amanda would still be eating her dessert. "Bye, honey. Sorry," Daisy would tell her.

Cal's first bill sent a flutter of panic through Daisy's chest, but it was worth it, of course. Just look at Donny's face when they picked him up: alight and full of interest. The principal telephoned Daisy to tell her how Donny had improved. "Of course, it hasn't shown up in his grades yet, but several of the teachers have noticed how his attitude's changed. Yes, sir, I think we're onto something here."

At home, Donny didn't act much different. He still seemed to have a low opinion of his parents. But Daisy supposed that was unavoidable—part of being fifteen. He said his parents were too "controlling"—a word that made Daisy give him a sudden look. He said they acted like wardens. On weekends, they enforced a curfew. And any time he went to a party, they always telephoned first to see if adults would be supervising. "For God's sake!" he said. "Don't you trust me?"

"It isn't a matter of trust, honey . . ." But there was no explaining to him.

His tutor called one afternoon. "I get the sense," he said, "that this kid's feeling . . . underestimated, you know? Like you folks expect the worst of him. I'm thinking we ought to give him more rope."

"But see, he's still so suggestible," Daisy said. "When his friends suggest some mischief—smoking or drinking or such—why, he just finds it very hard not to go along with them."

"Mrs. Coble," the tutor said, "I think this kid is hurting. You know? Here's a serious, sensitive kid, telling you he'd like to take on some grown-up challenges, and you're giving him the message that he can't be trusted. Don't you understand how that hurts?"

"Oh," said Daisy.

"It undermines his self-esteem—don't you realize that?"

"Well, I guess you're right," said Daisy. She saw Donny suddenly from a whole new angle: his pathetically poor posture, that slouch so forlorn that his shoulders seemed about to meet his chin . . . oh, wasn't it awful being young? She'd had a miserable adolescence herself and had always sworn no child of hers would ever be that unhappy.

They let Donny stay out later, they didn't call ahead to see if the parties were supervised, and they were careful not to grill him about his evening. The tutor had set down so many rules! They were not allowed any questions at all about any aspect of school, nor were they to speak with his teachers. If a teacher had some complaint, she should phone Cal. Only one teacher disobeyed—the history teacher, Miss Evans. She called one morning in February. "I'm a little concerned about Donny, Mrs. Coble."

"Oh, I'm sorry, Miss Evans, but Donny's tutor handles these things now . . ."

"I always deal directly with the parents. You are the parent," Miss Evans said, speaking very slowly and distinctly. "Now, here is the problem. Back when you were helping Donny with his homework, his grades rose from a D to a C, but now they've slipped back, and they're closer to an F."

"They are?"

"I think you should start overseeing his homework again."

"But Donny's tutor says . . ."

"It's nice that Donny has a tutor, but you should still be in charge of his homework. With you, he learned it. Then he passed his tests. With the tutor, well, it seems the tutor is more of a crutch. 'Donny,' I say, 'a quiz is coming up on Friday. Hadn't you better be listening instead of talking?' 'That's okay, Miss Evans,' he says. 'I have a tutor now.' Like a talisman! I really think you ought to take over, Mrs. Coble."

"I see," said Daisy. "Well, I'll think about that. Thank you for calling."

Hanging up, she felt a rush of anger at Donny. A talisman! For a talisman, she'd given up all luxuries, all that time with her daughter, her evenings at home!

She dialed Cal's number. He sounded muzzy. "I'm sorry if I woke you," she told him, "but Donny's history teacher just called. She says he isn't doing well."

"She should have dealt with me."

"She wants me to start supervising his homework again. His grades are slipping."

"Yes," said the tutor, "but you and I both know there's more to it than mere grades, don't we? I care about the whole child— his happiness, his self-esteem. The grades will come. Just give them time."

When she hung up, it was Miss Evans she was angry at. What a narrow woman!

It was Cal this, Cal that, Cal says this, Cal and I did that. Cal lent Donny an album by the Who. He took Donny and two other pupils to a rock concert. In March, when Donny began to talk endlessly on the phone with a girl named Miriam, Cal even let Miriam come to one of the tutoring sessions. Daisy was touched that Cal would grow so involved in Donny's life, but she was also a little hurt, because she had offered to have Miriam to dinner and Donny had refused. Now he asked them to drive her to Cal's house without a qualm.

This Miriam was an unappealing girl with blurry lipstick and masses of rough red hair. She wore a short, bulky jacket that would not have been out of place on a motorcycle. During the trip to Cal's she was silent, but coming back, she was more talkative. "What a neat guy, and what a house! All those kids hanging out, like a club. And the stereo playing rock . . . gosh, he's not like a grown–up at all! Married and divorced and everything, but you'd think he was our own age."

"Mr. Beadle was married?" Daisy asked.

"Yeah, to this really controlling lady. She didn't understand him a bit."

"No, I guess not," Daisy said.

Spring came, and the students who hung around at Cal's drifted out to the basketball net above the garage. Sometimes, when Daisy and Matt arrived to pick up Donny, they'd find him there with the others—spiky and excited, jittering on his toes beneath the backboard. It was staying light much longer now, and the neighboring fence cast narrow bars across the bright grass. Loud music would be spilling from Cal's windows. Once it was the Who, which Daisy recognized from the time that Donny had borrowed the album. "Teenage Wasteland," she said aloud, identifying the song, and Matt gave a short, dry laugh. "It certainly is," he said. He'd misunderstood; he thought she was commenting on the scene spread before them. In fact, she might have been. The players looked like hoodlums, even her son. Why, one of Cal's students had recently been knifed in a tavern. One had been shipped off to boarding school in midterm; two had been withdrawn by their parents. On the other hand, Donny had mentioned someone who'd been studying with Cal for five years. "Five years!" said Daisy. "Doesn't anyone ever stop needing him?"

Donny looked at her. Lately, whatever she said about Cal was read as criticism. "You're just feeling competitive," he said. "And controlling."

She bit her lip and said no more.

In April, the principal called to tell her that Donny had been expelled. There had been a locker check, and in Donny's locker they found five cans of beer and half a pack of cigarettes. With Donny's previous record, this offense meant expulsion.

Daisy gripped the receiver tightly and said, "Well, where is he now?"

"We've sent him home," said Mr. Lanham. "He's packed up all his belongings, and he's coming home on foot."

Daisy wondered what she would say to him. She felt him looming closer and closer, bringing this brand-new situation that no one had prepared her to handle. What other place would take him? Could they enter him in a public school? What were the rules? She stood at the living room window, waiting for him to show up. Gradually, she realized that he was taking too long. She checked the clock. She stared up the street again.

When an hour had passed, she phoned the school. Mr. Lanham's secretary answered and told her in a grave, sympathetic voice that yes, Donny Coble had most definitely gone home. Daisy called her husband. He was out of the office. She went back to the window and thought awhile, and then she called Donny's tutor.

"Donny's been expelled from school," she said, "and now I don't know where he's gone. I wonder if you've heard from him?"

There was a long silence. "Donny's with me, Mrs. Coble," he finally said.

"With you? How'd he get there?"

"He hailed a cab, and I paid the driver."

"Could I speak to him, please?"

There was another silence. "Maybe it'd be better if we had a conference," Cal said.

"I don't want a conference. I've been standing at the window picturing him dead or kidnapped or something, and now you tell me you want a—"

"Donny is very, very upset. Understandably so," said Cal. "Believe me, Mrs. Coble, this is not what it seems. Have you asked Donny's side of the story?"

"Well, of course not, how could I? He went running off to you instead."

"Because he didn't feel he'd be listened to."

"But I haven't even—"

"Why don't you come out and talk? The three of us," said Cal, "will try to get this thing in perspective."

"Well, all right," Daisy said. But she wasn't as reluctant as she sounded. Already, she felt soothed by the calm way Cal was taking this.

Cal answered the doorbell at once. He said, "Hi, there," and led her into the dining room. Donny sat slumped in a chair, chewing the knuckle of one thumb. "Hello, Donny," Daisy said. He flicked his eyes in her direction.

"Sit here, Mrs. Coble," said Cal, placing her opposite Donny. He himself remained standing, restlessly pacing. "So," he said.

Daisy stole a look at Donny. His lips were swollen, as if he'd been crying.

"You know," Cal told Daisy, "I kind of expected something like this. That's a very punitive school you've got him in—you realize that. And any half-decent lawyer will tell you they've violated his civil rights. Locker checks! Where's their search warrant?"

"But if the rule is—" Daisy said.

"Well, anyhow, let him tell you his side."

She looked at Donny. He said, "It wasn't my fault. I promise."

"They said your locker was full of beer."

"It was a put-up job! See, there's this guy that doesn't like me. He put all these beers in my locker and started a rumor going, so Mr. Lanham ordered a locker check."

"What was the boy's name?" Daisy asked.

"Huh?"

"Mrs. Coble, take my word, the situation is not so unusual," Cal said. "You can't imagine how vindictive kids can be sometimes."

"What was the boy's name," said Daisy, "so that I can ask Mr. Lanham if that's who suggested he run a locker check."

"You don't believe me," Donny said.

"And how'd this boy get your combination in the first place?"

"Frankly," said Cal, "I wouldn't be surprised to learn the school was in on it. Any kid that marches to a different drummer, why, they'd just love an excuse to get rid of him. The school is where I lay the blame."

"Doesn't Donny ever get blamed?"

"Now, Mrs. Coble, you heard what he—"

"Forget it," Donny told Cal. "You can see she doesn't trust me."

Daisy drew in a breath to say that of course she trusted him—a reflex. But she knew that bold-faced, wide-eyed look of Donny's. He had worn that look when he was small, denying some petty misdeed with the evidence plain as day all around him. Still, it was hard for her to accuse him outright. She temporized and said, "The only thing I'm sure of is that they've kicked you out of school, and now I don't know what we're going to do."

"We'll fight it," said Cal.

"We can't. Even you must see we can't."

"I could apply to Brantly," Donny said.

Cal stopped his pacing to beam down at him. "Brantly! Yes. They're really onto where a kid is coming from, at Brantly. Why, I could get you into Brantly. I work with a lot of their students."

Daisy had never heard of Brantly, but already she didn't like it. And she didn't like Cal's smile, which struck her now as feverish and avid—a smile of hunger.

On the fifteenth of April, they entered Donny in a public school, and they stopped his tutoring sessions. Donny fought both decisions bitterly. Cal, surprisingly enough, did not object. He admitted he'd made no headway with Donny and said it was because Donny was emotionally disturbed.

Donny went to his new school every morning, plodding off alone with his head down. He did his assignments, and he earned average grades, but he gathered no friends, joined no clubs. There was something exhausted and defeated about him.

The first week in June, during final exams, Donny vanished. He simply didn't come home one afternoon, and no one at school remembered seeing him. The police were reassuring, and for the first few days, they worked hard. They combed Donny's sad, messy room for clues; they visited Miriam and Cal.

But then they started talking about the number of kids who ran away every year. Hundreds, just in this city. "He'll show up, if he wants to," they said. "If he doesn't, he won't."

Evidently, Donny didn't want to.

It's been three months now and still no word. Matt and Daisy still look for him in every crowd of awkward, heartbreaking teenage boys. Every time the phone rings, they imagine it might be Donny. Both parents have aged. Donny's sister seems to be staying away from home as much as possible.

At night, Daisy lies awake and goes over Donny's life. She is trying to figure out what went wrong, where they made their first mistake. Often, she finds herself blaming Cal, although she knows he didn't begin it. Then at other times she excuses him, for without him, Donny might have left earlier. Who really knows? In the end, she can only sigh and search for a cooler spot on the pillow. As she falls asleep, she occasionally glimpses something in the corner of her vision. It's something fleet and round, a ball—a basketball. It flies up, it sinks through the hoop, descends, lands in a yard littered with last year's leaves and striped with bars of sunlight as white as bones, bleached and parched and cleanly picked.

Meaning

1. One or both of Donny's parents have to make several decisions during the story. Whose advice do they base their choices on? When do Donny's parents make their own decision?
2. At one point Daisy thinks, "The tutor had set down so many rules!" What is ironic about Cal setting down rules for Donny's parents?
3. During her last meeting with Cal, Daisy sees his smile as "feverish and avid—a smile of hunger." What do you think she means?
4. When Donny is expelled, Cal suggests that the school has betrayed Donny. In what way does Cal betray Donny?

Method

1. Reread the first paragraph of the story. What is the effect of beginning the story with this description of Donny? How does this description help to characterize Donny?
2. Explain the significance of the story's title.

3. Daisy is at odds with Donny, Cal, and Donny's school. All of these are *external conflicts,* or conflicts between the character and something or someone outside of the character. What *internal conflicts*—conflicts within herself—does Daisy experience? Are these conflicts ever resolved?
4. How would you describe Cal? What details in the story show Cal's true character?
5. Anne Tyler never tells the reader directly what Donny is thinking and feeling. How would the story be different if it were told from Donny's point of view?

Language: Description

Anne Tyler gives only brief descriptions of her characters in "Teenage Wasteland"; yet her precise language creates clear, meaningful images. For example, on page 207 she describes Cal as having a "brown handlebar mustache," "long and stringy" hair, "faded" jeans, and "wire-rimmed spectacles." What kind of picture do these words create in your mind? What does the description tell you about Cal, and how does it explain the appeal he has for his teenage students?

Give two additional examples from the story of descriptions that create a picture of a character as well as an impression of his or her personality. Point out specific words and phrases that contribute to the effectiveness of the descriptions.

Discussion and Composition

1. Whom, if anyone, do you hold responsible for Donny's expulsion from school? Do you think anyone is to blame for what happens to Donny at the end of the story? Explain.
2. Do you think that anyone—Donny's parents, his teachers, or Cal—might have done more to help Donny? If so, what might they have done differently?
3. Write a letter that Donny might write to his parents explaining why he has run away. Refer to specific events and details in the story, and have Donny tell how he feels about the things that have happened in his life. Use the style and tone that Donny would likely use in addressing his parents.

ROBERT CORMIER

(born 1925)

Robert Cormier has said of his childhood: "I was a skinny kid living in a ghetto type of neighborhood wanting the world to know I existed." Cormier was born into a large family in Leominster, Massachusetts, during the Depression. As a young boy, he found his "heroes" in the countless books he devoured at the library, and he aspired as early as the eighth grade to be a writer.

In 1948, Cormier began his writing career as a journalist, and his news stories earned him several awards. He published his first novel in 1960. With the success of his novel *The Chocolate War,* which was published in 1974, he was able to realize his dream of becoming a full-time fiction writer.

Cormier's novels and short stories have earned him numerous awards as well as a devoted readership of young adults. At the same time, several of his novels have provoked controversy because they present grim views of the world, depicting young people who struggle against powerful, negative forces in their environments. Like his novels, Cormier's short stories are often sobering; yet they also present a moving, realistic view of growing up. The following story is taken from Cormier's collection *Eight Plus One,* which was published in 1980.

THE MOUSTACHE

At the last minute Annie couldn't go. She was invaded by one of those twenty-four-hour flu bugs that sent her to bed with a fever, moaning about the fact that she'd also have to break her date with Handsome Harry Arnold that night. We call him Handsome Harry because he's actually handsome, but he's also a nice guy, cool, and he doesn't treat me like Annie's kid brother, which I am, but like a regular person. Anyway, I had to go to Lawnrest alone that afternoon. But first of all I had to stand inspection. My mother lined me up against the wall. She stood there like a one-man firing squad, which is kind of funny because she's not like a man at all, she's very feminine, and we have this relationship—I mean, I feel as if she really likes me. I realize that sounds strange, but I know guys whose mothers love them and cook special stuff for them and worry about them and all but there's something missing in their relationship.

Anyway. She frowned and started the routine.

"That hair," she said. Then admitted: "Well, at least you combed it."

I sighed. I have discovered that it's better to sigh than argue.

"And that moustache." She shook her head. "I still say a seventeen-year-old has no business wearing a moustache."

"It's an experiment," I said. "I just wanted to see if I could grow one." To tell the truth, I had proved my point about being able to grow a decent moustache, but I also had learned to like it.

"It's costing you money, Mike," she said.

"I know, I know."

The money was a reference to the movies. The Downtown Cinema has a special Friday night offer—half-price admission for high school couples, seventeen or younger. But the woman in the box office took one look at my moustache and charged me full price. Even when I showed her my driver's license. She charged full admission for Cindy's ticket, too, which left me practically broke and unable to take Cindy out for a hamburger with the crowd afterward. That didn't help matters, because Cindy has been getting impatient recently about things like the fact that I don't own my own car and have to concentrate on my studies if I want to win that college scholarship, for instance. Cindy wasn't exactly crazy about the moustache, either.

Now it was my mother's turn to sigh.

"Look," I said, to cheer her up. "I'm thinking about shaving it off." Even though I wasn't. Another discovery: You can build a way of life on postponement.

"Your grandmother probably won't even recognize you," she said. And I saw the shadow fall across her face.

Let me tell you what the visit to Lawnrest was all about. My grandmother is seventy-three years old. She is a resident—which is supposed to be a better word than *patient*—at the Lawnrest Nursing Home. She used to make the greatest turkey dressing in the world and was a nut about baseball and could even quote batting averages, for crying out loud. She always rooted for the losers. She was in love with the Mets until they started to win. Now she has arteriosclerosis, which the dictionary says is "a chronic disease characterized by abnormal thickening and hardening of the arterial walls." Which really means that she can't live at home anymore or even with us, and her memory has betrayed her as well as her body. She used to wander off and sometimes didn't recognize people. My mother visits her all the time, driving the thirty miles to Lawnrest almost every day. Because Annie was home for a semester break from college, we had decided to make a special Saturday visit. Now Annie was in bed, groaning theatrically—she's a drama major—but I told my mother I'd go, anyway. I hadn't seen my grandmother since she'd been admitted to Lawnrest. Besides, the place is located on the Southwest Turnpike, which meant I could barrel along in my father's new Le Mans. My ambition was to see the speedometer hit seventy-five. Ordinarily, I used the old station wagon, which can barely stagger up to fifty.

Frankly, I wasn't too crazy about visiting a nursing home. They reminded me of hospitals and hospitals turn me off. I mean, the smell of ether makes me nauseous, and I feel faint at the sight of blood. And as I approached Lawnrest—which is a terrible cemetery kind of name, to begin with—I was sorry I hadn't avoided the trip. Then I felt guilty about it. I'm loaded with guilt complexes. Like driving like a madman after promising my father to be careful. Like sitting in the parking lot, looking at the nursing home with dread and thinking how I'd rather be with Cindy. Then I thought of all the Christmas and birthday gifts my grandmother had given me and I got out of the car, guilty, as usual.

Inside, I was surprised by the lack of hospital smell, although there was another odor or maybe the absence of an odor. The air was antiseptic, sterile. As if there was no atmosphere at all or I'd caught a cold suddenly and couldn't taste or smell.

A nurse at the reception desk gave me directions—my grandmother was in East Three. I made my way down the tiled corridor and was glad to see that the walls were painted with cheerful colors like yellow and pink. A wheelchair suddenly shot around a corner, self-propelled by an old man, white-haired and toothless, who cackled merrily as he barely missed me. I jumped aside—here I was, almost getting wiped out by a two-mile-an-hour wheelchair after doing seventy-five on the pike. As I walked through the corridor seeking East Three, I couldn't help glancing into the rooms, and it was like some kind of wax museum—all these figures in various stances and attitudes, sitting in beds or chairs, standing at windows, as if they were frozen forever in these postures. To tell the truth, I began to hurry because I was getting depressed. Finally, I saw a beautiful girl approaching, dressed in white, a nurse or an attendant, and I was so happy to see someone young, someone walking and acting normally, that I gave her a wide smile and a big hello and I must have looked like a kind of nut. Anyway, she looked right through me as if I were a window, which is about par for the course whenever I meet beautiful girls.

I finally found the room and saw my grandmother in bed. My grandmother looks like Ethel Barrymore. I never knew who Ethel Barrymore was until I saw a terrific movie, *None But the Lonely Heart,* on TV, starring Ethel Barrymore and Cary Grant. Both my grandmother and Ethel Barrymore have these great craggy faces like the side of a mountain and wonderful voices like syrup being poured. Slowly. She was propped up in bed, pillows puffed behind her. Her hair had been combed out and fell upon her shoulders. For some reason, this flowing hair gave her an almost girlish appearance, despite its whiteness.

She saw me and smiled. Her eyes lit up and her eyebrows arched and she reached out her hands to me in greeting. "Mike, Mike," she said. And I breathed a sigh of relief. This was one of her good days. My mother had warned me that she might not know who I was at first.

I took her hands in mine. They were fragile. I could actually feel her bones, and it seemed as if they would break if I pressed too hard. Her skin was smooth, almost slippery, as if the years had worn away all the roughness the way the wind wears away the surfaces of stones.

"Mike, Mike, I didn't think you'd come," she said, so happy, and she was still Ethel Barrymore, that voice like a caress. "I've been waiting all this time." Before I could reply, she looked away, out the window. "See the birds? I've been watching them at the feeder. I love to see them come. Even the blue jays. The blue jays are like hawks—they take the food that the small birds should have. But the small birds, the chickadees, watch the blue jays and at least learn where the feeder is."

She lapsed into silence, and I looked out the window. There was no feeder. No birds. There was only the parking lot and the sun glinting on car windshields.

moaning sound and turned away on the bed, pulling the blankets around her.

I counted to twenty-five and then to fifty and did it all over again. I cleared my throat and coughed tentatively. She didn't move; she didn't respond. I wanted to say, "Nana, it's me." But I didn't. I thought of saying, "Meg, it's me." But I couldn't.

Finally I left. Just like that. I didn't say goodbye or anything. I stalked through the corridors, looking neither to the right nor the left, not caring whether that wild old man with the wheelchair ran me down or not.

On the Southwest Turnpike I did seventy-five—no, eighty—most of the way. I turned the radio up as loud as it could go. Rock music—anything to fill the air. When I got home, my mother was vacuuming the living-room rug. She shut off the cleaner, and the silence was deafening. "Well, how was your grandmother?" she asked.

I told her she was fine. I told her a lot of things. How great Nana looked and how she seemed happy and had called me Mike. I wanted to ask her—hey, Mom, you and Dad really love each other, don't you? I mean—there's nothing to forgive between you, is there? But I didn't.

Instead I went upstairs and took out the electric razor Annie had given me for Christmas and shaved off my moustache.

Meaning

1. At the beginning of the story, how does Mike feel about visiting his grandmother?
2. Whom does his grandmother mistake him for, and why?
3. Why does Mike grant his grandmother forgiveness instead of correcting her mistake? What does this decision reveal about his character?
4. How is Mike changed by his visit to the nursing home?
5. Why do you think Mike decides to shave off his moustache?

Method

1. As the title indicates, the narrator's moustache has a special significance in the story. What does the moustache *symbolize,* or represent?

2. An *epiphany* is a moment of illumination in a work of literature, usually involving a sudden realization on the part of the central character. What is the epiphany in "The Moustache"?

3. What is Mike's grandmother referring to when she asks for her husband's forgiveness? How does the author reveal this information?

4. What do you think is the *theme,* or underlying idea, of this story?

Language: Diction

Diction is a writer's choice and use of words. In "The Moustache," the author's diction includes the use of slang and informal expressions that help to make the narrator a convincing seventeen-year-old. For example, Mike says that his sister's boyfriend is "a nice guy, cool, and he doesn't treat me like Annie's kid brother."

Find other words and phrases in the story that help to characterize Mike as a teenage boy. Which of these expressions do you and your friends use?

Discussion and Composition

1. The relationship between younger and older generations is a recurring subject in literature. Discuss how some other stories you have read deal with this subject.

2. Do you think that your perceptions of older people, such as parents and grandparents, might change in ten years? Explain.

3. Study a photograph of an older person, and write a character sketch of the person as a teenager. First imagine how the person might have looked and acted as a youth. What kinds of interests, hobbies, dreams, and ambitions might he or she have had? Although the details of your sketch will be imaginary, you will want to make them specific and convincing to give your reader a clear impression of the person.

JOHN UPDIKE
(born 1932)

The stories of John Updike reveal a craftsman's attention to fine detail. His language has been compared to a newly minted coin. Every sentence is polished; his use of metaphor has been called brilliant and inventive.

Updike's fiction is usually set in small towns similar to Shillington, Pennsylvania, where he was born. He was an only child. His father was a high school teacher. Updike graduated from Harvard University summa cum laude and studied for a year in Oxford, England. After his return to America in 1955, he worked as a staff writer on *The New Yorker* magazine, which had published several of his pieces while he was still at Harvard.

Updike is no longer on *The New Yorker* staff although he still contributes his writing to the magazine, which seems to suit his ornately figurative, witty style. Since he was twenty-five, Updike has supported himself and his family with his prolific production of novels, short stories, poetry, and articles. His first book of short stories, *The Same Door,* was published in 1959. *Rabbit, Run* (1960), the story of an irresponsible husband who tries to escape from a life he finds boring, is considered his best novel. Many of Updike's stories, especially those about young people, contain elements of his own boyhood. He lives on Cape Cod in Massachusetts.

THE LUCID EYE
IN SILVER TOWN

The first time I visited New York City, I was thirteen and went with my father. I went to meet my Uncle Quin and to buy a book about Vermeer.[1] The Vermeer book was my idea, and my mother's; meeting Uncle Quin was my father's. A generation ago, my uncle

---

1. **Vermeer** (vər•mâr′): Jan (1632–1675), a Dutch painter who gave subtle significance to ordinary subjects by his skillful use of color and light.

had vanished in the direction of Chicago and become, apparently, rich; in the last week he had come east on business and I had graduated from the eighth grade with perfect marks. My father claimed that I and his brother were the smartest people he had ever met—"go-getters," he called us, with perhaps more irony than at the time I gave him credit for—and in his visionary way he suddenly, irresistibly, felt that now was the time for us to meet. New York in those days was seven dollars away; we measured everything, distance and time, in money then. World War II was almost over but we were still living in the Depression. My father and I set off with the return tickets and a five-dollar bill in his pocket. The five dollars was for the book.

My mother, on the railway platform, suddenly exclaimed, "I *hate* the Augusts." This surprised me, because we were all Augusts—I was an August, my father was an August, Uncle Quincy was an August, and she, I had thought, was an August.

My father gazed serenely over her head and said, "You have every reason to. I wouldn't blame you if you took a gun and shot us all. Except for Quin and your son. They're the only ones of us ever had any get up and git." Nothing was more infuriating about my father than his way of agreeing.

Uncle Quin didn't meet us at Pennsylvania Station. If my father was disappointed, he didn't reveal it to me. It was after one o'clock and all we had for lunch were two candy bars. By walking what seemed to me a very long way on pavements only a little broader than those of my home town, and not so clean, we reached the hotel, which seemed to sprout somehow from Grand Central Station. The lobby smelled of perfume. After the clerk had phoned Quincy August that a man who said he was his brother was at the desk, an elevator took us to the twentieth floor. Inside the room sat three men, each in a gray or blue suit with freshly pressed pants and garters peeping from under the cuffs when they crossed their legs. The men were not quite interchangeable. One had a caterpillar-shaped mustache, one had tangled blond eyebrows like my father's, and the third had a drink in his hand—the others had drinks, too, but were not gripping them so tightly.

"Gentlemen, I'd like you to meet my brother Marty and his young son," Uncle Quin said.

"The kid's name is Jay," my father added, shaking hands with each of the two men, staring them in the eye. I imitated my father, and the mustached man, not expecting my firm handshake and stare, said, "Why, hello there, Jay!"

"Marty, would you and the boy like to freshen up? The facilities are through the door and to the left."

"Thank you, Quin. I believe we will. Excuse me, gentlemen."

"Certainly."

"Certainly."

My father and I went into the bedroom of the suite. The furniture was square and new and all the same shade of maroon. On the bed was an opened suitcase, also new. The clean, expensive smells of leather and lotion were beautiful to me. Uncle Quin's underwear looked silk and was full of fleurs-de-lis.[2] When I was through in the lavatory, I made for the living room, to rejoin Uncle Quin and his friends.

"Hold it," my father said. "Let's wait in here."

"Won't that look rude?"

"No. It's what Quin wants."

"Now Daddy, don't be ridiculous. He'll think we've died in here."

"No he won't, not my brother. He's working some deal. He doesn't want to be bothered. I know how my brother works: he got us in here so we'd stay in here."

"*Really*, Pop. You're such a schemer." But I did not want to go in there without him. I looked around the room for something to read. There was nothing, not even a newspaper, except a shiny little pamphlet about the hotel itself. I wondered when we would get a chance to look for the Vermeer book. I wondered what the men in the next room were talking about. I wondered why Uncle Quin was so short, when my father was so tall. By leaning out of the window, I could see taxicabs maneuvering like windup toys.

My father came and stood beside me. "Don't lean out too far."

I edged out inches farther and took a big bite of the high cold air, spiced by the distant street noises. "Look at the green cab cut in front of the yellow," I said. "Should they be making U-turns on that street?"

"In New York it's OK. Survival of the fittest is the only law here."

---

2. fleurs-de-lis (floor′də•lē′): a design of three petals resembling an iris, bound together at the base; once the coat of arms of the French royal family.

"Isn't that the Chrysler Building?"

"Yes, isn't it graceful though? It always reminds me of the queen of the chessboard."

"What's the one beside it?"

"I don't know. Some big gravestone. The one deep in back, from this window, is the Woolworth Building. For years it was the tallest building in the world."

As, side by side at the window, we talked, I was surprised that my father could answer so many of my questions. As a young man, before I was born, he had traveled, looking for work; this was not *his* first trip to New York. Excited by my new respect, I longed to say something to remold that calm, beaten face.

"Do you really think he meant for us to stay out here?" I asked.

"Quin is a go-getter," he said, gazing over my head. "I admire him. Anything he wanted, from little on up, he went after it. Slam. Bang. His thinking is miles ahead of mine—just like your mother's. You can feel them pull ahead of you." He moved his hands, palms down, like two taxis, the left quickly pulling ahead of the right. "You're the same way."

"Sure, sure." My impatience was not merely embarrassment at being praised; I was irritated that he considered Uncle Quin as smart as myself. At that point in my life I was sure that only stupid people took an interest in money.

When Uncle Quin finally entered the bedroom, he said, "Martin, I hoped you and the boy would come out and join us."

"Hell, I didn't want to butt in. You and those men were talking business."

"Lucas and Roebuck and I? Now, Marty, it was nothing that my own brother couldn't hear. Just a minor matter of adjustment. Both these men are fine men. Very important in their own fields. I'm disappointed that you couldn't see more of them. Believe me, I hadn't meant for you to hide in here. Now what kind of drink would you like?"

"I don't care. I drink very little any more."

"Scotch and water, Marty?"

"Swell."

"And the boy? What about some ginger ale, young man? Or would you like milk?"

"The ginger ale," I said.

As I remember it, a waiter brought the drinks to the room, and while we were drinking them I asked if we were going to spend all afternoon in this room. Uncle Quin didn't seem to hear, but five minutes later he suggested that the boy might like to take a look around the city—Gotham, he called it. Baghdad-on-the-Subway. My father said that that would be a once-in-a-lifetime treat for the kid. He always called me "the kid" when I was sick or had lost at something or was angry—when he felt sorry for me, in short. The three of us went down in the elevator and took a taxi ride down Broadway, or up Broadway—I wasn't sure. "This is what they call the Great White Way," Uncle Quin said several times. Once he apologized, "In the daytime it's just another street." The trip didn't seem so much designed for sightseeing as for getting Uncle Quin to the Pickernut Club, a little restaurant set in a block of similar canopied places. I remember we stepped down into it and it was dark inside. A piano was playing "There's a Small Hotel."

"He shouldn't do that," Uncle Quin said. Then he waved to the man behind the piano. "How are you, Freddie? How are the kids?"

"Fine, Mr. August, fine," Freddie said, bobbing his head and smiling and not missing a note.

"That's Quin's song," my father said to me as we wriggled our way into a dark curved seat at a round table.

I didn't say anything, but Uncle Quin, overhearing some disapproval in my silence, said, "Freddie's a first-rate man. He has a boy going to Colgate[3] this autumn."

I asked, "Is that really your song?"

Uncle Quin grinned and put his warm broad hand on my shoulder; I hated, at that age, being touched. "I let them think it is," he said, oddly purring. "To me, songs are like young girls. They're all pretty."

A waiter in a red coat scurried up. "Mr. August! Back from the West? How are you, Mr. August?"

"Getting by, Jerome, getting by. Jerome, I'd like you to meet my kid brother, Martin."

"How do you do, Mr. Martin. Are you paying New York a visit? Or do you live here?"

My father quickly shook hands with Jerome, somewhat to Jerome's surprise. "I'm just up for the afternoon, thank you. I live in a hick town in Pennsylvania you never heard of."

"I see, sir. A quick visit."

3. **Colgate:** a university in Hamilton, New York, established in 1819.

"This is the first time in six years that I've had a chance to see my brother."

"Yes, we've seen very little of him these past years. He's a man we can never see too much of, isn't that right?"

Uncle Quin interrupted. "This is my nephew Jay."

"How do you like the big city, Jay?"

"Fine." I didn't duplicate my father's mistake of offering to shake hands.

"Why, Jerome," Uncle Quin said. "My brother and I would like to have a Scotch-on-the-rocks. The boy would like a ginger ale."

"No, wait," I said. "What kinds of ice cream do you have?"

"Vanilla and chocolate, sir."

I hesitated. I could scarcely believe it, when the cheap drugstore at home had fifteen flavors.

"I'm afraid it's not a very big selection," Jerome said.

"I guess vanilla."

"Yes, sir. One plate of vanilla."

When my ice cream came it was a golf ball in a flat silver dish; it kept spinning away as I dug at it with my spoon. Uncle Quin watched me and asked, "Is there anything especially you'd like to do?"

"The kid'd like to get into a bookstore," my father said.

"A bookstore. What sort of book, Jay?"

I said, "I'd like to look for a good book of Vermeer."

"Vermeer," Uncle Quin pronounced slowly, relishing the r's, pretending to give the matter thought. "Dutch School."

"He's Dutch, yes."

"For my own money, Jay, the French are the people to beat. We have four Degas[4] ballet dancers in our living room in Chicago, and I could sit and look at one of them for hours. I think it's wonderful, the feeling for balance the man had."

"Yeah, but don't Degas's paintings always remind you of colored drawings? For actually *looking* at things in terms of paint, for the lucid eye, I think Vermeer makes Degas look sick."

Uncle Quin said nothing, and my father, after an anxious glance across the table, said, "That's the way he and his mother talk all the time. It's all beyond me. I can't understand a thing they say."

"Your mother is encouraging you to be a painter, is she, Jay?"

4. **Degas** (dəˑgöʹ): Edgar (1834–1917), a French impressionist painter.

Uncle Quin's smile was very wide and his cheeks were pushed out as if each held a candy.

"Sure, I suppose she is."

"Your mother is a very wonderful woman, Jay," Uncle Quin said.

It was such an embarrassing remark, and so much depended upon your definition of "wonderful," that I dug at my ice cream, and my father asked Uncle Quin about his own wife, Tessie. When we left, Uncle Quin signed the check with his name and the name of some company. It was close to five o'clock.

My uncle didn't know much about the location of bookstores in New York—his last fifteen years had been spent in Chicago—but he thought that if we went to Forty-second Street and Sixth Avenue we should find something. The cab driver let us out beside a park that acted as kind of a backyard for the Public Library. It looked so inviting, so agreeably dusty, with the pigeons and the men nodding on the benches and the office girls in their taut summer dresses, that without thinking, I led the two men into it. Shimmering buildings arrowed upward and glinted through the treetops. This was New York, I felt: the silver town. Towers of ambition rose, crystalline, within me. "If you stand here," my father said, "you can see the Empire State." I went and stood beneath my father's arm and followed with my eyes the direction of it. Something sharp and hard fell into my right eye. I ducked my head and blinked; it was painful.

"What's the trouble?" Uncle Quin's voice asked.

My father said, "The poor kid's got something into his eye. He has the worst luck that way of anybody I ever knew."

The thing seemed to have life. It bit. "Ow," I said, angry enough to cry.

"If we can get him out of the wind," my father's voice said, "maybe I can see it."

"No, now, Marty, use your head. Never fool with the eyes or ears. The hotel is within two blocks. Can you walk two blocks, Jay?"

"I'm blind, not lame," I snapped.

"He has a ready wit," Uncle Quin said.

Between the two men, shielding my eye with a hand, I walked to the hotel. From time to time, one of them would take my other hand, or put one of theirs on my shoulder, but I would walk faster, and the hands would drop away. I hoped our entrance into the hotel lobby would not be too conspicuous; I took my hand from my eye and walked erect, defying the impulse to stoop. Except for the one lid being shut and possibly my face being red, I imagined I looked passably suave. However, my guardians lost no time betraying me. Not only did they walk at my heels, as if I might topple any instant, but my father told one old bum sitting in the lobby, "Poor kid got something in his eye," and Uncle Quin passing the desk called, "Send up a doctor to Twenty-eleven."

"You shouldn't have done that, Quin," my father said in the elevator. "I can get it out, now that he's out of the wind. This is happening all the time. The kid's eyes are too far front."

"Never fool with the eyes, Martin. They are your most precious tool in life."

"It'll work out," I said, though I didn't believe it would. It felt like a steel chip, deeply embedded.

Up in the room, Uncle Quin made me lie down on the bed. My father, a clean handkerchief wadded in his hand so that one corner stuck out, approached me, but it hurt so much to open the eye that I repulsed him. "Don't torment me," I said twisting my face away. "What good does it do? The doctor'll be up."

Regretfully my father put the handkerchief back into his pocket.

The doctor was a soft-handed man with little to say to anybody; he wasn't pretending to be the family doctor. He rolled my lower eyelid on a thin stick, jabbed with a Q-tip, and showed me, on the end of the Q-tip, an eyelash. He dropped three drops of yellow fluid into the eye to remove any chance of infection. The fluid stung, and I shut my eyes, leaning back into the pillow, glad it was over. When I opened them, my father was passing a bill into the doctor's hand. The doctor thanked him, winked at me, and left. Uncle Quin came out of the bathroom.

"Well, young man, how are you feeling now?" he asked.

"Fine."

"It was just an eyelash," my father said.

"*Just* an eyelash! Well I know how an eyelash can feel like a razor blade in there. But now that the young invalid is recovered, we can think of dinner."

"No, I really appreciate your kindness, Quin, but we must be getting back to the sticks. I have an eight-o'clock meeting I should be at."

"I'm extremely sorry to hear that. What sort of meeting, Marty?"

"A church council."

"So you're still doing church work. Well, God bless you for it."

"Grace wanted me to ask you if you couldn't possibly come over some day. We'll put you up overnight. It would be a real treat for her to see you again."

Uncle Quin reached up and put his arm around his younger brother's shoulders. "Martin, I'd like that better than anything in the world. But I am solid with appointments, and I must head west this Thursday. They don't let me have a minute's repose. Nothing would please my heart better than to share a quiet day with you and Grace in your home. Please give her my love, and tell her what a wonderful boy she is raising. The two of you are raising."

My father promised, "I'll do that." And, after a little more fuss, we left.

"The child better?" the old man in the lobby called to us on the way out.

"It was just an eyelash, thank you, sir," my father said.

When we got outside, I wondered if there were any bookstores still open.

"We have no money."

"None at all?"

"The doctor charged five dollars. That's how much it costs in New York to get something in your eye."

"I didn't do it on purpose. Do you think I pulled out the eyelash and stuck it in there myself? I didn't tell you to call the doctor."

"I know that."

"Couldn't we just go into a bookstore and look a minute?"

"We haven't time, Jay."

But when we reached Pennsylvania Station, it was over thirty minutes until the next train left. As we sat on a bench, my father smiled reminiscently. "Boy, he's smart, isn't he? His thinking is sixty light-years ahead of mine."

"Whose?"

"My brother. Notice the way he hid in the bathroom until the doctor was gone? That's how to make money. The rich man collects dollar bills like the stamp collector collects stamps. I knew he'd do it. I knew it when he told the clerk to send up a doctor that I'd have to pay for it."

"Well, why *should* he pay for it? *You* were the person to pay for it."

"That's right. Why should he?" My father settled back, his eyes forward, his hands crossed and limp in his lap. The skin beneath his chin was loose; his temples seemed concave. The liquor was probably disagreeing with him. "That's why he's where he is now, and that's why I am where I am."

The seed of my anger seemed to be a desire to recall him to himself, to scold him out of being old and tired. "Well, why'd you bring along only five dollars? You might have known something would happen."

"You're right, Jay. I should have brought more."

"Look. Right over there is an open bookstore. Now if you had brought *ten* dollars—"

"Is it open? I don't think so. They just left the lights in the window on."

"What if it isn't? What does it matter to us? Anyway, what kind of art book can you get for five dollars? Color plates cost money. How much do you think a decent book of Vermeer costs? It'd be cheap at fifteen dollars, even secondhand, with the pages all crummy and full of spilled coffee." I kept on, shrilly flailing the passive and infuriating figure of my father, until we left the city. Once we were on the homeward train, my tantrum ended; it had been a kind of ritual, for both of us, and he had endured my screams complacently, nodding assent, like a midwife assisting at the birth of family pride. Years passed before I needed to go to New York again.

Meaning

1. What do you learn about each of Jay's parents in the first two paragraphs of this story? What sort of boy is Jay?

2. In what way does Uncle Quin fit the image of a successful man? Where is there evidence that, in spite of success, Uncle Quin lacks character?

3. One minute Jay says that he didn't duplicate his father's mistake of offering to shake hands with Jerome. The next minute he is astounded that the Pickernut Club has only two flavors of ice cream, when the cheap drugstore at home has fifteen flavors. What does each reaction tell you about the boy?

4. What thoughts were running through Jay's mind just before he became temporarily blinded? What meaning would you attach to this incident? Give specific reasons for your answer.

Method

1. Explain the significance of the title. Who actually possesses the "lucid eye in silver town" at the time these three people meet?
2. How is the character of the father developed in the story? Does your opinion of the father change or remain the same?
3. What are the conflicts in the story?

Language: The Use of Allusions

An *allusion* is a reference to some person, place, or thing, usually from history or literature, that will give new meaning to a present topic. For example, if someone calls you Scrooge, you had better check your attitude toward money. If someone alludes to you as Cleopatra, it probably means that you are attractive.

In "The Lucid Eye in Silver Town," Uncle Quin calls New York "Gotham" and "Baghdad-on-the-Subway." Gotham was the name of an English village noted in legend for the "foolish" behavior of its inhabitants. In order to keep King John from building a castle there with its high cost to them, they deliberately pretended to be stupid when the royal messengers arrived. As used to designate New York, the word has come to mean "a place of fools."

Baghdad was O. Henry's synonym for Manhattan. Often in his stories he compared New York to the fabulous city of Baghdad, made famous in the tales of *The Arabian Nights*.

Team up with a group of your classmates, and have each member of your group research the story behind one of the following people. What are the person's striking characteristics or famous deeds? Share the information you find; then, for each of the people you have researched, explain what an allusion to that person would mean.

1. Helen of Troy
2. Einstein
3. Nero
4. Rip Van Winkle
5. Marie Curie
6. Lot's Wife

Discussion and Composition

1. What is your idea of a successful adult? Discuss the personal qualities and achievements that would mean success to you as an adult in our society.
2. Both "My Oedipus Complex" and "The Lucid Eye in Silver Town" are narrated in the first person, from the point of view of a

young boy. Compare and contrast the impression that each boy has of his father. What traits does each boy feel his father lacks? When, if at all, does each boy come to understand his father? Base your analysis on specific incidents from the story.

3. For centuries, people have discussed whether it is better to live in a big city, a small town, or the country. Write an essay discussing where you would prefer to live. As a prewriting activity, you might list the advantages of living in the place you have chosen; then list the disadvantages. Consider why the advantages outweigh the disadvantages.

KURT VONNEGUT
(born 1922)

His protests of war, environmental pollution, and dehumaniz-
ing occupations have made Kurt Vonnegut one of the most provoc-
ative writers of the twentieth century. Vonnegut was born in
Indianapolis, Indiana, the son of an architect who lost most of his
wealth during the Depression. Urged by his father to study
"something useful," Vonnegut majored in chemistry and biology at
Cornell University. In 1943, he enlisted in the army and was captured
a year later at the Battle of the Bulge. Imprisoned in Dresden, he was
one of the few who survived the Allied fire-bombing.

Returning to the United States in 1945, Vonnegut studied an-
thropology at the University of Chicago. In the late 1940s he did
public relations work at a large corporation in New York. In 1950,
his first story, "Report on the Barnhouse Effect," was published. The
following year he moved to Cape Cod, Massachusetts, where he
taught English, wrote advertising, and sold cars to support his family
until he was able to make enough money to spend all of his time
writing.

Vonnegut's first novel, *Player Piano* (1952), satirizes automa-
tion. His most innovative and best known work is *Slaughterhouse
Five*, which is based on his experiences in Dresden.

In addition to novels and short stories, Vonnegut has written
several plays and many articles. His work often contains elements of
fantasy, especially science fiction. Unlike much of Vonnegut's work,
"Tom Edison's Shaggy Dog" is not a pessimistic satire, but an example of the author's lighter, more humorous stories.

TOM EDISON'S SHAGGY DOG

Two old men sat on a park bench one morning in the sunshine
of Tampa, Florida—one trying doggedly to read a book he was
plainly enjoying while the other, Harold K. Bullard, told him the
story of his life in the full, round, head tones of a public address
system. At their feet lay Bullard's Labrador retriever, who further

tormented the aged listener by probing his ankles with a large, wet nose.

Bullard, who had been, before he retired, successful in many fields, enjoyed reviewing his important past. But he faced the problem that complicates the lives of cannibals—namely: that a single victim cannot be used over and over. Anyone who had passed the time of day with him and his dog refused to share a bench with them again.

So Bullard and his dog set out through the park each day in quest of new faces. They had had good luck this morning, for they had found this stranger right away, clearly a new arrival in Florida, still buttoned up tight in heavy serge, stiff collar and necktie, and with nothing better to do than read.

"Yes," said Bullard, rounding out the first hour of his lecture, "made and lost five fortunes in my time."

"So you said," said the stranger, whose name Bullard had neglected to ask. "Easy, boy. No, no, no, boy," he said to the dog, who was growing more aggressive toward his ankles.

"Oh? Already told you that, did I?" said Bullard.

"Twice."

"Two in real estate, one in scrap iron, and one in oil and one in trucking."

"So you said."

"I did? Yes, guess I did. Two in real estate, one in scrap iron, one in oil, and one in trucking. Wouldn't take back a day of it."

"No, I suppose not," said the stranger. "Pardon me, but do you suppose you could move your dog somewhere else? He keeps—"

"Him?" said Bullard, heartily. "Friendliest dog in the world. Don't need to be afraid of him."

"I'm not afraid of him. It's just that he drives me crazy, sniffing at my ankles."

"Plastic," said Bullard, chuckling.

"What?"

"Plastic. Must be something plastic on your garters. By golly, I'll bet it's those little buttons. Sure as we're sitting here, those buttons must be plastic. That dog is nuts about plastic. Don't know why that is, but he'll sniff it out and find it if there's a speck around. Must be a deficiency in his diet, though, by gosh, he eats better than I do. Once he chewed up a whole plastic humidor.[1] Can you beat it? *That's* the

1. **humidor** (hū′mə·dôr): a box for keeping tobacco moist.

240   *Kurt Vonnegut*

business I'd go into now, by glory, if the pill rollers hadn't told me to let up, to give the old ticker a rest."

"You could tie the dog to that tree over there," said the stranger.

"I get so darn' sore at all the youngsters these days!" said Bullard. "All of 'em mooning around about no frontiers any more. There never have been so many frontiers as there are today. You know what Horace Greeley[2] would say today?"

"His nose is wet," said the stranger, and he pulled his ankles away, but the dog humped forward in patient pursuit. "Stop it, boy!"

"His wet nose shows he's healthy," said Bullard. " 'Go plastic, young man!' That's what Greeley'd say. 'Go atom, young man!' "

The dog had definitely located the plastic buttons on the stranger's garters and was cocking his head one way and another, thinking out ways of bringing his teeth to bear on those delicacies.

"Scat!" said the stranger.

" 'Go electronic, young man!' " said Bullard. "Don't talk to me about no opportunity any more. Opportunity's knocking down every door in the country, trying to get in. When I was young, a man had to go out and find opportunity and drag it home by the ears. Nowadays—"

"Sorry," said the stranger, evenly. He slammed his book shut, stood and jerked his ankle away from the dog. "I've got to be on my way. So good day, sir."

He stalked across the park, found another bench, sat down with a sigh and began to read. His respiration had just returned to normal, when he felt the wet sponge of the dog's nose on his ankles again.

"Oh—it's you!" said Bullard, sitting down beside him. "He was tracking you. He was on the scent of something, and I just let him have his head. What'd I tell you about plastic?" He looked about contentedly. "Don't blame you for moving on. It was stuffy back there. No shade to speak of and not a sign of a breeze."

"Would the dog go away if I bought him a humidor?" said the stranger.

"Pretty good joke, pretty good joke," said Bullard, amiably. Suddenly he clapped the stranger on his knee. "Sa-ay, you aren't in plastics are you? Here I've been blowing off about plastics, and for all I know that's your line."

2. **Horace Greeley:** American newspaper editor (1811–1872) whose advice was "Go West, young man."

"My line?" said the stranger crisply, laying down his book. "Sorry—I've never had a line. I've been a drifter since the age of nine, since Edison set up his laboratory next to my home, and showed me the intelligence analyzer."

"Edison?" said Bullard. "Thomas Edison, the inventor?"

"If you want to call him that, go ahead," said the stranger.

"If I *want* to call him that?"—Bullard guffawed—"I guess I just will! Father of the light bulb and I don't know what all."

"If you want to think he invented the light bulb, go ahead. No harm in it." The stranger resumed his reading.

"Say, what is this?" said Bullard, suspiciously. "You pulling my leg? What's this about an intelligence analyzer? I never heard of that."

"Of course you haven't," said the stranger. "Mr. Edison and I promised to keep it a secret. I've never told anyone. Mr. Edison broke his promise and told Henry Ford, but Ford made him promise not to tell anybody else—for the good of humanity."

Bullard was entranced. "Uh, this intelligence analyzer," he said, "it analyzed intelligence, did it?"

"It was an electric butter churn," said the stranger.

"Seriously now," Bullard coaxed.

"Maybe it *would* be better to talk it over with someone," said the stranger. "It's a terrible thing to keep bottled up inside me, year in and year out. But how can I be sure that it won't go any further?"

"My word as a gentleman," Bullard assured him.

"I don't suppose I could find a stronger guarantee than that, could I?" said the stranger, judiciously.

"There is no stronger guarantee," said Bullard, proudly. "Cross my heart and hope to die!"

"Very well." The stranger leaned back and closed his eyes, seeming to travel backward through time. He was silent for a full minute, during which Bullard watched with respect.

"It was back in the fall of eighteen seventy-nine," said the stranger at last, softly. "Back in the village of Menlo Park, New Jersey. I was a boy of nine. A young man we all thought was a wizard had set up a laboratory next door to my home, and there were flashes and crashes inside, and all sorts of scary goings on. The neighborhood children were warned to keep away, not to make any noise that would bother the wizard.

"I didn't get to know Edison right off, but his dog Sparky and I got to be steady pals. A dog a whole lot like yours, Sparky was, and we used to wrestle all over the neighborhood. Yes, sir, your dog is the image of Sparky."

"Is that so?" said Bullard, flattered.

"Gospel," replied the stranger. "Well, one day Sparky and I were wrestling around, and we wrestled right up to the door of Edison's laboratory. The next thing I knew, Sparky had pushed me in through the door, and bam! I was sitting on the laboratory floor, looking up at Mr. Edison himself."

"Bet he was sore," said Bullard, delighted.

"You can bet I was scared," said the stranger. "I thought I was face to face with Satan himself. Edison had wires hooked to his ears and running down to a little black box in his lap! I started to scoot, but he caught me by my collar and made me sit down.

" 'Boy,' said Edison, 'it's always darkest before the dawn. I want you to remember that.'

" 'Yes, sir,' I said.

" 'For over a year, my boy,' Edison said to me, 'I've been trying to find a filament that will last in an incandescent lamp. Hair, string, splinters—nothing works. So while I was trying to think of something else to try, I started tinkering with another idea of mine, just letting off steam. I put this together,' he said, showing me the little black box. 'I thought maybe intelligence was just a certain kind of electricity, so I made this intelligence analyzer here. It works! You're the first one to know about it, my boy. But I don't know why you shouldn't be. It will be your generation that will grow up in the glorious new era when people will be as easily graded as oranges.' "

"I don't believe it!" said Bullard.

"May I be struck by lightning this very instant!" said the stranger. "And it did work, too. Edison had tried out the analyzer on the men in his shop, without telling them what he was up to. The smarter a man was, by gosh, the farther the needle on the indicator in the little black box swung to the right. I let him try it on me, and the needle just lay where it was and trembled. But dumb as I was, then is when I made my one and only contribution to the world. As I say, I haven't lifted a finger since."

"Whadja do?" said Bullard, eagerly.

"I said, 'Mr. Edison, sir, let's try it on the dog.' And I wish you could have seen the show that dog put on when I said it! Old Sparky barked and howled and scratched to get out. When he saw we meant business, that he wasn't going to get out, he made a beeline right for the intelligence analyzer and knocked it out of Edison's hands. But we cornered him, and Edison held him down while I touched the wires to his ears. And would you believe it, that needle sailed clear across the dial, way past a little red pencil mark on the dial face!"

"The dog busted it," said Bullard.

" 'Mr. Edison, sir,' I said, 'what's that red mark mean?' " 'My boy,' said Edison, 'it means that the instrument is broken, because that red mark is me.' "

"I'll say it was broken" said Bullard.

The stranger said gravely. "But it wasn't broken. No, sir. Edison checked the whole thing, and it was in apple-pie order. When Edison told me that, it was then that Sparky, crazy to get out, gave himself away."

"How?" said Bullard, suspiciously.

"We really had him locked in, see? There were three locks on the door—a hook and eye, a bolt, and a regular knob and latch. That dog stood up, unhooked the hook, pushed the bolt back and had the knob in his teeth when Edison stopped him."

"No!" said Bullard.

"Yes!" said the stranger, his eyes shining. "And then is when Edison showed me what a great scientist he was. He was willing to face the truth, no matter how unpleasant it might be.

" 'So!' said Edison to Sparky, 'Man's best friend, huh? Dumb animal, huh?'

"That Sparky was a caution. He pretended not to hear. He scratched himself and bit fleas and went around growling at ratholes—anything to get out of looking Edison in the eye.

" 'Pretty soft, isn't it, Sparky?' said Edison. 'Let somebody else worry about getting food, building shelters and keeping warm, while you sleep in front of a fire or go chasing after the girls or raise hell with the boys. No mortgages, no politics, no war, no work, no worry. Just wag the old tail or lick a hand, and you're all taken care of.'

" 'Mr. Edison,' I said, 'do you mean to tell me that dogs are smarter than people?'

" 'Smarter?' said Edison. 'I'll tell the world! And what have I been doing for the past year? Slaving to work out a light bulb so dogs can play at night!'

" 'Look, Mr. Edison,' said Sparky, 'why not—' "

"Hold on!" roared Bullard.

"Silence!" shouted the stranger, triumphantly. " 'Look, Mr.

Edison,' said Sparky, 'why not keep quiet about this? It's been working out to everybody's satisfaction for hundreds of thousands of years. Let sleeping dogs lie. You forget all about it, destroy the intelligence analyzer, and I'll tell you what to use for a lamp filament.' "

"Hogwash!" said Bullard, his face purple.

The stranger stood. "You have my solemn word as a gentleman. That dog rewarded *me* for my silence with a stock-market tip that made me independently wealthy for the rest of my days. And the last words that Sparky ever spoke were to Thomas Edison. 'Try a piece of carbonized cotton thread,' he said. Later, he was torn to bits by a pack of dogs that had gathered outside the door, listening."

The stranger removed his garters and handed them to Bullard's dog. "A small token of esteem, sir, for an ancestor of yours who talked himself to death. Good day." He tucked his book under his arm and walked away.

Meaning

1. A *shaggy dog story* is an anecdote that has a surprise ending (not always involving a dog) and containing humorously unreal behavior. How does "Tom Edison's Shaggy Dog" fit this definition?
2. Do you think the story is humorous? Why or why not?
3. What happened to Sparky? What was the source of the stranger's wealth?
4. Why does the stranger tell the story? How is the point of the story related to the conflict between Bullard and the stranger?

Method

1. At what point in the story does Bullard realize that he is being fooled? At what point do you realize that the stranger has made up the story to get even with Bullard?
2. "Tom Edison's Shaggy Dog" tells of two meetings between Bullard and a newcomer to Florida. How does the author convey the impression that Bullard is in control of the situation during the first encounter? How do you know that the roles of tormentor and victim have been reversed in the second encounter?
3. Point out some examples of ironic dialogue in the story.
4. Why are you told so little about the stranger, not even his name? Describe his character as it is revealed in the story.

Language: Repetition for Effect

Although repetition is more common in poetry than it is in prose, a short story writer may repeat words and phrases to achieve a particular effect. In "Tom Edison's Shaggy Dog," repetition is used to characterize Bullard. In the first conversation between Bullard and the stranger, notice that Bullard repeats, sometimes with slight variation, almost everything he says. Find the places in the story where Bullard repeats the following words and phrases:

"plastic"
"go"
"opportunity"
"Two in real estate, one in scrap iron, one in oil, and one in trucking"

How do these words help to characterize him? What is ironic about his repetition of the words *go* and *opportunity*?

Later, as the stranger tells his story to Bullard, the phrase "My word as a gentleman" is repeated. Why is this ironic?

Discussion and Composition

1. Discuss how our ideas of humor change as we get older. Begin by considering jokes that you found humorous when you were younger. If you have forgotten, ask children who are approximately five, eight, and twelve what they consider to be funny.

2. Write a story about a funny incident that has happened to you. Use dialogue to help your readers know the characters in your story. You should also use specific details to help your reader visualize the situation you are writing about. You might begin your essay with a paragraph that establishes the setting of your story.

3. In a paragraph, argue either for or against the stranger's treatment of Bullard. Begin your paragraph with a topic sentence stating your position. Then give at least two good reasons why the stranger is (or is not) justified in acting as he does.

LUIGI PIRANDELLO
(1867–1936)

His innovative ideas as a writer of plays brought fame to Luigi Pirandello when he was in his mid-fifties. His unique use of the "play within a play" allowed an unusual dialogue of ideas between characters and playwright, fiction and reality, which had a major influence on modern drama. Until his play *Six Characters in Search of an Author* was performed in the 1920s, Pirandello was known in Italy primarily as a realistic storyteller.

The son of a wealthy merchant, Pirandello was born in Sicily. He studied at the University of Rome and received a doctorate in linguistics in 1891 from the University of Bonn in Germany. Although he published some poetry and short stories in the 1890s, Pirandello did not have to support himself until 1903, when a landslide closed the mine that had been the source of his family's wealth. To supplement his writing income, Pirandello taught Italian at a college in Rome, and did translations. His wife, despairing over their financial problems, became insane. The stories and novels that he wrote during the next fourteen years, when he cared for his wife at home, explore the human personality, especially the subconscious forces that influence behavior.

After he began to achieve recognition as a dramatist, Pirandello opened his own theater in Rome and toured Europe with his acting company.

Pirandello believed that life is "a very sad piece of buffoonery." He pitied people who fool themselves by basing their lives on illusions. Yet he realized that each person creates his or her own reality.

WAR

The passengers who had left Rome by the night express had had to stop until dawn at the small station of Fabriano in order to continue their journey by the small old-fashioned local joining the main line with Sulmona.

At dawn, in a stuffy and smoky second-class carriage,[1] in which five people had already spent the night, a bulky woman in deep mourning was hoisted in—almost like a shapeless bundle. Behind her, puffing and moaning, followed her husband—a tiny man, thin and weakly, his face death-white, his eyes small and bright—looking shy and uneasy.

Having at last taken a seat, he politely thanked the passengers who had helped his wife and who had made room for her; then he turned around to the woman trying to pull down the collar of her coat, and politely inquired:

"Are you all right, dear?"

The wife, instead of answering, pulled up her collar again to her eyes, so as to hide her face.

"Nasty world," muttered the husband with a sad smile.

And he felt it his duty to explain to his traveling companions that the poor woman was to be pitied, for the war was taking away from her her only son, a boy of twenty, to whom both had devoted their entire life, even breaking up their home at Sulmona to follow him to Rome, where he had to go as a student, then allowing him to volunteer for war with an assurance, however, that at least for six months he would not be sent to the front, and now all of a sudden receiving a wire saying that he was due to leave in three days' time and asking them to go and see him off.

The woman under the big coat was twisting and wriggling, at times growling like a wild animal, feeling certain that all those explanations would not have aroused even a shadow of sympathy from those people who—most likely—were in the same plight as herself. One of them, who had been listening with particular attention, said:

"You should thank God that your son is only leaving now for the front. Mine was sent there the first day of the war. He has already come back twice wounded and been sent back again to the front."

"What about me? I have two sons and three nephews at the front," said another passenger.

"Maybe, but in our case it is our *only* son," ventured the husband.

"What difference can it make? You may spoil your only son with excessive attention, but you cannot love him more than you would all your other children if you had any. Paternal love is not like

1. **second-class carriage:** a coach-car, moderately priced. It is divided into separate compartments each containing two long, facing seats.

bread that can be broken into pieces and split among the children in equal shares. A father gives *all* his love to each of his children without discrimination, whether it be one or ten, and if I am suffering now for my two sons, I am not suffering half for each of them but double."

"True ... true ..." sighed the embarrassed husband, "but suppose (of course we all hope it will never be your case) a father has two sons at the front and he loses one of them, there is still one left to console him ... while...."

"Yes," answered the other, getting cross, "a son left to console him but also a son left for whom he must survive, while in the case of the father of an only son if the son dies the father can die too and put and end to his distress. Which of the two positions is the worse? Don't you see how my case would be worse than yours?"

"Nonsense," interrupted another traveler, a fat, red-faced man with bloodshot eyes of the palest gray.

He was panting. From his bulging eyes seemed to spurt inner violence of an uncontrolled vitality which his weakened body could hardly contain.

"Nonsense," he repeated, trying to cover his mouth with his hand so as to hide the two missing front teeth. "Nonsense. Do we give life to our children for our own benefit?"

The other travelers stared at him in distress. The one who had had his son at the front since the first day of war sighed: "You are right. Our children do not belong to us; they belong to the Country...."

"Bosh," retorted the fat traveler. "Do we think of the Country when we give life to our children? Our sons are born because ... well, because they must be born, and when they come to life they take our own life with them. This is the truth. We belong to them but they never belong to us. And when they reach twenty they are exactly what we were at their age. We too had a father and mother, but there were so many other things as well ... girls, cigarettes, illusions, new ties ... and the Country, of course, whose call we would have answered—when we were twenty—even if father and mother had said no. Now at our age, the love of our Country is still great, of course, but stronger than it is the love for our children. Is there any one of us here who wouldn't gladly take his son's place at the front if he could?"

There was a silence all around, everybody nodding as to approve.

"Why then," continued the fat man, "shouldn't we consider the feelings of our children when they are twenty? Isn't it natural that at their age they should consider the love for their Country (I am speaking of decent boys, of course) even greater than the love for us? Isn't it natural that it should be so, as after all they must look upon us as upon old boys who cannot move any more and must stay at home? If Country exists, if Country is a natural necessity, like bread, of which each of us must eat in order not to die of hunger, somebody must go to defend it. And our sons go, when they are twenty, and they don't want tears, because if they die, they die inflamed and happy (I am speaking, of course, of decent boys). Now, if one dies young and happy, without having seen the ugly sides of life, the boredom of it, the pettiness, the bitterness of disillusion . . . what more can we ask for him? Everyone should stop crying; everyone should laugh, as I do . . . or at least thank God—as I do—because my son, before dying, sent me a message saying that he was dying satisfied at having ended his life in the best way he could have wished. That's why, as you see, I do not even wear mourning."

He shook his light fawn[2] coat so as to show it; his livid lip over his missing teeth was trembling, his eyes were watery and motionless, and soon after he ended with a shrill laugh which might well have been a sob.

"Quite so . . . quite so . . ." agreed the others.

The woman who, bundled in a corner under her coat, had been sitting and listening, had for the last three months tried to find in the words of her husband and her friends something to console her in her deep sorrow, something that might show her how a mother should resign herself to send her son not even to death but to a probably dangerous life. Yet not a word had she found among the many which had been said . . . and her grief had been greater in seeing that nobody—as she thought—could share her feelings.

But now the words of the traveler amazed and almost stunned her. She suddenly realized that it wasn't the others who were wrong and could not understand her but herself who could not rise up to the same height as those fathers and mothers willing to resign themselves, without crying, not only to the departure of their sons but even to their death.

She lifted her head, she bent over from her corner trying to listen with great attention to the details which the fat man was giving

2. **fawn:** light grayish-brown.

to his companions about the way his son had fallen as a hero, for his King and his Country, happy and without regrets. It seemed to her that she had stumbled into a world she had never dreamed of, a world so far unknown to her, and she was so pleased to hear everyone joining in congratulating that brave father who could so stoically[3] speak of his child's death.

Then suddenly, just as if she had heard nothing of what had been said and almost as if waking up from a dream, she turned to the old man, asking him:

"Then . . . is your son really dead?"

Everybody stared at her. The old man, too, turned to look at her, fixing his great, bulging, horribly watery light-gray eyes deep in her face. For some little time he tried to answer, but words failed him. He looked and looked at her, almost as if only then—at that silly, incongruous question—he had suddenly realized at last that his son was really dead . . . gone forever . . . forever. His face contracted, became horribly distorted, then he snatched in haste a handkerchief from his pocket, and to the amazement of everyone broke into harrowing, heart-rendering, uncontrollable sobs.

3. **stoically** (stō′īk•ə•lē): apparently unmoved by pain.

Meaning

1. As the fat woman listens to the explanations of the fat, red-faced man, what aspects of the man's arguments appeal to her? Is her question really silly and incongruous?
2. An *allegory* is a story in which the characters are personifications of ideas or abstract values. What idea or value might the fat woman represent in this story? What might the fat, red-faced man represent?
3. What reason might the author have for not giving names to the characters?
4. In your opinion, what is the theme of the story? How does the story's title relate to the theme?

Method

1. What is the climax of the story? What is the dénouement? What hints of the fat man's true state of mind does Pirandello give early in the story?
2. There is very little physical action in this story, but there is movement on the part of the characters. How do the movements of the fat woman and the man with the fawn-colored coat reflect their feelings and attitudes?
3. The setting of the story is World War I, when Italy and the Allies were fighting against Germany and Austria. Do you think this is why Pirandello entitled his story "War"? Is there anything else in conflict or at war in the story?
4. Why do you think the author made his characters physically unattractive?

Language: Using Adjectives

Pirandello at times uses several adjectives that complement one another. Each adjective has a special meaning that provides an effect of mounting ugliness, horror, and despair.

Notice how the adjectives in the following descriptions have been carefully chosen to heighten the effect he wants to convey.

1. "... a tiny man, thin and weakly, his face death-white, his eyes small and bright—looking shy and uneasy."
2. "... a fat, red-faced man with bloodshot eyes of the palest gray."
3. "... harrowing, heart-rendering, uncontrollable sobs."

Discussion and Composition

1. The fat man says, "We belong to them [our children] but they never belong to us." Do you agree or disagree with this statement? Explain.

2. "It's better to die young and happy than to see the ugly side of life." Write an essay in which you agree or disagree with this statement. First, consider the following questions: Are all young people happy? Have some young people already been exposed to the ugly side of life? Is the fact that life is sometimes ugly any reason not to live it? Can positive rewards come out of negative experiences? As you write your composition, you will want to draw on specific examples from your experience.

EUGENIA COLLIER
(born 1928)

As an educator and writer, Eugenia Collier has used her considerable talents to further the cause of black people in America. In fact, she has said that her blackness has been the source of her creativeness.

Educated at Howard University, Columbia, and the University of Maryland, she has taught at Howard, the University of Maryland, Community College of Baltimore, Morgan State University, and Atlanta University, among others. For ten years she functioned as a case worker for the Baltimore Department of Public Welfare. She lectured on a television series called "The Negro in History" and was executive producer for another series on black American folklore.

"Marigolds," which won the Gwendolyn Brooks Award for fiction in 1969, presents a vivid portrait of growing up black and female in twentieth-century America.

MARIGOLDS

When I think of the home town of my youth, all that I seem to remember is dust—the brown, crumbly dust of late summer—arid, sterile dust that gets into the eyes and makes them water, gets into the throat and between the toes of bare brown feet. I don't know why I should remember only the dust. Surely there must have been lush green lawns and paved streets under leafy shade trees somewhere in town; but memory is an abstract painting—it does not present things as they are, but rather as they *feel*. And so, when I think of that time and that place, I remember only the dry September of the dirt roads and grassless yards of the shantytown where I lived. And one other thing I remember, another incongruency of memory—a brilliant splash of sunny yellow against the dust—Miss Lottie's marigolds.

Whenever the memory of those marigolds flashes across my mind, a strange nostalgia comes with it and remains long after the picture has faded. I feel again the chaotic emotions of adolescence, illusive as smoke, yet as real as the potted geranium before me now. Joy and rage and wild animal gladness and shame become tangled together in the multicolored skein of 14-going-on-15 as I recall that devastating moment when I was suddenly more woman than child, years ago in Miss Lottie's yard. I think of those marigolds at the strangest times; I remember them vividly now as I desperately pass away the time waiting for you, who will not come.

I suppose that futile waiting was the sorrowful background music of our impoverished little community when I was young. The Depression that gripped the nation was no new thing to us, for the black workers of rural Maryland had always been depressed. I don't know what it was that we were waiting for; certainly not for the prosperity that was "just around the corner," for those were white folks' words, which we never believed. Nor did we wait for hard work and thrift to pay off in shining success as the American Dream promised, for we knew better than that, too. Perhaps we waited for a miracle, amorphous in concept but necessary if one were to have the grit to rise before dawn each day and labor in the white man's vineyard until after dark, or to wander about in the September dust offering one's sweat in return for some meager share of bread. But God was chary with miracles in those days, and so we waited—and waited.

We children, of course, were only vaguely aware of the extent of our poverty. Having no radios, few newspapers, and no magazines, we were somewhat unaware of the world outside our community. Nowadays we would be called "culturally deprived" and people would write books and hold conferences about us. In those days everybody we knew was just as hungry and ill-clad as we were. Poverty was the cage in which we all were trapped, and our hatred of it was still the vague, undirected restlessness of the zoo-bred flamingo who knows that nature created him to fly free.

As I think of those days I feel most poignantly the tag-end of summer, the bright dry times when we began to have a sense of shortening days and the imminence of the cold.

By the time I was 14 my brother Joey and I were the only children left at our house, the older ones having left home for early marriage or the lure of the city, and the two babies having been sent to relatives who might care for them better than we. Joey was three years younger than I, and a boy, and therefore vastly inferior. Each morning our mother and father trudged wearily down the dirt road and around the bend, she to her domestic job, he to his daily unsuccessful quest for work. After our few chores around the tumble-down shanty, Joey and I were free to run wild in the sun with other children similarly situated.

For the most part, those days are ill-defined in my memory, running together and combining like a fresh water-color painting left out in the rain. I remember squatting in the road drawing a picture in the dust, a picture which Joey gleefully erased with one sweep of his dirty foot. I remember fishing for minnows in a muddy creek and watching sadly as they eluded my cupped hands, while Joey laughed uproariously. And I remember, that year, a strange restlessness of body and of spirit, a feeling that something old and familiar was ending, and something unknown and therefore terrifying was beginning.

One day returns to me with special clarity for some reason, perhaps because it was the beginning of the experience that in some inexplicable way marked the end of innocence. I was loafing under the great oak tree in our yard, deep in some reverie which I have now forgotten except that it involved some secret, secret thoughts of one of the Harris boys across the yard. Joey and a bunch of kids were bored now with the old tire suspended from an oak limb which had kept them entertained for awhile.

"Hey, Lizabeth," Joey yelled. He never talked when he could yell. "Hey, Lizabeth, let's us go somewhere."

I came reluctantly from my private world. "Where at, Joey?"

The truth was that we were becoming tired of the formlessness of our summer days. The idleness whose prospect had seemed so beautiful during the busy days of spring now had degenerated to an almost desperate effort to fill up the empty midday hours.

"Let's go see can we find us some locusts on the hill," someone suggested.

Joey was scornful. "Ain't no more locusts there. Y'all got 'em all while they was still green."

The argument that followed was brief and not really worth the effort. Hunting locust trees wasn't fun any more by now.

"Tell you what," said Joey finally, his eyes sparkling. "Let's us go over to Miss Lottie's."

The idea caught on at once, for annoying Miss Lottie was always fun. I was still child enough to scamper along with the group over rickety fences and through bushes that tore our already raggedy clothes, back to where Miss Lottie lived. I think now that we must have made a tragicomic spectacle, five or six kids of different ages, each of us clad in only one garment—the girls in faded dresses that were too long or too short, the boys in patchy pants, their sweaty brown chests gleaming in the hot sun. A little cloud of dust followed our thin legs and bare feet as we tramped over the barren land.

When Miss Lottie's house came into view we stopped, ostensibly to plan our strategy, but actually to reinforce our courage. Miss Lottie's house was the most ramshackle of all our ramshackle homes. The sun and rain had long since faded its rickety frame siding from white to a sullen gray. The boards themselves seemed to remain upright not from being nailed together but rather from leaning together like a house that a child might have constructed from cards. A brisk wind might have blown it down, and the fact that it was still standing implied a kind of enchantment that was stronger than the elements. There it stood, and as far as I know is standing yet—a gray rotting thing with no porch, no shutters, no steps, set on a cramped lot with no grass, not even any weeds—a monument to decay.

In front of the house in a squeaky rocking chair sat Miss Lottie's son, John Burke, completing the impression of decay. John Burke was what was known as "queer-headed." Black and ageless, he sat, rocking day in and day out in a mindless stupor, lulled by the monotonous squeak-squawk of the chair. A battered hat atop his shaggy head shaded him from the sun. Usually John Burke was totally unaware of everything outside his quiet dream world. But if you disturbed him, if you intruded upon his fantasies, he would become enraged, strike out at you, and curse at you in some strange enchanted language which only he could understand. We children made a game of thinking of ways to disturb John Burke and then to elude his violent retribution.

But our real fun and our real fear lay in Miss Lottie herself. Miss Lottie seemed to be at least a hundred years old. Her big frame still held traces of the tall, powerful woman she must have been in youth, although it was now bent and drawn. Her smooth skin was a dark reddish-brown, and her face had Indian-like features and the stern stoicism that one associates with Indian faces. Miss Lottie didn't like intruders either, especially children. She never left her yard, and nobody ever visited her. We never knew how she managed those necessities which depend on human interaction—how she ate, for example, or even whether she ate. When we were tiny children, we thought Miss Lottie was a witch and we made up tales, that we half believed ourselves, about her exploits. We were far too sophisticated now, of course, to believe the witch-nonsense. But old fears have a way of clinging like cobwebs, and so when we sighted the tumble-down shack, we had to stop to reinforce our nerves.

"Look, there she is," I whispered, forgetting that Miss Lottie could not possibly have heard me from that distance. "She's fooling with them crazy flowers."

"Yeh, look at 'er."

Miss Lottie's marigolds were perhaps the strangest part of the picture. Certainly they did not fit in with the crumbling decay of the rest of her yard. Beyond the dusty brown yard, in front of the sorry gray house, rose suddenly and shockingly a dazzling strip of bright blossoms, clumped together in enormous mounds, warm and passionate and sun-golden. The old black witch-woman worked on them all summer, every summer, down on her creaky knees, weeding and cultivating and arranging, while the house crumbled and John Burke rocked. For some perverse reason, we children hated those marigolds. They interfered with the perfect ugliness of the place; they were too beautiful; they said too much that we could not understand, they did not make sense. There was something in the vigor with which the old woman destroyed the weeds that intimidated us. It should have been a comical sight—the old woman with the man's hat on her cropped white head, leaning over the bright mounds, her big backside in the air—but it wasn't comical, it was something we could not name. We had to annoy her by whizzing a pebble into her flowers or by yelling a dirty word, then dancing away from her rage, revelling in our youth and mocking her age. Actually, I think it was the flowers we wanted to destroy, but nobody had the nerve to try it, not even Joey, who was usually fool enough to try anything.

"Y'all git some stones," commanded Joey now, and was met with instant giggling obedience as everyone except me began to gather pebbles from the dusty ground. "Come on, Lizabeth."

I just stood there peering through the bushes, torn between wanting to join the fun and feeling that it was all a bit silly.

"You scared, Lizabeth?"

I cursed and spat on the ground—my favorite gesture of phony bravado. "Y'all children get the stones, I'll show you how to use 'em."

I said before that we children were not consciously aware of how thick were the bars of our cage. I wonder now, though, whether we were not more aware of it than I thought. Perhaps we had some dim notion of what we were, and how little chance we had of being anything else. Otherwise, why would we have been so preoccupied with destruction? Anyway, the pebbles were collected quickly, and everybody looked at me to begin the fun.

"Come on, y'all."

We crept to the edge of the bushes that bordered the narrow road in front of Miss Lottie's place. She was working placidly, kneeling over the flowers, her dark hand plunged into the golden mound. Suddenly "zing"—an expertly-aimed stone cut the head off one of the blossoms.

"Who out there?" Miss Lottie's backside came down and her head came up as her sharp eyes searched the bushes. "You better git!"

We had crouched down out of sight in the bushes, where we stifled the giggles that insisted on coming. Miss Lottie gazed warily across the road for a moment, then cautiously returned to her weeding. "Zing"—Joey sent a pebble into the blooms, and another marigold was beheaded.

Miss Lottie was enraged now. She began struggling to her feet, leaning on a rickety cane and shouting, "Y'all git! Go on home!" Then the rest of the kids let loose with their pebbles, storming the flowers and laughing wildly and senselessly at Miss Lottie's impotent rage. She shook her stick at us and started shakily toward the road crying, "Git 'long! John Burke! John Burke, come help!"

Then I lost my head entirely, mad with the power of inciting such rage, and ran out of the bushes in the storm of pebbles, straight toward Miss Lottie chanting madly, "Old witch, fell in a ditch, picked up a penny and thought she was rich!" The children screamed with delight, dropped their pebbles and joined the crazy dance, swarming around Miss Lottie like bees and chanting, "Old lady witch!" while she screamed curses at us. The madness lasted only a moment, for John Burke, startled at last, lurched out of his chair, and we dashed for the bushes just as Miss Lottie's cane went whizzing at my head.

I did not join the merriment when the kids gathered again under the oak in our bare yard. Suddenly I was ashamed, and I did not like being ashamed. The child in me sulked and said it was all in fun, but the woman in me flinched at the thought of the malicious attack that I had led. The mood lasted all afternoon. When we ate the beans and rice that was supper that night, I did not notice my father's silence, for he was always silent these days, nor did I notice my mother's absence, for she always worked until well into evening. Joey and I had a particularly bitter argument after supper; his exuberance got on my nerves. Finally I stretched out upon the palette in the room we shared and fell into a fitful doze.

When I awoke, somewhere in the middle of the night, my mother had returned, and I vaguely listened to the conversation that was audible through the thin walls that separated our rooms. At first I heard no words, only voices. My mother's voice was like a cool, dark room in summer—peaceful, soothing, quiet. I loved to listen to it; it made things seem alright somehow. But my father's voice cut through hers, shattering the peace.

"Twenty-two years, Maybelle, 22 years," he was saying, "and I got nothing for you, nothing, nothing."

"It's all right, honey, you'll get something. Everybody out of work now, you know that."

"It ain't right. Ain't no man ought to eat his woman's food year in and year out, and see his children running wild. Ain't nothing right about that."

"Honey, you took good care of us when you had it. Ain't nobody got nothing nowadays."

"I ain't talking about nobody else, I'm talking about *me.* God knows I try." My mother said something I could not hear, and my father cried out louder, "What must a man do, tell me that?"

"Look, we ain't starving. I git paid every week, and Mrs. Ellis is real nice about giving me things. She gonna let me have Mr. Ellis' old coat for you this winter—"

"Damn Mr. Ellis' coat! And damn his money! You think I want white folks' leavings? Damn, Maybelle"—and suddenly he sobbed, loudly and painfully, and cried helplessly and hopelessly in the dark night. I had never heard a man cry before. I did not know men ever cried. I covered my ears with my hands but could not cut off the sound of my father's harsh, painful, despairing sobs. My father was a strong man who would whisk a child upon his shoulders and go singing through the house. My father whittled toys for us and laughed so loud that the great oak seemed to laugh with him, and taught us how to fish and hunt rabbits. How could it be that my father was crying? But the sobs went on, unstifled, finally quieting until I could hear my mother's voice, deep and rich, humming softly as she used to hum to a frightened child.

The world had lost its boundary lines. My mother, who was small and soft, was now the strength of the family; my father, who was the rock on which the family had been built, was sobbing like the tiniest child. Everything was suddenly out of tune, like a broken accordion. Where did I fit into this crazy picture? I do not now remember my thoughts, only a feeling of great bewilderment and fear.

Long after the sobbing and the humming had stopped, I lay on the palette, still as stone with my hands over my ears, wishing that I too could cry and be comforted. The night was silent now except for the sound of the crickets and of Joey's soft breathing. But the room was too crowded with fear to allow me to sleep, and finally, feeling the terrible aloneness of 4 A.M., I decided to awaken Joey.

"Ouch! What's the matter with you? What you want?" he demanded disagreeably when I had pinched and slapped him awake.

"Come on, wake up."

"What for? Go 'way."

I was lost for a reasonable reply. I could not say, "I'm scared and I don't want to be alone," so I merely said, "I'm going out. If you want to come, come on."

The promise of adventure awoke him. "Going out now? Where at, Lizabeth? What you going to do?"

I was pulling my dress over my head. Until now I had not thought of going out. "Just come on," I replied tersely.

I was out the window and halfway down the road before Joey caught up with me.

"Wait, Lizabeth, where you going?"

I was running as if the furies were after me, as perhaps they were—running silently and furiously until I came to where I had half-known I was headed: to Miss Lottie's yard.

The half-dawn light was more eerie than complete darkness, and in it the old house was like the ruin that my world had become—foul and crumbling, a grotesque caricature. It looked haunted, but I was not afraid because I was haunted too.

"Lizabeth, you lost your mind?" panted Joey.

I had indeed lost my mind, for all the smoldering emotions of that summer swelled in me and burst—the great need for my mother who was never there, the hopelessness of our poverty and degradation, the bewilderment of being neither child nor woman and yet both at once, the fear unleashed by my father's tears. And these feelings combined in one great impulse toward destruction.

"Lizabeth!"

I leaped furiously into the mounds of marigolds and pulled madly, trampling and pulling and destroying the perfect yellow blooms. The fresh smell of early morning and of dew-soaked mari-golds spurred me on as I went tearing and mangling and sobbing while Joey tugged my dress or my waist crying, "Lizabeth, stop, please stop!"

And then I was sitting in the ruined little garden among the uprooted and ruined flowers, crying and crying, and it was too late to undo what I had done. Joey was sitting beside me, silent and fright-ened not knowing what to say. Then "Lizabeth, look."

I opened my swollen eyes and saw in front of me a pair of large calloused feet; my gaze lifted to the swollen legs, the age-distorted body clad in a tight cotton night dress, and then the shadowed Indian face surrounded by stubby white hair. And there was no rage in the face now, now that the garden was destroyed and there was nothing any longer to be protected.

"M-miss Lottie!" I scrambled to my feet and just stood there and stared at her, and that was the moment when childhood faded and womanhood began. That violent, crazy act was the last act of childhood. For as I gazed at the immobile face with the sad, weary eyes, I gazed upon a kind of reality which is hidden to childhood. The witch was no longer a witch but only a broken old woman who had dared to create beauty in the midst of ugliness and sterility. She had been born in squalor and lived in it all her life. Now at the end of that life she had nothing except a falling-down hut, a wrecked body, and John Burke, the mindless son of her passion. Whatever verve there was left in her, whatever was of love and beauty and joy that had not been squeezed out by life, had been there in the marigolds she had so tenderly cared for.

Of course I could not express the things that I knew about Miss Lottie as I stood there awkward and ashamed. The years have put words to the things I knew in that moment, and as I look back upon it, I know that the moment marked the end of innocence. Innocence involves an unseeing acceptance of things at face value, an ignorance of the area below the surface. In that humiliating moment I looked beyond myself and into the depths of another person. This was the beginning of compassion, and one cannot have both compassion and innocence.

The years have taken me worlds away from that time and that place, from the dust and squalor of our lives and from the bright thing that I destroyed in a blind childish striking out at God-knows-what. Miss Lottie died long ago and many years have passed since I last saw her hut, completely barren at last, for despite my wild contrition she never planted marigolds again. Yet, there are times when the image of those passionate yellow mounds returns with a painful poignancy. For one does not have to be ignorant and poor to find that his life is barren as the dusty yards of our town. And I too have planted marigolds.

Meaning

1. What is Lizabeth's mood when she mounts her second assault on the garden?
2. How does Lizabeth's mood differ from that of the children she is leading?
3. Why do you suppose Miss Lottie's reaction to the second attack is different from her reaction to the first?

Method

1. Why does Lizabeth's anger focus on Miss Lottie's marigolds? What do the flowers symbolize in the story?
2. What are the advantages of having an older Lizabeth tell the story?
3. How do the last two sentences of the story point up its theme? How is the theme anticipated in the opening paragraph?

Language: Forming Adjectives from Nouns

Lizabeth describes her behavior as "childish." The word *childish* is an example of an adjective that is formed from a noun by the addition of a suffix. The suffix *-ish* means "tending towards or interested in." Examples are *Scottish, Turkish, bookish.* Notice that the *t* in Scot is doubled when the suffix is added.

The suffixes *-ian,* meaning "belonging to a class or order," and *-esque,* meaning "resembling or having the style of," are often added to nouns to form adjectives. When added to the proper noun *Arab,* for example, they form the adjectives *Arabian* and *arabesque.* (The latter originally meant "after the manner or style of the Arabs.") The horror stories of Edgar Allan Poe are referred to as tales of the grotesque and arabesque. How would you interpret the adjective *arabesque* as used here?

The addition of the suffix *-ian* often calls for a change in the accent or stress of a word; Arab (ăr′əb) becomes Arabian (ə•rā′bē•ən).

The suffix *-al*, meaning "pertaining to," is another addition, providing adjectives such as *musical, electrical,* and *adjectival.*

Make adjectives from each of the following nouns by adding the suffix *-al, -esque, -ian,* or *-ish.* Check your dictionary to see that you spell and pronounce the adjectives correctly.

1. anecdote   5. picture
2. Dane   6. Roman
3. Dickens   7. folklore
4. Finn   8. autumn

Discussion and Composition

1. The narrator in "Marigolds" says, "One cannot have both innocence and compassion." What do you think she means by this? Do you agree or disagree?

2. Write a composition about the conflict going on in the mind and heart of the narrator in "Marigolds." First explain the nature of her inner conflict, and then evaluate her success or failure in resolving the conflict.

A GLOSSARY OF LITERARY TERMS

Allegory: a narrative in which objects, characters, or actions stand for abstract ideas or moral qualities. In Luigi Pirandello's "War," for example, the fat woman represents emotion, whereas the fat, red-eyed man represents reason and duty.

Alliteration: the repetition of a sound at the beginning, in the middle, or at the end of words. Although it is mainly a poetic device, alliteration is sometimes used in prose. For example:

> "But that beard! That bristly, thick, square beard of a stranger!"

Allusion: a reference to a person, a place, an event, or an artistic work that the author expects the reader to recognize. An allusion may be drawn from literature, history, geography, scripture, or mythology. A statement is enriched by an allusion because in a few words an author can evoke a particular atmosphere, story, or historical setting. For example, in "The Lucid Eye in Silver Town," John Updike refers to New York as "Baghdad-on-the-Subway," evoking an image of the fabulous city made famous in *The Arabian Nights*.

Ambiguity: the possibility of more than one meaning. In literature, an author may deliberately use ambiguity to produce subtle or multiple variations in meaning. For example, the title of Kurt Vonnegut's story "Tom Edison's Shaggy Dog" is deliberately ambiguous: the words "shaggy dog" refer both to an actual dog and to a type of anecdote, a "shaggy dog story."

Analogy: a form of comparison that points out the likeness between two basically dissimilar things; it attempts to use a familiar object or idea to illustrate or to introduce a subject that is unfamiliar or complex.

Anecdote: a brief account, sometimes biographical, or an interesting or entertaining incident. A writer may use an anecdote to introduce or illustrate a topic.

Antagonist: the force or character opposing the main character or **protagonist.**

Atmosphere: the prevailing mental and emotional climate of a story; something the reader senses or feels. **Setting** and **mood** help to create and heighten atmosphere. Edgar Allan Poe is noted for creating stories of atmosphere. In "The Cask of Amontillado," for example, an atmosphere of foreboding tension prevails.

Autobiography and Biography: literature that presents an account of a person's life, usually in chronological order, using facts, events, and other information that is available. An *autobiography* is an account written by a person about himself or herself; a *biography* is an account written by another person.

Characters: persons—or animals, things, or natural forces presented as persons—appearing in a short story, novel, play, or narrative poem. Characters are sometimes described as *dynamic* or *static*. Dynamic characters experience some change in personality or attitude. This change is an essential one and usually involves more than a mere change in surroundings or condition. Static characters remain the same throughout a narrative.

Characters are sometimes classified as *flat* or *round*. Flat characters have only one or two "sides," representing one or two traits. They are often **stereotypes** that can be summed up in a few words, for example, an "anxious miser" or a "strong, silent type." Round characters are complex and have many "sides" or traits. They are individuals, and their personalities are fully developed.

Characterization: the techniques an author uses to develop the personalities of fictional characters so that they seem believable, act consistently, and speak naturally. These methods include characterization through:

a. direct analysis of a character's thoughts, feelings, and actions;

b. physical description of a character's appearance;

c. description of a character's surroundings, such as the room in which he or she lives or works;

d. the speech or conversations of a character;

e. the behavior or actions of a character;

f. a character's reactions to events, situations, and other people;

g. the responses or reactions of other people in the story to a character's behavior, and in some cases, their remarks and conversations about the character;

h. a combination of two or more of these methods.

Climax: the high point or turning point of a story. The author builds up to the climax through a series of complications.

Comparison and Contrast: a *comparison* shows the similarities between two things, while a *contrast* details the differences between things. In writing, this is a method used to clarify and illustrate a subject. Comparison and contrast are often used together, but can be used separately. (See **Contrast**.)

Complication: a series of difficulties forming the central action of a narrative. Complications in a story make a conflict difficult to resolve and add interest or suspense.

Conflict: a struggle between opposing forces, people, or ideas in a story, novel, play, or narrative poem. Conflict can be external or internal, and it can take one of these forms: **a.** a person against another person, **b.** a person against society, **c.** a person against nature, **d.** two elements or ideas struggling for mastery within a person, or **e.** a combination of two or more of these types.

Connotation: the emotion or association that a word or phrase may arouse. Connotation is distinct from **denotation,** which is the literal meaning of the word. The word *snowstorm,* for example, may arouse emotions such as fear or excitement.

Context: the words and phrases that closely surround a word and affect or suggest its meaning. Often, the intended meaning of a word can be determined from its context, as in the following examples.

> "The customer refused to buy the table because the edges were too *rough.*"
> "The students felt that the last two questions were too *rough.*"

For an event or incident, context includes the situation and circumstances that surround the event. For example, we often speak of a specific event in its historical context.

Contrast: a striking difference between two things. In literature, an author may contrast ideas, personalities, or images to heighten or clarify a situation. (See also **Comparison and Contrast.**)

Denotation: the literal or "dictionary" meaning of a word. (See also **Connotation.**)

Dénouement (dā·nōō·män′): that part of the plot that reveals the final outcome of the conflicts.

Description: any careful detailing of a person, place, thing, or event. Description is one of the four major forms of discourse. Descriptions re-create sensory impressions: sights, sounds, smells, textures, or tastes. Some description is direct and factual, but more often, description helps to establish a mood or stir an emotion.

Dialect: the speech that is characteristic of a particular group or of the inhabitants of a specific geographical region. In literature, dialect may be used as part of a characterization.

Dialogue: the conversation carried on by two or more characters in a story.

Diction: a writer's choice, arrangement, and use of words.

Epiphany: a moment of illumination in a work of literature, usually involving a sudden realization on the part of the central character. Epiphanies occur in James Joyce's "Araby" and Robert Cormier's "The Moustache."

Episode: one of a series of occurrences or significant events in the plot of a story.

Exposition: that part of a story or play in which the author provides background material about the lives of characters and about events that have taken place before the story opens. For example, in "A Flight of Geese," Leslie Norris provides background information about the life of the central character, Uncle Wynford.

As a form of discourse, exposition is writing intended to explain a subject or provide information.

Fable: a brief narrative in prose or verse intended to teach a moral lesson. Many fables, such as those of the Greek writer Aesop, are beast fables, in which animals speak and act as if they were human.

Fantasy: a work that employs highly imaginative elements and that deliberately departs from reality. A fantasy might take place in a dreamlike world, present unreal characters, or project scientific principles into the future (as in science-fiction stories such as Ray Bradbury's "The Toynbee Convector"). A fantasy can be a whimsical form of entertainment or can offer a serious comment on reality. It usually has more than one level of meaning.

Figurative Language: language that is not intended to be interpreted in a literal sense. Figurative language consists of imaginative comparisons called *figures of speech*. **Simile, metaphor,** and **personification** are among the most common figures of speech.

Flashback: a device by which an author interrupts the logical time sequence of a story or play to relate an episode that occurred prior to the opening situation.

Foil: a character who serves by contrast to emphasize the qualities of another character. For example, the appearance of a particularly lazy, shiftless, and unenterprising character will strengthen the reader's impression of an active, ambitious, and aggressive character.

Foreshadowing: hints or clues; a shadow of things to come. The use of foreshadowing stimulates interest and suspense and helps prepare the reader for the outcome. For example, in John Updike's "A Lucid Eye in Silver Town," Uncle Quinn's failure to meet Jay and his father at the station foreshadows Uncle Quinn's rude, selfish behavior during their visit.

Framework Story: a story that contains another story. Leslie Norris's "A Flight of Geese" is an example of a framework story.

Hyperbole (hī·pûr'bə·lē): a deliberate exaggeration for the purpose of emphasis or humor; overstatement. "I'm dying to hear what happened" is an example of hyperbole.

Idiom: an expression that has a special meaning different from the usual meanings of the words. *To turn the corner, to carry out,* and *to pull someone's leg* are examples of idioms. When the term is used in reference to an overall manner of expression, it refers to the language or dialect of a particular group of people.

Imagery: language that appeals to one or more senses and creates pictures and impressions in the reader's mind. Although imagery may create visual pictures, some imagery may appeal to the senses of touch, taste, smell, and hearing as well. Imagery often involves the use of figurative language and vivid description.

Irony: a contrast or an incongruity between what is stated and what is really meant, or between what is expected to happen and what actually does happen. There are three kinds of irony. With *verbal irony,* a writer or speaker says one thing and means something entirely different. For example, a writer might say of a character who has just taken several clumsy falls on the ice, "What a fine skater he turned out to be!" With *dramatic irony,* a reader or an audience perceives something that a character in the story or play does not know. *Irony of situation* involves a discrepancy between the expected result of an action or situation and its actual result. This kind of irony occurs in Shirley Jackson's "The Lottery," in which the lottery at first seems to be a pleasant community activity but turns out to be something terrible.

Jargon: the special vocabulary of an identifiable group. This vocabulary may include terms used by people who share a particular occupation, art, science, trade, sect, or sport. For example, sports fans may use special *football* jargon. *Jargon* can also refer to language full of long words and circumlocutions that serve little purpose other than to impress and bewilder the average person.

Local Color: details of dress, speech, locale, customs, and traditions that give an impression of the local "atmosphere" of a particular place.

Metaphor: a comparison between two unlike things with the intent of giving added meaning to one of them. Unlike **similes,** metaphors do not use terms such as *like* or *as* but compare two things directly. In Ray Bradbury's "The Toynbee Convector," Stiles uses a metaphor when he says that "the economy was a snail."

Monologue: speech or narrative by a person who reveals his or her own character while speaking or telling a story.

Mood: the prevailing feeling or emotional climate of a literary work. Mood is often developed, at least in part, through descriptions of **setting** and by the author's **tone.** In Rudolfo Anaya's "Salomon's Story," the mood of gloomy foreboding is developed through descriptions of the hot, oppressive jungle and through the author's ominous tone.

Motif: an image or phrase that recurs, and thus provides a pattern within a work of literature.

Motivation: the reasons, either stated or implied, for a character's behavior. To make a story believable, a writer must provide characters with motivation that explains what they do. Characters may be motivated by outside events, or they may be motivated by inner needs or fears.

Myth: a tale usually focusing on the deeds of gods or superhuman heroes. Myths played an important role in ancient cultures by helping to explain or justify the mysteries of nature and the universe. As a loose term, *myth* can denote any invented or grossly exaggerated story.

Narrative: the telling of an event or series of incidents that together make up a meaningful action; a story.

Narrator: one who narrates, or tells, a true or fictional story. The narrator may be a major or minor participant in the action of the narrative or simply an observer of the action.

Novel: a fictional narrative in prose, usually longer than a short story. A novel is similar to a short story in its use of characterization, plot, setting, mood, theme, and other literary elements. Because of its greater length, a novel may introduce several different groups of characters, a complicated plot or various subplots, multiple settings, or more than one mood or theme, while a short story usually focuses on one predominant effect.

Onomatopoeia: (on′ə•mat′ə•pē′ə): the use of words that imitate the sound, action, or idea they represent. Sometimes a single word sounds like the thing it describes, such as *cuckoo* or *twitter*. Sometimes several words are grouped together to imitate a sound, as "murmuring of innumerable bees."

Paraphrase: a rewording of a line, passage, or entire work, giving the meaning in shorter form, usually to simplify the original.

Personification: a figure of speech in which a nonhuman or inanimate object, quality, or idea is given lifelike characteristics or powers. For example:

> "The other houses of the street, conscious of decent lives within them, gazed at one another with brown imperturbable faces."

Plot: the arrangement of incidents, details, and elements of conflict in a story. Plot is usually divided into the following stages:

a. the *conflict*, or problem, usually introduced at the beginning of a narrative;

b. the *complications*, or entanglements, produced by new or complex events and involvements;

c. the *rising action*, or advancing movement, toward an event or moment when something decisive has to happen;

d. the *climax*, or most intense moment or event, usually occurring near a narrative's major *turning point*, or crisis, the moment when the main character turns toward a (good or bad) solution of the problem;

e. the *dénouement*, the final outcome in which the resolution of the conflicts is made known.

Point of View: the vantage point from which the story is told. Each viewpoint allows the author a particular range or scope. There are two basic points of view:

a. first-person point of view, in which the narrative is told by a major or minor character in his or her own words. The author is limited to the narrator's scope of knowledge, degree of involvement, and powers of observation and expression. Robert Cormier's "The Moustache" is an example of a story that uses first-person narration.

b. third-person point of view, in which the narrator serves as an observer who describes and comments upon the characters and action in a narrative. The **omniscient third-person narrator** knows everything there is to know about the characters—their thoughts, motives, actions, and reactions. Maurice Walsh's "The Quiet Man" is told by an omniscient third-person narrator.

Writers can also adopt a **limited third-person point of view.** An author using this point of view tells the inner thoughts and feelings of one character only, usually the main character. We are never told what other characters are thinking; we must infer this from their external acts. Anne Tyler uses the limited third-person point of view in "Teenage Wasteland."

Protagonist: the main character in a story or a drama. The word, which comes from the Greek *protos* meaning "first" and *agónistés* meaning "contestant" or "actor," was originally used to designate the actor who played the chief role in a Greek drama. (See also **Antagonist.**)

Repetition: the use of the same sound, word, phrase, sentence, idea (or some slight variation of these) to achieve emphasis or suggest order in a piece of literature. Repetition is most often used in poetry, but it is sometimes found in prose. (See also **Alliteration.**)

Rhythm: in poetry, the regular rise and fall of strong and weak syllables. (As the accent becomes more fixed and systematized, it approaches *meter*.) In prose, although rhythm is often present, it is irregular and approximate; prose rhythm is the effective and pleasing arrangement of meaningful sounds in a sentence.

Rising Action: the part of the plot that leads to a turning point in the action that will affect the fortunes (good or bad) of the main character.

Satire: the use of ridicule, sarcasm, wit, or irony in order to expose, set right, or destroy a vice, folly, breach of good taste, or undesirable social condition. Satire may range from gentle ridicule to bitter attack. In "Everyday Use," Alice Walker satirizes superficial, merely fashionable interest in heritage through the character of Dee.

Science Fiction: a type of **fantasy** that includes speculation about the impact of science—or of any imagined future development—on society or individuals. Ray Bradbury's "The Toynbee Convector" is a science fiction story.

Setting: the time and place of the events in a story; the physical background. The importance of setting as a story element depends on the extent of its contribution to characterization, plot, theme, and atmosphere. For example, the setting of "In Another Country" is foreign to the characters, reinforcing the inner sense of isolation and alienation that the characters feel.

Simile: a stated comparison or likeness expressed in figurative language and introduced by terms such as *like, as, so, as if, resembles,* and *as though.* For example, Amy Tan uses the following simile in "Rules of the Game":

> ". . . yellow lights shining from our flat like two tiger's eyes in the night."

Sketch: a short, simply constructed work, usually about a single character, place, or incident. A *character sketch,* for example, may be a brief study of a person's characteristics and personality. As in art, a sketch may also be a "rough" or preliminary draft for a longer, more complex work.

Style: a writer's distinctive or characteristic form of expression. Style is determined by choice and arrangement of words, sentence structure, tone, rhythm, and the use of figurative language.

Surprise Ending: in fiction, an unexpected twist of plot at the conclusion of a story; a trick ending. It should be carefully foreshadowed to produce its striking effect.

Suspense: the feeling of uncertainty, interest, or anxiety that is created in the reader by events or complications in a literary work. Suspense makes readers ask "What will happen next?" or "How will this work out?" and impels them to read on.

Symbol: a person, place, event, or object that is real in itself and also represents or suggests something larger than itself, such as a quality, an attitude, a belief, or a value. For example, a heart symbolizes affection and love; a horseshoe, good luck; a lily, purity; a skull, death; and a dove, peace. In fiction, some symbols have *universal* meaning, such as the association of spring with youth and winter with old age.

Some symbols have a special meaning within the context of a story. A character's name, for instance, may suggest his or her personality. "Prince Prospero" may be a name associated with a wealthy, royal, and "prosperous" character. The action of a story may also be symbolic. A long trip might, during the course of a story, come to symbolize a person's journey through life.

Theme: the main idea of a literary work; the general truth behind the story of a particular individual in a particular situation. The theme of a story is usually implied rather than stated.

Tone: the attitude of the writer toward his or her subject, characters, and readers. An author may be sympathetic and sorrowful, may wish to provoke, shock, or anger, or may write in a humorous way and intend simply to entertain the reader. Tone is created through the writer's choice of words and details.

Understatement: the representation of something as less than it really is for the purpose of emphasis or humor. For example, in agreeing with a friend's praise of a new sports car, the owner might say, "Oh, it will do, I suppose."

Vignette: a brief but significant sketch of a person or event. The meaning of a vignette is usually subtly implied rather than stated. It often forms part of a longer work.

THE LANGUAGE ARTS PROGRAM
LIST OF SKILLS

Throughout the text, language arts have been integrated with the presentation of literature. The majority of language-arts activities appear in the end-of-selection questions and assignments under the headings **Meaning, Method, Language, Composition,** and **Composition and Discussion.** Others are introduced and discussed in the general introductions, and still others, especially those concerning word origins and derivations, are covered in text footnotes.

The following indexes are intended to serve as guidelines to specific aspects of the language-arts program in *A Book of Short Stories—2*.

VOCABULARY DEVELOPMENT

COMPOSITION

Narration:

Description:

Exposition: